Second Death

DONNA K. FITCH

Published by Passarola Media
in association with the Alexandria Publishing Group

ISBN: 0615997031
ISBN-13: **978-0615997032**

DEDICATION

To my husband Thomas, for his love and support always.

AUTHOR'S NOTE

Most of the locations in this book are based on actual places,
although a few of the names have been changed.
While their fictional counterparts remain static,
the real locations evolve and grow, and may not be entirely recognizable.
Please think of their presence here as a snapshot in time.

ACKNOWLEDGMENTS

I'm an inveterate researcher when I write fiction. Or pretty much anything. The Civil War research for this novel was done at the Samford University Library. I've obsessed over genealogy for years, and that research took place at the Linn-Henley Research Library of the Birmingham Public Library.

A good editor's price is beyond rubies: Kathryn Ptacek edited the manuscript, helping me shape it into a compelling story. J.P. Edwards, my agent, contributed market-savvy comments.

Thanks to R. Barratt of The Cover Counts for the new cover design. Thanks go to my early readers, especially Rick and Jeanette Roach, Karen Perreault and Janica York Carter, for their enthusiasm and encouragement. Thanks also to Scott Carter, my oft-times writing partner, whose creativity and boundless store of ideas never fail to inspire me.

PROLOGUE

Monday, February 8, 2010.

He couldn't call the bookstore haunted.

Which Mark Richards considered a shame, really. He clenched his teeth against a shiver that had nothing to do with the cold and plunged his hands deeper into the pockets of his barn jacket. No matter how many times he'd painted the storefront, it still looked its eighty years, and then some. The second story windows cried out for a shadowy face in a sealed room or a lightning-etched visage peering out in terror.

Mark crossed the street and entered "Pages of Wisdom: A Holistic Bookstore, Janet Richards, Proprietor." The front door bell and a squeal from WD-40-immune hinges announced his presence. The clerk behind the cash register, a college student named Penny, waved at him with a bright smile. Mark stretched his numb lips in return, but Penny's raised eyebrows told him the result was more of a grimace. "She's over there." Penny pointed to the rear of the shop.

Mark rounded the row of bookshelves. Despite his present state of mind, the sight of his wife quickened his pulse. She stood in profile, cradling a tiny baby under the watchful eye of a woman who had to be the mother. Janet's lustrous brown hair was knotted back with a wide turquoise barrette, and her full lips, shiny with rose gloss, curved in a tender smile. Mark knew how much she wanted one of their own, how good she would be as a mother.

God, I love her. The vehemence of his need for her frightened him for a moment.

As if sensing someone behind her, Janet turned. "May I help—oh, hi, honey..."

Her brown eyes narrowed, smile changing to concern when she saw her

1

husband's expression. She turned back to the woman. "It was nice to see you again, Lynn. Thanks for bringing Max to see me." Janet slipped the baby back into his mother's arms.

"If I remember that other thing I wanted to tell you," Lynn said, "I'll call you."

"Thanks."

Janet grabbed his arm, her hand warm against his chilly skin. "What's wrong, Mark?" she asked. "You look terrible."

"I saw him," he breathed, unsure if he spoke loudly enough for her to hear.

"Your father?" Janet frowned, then said in a louder voice to Penny, "I'll be upstairs. Let me know if you need me."

Penny waved her assent, and Janet took his hand, pulling him up the stairs to the combination storage room/office/break room, her touch warm and dry and comforting. She shut the office door behind them.

"What's wrong?" Janet asked. "You saw your father at the hospital?"

Mark blew out a long breath. "They released him to the psych ward."

"How was he?" She unbuttoned his coat and hung it on the coat rack on top of hers.

"Not very coherent, Mom said." He stared at a knot in the floorboard, trying to control the shaking of his hands.

"Why didn't you talk to him?" Janet asked, steering him around a stack of shipping crates to an overstuffed armchair.

Collapsing into the chair, Mark gazed up at her. "You always know, don't you?"

"I've been married to you for eleven years." She pulled the second armchair closer and sat, tucking one leg underneath her. "I know how you think."

Mark leaned forward, elbows on knees. He felt an overwhelming urge to cry.

"Janet," he said in a small voice. "He really scared me. What is going on in his head?" He twisted his fingers together and looked up at her. "Mom brought it up again...having him committed. But I'm just not sure..."

She rested her hand on his arm. "You've got to make a decision. I'll support you whatever you decide, but just decide."

Was that a hint of exasperation in her voice? He frowned. "You make it sound so easy." He pushed out of the chair and paced across the room. "I can see so many consequences either way. If I knew how it would turn out..."

Janet chuckled. "Maybe you should consult a fortuneteller."

Mark laughed, too. "Like your old boyfriend." The sound turned a little shrill, and he shut his mouth when Janet frowned at him. He wandered back to the chair and eased into it.

"Has Natalie been to see him?" The phone rang. She reached for it across the old army surplus desk. "Hello? Hi, Lynn."

His mind drifted to his father's white, staring face. Mark had braced himself in the door frame of the hospital room, hands and jaw clenched, afraid to go in. Afraid of what he might say to the man, afraid—

"Is he."

Janet's flat tone caught his attention. She had a good poker face, except for the slight flush. "I appreciate you telling me, Lynn." She glanced sideways at Mark, looked away.

"Jan?"

She hung up and folded her hands on the desktop. "Lynn forgot to tell me something."

"Oh, yeah?"

Looking him in the eyes seemed to be an effort for her. "Daniel's back in town."

"Daniel...as in, your Daniel?"

"He's not my Daniel." She rolled the chair back, almost banging into the microwave oven perched atop a stack of crates. "Hasn't been for a long time. I didn't think he'd be moving back, is all. Sorry for the interruption." She settled her gaze back on him. "We were talking about your father."

The mention of Daniel reawakened his frantic heartbeat. He stood, pulled her to her feet, and wrapped his arms around her.

"I love you, Janet," he whispered, wincing at the desperate edge in his own voice. "I don't know what I'd do without you."

She stroked his hair. "You don't have to find out, Mark," she murmured. "I married you for better or worse. I'm not going anywhere."

"Neither am I, Jan," he said, unfastening the barrette from her hair. The bit of plastic fell to the floor. He gripped her shoulders and repeated, "Neither am I."

CHAPTER 1.

The impact of solid earth against his knees shocked his entire body, and warm fluid spread through his mouth as his teeth clamped on his tongue. He spat blood and clawed at the nearest tree trunk. Jagged rocks underfoot lanced the thin soles of his boots as he scrambled for purchase on rain-slimed leaves. A twig snapped. The attacker sprang toward him. His heart thudded as he ducked under the arc of the knife blade and rolled—

Mark's father peered at him, eyes narrowed. "Demarcus?"

Mark stood on the porch of his father's house, but even the memory of that morning's dream or vision or whatever it had been clung to his consciousness with more reality than the old man hunched over on the porch swing.

"Sorry, Dad," he said. "My mind keeps wandering today. What were you saying?" He'd lost track when his father veered from a recitation of his new model train acquisitions to the familiar refrain about the importance of family and the past.

Thomas Richards rubbed his tanned face with both hands and sighed. "You tune me out when I try to talk to you about this, so I always give up. I can't this time." He took a deep breath. "Demarcus, there's a curse on the Giles family."

Eyes fixed on his father, Mark leaned back against the railing. It was the last thing he'd expected his father to say. He laughed. "What, a gypsy curse? Or the curse of the mummy?"

"I am not joking," Thomas snapped, straightening for a moment. "This is serious."

Mark slid down the railing, curled paint chips crackling behind him, and sat on the wooden floor. The sound of the chips reminded him of the breaking twig in the dream. With sheer force of will, he dragged his attention back to his father's face.

Thomas hunched forward again, hands dangling between his knees. "I must explain myself to you, Demarcus."

"Mark," he corrected. "My name is Mark."

"No, it isn't. You're named for your grandmother and your great-grandfather, who—"

"Dad, I've heard the dead ancestors speech a hundred times."

His father looked at him. "Our past is your responsibility. As it was mine. I have tried to fulfill my obligation to the past, but I've failed time and again."

Mark shook his head. "I'm not following you."

Thomas hissed out a long breath through clenched teeth, knuckles white on his knees. "My mother died twenty-six years ago today. When I turned twenty-one, she sat me down and revealed to me something that happened long ago, before her father's time, something horrible that brought a curse down on the Giles family."

Thomas closed bleary blue eyes, and Mark noticed the baggy skin under them, the deepening grooves bracketing his mouth.

"I've waited far too long to tell you this. Twelve years too long. I thought I could stop the curse, thought I knew how. But I've always failed." He blinked, fixing Mark with a stare. "Story of my life."

Mark wrapped his arms around his own knees, the same feeling in the pit of his stomach he had as a kid when venturing across his dark bedroom at night. "Dad..."

Thomas raised his hand, palm outward, like a bailiff swearing in a witness, and the sunlight illuminated the ridged white scar across his wrist. "The responsibility is yours, son," he intoned, his voice husky. "You must not fail, as I have. Do you hear me? You must not fail. Or your children are doomed."

I love my father, Mark reminded himself. But he has scared me so many times...

"You know I don't have any children," he said aloud. "I don't plan to have any. So it's just me that's doomed."

"And Natalie Clarice."

He stood up. "Yeah. And you already took care of Tommy." The words slipped out. He hadn't meant to say them, hadn't even thought he harbored as much bitterness about his brother's death as evident in those words.

His father's eyes went cold. "It was an accident, and you know that. The streets were slick. Doesn't his death help convince you of what I'm saying?"

A 1960s vintage car accelerated down the street where Mark grew up and he felt a surge of *deja vu*. "How am I supposed to end this curse?"

Thomas wet his bottom lip with the tip of his tongue. "Well...it involves the—the suicide attempts," he stammered.

Mark backed away, a ringing in his ears. "No, Dad, no. I don't want to hear about it." He banged into the railing, slipped sideways. "Janet," he called toward the screen door. "Janet, we're leaving now."

His father stood, mouth twisted. "Son, you must know—"

Mark pounded on the screen door, fighting the childish urge to cover his ears with his hands. "I found you all those times," he said, panic slicking his palms. "Isn't that enough torture for me? Do you have to dwell on it? Janet!"

His wife appeared in through the screen, her expression puzzled. "What's wrong?"

He tugged open the door. "We're leaving. Now. Come on."

She glanced from his father's anguished expression to Mark. "But did you—"

"Yeah, we talked." He stopped, noticing the crease between her eyebrows, the paleness of her face. "Are you sick?"

"Just a little stomach flu. Aren't you going to tell your mother and sister good-bye?"

Thomas grabbed his arm. "Demarcus—"

Shaking his head, Mark slid away and backed down the steps to the car. He tugged at the handle, dug in his pockets for the key, then remembered. Janet drove. His father was staring at him. Mark turned away.

Janet clicked the doors open with the remote. He glanced at his father, winced at the pain in the man's eyes, visible even from this distance.

"What on earth is wrong with you?" Janet demanded as they got inside and shut the doors. "You haven't seen him for three months. I thought you were going to make up with him."

"Why should *I* make up with *him*? *I* wasn't the one who OD'd on sleeping pills and spent a month in the hospital."

"You don't have to shout." She fastened the seatbelt and switched on the ignition. "Did he talk about it?"

"Yeah." Mark sighed, rubbed his sweaty palms on his jeans. "He tried. But I can't. Suicide freaks me out. He knows that."

"You know, I'm sure a psychiatrist would—"

"No, you don't." He waved to his mother, who'd appeared on the porch. "Don't start talking about psychiatrists again. Forget it." As Janet backed out of the driveway, he watched his parents walk inside the house, arm in arm. "I hope *he's* still seeing a psychiatrist. He needs it. He told me the Giles family is cursed."

"Oh?" She sounded distracted as she backed onto the street.

"Yeah. My grandmother told him about it. Goes back to before her father's time, or so he claimed. I mean seriously, who believes in curses?"

Janet glanced at him. "Well, Daniel once said negative energy must go somewhere, and it can manifest itself as—"

"Oh, please." Mark folded his arms. He felt sick at the mention of his wife's former lover. "Shoulda known Daniel would believe in curses."

She sighed and frowned at the road ahead. Mark slouched in his seat, trying to will away the edginess tickling his brain. He shivered as the vision of desperate self-preservation claimed his attention once more. In that instant, he was convinced the painstakingly constructed wall buffering him from the traumas of his life was about to be demolished, with consequences he couldn't even conceive of.

Maybe it would be a kindness if someone were to kill me right now, he thought.

CHAPTER 2.

Friday, April 23.

"I still think it would be a kindness to kill him, Sylvia," Victoria said, lowering herself onto the worn flowered couch, bracing for her aunt's response.

Aunt Sylvia looped yarn through yet another needlepoint canvas. She never finished, and Victoria wasn't certain what the end result was meant to be, if anything at all.

"Victoria, this is pointless if we do not see it through to its conclusion," the old woman answered, cold eyes piercing her. At least she didn't sound angry. "What did I teach you about the scientific method?"

Scientific method be damned, Victoria thought, shaking ash blonde hair out of her eyes. This is real life. But as she valued hers, she said instead, "It's so cruel. I feel like a...like a black widow spider in a lab coat."

"What a bizarre simile." Sylvia flipped the stretched canvas over and snipped the yarn with a tiny bird-shaped pair of scissors. "Cruelty does not enter into it. The time for action is drawing closer, according to my calculations," the woman went on pedantically. "But you must make certain it is the right man. You have made mistakes before."

Victoria snapped, "I know, damn it—"

Sylvia's slap across her face threw her back against the couch cushions.

"You have not learned to control your temper or your language," Sylvia said emotionlessly. "Have I wasted nineteen years of my life on you for nothing?"

Victoria fought back tears. "I'm sorry," she murmured. "It won't happen again."

Sylvia threaded a needle with dark green yarn. "It's a fairly common name. And you still have not learned if he has any children. You've been

8

seeing him how long now? A month?"

Victoria suspected the old woman knew down to the hour how long, and was testing her. "Five weeks. I've brought up the subject. But I'm young enough to be his daughter," she added. "I doubt he's anxious to tell me all about his children." Victoria chewed on a strand of hair, hesitant to offend further. "Why can't you just calculate the information we need?" she asked.

The old woman narrowed her eyes and set the canvas frame on the floor beside her. "The program operates on facts," Sylvia answered, "and extrapolates from those facts using a complex series of stochastic functions, as I'm certain I've told you before, Victoria. Until you gather additional data to feed into the program, I cannot forecast and manipulate events."

Sylvia rubbed her temples, and Victoria wondered again how old the woman really was. "The program has sensed him," she went on, "to use an extremely imprecise term. Indications are that someone related to him, perhaps his son, will become curious about the family soon and begin researching it. That should give you the necessary clue to find him. Which reminds me. Were you successful in your job search?"

"Yes," Victoria nodded, hoping for a bit of approval. "I've already started at the public library downtown. That's what I came by to tell you. Their genealogy collection is one of the best in the Southeast."

"I told you your experience would pay off."

The wooden floor shook as a stocky man strode into the living room, all blonde hair and white teeth. He looked like a walking advertisement for athletic equipment, from his white polo shirt to his perfect, unblemished white Nike shoes. "Good afternoon, Mr. Sweeney," Sylvia greeted the huge man. "Must I remind you yet again about slamming the front door?"

"Sorry, Miss Dee. I came by, like you asked." Andrew Sweeney smiled at Victoria. "Hey, babe."

Victoria dug her fingernails into her palms, but managed a civil, "Hello, Mr. Sweeney."

She stood and smoothed down her short red skirt, feeling Andrew's devouring gaze on her. "I have a date," she told Sylvia, pointedly ignoring the man. "I'll report to you later." She walked a wide circle around him, and hurried across the foyer, closing the front door behind her.

The air was warm outside, not too humid, a slight breeze rustling the oak trees lining the street. Victoria stepped over cracks in the sidewalk where roots thrust out of the ground, unclenched her fists and forced herself to breathe. Anger causes wrinkles, she reminded herself.

The warning signal at the railroad crossing flashed and clanged as she neared it. She was grateful for a chance to pause. Spike heels, she thought. Part of the uniform for all good whores.

A middle-aged man in a navy polo shirt and khaki slacks approached her as the train rumbled into view. Iron gray hair curled over his collar.

"Hi, Tom," she smiled at him, looking up into his silvery-blue eyes.

"Victoria, good to see you." Tom Richards grinned and squeezed her arm.

Three blue and yellow locomotives trundled past, followed by squealing and squeaking boxcars and coal cars and empty flatbeds.

"I love to watch the trains," she shouted in his ear over the noise. "My aunt lives nearby, so I see them pretty often. " She rested her fingers on his arm, "I prefer steam trains, though."

"When would you have seen a steam train?" Tom laughed, glancing down at her.

"Oh, I've never seen them in person. Just in books and on TV. You like trains?"

The little flashing light on the back of the last car sped away and the striped bar raised itself. Tom took her arm and helped her across the tracks to the sidewalk on the opposite side.

His cheeks reddened. "I collect model trains. Is that silly for an old man?"

She stopped in front of him on the sidewalk, palms on his chest. "Maybe for an old man," she said. "Do you know any old men? I don't."

"I can't imagine why you flatter me like this." His eyes crinkled shut when he laughed. "But I don't mind it."

Victoria grasped his callused hands and studied the white ridged scars on both wrists. She said, "Most men I've met in the past have been boys with no hobbies beyond women."

"I used to be that way, long ago." His smile faded. "Let's get a cup of coffee, okay? I want to talk to you."

Victoria linked her arm through his and they walked toward the coffee shop past houses new when he was a boy.

CHAPTER 3.

"Doctor, you've been spouting medical terminology at me for the last five minutes," Mark said. "Do you know what's wrong with me or not?"

Dr. Hollinger leaned forward. "Mark, I'll be honest with you. We've done every test in the alphabet, from ECG to MRI. The results show nothing wrong with your cardiovascular system, and no evidence of neurological problems." He straightened a stack of papers on one side of the desk. "I've been your doctor for, what, eight, nine years now? It's my professional opinion that you're as healthy as any thirty-three-year-old man. Well," the doctor amended, "you could use more exercise, but who couldn't?"

Mark clenched his hands on his knees, unable to keep his frustration out of his voice. "Is that your diagnosis? I keep passing out and having bizarre dreams for no apparent reason? I've scared my wife half to death, and the people I work with are so solicitous I may kill them. And I'm perfectly healthy?"

A frowning nurse stepped into the doorway. "Is anything wrong, Doctor?"

Hollinger crossed to the door and spoke to her. Mark realized he was standing, every muscle rigid. He emptied his lungs and sagged back into the chair as the doctor shut the door.

"Sorry," Mark muttered. "I'm not usually like this."

Dr. Hollinger sat on the corner of the desk. "I know. You under a lot of stress at work?"

A dragon carved in rust-red soapstone sitting on a shelf caught Mark's attention. "No more so than usual," he answered. He studied the dragon's sinuous lines, then dragged his gaze from the carving to the doctor's face. "I have two more days to finish upgrading software on about fifty computers. I've spent so damn many hours having needles stuck *in* me and electrodes stuck *on* me that I probably won't finish the report that's three days overdue--"

Mark took a deep breath, held it, and slowly let it out. He tried to smile. "Okay. I'm under a little stress lately."

"What about Janet?"

Mark's smile widened into a grin. "Oh, she's pretty stressed, too."

Hollinger grinned back. "You know what I mean. How are you getting along with her?"

Mark draped his arm over the back of the chair, stared at the ceiling. "Not too well. I've been so irritable lately I'm picking fights with her constantly. But that's not causing me to pass out and hear voices and see visions."

The doctor folded his arms. "That's twice now you've mentioned visions. You've only mentioned the blackouts before."

"I was at home, talking with Janet," Mark began, pushing the hair out of his eyes. "Suddenly I was somewhere else, maybe even someone else. I was running for my life. I knew if whoever was chasing me caught me, I was dead." Just remembering, his chest felt tight and he was panting. "I felt a searing pain in my shoulder and--" He rubbed his eyes.

"And?" the doctor prompted.

"Next thing I knew, I was on the living room floor with Janet hovering over me. I'd been out for about fifteen minutes, but despite the pain I'd felt, I wasn't hurt. She said I'd passed out in mid-sentence. It happened the next day, too, in the car. Thank God, I wasn't driving."

"Have you considered seeing a psychiatrist?"

Mark gritted his teeth. "She wants me to."

"There may be a psychological reason for these incidents." The doctor leaned back in his leather chair, frowning.

His mouth was dry. "Are you saying I'm crazy?"

"Of course not."

It sounded like a lie to Mark. "No, you don't ever say that. But the result is the same."

"Let me give you the name of a psychiatrist who--"

"No, thanks," Mark said, getting up to head for the door. "I don't think I'll get that desperate. Thanks for your time."

What scares you, he thought as he rode the elevator to the parking deck, is here's a situation you can't do anything about. You can't substitute a new motherboard or add more RAM. You're powerless to stop yourself from blacking out right this minute.

In the car, Mark went through the motions of driving home. He'd tried to banish the memory of his father's most recent suicide attempt, but it surfaced regularly these past three months. Mark arrived seconds before the paramedics in response to his mother's frantic phone call. He ran into the bedroom, braced for the spray of blood, rope burns or some new horror. Instead, he froze in the doorway, transfixed by the heap of dirty laundry that was his father. An open bottle spilled from his limp fingers and little yellow pills were scattered about his fingertips, like confetti after a party.

His mother told him later the EMTs dragged Mark bodily from the doorframe before they could bring his father out. All he recalled was the pale stillness of the unconscious man disappearing into an ambulance yet again. The ordinary attempt haunted him more than his father's two other dramatic acts of self-destruction.

The unsuccessful suicide left his father muttering as he stared out through the safety bars on the hospital window, "I couldn't save my family by killing myself. I can't even succeed when it's a selfish attempt to end my life."

That's when Mark closed off his emotions toward Thomas Richards. Mark told himself he was disgusted at his father's lack of consideration for his family, but deep down he knew the truth. Deep down, Mark was afraid. Afraid he could become just like him. Afraid he could lose control of his life without warning.

Afraid it was already happening.

CHAPTER 4.

Janet started, surprised by the sudden rattle of Mark's keys on the table by the door. She leaned over and picked up the paperback book she'd dropped. "I was getting worried," she said.

"My appointment was this afternoon." Mark stretched out full length on the couch, tensing for the discussion he knew was coming.

"You finally made an appointment? Why didn't you tell me? I would've gone with you. Was the news bad?"

Mark stared at the ceiling. "It was pretty bad."

She knelt next to him, a little crease forming between her eyebrows. "Oh, my God," she breathed. "Mark, is it a tumor?"

"No. He said there's nothing wrong with me. Ow!" he cried as she slapped his arm. "Why'd you do that?"

"Damn it, you scared me to death. Nothing's wrong?"

"All the tests were negative. I'm healthy." Mark folded his arms across his chest. "So basically I know shit."

She sat on the couch beside him and tucked a strand of shoulder-length hair behind her ear. The warmth of her body against his thigh annoyed him.

"I'm sorry. Didn't he give you any advice?"

He could see her concern, but hated to even mention what the doctor suggested. He might as well get it over with, though. "He told me to see a psychiatrist."

She nodded, as if she'd expected it. "Who did he recommend?"

Mark shrugged. Her closeness made him claustrophobic. He sat up and

14

nudged her out of the way. "Didn't find out."

"Well, call him back and find out." She used her schoolteacher voice.

"Nope."

Mark tugged off his hiking boots and padded into the kitchen. Janet followed. "You would've gone to see a neurologist if he'd recommended it, wouldn't you?"

He pulled a bottle of beer from the refrigerator, found an opener in the neatly arranged drawer. When the cap bounced across the floor, Janet tossed it in the trash can.

"Don't go all logical on me," Mark said, stopping to down a swallow of beer. "I'm not crazy. I'm not imagining things and I'm not dreaming."

"It doesn't mean you're crazy," she replied, exasperation creeping into her voice. "Just because your father--"

"This has nothing to do with my father." He swigged from the bottle again and the cool liquid eased the tightness of his throat.

"Yes, it does." She folded her arms beneath her breasts, fingers locked tight at her elbows. "You're afraid you'll end up like him."

Mark never hit a woman in his life, except maybe his kid sister, but an impulse to smack Janet with the back of his hand overwhelmed him. He set the bottle down on the counter with exaggerated care and grabbed her shoulders.

"I'm not going to see a psychiatrist," he whispered, staring into her eyes. Fear flickered across her face. "Understand?"

She backed away, expression troubled. "If you don't, Mark Richards, I'll--"

"You'll what?" he asked.

The doorbell rang, shattering his challenging pose.

Janet gasped, then stammered, "I-I forgot I invited your sister for dinner."

Mark grabbed her arm as she turned away. "Don't tell her anything about the blackouts."

"She doesn't know?" Her eyes were wide, fright still shimmering in their brown depths.

He growled, "I'll tell her eventually."

His wife glared back, then hurried to open the front door as the bell rang a second time.

"It's no good. I knew you were home. You can't hide." Natalie darted into the living room, tossed a bulging backpack onto the floor and kicked off her platform sandals. "When's dinner? I am *so* starving to death."

Janet hugged the tall young woman and said, "I ordered pizza. It should be here any minute."

"Did you order pineapple on it?" Natalie perched on the arm of a chair and ran her fingers through her short hair.

Mark settled his emotional mask into place and stretched out on the couch again. "Sorry, Nat. You're the only one in this house who likes pineapple on pizza."

Natalie slid to the floor and squinted at him. "You got something against fruit?"

"On pizza, yes."

Janet sat on the opposite end of the couch. "How's school?" she asked Natalie.

"I'm auditioning for a part in *Oklahoma* next week. Just a small part in the chorus." Natalie rummaged through her backpack. "By the way, I was cleaning my room--hey," she said as Mark raised his eyebrows. "It happens occasionally. Anyway, I found something for you."

She extracted a yellow spiral-bound notebook and handed it to Mark. The hand-printed cover read, "The History of My Family, by Thomas Demarcus Richards."

"What's this?" Mark asked. The pages were covered with his father's angular scrawl.

"I had to write a paper on our family last semester, so Daddy wrote this out for me." Natalie smiled, sitting up on her heels. "Got an A on the paper. You're always going on about the family history, so I thought you'd like to have it. What was it you said that made Daddy so mad?" She dropped her voice into a fair imitation of Mark's. "With all the bad things that happen to this family, there must be some pretty weird skeletons lurking in the closet.'" Natalie giggled. "I've never seen him so mad at you. I think he almost slugged you. After reading it, you'll see you were just about right."

The doorbell rang. Janet paid the pizza delivery woman and carried two fragrant boxes into the kitchen. Natalie popped up and bounded after her.

Mark stared at the notebook a moment before setting it on the couch and wandering across the room. "What do you mean, you understand why?" he asked, watching the women get out plates and glasses.

"Mark, our family is cursed." Natalie held up a cola bottle after this pronouncement. "Hexed. Jinxed. Born under a bad star."

"Thank you, Ms. Roget," Mark said. He skirted Janet, who was distributing slices of pizza, and snagged another bottle of beer from the refrigerator. "You sound just like Dad. On what do you base this amazing conclusion?"

He shook his head when Janet tried to hand him a plate. "Not hungry," he mumbled.

Natalie said around a bite of pizza, "Well, Daddy's Exhibit A in our Hall of Cursed Relatives. You can't deny that."

"Hardly," Mark said.

"And there's Tommy." The smile vanished from her eyes. Their middle brother had been dead for over ten years. Natalie was nine years old when their father left at two a.m. to pick Tommy up from his summer job. No one witnessed the accident, but the streets were slick with rain. The elder Richards walked away without a scratch. His namesake died in the ambulance on the way to the hospital. Thomas Richards' second suicide attempt occurred two weeks later.

Mark's vision swam briefly and he closed his eyes, reopening them as Natalie continued, "Daddy only went back as far as his parents and his brothers and sisters in the family history. He has a page about each person."

"Brothers and sisters?" Mark clutched the countertop, as the floor inexplicably tilted.

Natalie nodded. "Daddy was the youngest of seven children."

The beer bottle shattered on the linoleum floor. He knelt to pick up the pieces, but his hands were shaking.

"Mark, you're bleeding," Janet said.

"What?"

Janet dragged him to the sink, washing the smear of blood from his palm. "Don't listen to her," she said, drying the small cut. "If there's a curse--"

"There's no damn curse."

"If there is," she persisted, "it can be dispelled. All curses can be." Janet bandaged his hand, opened another beer for him, and steered him to the couch. "Sit down and read the notebook before you jump to conclusions," she said. "You know how melodramatic your sister is. She likes to scare people." She left him there, steering his chastened sister back into the kitchen with her.

He nodded, settled down on the couch again, and drank half the bottle before opening the notebook. Unfamiliar names leapt from the pages as he read about his grandparents, both of whom died when Mark was a child. They had seven children, and within a span of seven years, all but his father were dead.

The eldest child fell through an ice-covered creek and drowned. Mark's father failed to rescue her. Two others died in a car crash Mark's father survived. His remaining sister disappeared on her way home and was never seen again.

Mark drank the rest of the beer, afraid he would drop the bottle if he didn't. His face felt cold and numb, but he needed to find out what happened to the other children. Janet and Natalie's chatter sounded far away, distorted and unreal.

When his father was eighteen, he was babysitting his nine-year-old brother. The child fell from the tree he was climbing and broke his neck.

Two years later, Thomas accompanied his only living brother on a hunting trip. According to Thomas, his brother climbed over a fence, shotgun in hand, and the gun discharged. The nineteen-year-old lingered for three days in the middle of the wilderness with the side of his head shot off before he died.

The family moved every time one their children died, the only explanation Mark could find for why police or social services hadn't investigated. Nowhere in the terse narrative did Mark's father mention his feelings toward witnessing the deaths of his siblings. Mark wondered if his father thought he should be dead, too, and if the suicide attempts were to make reality square with his perceptions. He lost track of time as he stared at the ceiling. At some point, Natalie appeared beside him, expression anxious.

"Are you okay, Bro?" she asked.

Mark sat up. The room spun and he shut his eyes, which only made it worse. His tongue felt huge and tingly. "There's no curse, Nat," he enunciated carefully. "One generation of bad luck doesn't mean anything. Okay, really rotten luck. But--"

The abrupt ringing of the phone on the table next to him made painful vibrations in the bones of his face. Sweat beaded his forehead and his heart shifted gears. Such a simple thing to bring so much fear.

Janet picked up the receiver. She listened a moment, then said, "We'll be right over."

"Oh, God," he whispered. "What's he done now?"

Janet's face was pale as she hung up the phone. "Your father's missing."

CHAPTER 5.

Mark burst into his parents' house. "Mom! Mother!" He skidded on the throw rug inside the door. Janet caught his arm before he fell. "She's not here."

The swinging door from the dining room opened, and his mother said with a tired sigh, "I'll be right there, I'm on the phone." Her pale face accentuated the redness of her eyes.

Natalie collapsed onto the couch. Mark sat beside her, watching Janet straighten the rug. The plastic slipcover crinkled beneath him, reminding him of interminable Sunday afternoons spent sitting as still as possible while his parents discussed grown-up things with the neighbors.

"What do you suppose triggered it this time?" Janet asked, rearranging the glass figurines in the curio cabinet.

Natalie slapped the couch. "Maybe he just went out somewhere," she said in a thin voice. "Why do we have to assume he's killed himself?"

She folded forward, dissolving into great hiccupping sobs. Janet squeezed between brother and sister, wrapping her arms around Natalie. "I'm sorry, I didn't mean to upset you."

Delia Richards walked into the living room.

"What happened, Mom?" Mark asked.

She lowered herself into the armchair, took off her glasses, and rubbed her eyes. "We closed the office early today. The air conditioning broke down again, and you know how it is in there. No ventilation. Your father insisted on keeping the car today and I called him to pick me up, but there was no answer, so I had to get a ride with Miriam. He wasn't here, though, and neither was the car."

"He didn't leave a note, did he?" Natalie raised her head, mascara

19

streaking her cheeks.

Delia sighed, fingers twisting together in her lap. "No, honey, he didn't."

Mark's sister swiped at tears. "Then maybe he's gone to get a new train or something."

"We can't even call the police yet," the ever-practical Janet said. "It hasn't been twenty-four hours yet."

"It doesn't matter," said Mark, pacing across the room. "He's already dead."

Three female faces glared up at him, and he turned away. "Look, he's tried to kill himself four times already. Maybe this time he decided to get it right without interruption."

Janet and Natalie both began talking together, making his ears ring, until his mother said, "Sit down, Mark," in that soft-but-stern voice he remembered from years of broken lamps and disobeyed directives.

But I'm thirty-three now, he thought. You can't make me sit down. Aloud, he said, "Just accept it. He's gone. And he's not out buying new trains." Mark strode from the room, up the stairs, and into his father's study.

The room hadn't changed in years, the same oversized desk topped with an elaborate model train layout, the same bookcases overflowing with books and papers, the same smell of model glue and paint. The chair's squeal of protest flayed his raw nerves as he flung himself into it. Mark's elbow hit a book lying open on the desk's pull-out extension. The oversized pages held black-and-white photographs, white borders neatly tucked into arrow-shaped holders. His father was younger and thinner in the pictures, smiling broadly, his eyes crinkled against the sun, alongside a huge steam engine, sitting under a tree beside railroad tracks with Delia.

"Demarcus--"

He jumped at the sound of Delia's voice as if the woman in the photo had spoken. The scrapbook spun to the floor.

"Demarcus, I want you to find your father."

A distant shot of a Seaboard Air Line engine and string of boxcars had fallen from the book and he slid it back into place. "No," Mark answered. The corner of the photograph sprang out of the holder, as if it wanted to be anywhere but trapped between the pages of the scrapbook.

A clock ticked somewhere in the room. Mark's mother was a patient woman, and he knew she would stand and look at him until he finally spoke.

But she broke the silence first.

"You must find him," she said. She could have been discussing a meatloaf recipe. "He could be hurt somewhere."

"No!" Mark shoved himself to his feet. The chair clanged in metallic protest against the bookcase. "He's dead. Let someone else find him this time."

One of her hands brushed the little green hill on the diorama table, trailed to the miniature tracks below it. She watched the motion of her fingers, but her jaw muscle rippled. "I know this isn't easy for you."

Something screamed inside his head. Mark turned his back on her, gripped the sill, and stared out at the dark street. "No, it's not," he whispered. "Do you know how many times I've dreamed of blood and rope-burned skin and--"

He swallowed hard. "Damn it, Mom, I can't do it again. I don't have the strength."

"I can't do it myself," she said. "And you know Natalie and Janet will insist on--"

"Oh, they're women, so they can't do hard work like that."

She picked up a length of track, and the plastic snapped between her fingers. "That's not what I meant." Delia dropped the pieces on the layout's artificial grass. "It's not safe for them to be out wandering by themselves. I've called everyone we know, including the man at the hobby shop, and no one's seen him."

Mark sagged back into the chair. "I'll think about it," he murmured.

His mother nodded, lips compressed, and left the room.

He's probably shot his head off this time, Mark thought. Won't that be something to see?

A sharp pain lanced from his groin to his head, arching his body off the seat, fingers spasming on the chair arms. He cried out, agonized, as every neuron fired at once. The pain flipped off like a switch. He slid to the floor, and kept on sliding into an inky black void.

CHAPTER 6.

She's laughing again. If my jokes were as funny as she thinks they are, I could be a stand-up comic, he thought. Tom Richards smiled at the beautiful young woman, part of him wondering why she was spending the afternoon in his company, as he did every time they'd met in the last five weeks. But most of him simply enjoyed the experience.

"It's too bad," Victoria said, setting her coffee cup on the café table, "that there's nowhere peaceful and quiet where we could walk along train tracks."

"That's what you want to do this afternoon?" he asked. "We could go down to Helena." He pronounced it with the accent on the second syllable, Hell-EE-na.

Victoria squinted her eyes in thought, blonde eyebrows almost joining at the center like a bird's wings. "Helena? South of town?"

He nodded. "That's where I grew up. Nice little place."

She scooped up her huge purse.

What do women carry in those things? he wondered absently. Even after thirty-four years of marriage, he wasn't sure, and wasn't sure he really wanted to know.

"Let's go then."

Tom gaped. "You'd like to?"

She smiled. "Sure. I've never been down there. It'll be fun."

He fumbled in his wallet and dropped a five-dollar bill on the table to cover the coffee and tip and followed her out to his big brown Ford LTD. As he opened the door for her and walked around to the driver's side, a thought occurred that flamed his cheeks.

"I'm embarrassed to say this," Tom said, starting the car, "but I don't know your last name after all the times we've ... been intimate." The engine roared as he pulled out into traffic.

"Giles," she smiled. "Victoria Giles."

"Giles? My mother was a Giles."

Victoria was silent. He glanced at her, uneasy about bringing relatives into their secret world. But she was looking at him, green eyes wide, lips parted.

"Oh?" she said at last. "What was her name?"

Tom accelerated up the on-ramp. "Clarice Demarca Giles. Unusual, huh? Demarcus is my middle name and my son's first name, after her. I think that was her father's name." Tom laughed as he sped around a slow-moving utility truck. "He hates it, though, my son does."

There, he'd done it. Slipped in the idea he had children and probably wasn't as young as she might've thought.

"People are funny about their names, aren't they?" she observed, fumbling with her seat belt. He wondered if his driving made her as nervous as it did Delia.

Delia.

He glanced at Victoria, her legs tucked beneath her on the wide seat, skirt hiked up to reveal creamy thighs, and the image of his wife's face vanished. He forced his eyes back onto the road, swerving away from the gravel shoulder.

"So your son's name is Demarcus Richards." Her hair hid her face as she rummaged in her purse, producing a pair of red flats.

Tom tried to watch her change shoes, but the honk of an angry driver distracted him away from a glimpse of lace under her skirt, and when he looked back, she was stuffing the spike heels into the purse, her skirt concealing the well-muscled thighs.

"Do you have any other children?" she asked.

"Two. No, one," he amended.

His error brought a laugh from her. "Don't you know how many children you have?"

He chewed his lip and squinted through the windshield. "I lost a boy, several years ago. In a car crash."

Her manicured hand appeared on his leg. "I'm sorry. I shouldn't have laughed."

Tom cleared his throat. "You didn't know."

Despite his unease at the subject matter, his heart was pounding and he tingled from the warmth of her hand on his leg. He didn't remember ever feeling quite this way about Delia, even when they first met. His feelings for his wife were calmer, gentle and familiar and safe.

"My other child is a girl, Natalie Clarice," he went on, gripping the steering wheel. "She's a sophomore in college."

"That's nice," Victoria murmured. She unfastened her seat belt and slid next to him, the heat of her thigh burning through his pants. A wave of pure lust washed through his body and he wiped beads of sweat from his brow.

They rode in silence as he turned off the interstate next to rows of enormous fuel storage tanks, a faint petroleum smell filtering into the car. Mostly to distract himself from the tightness in his trousers, he pointed out the railroad tracks paralleling the road on the left as a train boomed into view, rattling along in the opposite direction.

The road wound up and down hills, past housing developments and apartment complexes. "This is all new," he explained, grimacing. "These were fields not too long ago."

"Why don't you live out here, Tom?"

He shivered agreeably as her fingers caressed the back of his neck. "I had a hardware store in town years ago, when I was younger. It was too far to commute every day, and Delia didn't want to live 'in the middle of nowhere,' as she called it." He sighed, waiting for a bus to pass before turning right. "My hardware business went bust, and I guess I did too."

He slowed the car, gesturing at the ramshackle buildings in the twilight. "Some of these were really nice, once. A tornado came through in 1933 and blew most of the town away." He fell silent and parked the car in the gravel lot of the Masonic Lodge, a two-story whitewashed structure. The walls were slotted with tall narrow windows, dark behind cheery yellow curtains.

"Tom, what's wrong?"

He shook his head, staring into the distance. "I just remembered a dream I had last night-a recurring nightmare. About a tornado."

Victoria giggled. "Those are supposed to be sexual dreams."

"Not this one," he said, and her smile vanished. "I was standing in a field, at one end, and scattered through it were family members ... my parents, my brothers and sisters, my grandparents. Closest to me were Delia, Natalie and Demarcus, with Tommy a little further out. Suddenly the sky went green and a tornado dropped down out of the clouds and scooped up people, one after another. It drew closer and closer. I woke up just after it took Tommy."

The terror of the dream was still too real.

"But it was just a dream," Victoria whispered, hand on his arm.

"It's the same sort of dream my mother had. She told me about it once. I've had it a few times before, right before ... right before something bad happens." He cleared his throat again and looked into her eyes. "I don't know if it's possible, but the dream is genetic."

Her eyes mirrored his pain. She's actually listening, he marveled. She cares about my dream. He leaned over and kissed her lips gently. "Let's not talk about it anymore."

"Where are the train tracks?" she asked, craning her neck. "Oh, I see the sign now."

Tom opened the car door for her. "Let's walk down there. It's staying light so much longer now, we should be able to see really well." He hauled out his old pocket watch and squinted at it. "Nearly five o'clock," he announced, thinking, Delia's going to be upset, but right now, I don't care.

"What a beautiful watch." Victoria slipped her fingers around his, pulling it closer.

"My mother gave it to me. It was her great-grandfather's, passed down from father to son. I guess I always thought of it as a kind of--don't laugh now--a magic talisman." He darted a glance at her lovely face.

She nodded solemnly, releasing his hand.

"She gave it to me after ... after all the horrible things happened. I always felt if I kept it with me, nothing else horrible could happen to me." Tom shook his head.

He sighed heavily, put the watch back in his pocket and took Victoria's hand, leading her two blocks down to the tracks, pointing out the old city hall and the dry goods store and the bridge near which a rolling mill used to stand.

When they reached the tracks, they walked down the middle between a gravel slope on one side and a brushy hill on the other. The air was breezy and warm, dinner cooking in the houses up the hill mingling with pine smell and diesel fumes. Sounds of children playing drifted to them from a distance.

"Let's stop here," Victoria suggested after about fifteen minutes. She stepped off the tracks and climbed a little ridge to a flat, tree-surrounded area with a view of dark green pines and bright green oaks and maples. She tugged at his hand and sat down on the brown grass. He joined her with a grunt, wincing as his knee joints popped.

"I'm getting too old to sit on the ground.'

"Just how old are you, Tom?" she demanded, tossing her purse on the ground and leaning close to him. "You've never told me."

"Fifty-three."

"You talk like you're eighty-three. Shut up and kiss me."

He'd never made love to anyone outside a bedroom, especially not outside in broad daylight, but he grasped her shoulders and pressed his lips to hers. He moaned as she unbuckled his belt, unfastening the buttons of her blouse with trembling hands. She writhed against him and his thoughts dissolved in a black blur of passion. The bushes surrounding them shaded them from the glaring sun and dappled a pattern across their clothing and her soft, hot skin.

Moments or days or years later, he couldn't be sure, he lay back on the grass, spent and gasping, warm air rasping his lungs. Her head rested on his chest, hair tickling his nose. Finally his breathing slowed and he opened his eyes. He must've dozed; her back was to him as she combed her blonde hair, luminous in the filtered rays of the setting sun. He reached up and tweaked grass from the back of her head, and she turned and smiled.

"I enjoyed that, Tom," she said, thrusting her comb back in her purse.

He was disappointed she'd already fastened her blouse and smoothed her skirt. He sat up and zipped his pants. "That was my first time outside," he admitted.

She brushed debris from his hair, looked down the track. "Do trains ever come by here?"

As if in answer, they heard a whistle in the distance. "Sure do. Maybe we should move away from the track."

"No, I want to be close to it when it comes by," she insisted.

He shrugged and stood, tucking his shirt into his waistband.

The roar grew louder as the train approached, its cyclopean eye glaring at them. The ground vibrated. Tom reached for Victoria's hand, and turned to see her standing just behind him. The train was nearly upon them as she stepped toward him. She darted forward --

And he was falling from the ridge into the path of the train. But this time I don't want to die, he thought in mild protest as his head struck the steel rail.

~*~*~

Victoria crossed the tracks and slid down the gravel on the other side. The train screeched to a halt up ahead. By the time she reached the street, the keening of sirens split the evening air. She sagged against the wall of a building in the long late shadows as deep sobs wracked her body. Her fingers and toes were numb, and she was shivering. A Helena police car screamed past as she ducked farther back into the shadows.

Sylvia's not going to like this, she thought, rubbing her arms. Every nerve pleaded with her to give in, to sink to the ground into oblivion. She forced away the memory of Tom's gentle hands on her body, dug her long fingernails into her palms and pushed herself away from the building. When she passed the old brown LTD parked next to the Masonic Lodge, she paused, tears welling up as she relived the moment of Tom's death. I had to do it, she reminded herself. I had to save him from himself.

Red and blue light stained the road and trees as an ambulance tore past her, but the siren was silent. He's dead, most likely in several pieces, she told herself. No reason to hurry now.

Still watching the ambulance, she collided with what felt like a brick wall.

"Hey, babe. Guess I'm too late. What've you done now?"

"Let go of me." Victoria struggled in his grip.

"Miss Dee ain't gonna look kindly on either of us, darlin'." Andrew yanked her along.

"You don't have to drag me."

"Rather I carried you to the car?"

She sighed, her body slumping. "No." With a final glance at the light show, she asked, "What do you think Sylvia will do?"

"Ain't gonna be pretty, babe." He wiped a tear from her cheek as they neared his pick-up truck. "You really were sweet on that guy, huh?"

"Go to hell, Sweeney."

~*~*~

Victoria resisted the urge to kick Andrew's muscular ass as he preceded her into Sylvia's house. She noted with some satisfaction he was limping, and she scraped bits of his skin from under her nails. Her own blouse was torn, her cheek ached, but her nose stopped bleeding at last.

"He attacked me," she snapped, throwing herself into an overstuffed armchair.

"Victoria." Sylvia folded her arms across her sagging bosom, sparse eyebrows crowding her tiny dark eyes. "You disobeyed me. He was acting on my orders."

Victoria licked her lower lip and tasted blood. "Did you tell him to try to rape me?"

"Now, wait just a minute. I didn't--" Andrew broke in from his position by the door.

"Mr. Sweeney," Sylvia said, "when we spoke on the telephone, I authorized discipline, nothing more. I suggest you leave. Quickly."

Victoria laughed. "He won't be doing anything quickly. I kicked him in the nuts."

Andrew glared, nodded to the older woman and left the house. Sylvia hobbled to stand beside Victoria. "I hope you learned something useful since you so flagrantly disobeyed me."

"I don't care. You knew what was going to happen, what he would do," Victoria argued, digging a brush from her purse and unsnarling her hair. "I didn't want him put through that, not even for your precious experiments."

"What did you find out from him? Did he have any children?"

She exchanged the brush for a mirror. "He started with three. Now he has two."

"Oh?" Sylvia leaned forward. "So the curse is still working, still gathering strength. Very interesting. Was it the eldest child who was dead?"

"I'm not sure. Somehow I don't think so." She crossed her legs, swallowing against the tightness in the back of her throat. "Demarcus

Richards is his son's name. He's married. His daughter is Natalie Clarice, a sophomore in college. And no, I don't know what college."

"A daughter? A daughter could be useful."

"Useful? How?" Victoria asked.

"Never mind," Sylvia said. "Now go home and clean yourself up. I expect you to redeem yourself when you meet the son. Your particular seductive power should work on him just as well as it did on the father."

CHAPTER 7.

Mark opened his eyes and stared at the ceiling, trying to figure out where he was. I didn't hear the alarm go off, he thought in a panic. Did I oversleep?

The bare bulb of his father's train room glared down at him. A searing band of agony scored his upper chest and calves, like nerves exposed to raw current. He rolled out from under the chair and frantically hiked up his shirt, expecting to see blackened, charred flesh. The skin was undamaged beneath, the pain fading even as he examined it. He crawled up into the chair, wondering what happened to him. The other blackouts were more like fainting spells, the pain disappearing when he regained consciousness.

A phone rang somewhere in the house. Mark shoved his shirttail back into pants, and skirted the train layout. He was leaning on the doorframe of the room when Janet appeared at the top of the stairs moments later.

"They've found your father," she said, reaching out to him.

~*~*~

Monday, April 26.

The night air was still cool, but the wind had died down. Mark gently rocked the swing, his feet braced on the porch, his arm around his mother's shoulders. Friends and acquaintances who stopped by after the funeral dispersed a few hours ago, leaving him numb and distracted.

The sad little funeral went as well as he expected, the minister struggling valiantly to say something positive about a man successful on his fifth suicide attempt. Many of Mark's coworkers attended, their presence inhibiting any emotion he might've shown. He shrugged off their condolences until his mother took him aside and reprimanded him for being rude.

A quiet noise brought his gaze to the woman next to him.

His mother reached into the pocket of her denim skirt. "Your father wanted you to have this." She unwrapped a handkerchief to reveal a familiar gold pocket watch.

Mark took it, rubbed the brushed gold surface, squinted at the dent in the back. He pressed the catch and the cover popped open, revealing a white face with stark black numerals.

"It's a miracle the crystal wasn't broken. The dent is the only damage it suffered. The chain was twisted, too. I'll buy you a new one."

He cleared his throat. "Thanks, Mom, I'm really touched. Did his dad give it to him?"

"His mother did. It belonged to her father, and his father before him and his father before him."

He closed the cover. "I never wanted to pry back then, but what started Dad's problems?"

Delia slipped off the swing, clasping her hands in front of her. She walked to the top of the steps and back, shaking her head. "You certainly are your father's son. You think asking about another family member's welfare is prying." She raised a hand to stop his protests. "Not a criticism, Demarcus. You're a very private person, always have been. Your father was too."

Buttoning her sweater absorbed her attention for several moments before she continued. "What started his problems? Well, your brother's death contributed, but the blackouts and nightmares started before the accident--Demarcus? What's wrong?"

His pounding heart almost drowned out her words. Sweat prickled his forehead and palms. "Blackouts?" He dropped the watch into the pocket of his chambray shirt and wiped his hands on his jeans.

"You're pale as a ghost," his mother said. "Maybe we should talk later."

"No, no, go ahead," Mark insisted. "I'm fine."

Delia folded her arms and leaned against the porch railing. "He passed out several times about a month before the accident. Tom had all sorts of tests run, but the doctors couldn't find any reason for it. They referred him to a psychiatrist. Before he could go, he had the accident with Tommy." She sighed. "He never said, but I think a blackout caused the accident. It makes more sense than any other explanation I can come up with."

"Did he ever talk about the nightmares?" Mark wondered if he'd have them too.

"Some." She pushed herself off the railing and sat beside him again. "They weren't actually nightmares; that's just what he called them. I mean, they didn't happen while he was asleep. They happened during some of the blackouts." She stared up at the night sky. "It was all connected with family history. He was convinced, whether by the dreams or apart from them, I don't know, that the family was cursed. Not the Richards side, but the Giles side. You know how obsessive he was. Again, like you."

She paused, swallowed, went on, "Sometimes after a blackout he'd rave about murder and blood and throats being cut--"

She shivered. "I think he got the idea from his mother. She used to go on about curses and black magic." Delia leaned closer as if someone were listening. "I was never comfortable around her, to tell you the truth. I tried not to let Tom see, but ... well, she gave me the creeps."

Mark squinted his eyes shut, remembering his last conversation with his father. "That sounds like Natalie. She's convinced of the family curse too. It's silly. Just a lot of coincidence and tragedy, that's all. No need to make it into a curse. I mean it," he protested as she continued to eye him with what he thought of as the "Mom-knows-I'm-lying" look. "Although I must confess, it is strange he was present when all but one of his siblings died."

She snapped her head toward him. "Did he tell you that?"

"Whoa, easy, Mom! He wrote it down for Natalie for a paper of hers. You know, the last time I saw him, last Sunday, he started to tell me something. He wasn't ... he wasn't involved in any way with their deaths, was he?"

"I don't honestly know, dear," Delia answered. "I've always wondered. And to tell you the truth, when Tommy died--oh, I shouldn't say this so soon after the funeral."

"Say what?" Mark asked.

"I wondered if your father killed him intentionally." She sat next to him again.

"Mom!"

"Sit down, Demarcus." She tugged at his shirt until he slumped back onto the swing. "It was just the momentary reaction of a grieving mother. The police gave no indication at the time that it was anything other than an accident or a blackout."

He sat, watching a pair of joggers huffing down the street, then wrapped an arm around his mother's shoulders again and changed the subject. "How are you holding up?"

She twisted her wedding ring around her finger, attention focused on the motion. "I don't really know yet. I prepared myself so many times to be ready for this moment, but ..."

She trailed off into silence. "I'll know better in the coming weeks. How about you?"

He shrugged. "I'm fine. I probably shouldn't say this, but I'm a little relieved--"

"Demarcus!"

"I'm sorry, Mom," Mark said, "but I know it's been a strain on you, too, wondering when it would happen again and if he'd be successful. Preparing, as you said."

She shifted her position on the swing so she could look into his face. "You're going to think I'm a crazy woman in denial, but I'm not so sure I believe the verdict on your father."

He frowned. "What do you mean?"

"The other times he tried, he was so depressed...quiet...listless beforehand. I knew something was going on." She shook her head and looked up at the diamond-studded sky. "He wasn't depressed this time. In fact--"

Her voice faltered. She cleared her throat and started again. "In fact, I think he may have been seeing someone else."

Mark stopped the swing's motion with his feet and stared. "Seeing... someone...else," he repeated. Okay, they're all English words, he thought, but what do they mean strung together like that? "I'm not following you, Mom."

Delia took his hand. "Having an affair."

He leapt off the swing, setting it rocking. "That's just ridiculous, Mom. Why would Dad have an affair? And who with? Did you see him with someone?"

"I knew you'd overreact," she said. "Sit back down."

"Overreact? Should I take it calmly?"

She tugged him down. "I have no proof. Just a feeling. Anyway, it doesn't matter now."

He leaned his head back on the swing chains, eyes closed, listening to the distant murmur of traffic, the squeak of the swing. His jumbled thoughts fell into a nice, neat pattern and his breath caught in his throat. "Mom..."

He was scared to say it. "If it wasn't suicide...and he was with someone... Do you realize what you're saying?"

Delia looked away, but nodded. "Your father may have been murdered."

CHAPTER 8.

Tuesday, April 27.

"Mark! Come look at this terminal. Why's it doing this?"

Mark grinned as he walked into the library. The place was a juxtaposition of warm wood paneling and mismatched wooden furniture against forty-year-old linoleum. I'm away for an extra day and they can't live without me, he thought. That's either job security or poor staff training on my part. The owner of the perplexed voice was the head of the library's circulation department, a heavy-set woman with highlighted blonde hair.

"Good morning to you, too, Tina." He walked around behind the main desk.

Tina smacked her forehead with her palm. "Oh, sorry, Mark. I'm too busy worrying about how we'll cope if the system's down today." She patted him on the shoulder. "Good to have you back. I'm sorry I couldn't make it to the funeral, but somebody had to hold down the fort."

"The flowers were nice. Mom commented on them."

"Oh, good." She shook her head. "I think the catalog's down. Again."

"I'll see what I can do." He glanced down at the keyboard and tapped a few keys.

Tina moved away. She was good about not hovering around him as he tried to fix problems. "There," he announced several minutes later to no one in particular. "I've saved the universe yet again."

"Thanks, Mark," Tina said with a smile. "I was afraid it was down for the rest of the day." She looked at him, brow furrowed. "Are you okay? Are you sure you shouldn't have taken some time off?"

"Okay?" He forced a grin. "Yeah, I'm making it. As well as can be expected."

"But I heard about the circumstances," she persisted. "That must be terribly upsetting."

He glanced at the front counter, desperate for a distraction. "You have a customer," he said, noticing a student standing on the other side of the counter.

Tina took the books the student slid across the counter. "You're sure I can use the system now?" she called over her shoulder, and Mark nodded. "How's your mother taking it?"

"I don't think the reality's set in yet. She's trying to be strong for Natalie's sake. My sister's a mess," he answered.

"They're due back on May 12th," Tina told the student. "I'm sorry," she said, turning back to Mark. "Your sister is such a sweet and lively person, I hate to see her upset."

Mark slid past the swinging panel between counters. "I'm sure she'll bounce back. At least, I hope so. See you later, Tina."

The phone rang. "Hang on, Mark, this could be for you."

He paused in mid-stride. Tina answered. "Okay, Fran. I'll tell him," she said, and hung up. "You have to save the universe again, Captain Kirk. Fran's having a computer problem."

"A hero's work is never done." He hauled the dented gold pocket watch from his khaki slacks and observed, "I've been here seventeen minutes and already saving the universe twice. What on earth did you do yesterday?"

Mark strode down the hallway, sidestepping two giggling girls in sorority T-shirts. A voice to his right demanded his attention. "Mark? Good to see you back. How are you?"

He stopped with a mental sigh and smiled at the library director. "Hi, Barbara. I'm okay, thanks. A little tired."

She nodded. "I'm sure you've had a very stressful weekend. Take care, okay?"

Mark was relieved when she left it at that. Barbara Williams was not a woman who wasted much time with sentiment. "When you've had a moment to settle down, would you come to my office? I have something to discuss with you."

"Let me see to Fran's computer, and I'll be right there."

Barbara rolled her eyes. "What has she done to it now?"

"I'm not sure. It's always something, isn't it?"

Mark walked toward the elevator and was stopped by a tall woman with stringy hair. She hugged him and gushed, "Oh, Mark," held him at arms' length and gazed at him. "You really shouldn't be back this soon, you know."

"Hi, Antonia." She ignored or, more likely, did not perceive his lack of enthusiasm.

"I heard it was suicide. That is oh so tragic!" Her tone of excitement belied her words.

He pulled away from her grasp. "I need to go, Antonia."

Antonia persisted. "And I heard he was with someone, a woman. Was it your mother? For her to witness--ouch!"

Mark grabbed her wrist hard. "Where did you hear that?"

Eyes wide, she shrank back against the journal stacks. "My son works for the paper," Antonia said. "You remember Billy? He graduated last year. Graduated cum laude, too. He--"

God, the woman is obtuse. "Where did he hear it?" His voice was almost a growl as he squeezed her wrist.

"You're hurting me," she wailed.

He released her as a passing student stared. Mark glared, and the student edged away.

"Billy talked to the reporter who covered the story, since he knows I work with you." Antonia rubbed the red mark on her wrist. "A witness saw a man fitting your father's description walking with a woman or having coffee or something some time before it happened. But the witness didn't get a good look and couldn't describe her very well. So it wasn't your mother?"

"Thanks for the information, Antonia." He slipped into the elevator door as it opened across from him and sagged against the wall. That story would be all over the library by ten. Sooner, if Antonia's not busy. It looks like Dad was seeing someone. Someone who killed him?

The elevator doors creaked open. Nodding to the librarian at the reference desk, Mark whisked around the corner before anyone else could extend sympathy. Fran had attended the funeral, so maybe she wouldn't dwell on condolences.

"Hi, Fran," he greeted the plump woman hunched over a keyboard. "What have you done to your poor computer now?"

"I don't know," she yelped, vacating her chair so he could take her place. "Computers hate me." Fran leaned against the wall. "Can you fix it? I think I lost the file I was working on."

"What was it called?"

"Serials. I think."

Mark tapped the keys, distracted by the memory of identifying his father after the accident. His face was almost unrecognizable from loss of blood, white and waxy and still, his body mercifully hidden beneath the sheet. A policeman confided, out of his mother's hearing, that the train wheels had sliced him into three pieces, across the chest and lower legs. The pain he experienced at his mother's house flashed into his mind, forgotten until that moment. He'd felt it in the exact places as his father's wounds.

"What's wrong?" Fran was shaking his shoulder. "Mark? You're white as a sheet."

He waved her off. "I'm just amazed at what a mess your files are." He savaged the left mouse button and watched the result on the screen. "There's your file, Fran," he gestured. "Now if you'll excuse me, I have a meeting with Barbara."

As he took the stairs down to Barbara's office, the incident at his mother's house replayed through his mind. He'd never experienced anything resembling a psychic link with his father. They hadn't even been that close. Tommy was his father's favorite. But he felt his father's pain, at the precise moment the train struck him.

When he reached the office, Barbara motioned him in. "I hate to do this so soon after the funeral," she began as they sat in upholstered armchairs grouped around a small cherry table. "But I suspect you'd rather work than brood."

"You're right," he agreed. "What do you need me to do?"

She opened a file in front of her. "The Development Office informed me of a new government grant program for university technology improvements. Unfortunately I didn't find out about it until yesterday, and the deadline is June 5th. We must submit it to Development by May 20th. It's a two million dollar grant. You're the only one qualified to write the proposal."

"Two *million*?" Mark whistled and shook his head. "I've never written a grant before."

Barbara pushed the folder toward him. "Our contact in Development said she's willing to go over it when you've completed it and let us know of any corrections, which is why we have about a month's lead time. No one in their office has the expertise you have."

"That's an incredible amount of money."

She picked up another file. "You don't have to start from scratch. How many times have we talked about what we could do with more money? Here's my folder on some of the more recent proposals to give you an idea of what to ask for." She leafed through a few pages. "I don't see a copy of that report you did last year. You wrote up a very good justification, as I recall."

"Not good enough to get us any money," he said. "I think I have it in on a CD down in storage. I'll dig it out."

"Good. I'd like to see a rough draft by ..."

Barbara flipped pages in her desk calendar. "How about May 10th? That way we can make sure you're headed in the right direction."

"In two weeks?"

The woman smiled. "I have every confidence in you, Mark. And try to finish that software upgrade of the catalog as soon as possible."

"Sure. I'm nearly through." He picked up the folder she'd pushed across the desk.

"And I still need that annual report."

Mark groaned. "I'd almost forgotten about it. You'll have it by Friday, I promise."

"Well, the provost's office needed it last Friday, so can you have it by Wednesday?"

"That's tomorrow," Mark said.

"So it is. Try for tomorrow then." She rose, scooped up the two files, and handed them to him. "Thanks, Mark. I really appreciate this. Oh, and Mark--"

He paused as she added, "Don't bully Antonia again, okay? I know she's annoying, but keep a professional attitude."

"Yes, ma'am."

Mark left the office, slapping the folder against his leg. Am I the only one who works here that she gives me everything to do, he wondered, clenching his teeth. He yanked open the heavy door to the front stairs on the way to his office and stomped halfway up when his vision blurred. Mark shook his head to clear the vertigo-- major mistake --and hauled himself around the railing to the next landing, points of light sparkling across his field of vision. Oh, no, not another blackout, not now. I've got too much work--Mark almost reached the top of the stairs between the second and third floors when he—

--pulled up short as he stumbled to the edge of a clearing near the bank of the river. Staring up at him, with varying expressions of surprise, were about a dozen men in dusty blue uniforms. What in the hell, he wondered as it dawned on him he'd crashed into the midst of a Yankee patrol. Panic welled inside him as he clutched the stock of his rifle and turned to dash away, but one of the men was quicker, leaping for his legs. His breath blew out in a ragged gasp as he was slammed face down to the earth, landing on his right arm, the rifle barrel sandwiched between it and his chest. Pain flared as something in his arm snapped audibly.

"Looks like a bushwhacker to me," growled a voice. Weather-gnarled hands flipped him on his back. Darkness tunneled his vision, lit with bright flashes of pain as someone grabbed his right wrist. He struggled to stay conscious, desperately afraid of the consequences if he did not. A face loomed over his, close enough to see the bits of food caught in the drooping mustache.

"No," he gasped in protest. "I'm not a bushwhacker. I have to get to my wife--"

Derisive laughter greeted his words. "Yeah, I want to get to my wife, too, Rebel," someone off to his right snapped. The pinned man twisted his neck to look in that direction, squinting against the pain in his arm.

"But she's very ill--" he tried again.

"Our orders are to clear these woods of all bushwhackers," the man in the mustache intoned as if quoting a regulation, his eyes dark. "We are to hang them in the area where they operate. I hope you're ready to die, Rebel."

He writhed in his captors' grasp, howling as the one on his right twisted the arm that now felt as if he had thrust it in a campfire. "You can't hang me," he panted when the pain subsided, throat raw. "Please, I'm not a bushwhacker."

The man in the mustache dragged him to his feet, catching him as he swayed toward unconsciousness from the sudden change of position. A slap across the face jarred his teeth. "His arm's broken," he heard someone call out from what seemed like a long distance. "Shouldn't we wait--"

"Heal him up before we hang him?" the mustachioed man snarled. "We got more important things to do. Get the rope."

He struggled feebly, his limbs refusing to cooperate. The scratchy fibers of a thick rope raked his hair and face as the noose was shoved onto his neck. He cried out in despair as they dragged him toward a tree at the edge of the clearing—

--and he stared at the white ceiling tiles. Mark shut his eyes and reopened them, disoriented. He flinched back as a face hovered over his.

"Mark! Are you okay?"

Janet's voice, he thought. I'm not in the forest anymore. So where the hell am I? My wife is Janet and she's not sick, and I'm not about to be lynched by Yankees. He flinched again as she rested her hand on his right arm, but was surprised when it didn't hurt. His forehead felt stiff and prickly; he dragged his hand up and rubbed the slick surface of a bandage.

"I was at work ..." he recalled, his voice a whisper. He cleared his throat and went on, "so how did I get here? Wherever I am." Mark turned his head toward her voice.

"You're in the emergency room, honey. You fell on the stairs at the library." The vertical wrinkle formed between her eyebrows. "They put fifteen stitches in your forehead. What happened? Did you black out?"

Fifteen stitches, he laughed to himself. That was Janet, worrying about the precise number of stitches when his arm was broken. "Did you count them?"

No, wait, my arm's not broken.

"Count what?" Janet asked.

"The stitches."

"You're talking nonsense, Mark. I'll call the doctor--"

He sighed. "I was trying to cheer you up, Janet. You look so serious." He struggled up onto his elbows, but his head throbbed with the effort and he slid back down onto the hard hospital bed. "I guess I blacked out, but it was more than that. I had another ..." he fumbled for an appropriate word to describe the bizarre experience, "hallucination, vision?"

Janet leaned on the bed. "Like last time?"

Mark raised his head again, squinting against the throbbing pain. "Similar. One minute I was walking up the steps to my office, and the next minute I was a rebel soldier about to be hanged by a bunch of Yankee troops."

She stared at him, frowning. "A rebel soldier."

"I think I was the same person as in the last event. I--"

"Glad you're conscious," the doctor said, glancing at the chart she carried.

"He woke up a few minutes ago," Janet explained.

Mark sucked in a breath as the doctor leaned over him, peering into his eyes. "Headache?" she asked.

"No, thanks, I already have one."

The doctor grinned at him. "There was some blood loss, but head injuries bleed freely anyway." She turned to Janet. "Make him lie down for the next twenty-four hours and watch him for any changes in behavior. Any nausea or vomiting, bring him back in immediately. He needs to see his primary doctor in a week to have the stitches removed."

"Thanks, Doctor."

Janet and a nurse helped Mark into a wheelchair. The pounding in his head subsided by the time they shut the passenger door of Janet's car and she started the engine. Mark pulled down the visor mirror and recoiled at the face staring back at him. The white rectangular bandage across his forehead emphasized the pallor of his skin, and his thick shoulder-length hair was matted with dried blood around his face and neck, stuck together like dreadlocks. The yoke of his shirt was dyed a stiff rusty red.

"God, I look like I've lost a war," he said. "I'll bet I nearly gave you a heart attack."

She sighed, shaking her head as she pulled out of the emergency room parking lot. "I thought you were dead, Mark. Tina called me. A student found you in the stairwell in a pool of blood and was absolutely hysterical. I think Tina said the paramedics sedated her." Janet was silent until they stopped at a red light. "Mark--"

He knew what was coming and gritted his teeth.

"This is getting serious. It's one thing to pass out at home, but when you injure yourself at work--you could've broken your neck!"

"I know that, Janet," he responded through clenched teeth.

She accelerated onto the interstate. "You have to get professional help. I insist."

He studied her from the corner of his eyes-- jaw set, her knuckles white on the steering wheel. She would not let this go easily. Well, let her be stubborn, he thought. He'd won prizes for stubborn. They'd asked him to join the Olympic Stubborn Team while still in elementary school. "I don't feel like arguing about this now."

"Then I'll call and get the name of a psychiatrist."

"Whatever." He rested his throbbing head on the headrest and tried to forget the feel of rope tightening around his neck.

CHAPTER 9.

Wednesday, April 28.

"You didn't eat much," Janet said, clearing away the dinner dishes.

Mark sat at the kitchen table, watching his wife. He knew every step of her routine.

"Is your head still hurting?" she asked, rinsing the plates.

"No, I'm fine," Mark answered. "Just thinking."

"Thinking about your dad?" she asked.

Mark rested his chin on his stacked fists. "Why would I be thinking about him?"

Janet twisted her neck toward him, soap bubbles dripping from her hand and said, "You didn't cry at the funeral. Or since. It's not healthy to-"

"Keep it bottled up inside. I know, I know." Mark leaned back in the chair. He didn't feel like crying. He felt removed from his emotions, as if they belonged to someone he knew, someone he sympathized with, but whom he didn't quite understand. "If I had a dollar for every time you've told me that--"

"--you'd spend it on computer stuff." She smiled and swabbed out a glass. "You know, it occurs to me that maybe repression of your feelings is causing these blackouts and visions."

Mark rocked the chair onto its back legs, a faint queasiness seeping into his stomach. "Whoa, that's a Freudian analysis if I ever heard one. You missed your calling."

"Don't do that, you'll break the chair."

"Yes, Mom." He stood, yawned against the nausea. "How on earth did you arrive at that conclusion?"

Janet scrubbed the table with a rag. "You dreamed about a hanging, right?"

"I didn't *dream* it." His frown only made his head throb more.

"Your dad tried to hang himself once, didn't he?"

He rubbed a hand across his belly and said, "Yeah, but--"

Janet said, "I think you're feeling guilty about your relationship with him, and--"

"Guilty?" Astonishment replaced the nausea. "What the--why the--what the hell do I have to feel guilty about?"

Janet frowned at him, then shook the rag over the sink and went to work on the countertop. "You never had the most civil relationship with the man."

"He was nuts, Jan." He folded his arms. "I was as civil as I could be."

"Mark." Janet dried her hands and said, "What really happened between you two? I've always had the feeling there's something you never told me."

Mark tucked his hands in his armpits, casting around for a way to say aloud what he'd only feared in the dead of night, in his darkest moods. "Oh, lots of little things. Like the suicide attempts. Why was it always *me* who found him? It's like he planned it that way."

He pushed away from the counter, sorting through the words racing through his head. "When Tommy died, in the accident ... when I saw Dad, looked into his eyes ..."

He cleared his throat and grabbed the back of the chair. "I knew he was lying."

Janet stood close. "Lying about what?"

"It wasn't an accident. He ..."

Mark took a deep breath. "He killed Tommy. He killed my brother. His own son."

She lowered herself into the chair, resting her hand on his and speaking in a precise voice, as if he were a rambunctious child holding a priceless vase off a balcony. "Mark, you were under a lot of stress. You don't know that. You were upset--"

He couldn't breathe. Mark snatched his hand away, lurched a step backwards. "You never believe me, do you?" he whispered. "I *know* he killed Tommy. I don't know how I know, but I *know*. And I was always afraid I was next. Or Natalie. God, if he'd hurt Natalie--"

Janet sound calm and logical. "What did you do about it? Did you tell anyone?"

"What could I do?" Mark asked. "I figured no one would believe me. You don't."

"When will you learn that sometimes you need to act?"

"The Book of Janet, chapter two," Mark muttered.

"Why didn't you have him committed?" she asked. "After all the suicide attempts? I know you and your mother talked about it."

He thrust his hands into the pockets of his jeans. "Mom wouldn't do it unless I consented. I've told you that. I never was sure if it was the right thing to do--"

"So you never did anything." Her lips twitched in annoyance. "Well, I don't have that problem. I'll be decisive for both of us."

"What do you mean?" Mark's stomach went cold. "You're going to commit me?"

"God, Mark, you're white as a ghost. I'm just taking you to a psychiatrist."

He couldn't move. "So *he* can commit me."

"No, silly," she said with a smile. "So we can find out why the blackout spells."

"What," he said, anger finally galvanizing him. "'Hi, I'm Mark and I'm a schizophrenic'?" He backed toward the hallway, strode into the bedroom.

Janet followed. "Oh, honey. Nobody thinks you're a schizophrenic."

He whipped his head toward her, hands clenched at his sides. "Hey, I'm a librarian, remember? You should. After all, you chose my career for me. I know where to find medical books, how to read the symptoms. Hearing voices, seeing things that aren't there--what else are they gonna call it?" He sat on the bed and glared at her.

"Maybe if your father had seen a psychiatrist--"

"He did. Regularly. Didn't help him much, did it?"

The crease between Janet's eyebrows deepened. Did she have to sound so calm? Couldn't she get a little upset?

"Don't be so bitter about him. He really loved you, I'm sure."

"Funny way of showing it. Know what he said when I told him we were engaged?" Mark laughed, like a short cough. "'Course you don't, I never told you." He rested his left ankle on his right knee. "After years of being the one-date wonder--or maybe it was two, it was so hard to keep track--I finally fell in love. With you. Proposed. You inexplicably accepted the second time I asked. I told Dad, and he said, 'I thought she was living with that psychic fellow. You must've caught her on the rebound.' Then he warned me that you're older than me and were probably just desperate to get married. That Daniel wouldn't marry you, so you latched on to me. How's that for fatherly love?"

She was silent.

He looked up at her, startled by her lack of retort. "Jan? Honey?" Her body was rigid, her eyes downcast.

"That's a terrible thing to say," she stammered at last.

A cold chill swept his body. He stood up. "Jan? It wasn't true, was it?"

"No, of course not."

But he knew, the same way he knew his father killed Tommy, that she was lying. He walked to the dresser.

"We're talking about you, though," she said, "not me." Her calm evaporated, but now he wanted it back. "If your doctor recommends it, then you should see a psychiatrist."

"Shut up about the damn psychiatrist." Mark slammed his fist on the dresser. Their wedding picture fell over with a loud snap.

"But it makes sense to just let him--"

"Nothing makes sense anymore," Mark said, slamming open the closet door. He hauled down a worn suitcase from the top of the closet.

"Mark--Daniel and I--the relationship wasn't going anywhere. We weren't--"

More photos toppled over as he wrestled open drawers, scooped out clothes and threw them on the bed. "Don't lie to me, Jan. I can't take being lied to."

"What are you doing?"

Mark opened the suitcase and stuffed his clothes into it. "I need to sort out my thoughts. I'm going to stay at Dave's for a while."

Janet tugged at his arm. "Running away won't solve anything," she said.

He spun toward her, glaring into her dark eyes. "It's always worked before." Then he noticed his favorite photograph hanging on the wall, taken on their honeymoon, of the jeans-clad couple entwined in each other's arms, smiling joyfully.

As he stared at the photo, his forehead throbbed under the bandage, his throat tight again. Janet was the one stable element in his life. Now even that was cast into doubt.

He coughed. "I need to think," he said. "I can't do it here." Snapping the latches on the suitcase he added, "At least I'm taking action."

"That's not what I meant. Mark, please, give me a chance to explain--"

She sounded scared.

Mark smiled and shook his head. "No, I think I understand. Just tell me where my keys are. You said Tina and Dave brought my car home last night?"

She nodded, a tear trailing down her cheek. "The keys are on the kitchen counter."

"Thanks." He slid the suitcase off the bed.

"Mark--don't do anything stupid, okay? Don't go doing anything you'll regret."

He walked out of the room and whispered, "I already am."

CHAPTER 10.

Janet heard Mark's boots plod across the living room floor and the slamming of the front door. She walked backward until she felt the bed against her legs and sank down onto it, wrapping her arms around one of the pillows. She refused to acknowledge the truth in Mark's words, that she married him mainly to get back at Daniel. Instead she focused on Mark's refusal to discover the reason for the blackouts. He wants to pretend none of this has happened, she thought, that it'll just go away.

"I don't care what he wants," she said aloud, grabbing the phone. "I'll get him help whether he likes it or not." She dialed the number of Mark's doctor, an old family friend.

"Hi, Dr. Hollinger? This is Janet Richards, Roger Mitchell's daughter. I'm sorry to bother you at home--"

"It's no bother at all," he replied. "How's your husband?"

She sighed. "He blacked out yesterday at work and fell on the stairs. Fifteen stitches."

"I heard. The E.R. physician told me."

"He absolutely refuses to see a psychiatrist. He told me you recommended it."

"He has nothing physically wrong with him that I can determine." The older man's voice took on a worried tone. "When he mentioned the blackouts and hallucinations, though, the first thing I thought was schizophrenia."

Janet shook her head, her mouth dry. "You actually think he's schizophrenic?"

45

"Not really. The perceptual symptoms are there, but his reasoning seems normal. He's obviously very stressed out--"

Her laugh sounded bitter, even to her. "You can say that again."

"But he doesn't seem to be impaired in his functioning. If you want the truth, I'm baffled." He chuckled. "Maybe he needs to see a psychic."

"What?" She slowly pushed the pillow away from her.

"Only joking, Janet. He really needs help, though, especially if he's having accidents caused by these spells. And he should not be driving."

"Don't I know it! He is so stubborn." She leaned back on her elbows, supporting the phone between her shoulder and ear. "I'll keep trying, though. Thanks for your help."

"Any time, Janet. You know that. How are your parents?"

She sighed. "Fine, thanks for asking. I think I need to spend some time with them to remember what normal life is like."

"Mark said you were stressed, too. Take care of yourself."

"I sure will. Thanks again." She hung up and flopped flat onto the bed. A psychic. Imagine him suggesting a psychic. She stared at the ceiling a moment.

That's actually not such a bad idea. Maybe Daniel would know what Mark's problem is.

Janet rolled onto her side and punched in the number, long stifled guilt filling her. She stared at the honeymoon picture on the wall and grimaced.

"So, Mark, how will you feel when my ex-lover finds out what's wrong with you?"

She shoved the guilt away and added, "But it's for your own good."

CHAPTER 11.

Saturday, May 1.

Mark leaned on the balcony overlooking the reading room of the Lynn-Henley Research Library, part of the Birmingham Public Library, and studied the murals depicting characters from world literature. Ruby and gold decorated the beams of the second-story ceiling, far beneath which women and men pored over volumes of genealogical knowledge. Dave had good-naturedly thrown Mark out of his house, requesting he "please go do something constructive, just for the day."

Mark knew what was going on: Dave wanted to spend some time alone with Tina.

"Work on genealogy," Dave suggested when Mark asked what there was for him to do. "You've been saying for two days you want to prove to your sister your family's not cursed. Go down to the public library and do some research. That'll kill a few hours."

So Mark reluctantly set off for the library.

Mark went down the stairs and crossed to the reference desk. A young black man in a white and blue-striped dress shirt and navy blue tie smiled a greeting.

"Hey, Mark! I haven't seen you since the convention. How've you been?"

Grinning, Mark shook the man's hand. "Hey, Kynon! How's the genealogy business?" He leaned on the counter.

Kynon sighed. "Busy. Doesn't anybody know who their relatives are?"

"If nobody researched family history, Kynon, would you have a job?"

"Yeah, yeah, the voice of reality crashes in." He paused to point out the copy machine to an older woman, then turned back to Mark. "So, what can I do for you today?"

"I'm actually starting research on my family tree." Mark snagged a nearby chair with his foot and straddled it.

Kynon convulsed with laughter, drawing disapproving stares from nearby patrons. "Last time I saw you, didn't you say you'd never scrounge through old records like ... what did you call them? Oh, yeah, 'those desperate people who do genealogy'?"

Mark leaned his forehead on the counter. "I know, never say never. But keep your voice down. These people may lynch me."

"Where do you want to start? Do you know yet?" Kynon looked up as an attractive woman wearing a black blouse and short white skirt strolled into the room carrying an armload of books. "Hi, Victoria."

"Hi, Kynon. Here's some books from my floor. I thought somebody might need them before the end of the day." She set the stack on a nearby cart and glanced at Mark, tucking a strand of long ash blonde hair behind her ear. "Hello."

Mark smiled back. "Victoria," Kynon said with a flourish of his hand, "this is Mark Richards, a colleague of mine and now one of those desperate genealogy folks. Victoria works in the microfilm room."

"Nice to meet you," Mark replied. "I thought I knew everyone who works here."

"I haven't been here long." Sliding a pencil from behind her ear, she gestured with it toward his forehead. "Has genealogy already got you beating your head against the wall?"

"What?" He fingered the bandage. "Oh, this. Not yet. I fell at work."

"Who are you researching?" she asked.

He rested an arm on the desk. "The Giles family. I've just started, though." The woman dropped her pencil and stooped to retrieve it.

"That's interesting." She tapped the pencil rapidly on the back of her other hand. "Well, I'd better get back upstairs." She flashed a brief smile at Mark, and strode out of the room, throwing a "It was nice to meet you, Demarcus" over her shoulder as she went.

Mark sat bolt upright and said, "Did you tell her my name was Demarcus?"

Kynon folded his arms across his chest. "Now, why would I do that? I don't have time to sit around and talk about you with other staff members."

Mark gazed after her, until Kynon's voice broke his reverie, "If you're through daydreaming about Victoria, would you like me to help you?"

"I wasn't--"

Kynon narrowed his eyes and Mark grinned. "Okay, so I was. Damn, she's hot. I'm not sure what it is ..."

"She's single and you're not."

"True. Almost." At the man's raised eyebrows, Mark went on, "I ... I sort of ... walked out on Janet this week."

"And who is it that used to give *me* lectures on finding the right woman and sticking with her, using yourself as a prime example?" Kynon gestured at the bandage on his forehead. "Is that how that happened? She beat you up?"

"No. You heard me say I fell on the stairs at work." He brushed his bangs down.

"If you're on the prowl, then, you might like Victoria."

"I am not 'on the prowl,' Kynon. Janet and I are just having a little ... cooling off period."

Kynon shrugged. "Whatever. Anyway, Victoria's kind of quiet, but very intelligent. I went out with her a week ago, right after she started here."

Mark cocked an eyebrow, smiling. "Oh? And yet you're anxious to give her to me? Assuming I was available, of course."

Kynon dismissed his question with a wave of his hand. "She wasn't my type. And there's no 'give' to it. She doesn't *belong* to anybody. There's something ... I don't know, *intense* about her that I couldn't deal with. But you're such an intense guy it might work for you."

"Me, intense?"

Kynon snorted. "Of course, she's much too young for you."

Mark glared. "And how old do you think I am?"

Kynon ran a hand over his shaved head, squinting into the distance as if calculating. "Forty, forty-five."

"You won't live to see thirty with that attitude. How old is she?" Mark asked.

"Well, I've seen her driver's license. She's twenty-five."

"I'm thirty-three, man. She's not that much younger."

"Thirty-three?" Kynon shook his head. "It's definitely the mileage."

"All right, enough insults. Do your job and help me."

"What, telling you about Victoria's not enough? What do you want to know?"

Mark shrugged. "Where do I start?"

Kynon leaned forward, adopting his professional persona. "You start with yourself and your family and work backward."

"Already done that."

"Bright boy." The other man smiled. "Okay then, try the catalog. Maybe someone's already done a book on your family. Check the books of county records, too, once you know what county you're looking for."

"I don't."

"Well, start with the catalog, and come back when you get stuck." Kynon gestured toward a nearby computer. "But don't be too disappointed if you don't find a book on your specific family. The odds are pretty slim, with as many surnames as there are."

Mark grinned his thanks and moved over to the terminal. Victoria's smile had done wonders for lifting his gray mood. He typed in "Giles family." The result was three citations, including *My Giles Family: A Personal History*, written by Demarcus Giles and published in 1909.

A chill raced down his spine. How many other families could have someone in them named Demarcus? Kynon was busy, so he wandered around until he found the slim pamphlet on the shelf. He stared in amazement at the cover before he finally sat down with his find.

The author's introduction began with a bang: "Rumors continue to circulate that my family is cursed. This could not be further from the truth. I have written this account to set out the facts and lay these rumors to rest."

This has to be my family, Mark thought, wiping his palms on his pants before digging a pen and notepad out of his briefcase.

"Eight years into a new century, these superstitions should not exist," the writer continued. "But you, the reasoning, thinking person, may judge for yourself."

Demarcus Giles introduced himself in the first chapter as a citizen of Demopolis, Alabama, born in Ohio to James Stuart and Elizabeth Bowman Giles. He married Clarice Hawthorne. Demarcus, Jr. was born the following year, and Elizabeth three years later. He was proud of his work as a surveyor for a railroad, using the career and his wife and children as evidence that his family was not cursed. Mark grinned. So far, so good. I believe you, Demarcus. No curse.

He turned to the next chapter, in which Demarcus discussed his parents. With a sinking feeling, Mark read about James Stuart Giles, orphaned at age two when his parents were murdered in 1863. The murderer or murderers were never caught, but the rumor was the deed was committed by marauding Yankee soldiers. His parents had sent James to stay with his aunt when the war moved closer to their home, saving his life.

Okay, but not necessarily a curse, Mark reasoned. Lots of people died during the Civil War. If it was really a curse, James would have died too. He scribbled the particulars of the family's move to Ohio, his move to Tennessee after his aunt died, and his marriage and eventual relocation to Alabama.

Mark's eyes widened as he read the next page.

"James Giles was reported to be a quiet and serious man, hard-working and normal, except for his obsession with the idea that the family was under a curse. No one in the family would talk about the reasons for his belief, which seemed to have its origins in an estrangement between James' father and grandfather."

Mark's forehead throbbed. Great. In every generation someone believed in a curse--except Demarcus. And me. Nothing in the book indicated when the estrangement occurred, but it had to be before 1863, when James Sr. died. What could have happened between a father and son to cause family members to believe in a curse?

To his chagrin, his hands shook as he read about Demarcus' father's death in a steamship accident on the Mississippi River in 1888. The accident also claimed the life of the uncle who had raised him as his own son. Rounding out the cheery pamphlet was a family tree listing James and Elizabeth, James' parents James and Alice, and James' grandparents Samuel and Lavinia Giles, with birth and death dates.

Mark carefully closed the booklet and stretched in his chair. I guess I should be grateful, he thought, staring up at the red and gold ceiling. I've found a huge chunk of my family tree already grown for me. Trouble is, I don't like the implications of it.

The estrangement between Samuel and his murdered son seemed an important event to research. He wandered back to Kynon's desk. "Census records. Where are they?"

"You're in luck," Kynon grinned. "They're in the microfilm room on the third floor. Where your girlfriend works."

Mark started to deny Kynon's words, decided it would sound too juvenile, and instead thanked the man for the information and moved toward the stairs.

A vague sense of guilt sifted through Mark's mind as he made his way to the upper floor. He hoped no one heard Kynon's 'girlfriend' banter and reported back to Janet. On the other hand, he snorted to himself, what harm could it do? It might give her something constructive to worry about instead of his brain.

The room at the end of the hallway was filled with the high-pitched hum and intermittent snap of four rows of microfilm readers. Researchers staring bleary-eyed at bright white screens filled all but a few chairs. Victoria raised dark blonde eyebrows and stretched her lips in a Mona Lisa sort of smile in response to Mark's wave. He threaded his way down the row to an empty chair and planted his briefcase in it.

Was that a greeting or not? He selected an index volume from a shelf, guessing at a possible date for his ancestor. Maybe she thinks I'm coming on to her, he thought. I've been out of circulation so long I can't read the signs. Not that I was ever very good at it. He flipped through the volume and found the name Samuel Giles, but discovered that the reel of film he needed was missing from the drawer.

Victoria was sliding microfilm boxes into large metal drawers when he approached her. "Excuse me," he said, "do you have the Marengo County reel for the 1850 Alabama census?"

A spark of static electricity jumped from her hand to his as she handed him a box from the top of the cabinet. "Is that what they call an electric personality?" she smiled.

Mark picked up the box from the floor where he'd dropped it, his hand still tingling. "No harm done, I guess."

Their eyes met. He fell into her gold-flecked green eyes, the scent of her skin reminding him of an incense-laden shop he once visited that sold exotic merchandise.

"Excuse me." The moment evaporated as a bespectacled older man pulled out a drawer between them. Victoria stepped back and continued her filing as if nothing had happened.

His heart raced as he wandered toward the microfilm machine where his briefcase waited. She's not that much shorter than me. I'd hardly have to lean down at all to kiss her. The black words illuminated on the white screen made no sense to him. Of course not, you fool. You threaded the film on the machine wrong. Damn it, quit thinking about her, he castigated himself. She's a kid. Beautiful, yes, but way too young for you. He unwound the film and threaded it onto the machine correctly. The film gate shut with a clank as he spun the dial forward. Too young for you. You're acting like you could actually ask her out. Janet would never approve.

Mark forced his mind back to the research. It was strange to think of a family--their hopes, dreams, fears, conflicts--summarized in a few lines of sprawling, handwritten statistics. He found the family of Samuel Giles, a 30-year-old farmer living in Marengo County, Alabama, a decade before the outbreak of the Civil War. His wife Lavinia was a year younger than he. They had four children, Rachel, twins James and Rebecca, and Beatrice.

He didn't see Victoria as he returned the film to the top of the cabinet. His knees popped in protest as he squatted down and dragged open the heavy bottom drawer to retrieve the 1860 reel. Sensing someone beside him, he turned to his left and found himself looking at a pair of long, slender legs. She stood so close he wasn't sure how he could stand without pulling her skirt up with his shoulder. Face reddening, he squirmed up to a standing position. Victoria smiled at his discomfort, but didn't move.

"Find what you were looking for?" she asked. One earring caught the light as she tilted her head and squinted at him. "You're not blushing, are you?"

He shoved the drawer shut with his foot, ignoring her second question.

"Yes, I found it," he replied, holding up the census reel. "Do you always hover over your patrons?"

She smiled that mysterious little smile and turned to help another patron.

Mark hesitated. She disappeared with the woman behind another row of cabinets. He sighed, flipped his hair out of his collar, and strolled back to his chair.

In the April 1860 census, all the children still lived with their parents. The oldest was nineteen, while the twins were eighteen and the youngest sixteen. Mark was surprised the two older girls hadn't married yet.

When he retrieved the 1870 census, Victoria had again disappeared. He squinted at the scrawled letters of the 1870 census, cursing the penmanship of census takers and jumped, dropping the pen as warm fingers stroked the back of his neck under his hair. Victoria smiled down at him. "Did you find what you needed?"

He opened his mouth, but she said, "Good. Let me know if you need anything else," and walked away. He retrieved his pen, wrenching his mind from the feel of her fingers on his skin.

The Giles family in 1870 consisted only of Lavinia Giles and her unmarried daughter Rachel. Mark knew from the scary little pamphlet that Samuel was dead by this time, but where were the others? Hauling out his pocket watch, he noted the library would close soon.

When he stood, Victoria hurried toward him, her eyes wide.

"What's wrong?" Mark asked.

She chewed her lip. "You'll think I'm crazy, since I don't even know you, but you are a friend of Kynon's ..."

"I won't think you're crazy," Mark assured her, inhaling the musky scent of her skin.

"You're so sweet," she smiled, grasping his arm. "Would you walk me out to my car when we close?"

"Sure, but it's still light outside--"

Victoria glanced around at the now-empty room and linked her arm with his. His heart thudded in his chest. "See, I've only been in town a couple of weeks. I came here from Atlanta to get away from my boyfriend. He ... he threatened to kill me if I broke up with him."

"I see--"

"And I'm afraid he might have followed me here. When I came in this morning, I thought I saw him on the street. He wouldn't dare come inside the library, with all the security, but he might be out there waiting for me. Please?"

Mark stared into the green-gold eyes, conscious of the warmth of her body pressed against his side. "No problem," he answered. "I'll play bodyguard."

"Great. I'm nearly ready."

He felt colder as she slid away from him, but as he waited, a shade of doubt crept in. Why me? Why not ask one of the security guards to walk her out? They've got guns. By the time she reappeared, he had an answer. This is her way of getting to know me better. I'll bet there's not really a jealous boyfriend either.

"All finished." She looked worried as she returned to his side. "I'm parked out back."

"So am I."

She took his hand and pulled him after her. Her high heels echoed on the marble steps. "I really appreciate this," Victoria went on as they reached the bottom. "I guess I could have gotten one of the security guards to escort me out," and she waved at two of them as they passed the check-out desk, "but this way we can chat. That's my car."

They walked about half the distance toward the dark blue Honda when she clutched his arm, nails biting his skin. "There's someone in it."

"The door's opening." Mark grabbed her hand. "Let's take my car."

Heart pounding, he fished for his keys with his free hand, grateful for the remote opener. They crossed two rows of parking spaces and dove into the Saturn as a bulky figure emerged from the Honda. The man's call, "Vicki! Wait--" was cut off by the simultaneous slamming of the car doors.

"He's getting into another car! Hurry!" The bar at the exit to the lot raised slowly. "Turn right!" she directed.

"Does he know where you live?" Mark peered in his rear view mirror.

"Turn right again!" She twisted in her seat to look out the back window. "No, he doesn't know. That's where we're headed."

Mark slipped under the traffic signal as it turned red.

Victoria giggled. "He got stopped by the light," She straightened in her seat. "Turn left when you get to University Boulevard. Maybe we've lost him."

"I doubt it. It's pretty much a straight shot to University." He turned at the last moment down a side street, then headed north again. "That might confuse him." He smiled and relaxed his grip on the wheel. "What is it with this guy?"

Victoria puffed out an annoyed sigh. "I dated him for a couple of months, but I got tired of his possessiveness. If I didn't call him every day, he'd call me, all suspicious about who I'd seen. He loved to say he'd castrate any guy he caught me with. Isn't that silly?"

"Uh, yeah, that's silly all right."

"With that kind of attitude, I had to dump him. But he came after me-- oh, veer left when the road forks at Claremont."

"Were you on a date when he came after you?" Mark squinted at every car.

"Unfortunately," Victoria said. "Oh, but the guy I was with is okay."

"That's good to know. So he's all talk?"

Victoria shook her head, long hair brushing Mark's shoulder. "No, Andrew broke his arm. Or rather his arm broke when Andrew threw him over the bar at the club where we were."

Mark slowed to take the curve in the road. "Well, hey, a broken arm's better than castration." He glanced in the mirror again. "What color was his car?"

"Dark red. Why?"

"I think I see him." He pressed the accelerator, swerving into the turn lane around a slower car. "How much farther?"

"Turn right at the next light. I don't see--wait, there he is." Her fingers pressed into his arm as she braced herself against the turn. "Park in the circle there," she pointed. "He won't know which house."

"Neither do I," he panted, adrenaline rushing through his veins as he shoved the gearshift into park.

"That one with green shutters and door. Run around to the back. It'll take less time."

They slammed the doors. Mark pocketed the keys and grabbed Victoria's hand, ducking under tree limbs and skirting bushes across two intervening lawns. She pounded up a short flight of wooden stairs to a tiny wooden porch. He scanned the backyard, screened from the next street by foliage, willing his breathing to slow. No sign of their pursuer from that direction.

Victoria yanked on his arm and drew him inside after fiddling with a balky lock. She slammed the door shut and locked it. "I think we made it," she breathed. "What do we do now?"

Fear is definitely an aphrodisiac, Mark thought, admiring the way her blouse wrinkled and unwrinkled across her breasts with each breath. I know what I want to do now.

A knock sounded from the front of the house. Both of them jumped at the unexpected sound. She leapt toward him and drew him to the floor. "He won't be able to see us in here if we stay down," she assured him in a whisper.

Mark felt foolish, cowering on the floor of a kitchen. "Couldn't we reason with him?"

Victoria shrugged. "Maybe so. If you're anxious to sing falsetto permanently. I wonder if he still carries that gun ..."

"Okay. Can he see through those curtains?"

"I don't think so, but let's go into the dining room to make sure." They crawled through a doorway to the right, where the only window was hung with heavy drapes. The room was empty except for a few shipping boxes.

"Dining room, huh?"

"Well, it's supposed to be the dining room," she said, wrinkling her nose. "I don't have a dining table yet." The front door shook, accompanied by a muffled shout. "I hope he doesn't try kicking the door in like last time."

Mark grinned. "Oh, I seriously doubt--"

He broke off as a rhythmic banging shook the house.

A splintering crash launched them to their feet. Mark's pulse raced with a primitive urge to protect the woman at his side. This doesn't happen in real life, he thought. No one breaks into someone's house--

Well, apparently they do. The doorway filled with the bulk of a man dressed in black muscle shirt and camouflage pants. This guy shops at the big-and-tall stores, Mark thought. And he's gonna break me in half.

Victoria's voice was calm. "Andrew, I cannot believe you would break into my house like this. Why on earth--"

Andrew studied Mark. "Who's he? Your new boyfriend?"

"Get out," Mark gritted through clenched teeth. "Stop bothering her." He stepped forward, lurching to a halt as the room dipped and spun like a Tilt-a-Whirl ride. The floor gave way as he fell through a vast blackness.

CHAPTER 12.

Janet's heart thudded. Eleven years since we broke up, she thought, and he still has this effect on me. He smiled, thin lips behind a closely-cropped blond beard, and strolled toward the cash register counter with the confident air she admired. His hair was thinning a little on top, but otherwise he still looked like a German exchange student.

He reached across the counter and grasped her hands. "Janet, it's so good to see you again. You haven't called me in almost a year."

"I'm sorry, Daniel. I started to call dozens of times, but after the last time ..."

You left town rather than face me again, she added to herself.

"That was wrong of me, I know." Daniel slid his hands from hers as a customer approached. After Janet rang up the purchases, he stepped closer again. "I shouldn't have tried to press my advantage when you were vulnerable. How are you and Mark getting along now?"

Her mouth was dry. "Penny should be here any minute to take over for me," she said. "Then we can go upstairs and talk."

"I'll wander around. Anything new I'd be interested in?"

"There's a new multi-volume history of the Tarot up there." She pointed to the balcony of the narrow building, watching as he climbed the creaky staircase. He always did have a nice butt. Despite herself, she grinned.

After Penny arrived a few minutes later, Janet found Daniel in the aisle, seated cross-legged on the floor, hunched over a large hardback volume. "We do have chairs available." She smiled down at him.

He stood up, closing the book and replacing it on the way up. "Thanks for telling me about this set. I'll have to buy it on my way out."

She led him across the well-worn wooden floor to the back room, then grabbed a pillow and sank into one of the armchairs. Daniel folded himself into the other chair.

"Pillow hugging already, are we?" he asked.

Janet laughed and set it beside her. "I told you on the phone the other night Mark was having trouble, but I didn't tell you what kind of trouble."

"I gather it is unusual, otherwise you wouldn't have called me." He was sitting with his elbows on the chair arms, fingers steepled in what Janet thought of as his "Mr. Spock pose."

"You're the only psychic counselor I know. Besides, I know that whatever your feelings about Mark, you'll be objective and professional."

He nodded during her description of the blackouts and his accident at work, but by the time she'd finished, Daniel's eyebrows were well up his high forehead. "I'm sure you've already sent him to a doctor."

"Many doctors. Many tests. They can't find a physical cause. His doctor recommended he see a psychiatrist, then jokingly suggested I talk to a psychic."

Daniel's laughs were infrequent, but the hearty guffaw always warmed her spirit. He rubbed his hands on his thighs. "My first thought is it sounds like some kind of psychic overload. Maybe he's processing some kind of signals he can't handle."

"Signals?"

He shrugged. "Either messages from someone or something he's sensing. It's hard to tell without talking to Mark or being in his presence. I'll really have to do that to know precisely what's going on."

"Psychic overload," she repeated. "Maybe that's connected with the visions."

"Visions?" He leaned over the chair arm toward her. "Tell me about them."

"I know of two. If he's had more, he hasn't told me about them." She clutched at the pillow, and sketched for him the incidents Mark experienced. "The second one was when he fell on the stairs," she finished.

Daniel stayed silent for several minutes, eyes closed, while Janet listened to the rattle of the old air conditioner and wondered what Mark was doing.

"I don't really think he's channeling," Daniel said, as if arguing with someone. "The messages seem intended for him, not for anyone else, at least as far as I can tell without talking to him. They seem so detailed--and I suspect there's more detail there than Mark conveyed to you-- I think the events really happened. To someone. Maybe they happened to Mark in another life? I'm not certain. I must speak with him first. Can you arrange it?"

Janet tossed the pillow onto an orange beanbag chair. "That could be tough. He is so stubborn. And, even though he's never met you, he feels threatened by our relationship. But I'll see what I can do. How much do I owe you for this session?"

Daniel looked at her sideways. "Janet, I'm hurt. For an old friend like you, nothing." He took her hand. "I just want you to be happy."

His kindness made her want to burst into tears. Instead, she smiled and placed her other hand on top of his. "Thanks, Daniel." She gazed into his dark violet eyes, feeling the years slip away. "Do you ever wonder why we broke up?"

"I know why. You were three years out of college and still unmarried. I wasn't interested in marriage. Then Mark came along and he *was* interested."

"Oh, God," she groaned. "Mark told me that's what his father thought when we got engaged. Why weren't you interested? We lived together for two years."

"I've told you many times, my love. I didn't wish to join myself to anyone in that way. It interfered with my counseling work at a time when I was not as strong in my abilities." The ceiling fan squeaked as it turned above their heads. "How long have you two been separated?"

Damn. I'd forgotten how perceptive he can be, she thought. "Four days. Since Wednesday night. He walked out."

"Then I presume you haven't told him."

"Told him?" she asked.

"About the baby."

She stared at him again, open-mouthed. "How--"

"Three months, isn't it? He would not leave if he knew you're pregnant."

"Ten weeks, actually," Janet said. "And no, I haven't told him. The time hasn't been right. So much has happened."

Daniel smiled. "You'll recall I warned you about him when you met him. That he wouldn't appreciate that you are--"

"A control freak?"

"No, an achiever. You're driven to accomplish things. Like buying this bookstore when the previous owner ran it into the ground and said no one could revive it."

She smiled back, feeling the undeniable attraction after all these years, strong now when she was in desperate need of warmth and love. She rose from the chair to escape his eyes.

Daniel took the hint and rose, too. "Call me when you set up a meeting with Mark. Or anytime." He kissed her lips, squeezed her hand, and was gone. As soon as the door shut behind him, Janet sank back into the chair and allowed herself the luxury of tears.

~*~*~

Mark blinked up at the solid white sky as the heaving of his labored lungs slowed. The fiery welts of rope burn around his neck faded as his spine sagged down against hard flat wood. If he concentrated hard enough, he could focus on that weird sky--no, he corrected, skies don't have brass chandeliers hanging from them. He sneezed when Victoria's hair tickled his nose as she knelt over him.

Reality snapped back into place. Oh, God, no, he thought. Don't tell me I passed out when Andrew--oh, yeah, women love guys who black out instead of defending them.

He must have groaned aloud, because the next thing he knew, she cradled his head in her lap, stroking his face. "Mark? Are you awake?" she asked.

Those green and gold eyes ... "I think so. Where's Andrew?"

"He left. I managed to convince him you weren't my lover." She rested her hand on his chest. "I think you scared him when you passed out. Are you okay?"

Let's see, he thought. How do I answer that? My head's in the lap of a gorgeous blonde with hypnotic eyes. "Yeah, I'm okay." He sat up, leaning back against her as the room tilted. "Honestly, it wasn't because of Andrew. I didn't faint, or anything."

Victoria eased him back into her lap. "So what did happen?"

Halfway through his explanation of the blackouts and the medical tests, he stopped. Why was he telling her all this? He had not even told his sister. But the expression in her eyes was so kind and concerned ...

He shoved aside his reservations and finished up, omitting any mention of the vivid vision of dangling by his neck from a noose as he gasped for air through a crushed windpipe.

Victoria nodded. "Sounds like psychic interference, to me."

On the other hand, he thought, why the hell did I just spill my guts to her? "You're kidding, right?"

She ran her fingers under his hair, lifting it out of his collar. "Some sort of psychic transmission you're picking up that's either too strong for you to handle, or too weak for you to process clearly. That's just a guess."

"A transmission." Mark squinted up at her. "You mean a message?"

"That's what it sounds like. I've dabbled in various fields of parapsychology," Victoria admitted with a shrug. "I know just enough to be dangerous."

Oh, you're dangerous, all right, he thought. And if I stay here in your lap one more minute, danger won't even begin to describe it. Mark sat up,

60

and this time the room stayed in place. "Do you think Andrew will bother you again?"

"Well, he knows where I live, which isn't good." She stood, helped him to his feet, then sighed. "I'll have to get the door fixed."

He slid his hand from hers, but still felt an electrical current flashing between them. He glanced at his pocket watch as a distraction. Seven-twenty. "I'd better go."

"Would you like to stay for dinner?"

"No!" His answer sounded more abrupt than he intended, to judge from her startled expression. "No," he said with a smile, "I'd better get going."

"Thanks for bringing me home," Victoria whispered. He suppressed the urge to kiss her and bolted, barely noticing the splintered doorframe from Andrew's flamboyant entrance.

On the lawn, he let out the breath he'd been holding and walked to his car, fighting the impulse to run back into the house, rip her clothes off and possess her there on the dining room floor. Instead, he climbed into the driver's seat and rested his head on the steering wheel.

CHAPTER 13.

Tuesday, May 4.

Natalie already waited for him at their usual table. The student center was a hive of activity, the blurred roar of talk sharpened occasionally by called greetings and shrieks of laughter. Mark threaded his way expertly past the knots of conversation, paid for a chicken sandwich and fries, and joined his sister.

"Why didn't you tell me you weren't living at home?" she demanded with an injured air as soon as he sat down.

Mark grimaced. "Sorry, Nat. I forgot."

"'Sorry, Nat. I forgot,'" she mimicked. "What else did you forget to tell me?"

He watched her pop a chicken nugget in her mouth and said, "I know I should have called you. I've been staying at Dave's, trying to stay out of his way when Tina's there, and I was really swamped here yesterday. I throw myself on the mercy of the court."

"Don't joke about this," Natalie said, frowning. "I can't believe you left Janet."

"Don't make a bigger deal out of it than it is."

"I don't have to," she said. "It's already a big deal."

"I don't want to talk about her right now." Mark squeezed a packet of mayonnaise onto the chicken breast and squashed the bun around it. "I'm researching the family history."

"I see. Testing out the curse theory?"

He swallowed a bite and gulped his Coke. "I was lucky enough to find a booklet written about the Giles family."

"You're kidding."

"Nope." He munched on the sandwich, watching her stare at him.

"Tell me, or I'll bug you about Janet again."

Mark recapped his research, skimming over the tragic parts and embellishing what little positive angles he could without flat-out lying. She knew what he was doing, though, and triumph glittered in her eyes as she listened and ate. She popped the last chicken nuggets into her mouth as he finished telling of his census research, omitting any mention of Victoria.

"Terrible stuff *has* happened to our family since the dawn of time!"

Mark grimaced. "I'd hardly say since the dawn of time," he said. "Unless you consider the 1860s the dawn of time. I think most historians would disagree with you there."

"How's your head?" she asked in a complete *non sequitur*. Janet called her with the news of the accident, which occurred on their usual lunch day.

"I got the stitches out this morning," he answered, smacking her hand as she tried to sneak a French fry.

"Oh, good. You have enough holes in your head already without another one," Natalie said, grinning. "So our--how many times great-grandfather?--thought the family was cursed."

"Just great-grandfather. No, he *didn't* think the family was cursed. Other people did. He was trying to prove them wrong."

"And did he?" she asked. "Prove it, I mean?"

Mark gobbled down the remainder of his sandwich, then wiped mayonnaise from his hands, conscious of Natalie's inquisitive stare. "Well, I don't know that the case against a curse would stand up in court," he admitted, offering her his last fry. "But my namesake seemed pretty confident his success in life was proof no curse existed."

"But when was the book written?" Natalie wanted to know.

"1909."

She chewed thoughtfully. "Have you ever heard of--What were his kids' names again?"

"Oh, yeah, real hard names," Mark retorted, unhappy with the turn the conversation was taking. "Demarcus and Elizabeth."

"Well? Have you heard of them before? They'd be our ... great-uncle and great-aunt."

"Well, no--"

"And where's our grandmother in all this? Our great-grandmother's name was Clarice, so they obviously had a child after this book was written and named her after her--uh, Clarice, I mean. I rest *my* case!"

Mark folded his arms and eyed her skeptically. "What case? Just because we haven't heard of them doesn't mean anything terrible happened to them. They'd have to be a hundred. Even in normal families, not everyone lives that long. I rest my case."

She dismissed his argument with a wave of her paper cup. "Let's just find out first what happened to them before we entirely discount the curse theory."

"Oh, speaking of research, I discovered we had ancestors in Marengo County, so I thought I'd sneak down there for a day for some courthouse research. Want to come with me?"

"During the week? Getting obsessed, are we?"

"You sound like Mom," he shot back. "She said I'm obsessive like Dad. She--Natalie? Sis, are you okay?"

Tears rolled down her cheeks as her shoulders convulsed. Mark wrapped his arms around her, holding her until the sobs subsided. She wiped her eyes and blew her nose on a napkin. "Sorry, Mark. It's just ... when you mentioned him ..."

"I know. Don't apologize. It's good to let it out."

"Which I'm sure you've done?" she challenged, her normal tone creeping back. "You didn't cry once during the funeral."

"I'm dealing with it in my own way," Mark replied. "Doesn't mean I'm not upset, too." He cleared his throat and changed the subject. "Do you want to go with me or not?"

"I'd love to. Oh, what day?"

He closed his eyes a minute, then opened them again. "I was thinking this Friday."

"Great! My exams don't start until Monday." She rummaged through her backpack, producing a datebook. "Oh, I can't have lunch with you next Tuesday. Exams, you know."

"Okay, I'll treat you to lunch while we're on the road."

"Thanks. You're the best." She caught sight of the clock on the wall and squealed. "Uh, oh, gotta dash. Talk to you later." Natalie swept up the backpack and whirled away, leaving her brother laughing and shaking his head.

She cannot be right, he mused as he threaded his way back to the door. I refuse to believe someone could actually bestow a curse on a family. Why? It would have to be some really horrible event--or a totally deranged mind. Mark smiled at an acquaintance, waved to a coworker, barely registering their presence as he climbed up the front steps of the library.

Tina's expression as he passed the front desk stopped his current train of thought. Funny how quickly people get tired of you when you're staying with their boyfriend. I've either got to reconcile with Janet or move elsewhere, otherwise Tina won't be speaking to me. Dave either.

The phone was ringing as he unlocked his office.

"Hi, honey."

He sank down into the chair behind his desk, a wave of guilt fluttering through his stomach. "Hi, Jan. How are you?"

"Okay, I guess. How are you?"

I miss you, he nearly blurted out, but instead he said, "Not bad, considering."

"Mark ..." She seemed to be having trouble coming to the point. "Mark, there's somebody I'd like you to talk with."

"Who's that?" He draped an arm over the back of the chair, wondering which psychiatrist she selected for him.

"Daniel."

Mark leaned forward on top of a week's worth of unopened mail. "Why do you want me to talk with him?"

"He thinks you're experiencing psychic overload," she said, sighing as if expecting him to laugh at her. "That you're processing some kind of signals your brain can't handle."

Mark nearly dropped the telephone. His palms were sweating. "Psychic overload," he repeated at last.

"Of course, he couldn't tell conclusively without talking with you personally. I know you probably don't want to follow any of my suggestions ..."

This was too weird. "I couldn't until the weekend ..."

Her voice brightened. "I'd have to check with Daniel to see what his schedule is like ..."

"Okay, Jan," he relented, sighing. "I'll talk to him, if it'll make you happy. Give me a call, and let me know when he can see me."

"Thanks, Mark. I think you'll be glad you talked to him. Maybe he can put a stop to these episodes." There was an awkward pause, and then she added, "Well, I'll talk to you later."

"Janet, I--" There was so much more he needed to say.

"Yes, Mark?"

"Um, I still ... take care, okay?" He hung up and rested his cheek on the layer of mail.

The phone rang again a minute later. Mark picked it up without moving his head.

"I just wanted to remind you the annual report's due tomorrow," Barbara said in a tone that meant she'd scream if he didn't get it done today. "Giving you an extension because of an accident is one thing, but I can't wait much longer."

He sat up straight. "I know. I'll have it for you first thing in the morning."

"I hope so. I'd hate for us to look bad on campus."

"I'm on it. Don't worry." He hung up and turned to his computer. He felt heavy and lifeless. Don't know why I'm tired, he thought. My father's funeral, a trip to the emergency room with accompanying vision, and a high-speed chase by the insanely jealous boyfriend of a beautiful blonde all in one week. Sure, I should be able to cope with that.

CHAPTER 14.

Afternoon melted into evening. Mark saved the file and glanced at the time on the computer screen: 6:07 p.m. He issued the "Print" command and stretched, frozen joints protesting movement after sitting for five hours with only a few bathroom breaks. The printer hummed to life. He watched for a moment to make sure it was actually printing, then slipped out of the office to check his mailbox.

The periodicals area buzzed with activity as he emerged from the mailroom with a handful of junk mail, a journal, and a supplies catalog. A student worker sat at the desk Antonia occupied in the daytime. I've got to remember to track down her son, he thought, threading his way past students on their way to the copiers. I need to find out what he knows about my dad being with someone before he died.

Passing the main desk, he bumped into a woman hunched over the counter.

"Oh, excuse me," he said. "I wasn't look--Victoria?"

The blonde woman turned, finger securing her place in the white pages of the campus directory. She wore a skin-tight sleeveless lavender sweater and an ankle-length denim wrap skirt. "Mark!" she said. "I didn't think you'd be here so late. I found this directory so I could look you up. You never gave me your number."

Mark grinned, savoring the thought of this alluring woman trying to track him down. He tucked his mail under his arm, and reached for the directory. "Well you wouldn't have found me in the white pages," he pointed out, sliding the book from where her finger held the place in the

R's. As he did, he knocked off an open copy of the spiralbound facebook of all the students, faculty and staff.

"How did this get here?" he wondered aloud as he picked it up, noting the smiling face of his sister on one of the pages before he laid it on the main desk. "That's the student section you were looking in. I'm in the blue pages. But I've got something better." He reached into his breast pocket, and presented her with one of his business cards. "I should've given you this, but what with all the adventure, I forgot."

"Thanks." She slipped it into her purse. "I wanted to ask you--"

Several students clomped past.

He tugged her around the corner to a quieter corridor. "What did you want to ask me?"

Victoria brushed hair from her eyes. "Would you like to come over for dinner?"

He was tempted, until he remembered Janet's anxious voice on the phone. Victoria stepped closer, her breath warm and cinnamon-scented. The little stack of mail under his arm slithered to the floor. They ducked to retrieve it simultaneously and nearly bumped heads. Mark struggled to recover his balance at the exact moment she straightened up, and caught himself against the wall with one hand on either side of her shoulders.

"Sorry to interrupt your little conversation." Tina stood a few feet away, arms folded, her lips pressed into a disapproving line. Mark backed away. Victoria did not move.

"Hi, Tina," he managed. "You're working tonight?"

"John's sick, so I'm in for him." She glared at Victoria, then back at Mark. "Dave wondered what time you're coming home. He's got his book discussion group coming over tonight, and wanted to warn you there might not be a place to park."

"Oh. I'm finishing up a report for Barbara. It's printing out now, so I'll probably be another thirty minutes," he answered, thrusting his hands into his pockets for want of anything else to do with them.

"I'll tell him." Tina glared at Victoria again and left.

Victoria handed him the stack of mail. "Who's that?"

"My current roommate's girlfriend. I get the feeling I'm wearing out my welcome."

"But I thought--"

She broke off and pointed at the third finger of his left hand.

"I'm separated at the moment," he replied. "Staying with Dave for now."

"I see," she smiled, pressing closer. "So--dinner? Tomorrow night?"

He shook his head. "I'd better not. The offer's very tempting--"

"This weekend?"

Mark took a deep breath. "Victoria, I--"

"Monday, then. How about Monday?"

"But I--"

"It's settled, then." She brushed her lips against his cheek. "I'll call you Monday."

"But, Victoria--"

"Bye, Mark."

He watched her hips sway until she turned the corner.

"Tina--" he started as he went past her at the main desk. "It wasn't what you think."

"I *think* you should be more discreet," she replied.

He placed his mail on the counter. "We were just talking."

"It didn't look right. You were practically on top of her."

Mark shrugged. "It was an accident. I dropped my mail and she was helping me pick it up and I lost my balance. She's just a friend. She works at Birmingham Public." Tina still eyed him. "I met her last Saturday. Honest, there's nothing going on between us."

"What's that saying about protesting too much?" Her expression softened her words.

"Thanks for worrying about me, Tina. I appreciate it."

She smiled a little and returned to her computer. Mark scooped up his mail, skirted a knot of conversing students and dashed up the stairs to his office. He shut the door behind him and dropped the mail on top of the pile already there, then stared at the printer. Fourteen pages of his sixty-page report printed. A dialog box on the screen said the printer was out of paper.

"Damn. Why didn't I check that?" He slammed his fist on his desk, then winced as pain shot up the side of his hand. He refilled the printer and buried his head on his folded arms to await the completion of the report.

~*~*~

Laughter from the distant dorms drifted across the still campus as Natalie walked back from a meeting of the theater club. The night air was warm and humid, smelling faintly of honeysuckle and freshly-mown grass. Pools of lamplight illuminated the sidewalks, casting the vast stretches of lawn in between into denser darkness. Natalie stopped in the middle of the quad and looked around her. Where is that voice coming from? No one stood anywhere near her. She shrugged her backpack higher on her shoulder and trudged across the wet grass.

A sharp pain knifed through her temples. Natalie whimpered, fingers knotted in her hair. The weight of her backpack pulled her to her knees as the voice echoed again through her head. Rebecca? Oh, what is happening—

This curse had better work, Rebecca thought, slipping the Bowie knife across the whetstone once more. She squinted at the blade, sliding her thumb across it and sucking at the bright bead of blood. No one deserves it more than my dear brother. She slid the weapon back into the sheath on her worn leather belt, stolen from a dead Yankee days ago--or was it weeks? Time no longer had meaning for her, here in the tangled undergrowth of the forests of Alabama and Georgia and Tennessee, where she'd tracked James for what seemed an eternity.

The man who supplied her with the knife was not yet dead when she found him lying by the side of the road, blood flowing from a massive chest wound. She marveled at the tenacity of the spirit that allowed so desecrated a body to live. His eyes pleaded, his parched mouth worked, but he looked too much like James for her to offer her canteen. He had James' dark hair with just enough curl to wave it, the same dark brown eyes with pupil almost indistinguishable from iris. She stared at him impassively, then snatched the foot-long knife from his belt and slit his throat.

Such a lot of blood, she marveled, fighting the waves of nausea that invariably followed a killing. She could not seem to get used to it. Rebecca dropped to the ground next to the body and concentrated on cleaning the knife until the dizziness subsided. His belt, cinched to its smallest size, rode on her hips until she punched another hole into with the knife. Nothing else he had seemed worth taking, so she set out again.

She peered up through the trees at the sky. Just past noon, she decided. He's obviously following the river, but she lost him in that rain storm yesterday, damn it. Rebecca whipped off her slouch hat and ruffled her hair, chopped off so she could pass for a soldier. She was still not used to feeling the wind on her neck. This is the most logical path for him to follow if he's headed home, she told herself. Which I'm sure he is. He believed the message telling him his beloved wife was deathly ill. She spat on the ground, 'Beloved wife.' That's what they'll carve on her tombstone after I'm through with her, she thought. James is a fool for refusing me. I could have given him more power than he could dream--

Her reverie was cut off by a sound in the underbrush. It could be an animal, but better safe than sorry. She avoided a Yankee patrol the day before and remained alert to the danger of being captured or even hanged as a bushwhacker. Rebecca slung her Enfield across her shoulder, pulled the hat over her hair, and crept toward the sound, swiftly but silently. A rabbit leaped across her path. She chuckled to herself, then pushed off toward the trickling sound of the river to fill her empty canteen.

Early afternoon sun shone down, sparkling the water and dazzling her eyes after the dimness of the forest. Rebecca peered out at the river, squinting up at the bluff across the way for alert soldiers. A rhythmic creaking caught her attention. She stepped around the last of the trees into a clearing and stopped short, locating the source of the sound. Suspended from a rope hung the body of a Rebel soldier, clad in a ragged butternut shirt and dark blue trousers, probably pilfered from a dead Yankee. His wrists were bound behind his back.

Rebecca's first impulse was to ignore the body, but something prompted her to draw nearer. She steadied its swaying and peered up into the darkening face. The blood froze in her veins. Despite the distortion of features, she recognized the wavy dark hair of the man whose death she wanted more than anything else. She dropped to her knees, hands clenched in rage. No, not after all my work, my plans.

She heard a low moan and looked up. His lips were moving.

CHAPTER 15.

Mark awoke with a start. Rubbing the crick in his neck and stretching, he remembered the report. To his relief, he saw the neat stack of pages in the tray and pounded a staple into them. Then he closed the word processing program and glanced at the clock.

10:13 p.m.

Good grief, he thought. I've been asleep for three hours? What the hell is wrong with me? He placed the report in a cleared spot on his desk, ready for Barbara in the morning.

Tina's eyebrows rose as he strode past the main desk. "I thought you'd left hours ago. You told me thirty minutes--"

"I know. I fell asleep at my desk."

"I hope you've got a key," she said. "If Dave doesn't get his beauty sleep ..."

Shaking her head, she added, "To tell you the truth, he's finding he's not too thrilled with having a roommate. It's nothing personal."

"And what promise does that hold for *your* relationship with him?" he inquired, raising his own eyebrows.

"A wife's different," Tina insisted with a shrug. "Anyway, he still hasn't brought up the subject of marriage yet. He's a stubborn old cuss."

"Don't I know it. Well, I have a key. God knows he could use some beauty sleep."

He took the front steps two at a time and cut across the lawn toward the parking lot. Something pale on the dark, damp grass sloping away from the sidewalk caught his attention. As his eyes adjusted to the faint light, a single word popped into his head: *Natalie.*

Mark raced down the slope, feet slipping on the wet grass. He knelt beside the figure on the ground, rolled her onto her back. "Natalie?" He shook her, kept calling her name.

At last she blinked up at him. "Mark? What happened? I don't feel so good." Her voice was low and faint, so he had to lean closer to hear.

"Nat, what happened to you? Are you sick?"

Mark helped her sit up as she rubbed the back of her head. "I was crossing the quad. I ... heard voices ..."

"Behind you?" he demanded. He sat in the wet grass beside her.

"I think they were in my head."

"In your head? What are you talking about, Nat?"

She frowned. "There was a buzzing ... in my head. I guess I passed out."

Great, he thought, don't tell me this passing out stuff is hereditary. "Are you sick?"

"I think I'm okay now," she said. "Maybe ... maybe it's just stress."

"Think you can stand?" At her nod, he helped his sister to her feet, and slung her heavy backpack over his shoulder. "I'll drive you to your dorm. You sure you're okay?"

"Sure. No buzzing, no voices."

Mark took her hand as they walked toward the parking lot. "This hasn't happened to you before, has it?"

"No. Never. I still feel a little light-headed. But don't worry about me, Bro. We Richardses are survivors. Right?"

God, I hope so, he thought.

CHAPTER 16.

Wednesday, May 8.

"Decaffeinated, please," Janet answered, twisting the tissue between her fingers. "Lemon, no sugar. Thank you, Delia."

Mark's mother slipped into the kitchen. Janet looked around the living room and wondered just how she was going to tell her news. Delia was always kind, the perfect mother-in-law, in fact, but the woman was already under so much strain Janet felt guilty adding it.

"I understand in England," Delia said, returning with a teacup-laden tray, "they drink milk in their tea. I don't think that sounds very pleasant." She set the tray on the coffee table and handed Janet a delicate floral-patterned cup and saucer.

Janet sipped the hot liquid, wondering how to begin, when Delia said, "I should be grateful for the company and not pry, but I'm not like my children. What's wrong, dear?"

Tears sprang up at the woman's gentle question. Janet set the cup on the table and dabbed at her eyes. "Everything," she said. "Delia, Mark's left me."

Delia blinked. "Left?"

"He's been so upset about these spells and we had a fight and he walked out and it's been over a week and--and--"

Janet bit her lip. "And I'm pregnant."

As she dissolved into choking sobs, Janet felt Delia's arm around her shoulders, but the older woman's voice was hard when she spoke. "My son left you and you're pregnant?"

74

Janet looked up. "No, Delia, no. Mark doesn't know. I-I wanted to tell him, but things were so confusing with his fainting spells and all, I wanted to wait until--"

She heaved a sigh, dabbed her nose. "I thought he'd come back the next day, but he didn't. I think he's staying at Dave's. I-I just don't know what to do."

Delia was silent for several minutes. "My son is a stubborn man," she said at last. "I know he loves you, though, Janet. If it weren't for you, I don't know what would have become of him. He always was a lonely child, and you brought him out of himself. I'll admit, Thomas and I had our doubts about you, but only because it happened so suddenly. He never did tell us what was going on in his life then, and that hasn't changed." Delia handed Janet another tissue. "I think he'll come around, dear, but in his own time."

"You won't tell him, will you?" Janet said.

"No, that's for you to do. But he really needs to know."

Janet shook out her cramped fingers and smiled at her mother-in-law. "Thank you, Delia. I always feel better talking to you. When the time is right, I'll tell him."

"If you need me, dear, I'm here."

Janet nodded and picked up her cup, feeling lighter than she had in days. Now, she just had to figure out how to talk to Mark. But it would wait until he'd seen Daniel.

CHAPTER 17.

Friday, May 7.

Tension drained from Mark's knotted shoulder muscles as the highway flashed under the wheels of his dark green Saturn. The day was perfect for driving, the sky overhead achingly blue, tinting down to translucency at the horizon. Clouds feathered the sky like daubs of titanium white on an artist's palette. He glanced over at his sister writhing in the seat in time to music on the car stereo, her eyes closed behind mirrored sunglasses. She seemed to have suffered no ill effects from the fainting spell on the quad four days ago.

He yawned, flexing his fingers on the wheel and envying her exuberance. When the alarm went off at six, he almost threw it across the room in a fit of frustration brought on by too little sleep. He tossed and turned on the lumpy couch, wide awake and replaying his life with Janet, until he dozed at about three a.m.. Their lunch of hearty country-style food at a local restaurant did nothing to help him stay alert. If not for Natalie's presence, he would have spent the afternoon accordioned between the car's dash and a tree.

Mark climbed out of the car in front of the Marengo County Courthouse and appraised the building, obviously the product of a 1960s building project. Smooth concrete aggregate pillars rose incongruously to the flat, second-story roof. A round disk with no numbers and two tapered slivers over the massive wooden doors approximated the time as either one-

76

forty or five after eight.

"I don't want to go in."

He gaped at his sister. "Then why did you come with me all the way down here?"

She shrugged. "I'll be in later. I need some air. I'm feeling kind of strange. Hyper and dizzy at the same time."

"You're not going to pass out on me, are you?"

She glared at him.

"Just be careful," Mark cautioned with a shrug. "Don't get into trouble."

Inside the building he smelled mildew and fresh coffee and the miasma of stale cigarette smoke. His steps in the hallway were muffled by the rubber soles of his boots, and only a distant hum of conversation from a few offices ahead told him the building was inhabited. Mark took a guess and turned left at the intersection of two hallways. At his inquiry, a gray-haired woman behind a counter pointed him toward a wide doorway a dozen feet away.

As he crossed the marble threshold, Mark realized the room was essentially a vault-steel door attached by large metal hinges to a foot-and-a-half-thick jamb, deep window ledges. The temperature inside was ten degrees cooler. At either end of the room, huge ledgers rested on waist-high counters. Metal shelving stacked with bound back issues of newspapers dominated the center of the room.

Mark sat at an old library table, wincing at the squeak of the chair joints, and fished a spiral notebook from his briefcase. He turned to the counter behind him and selected a book of probate records from the 1860s, wrestling the three-inch-thick ledger onto the wooden table.

The index in the front of the volume consisted of a list of handwritten names grouped by initial letter of the last name. Handwriting changed as new clerks came and went over the years. Mark flipped the page at the "G" tab and trailed a forefinger down the lines of 140-year-old writing, locating the entry for "Giles, Samuel." At the bottom of the indicated page, he found the words "The Estate of Sam'l Giles, Dec'd." Just as he began mentally translating the rounded letters and unfamiliar abbreviations, Mark jumped as a voice at his elbow intoned, "I am the ghost of your ancestors."

"Don't *do* that, Natalie," he gasped. "I'll be the next in the family to die--of a heart attack brought on by you."

Natalie flopped into a chair beside him. "Find anything?"

"In 1859, Samuel Giles wrote his last will and testament."

She exclaimed, "Oh, you were just talking about him!"

"Keep your voice down."

"Librarian." She stuck her tongue out.

"Giles left the bulk of his estate to his wife Lavinia," he read, "with bequests of a buggy and horse to unmarried daughter Rachel Giles, an iron bedstead to another unmarried daughter Rebecca, a mule to son James Giles, and another horse to daughter Mrs. Elmer Nations."

"Wow, I wish someone would leave me a buggy. Is that him?" She leaned toward the book for a better look.

"Yes. Our great-great-great grandfather, James Giles. Oh, wait, there's a codicil." He peered closer at the writing. "This is interesting."

"What? What?" Natalie shoved up against him.

"March 1st, 1861. He revokes the previous bequest to James, whom he renounces as his son and leaves everything else to his wife and daughters Rachel and Mrs. Elmer Nations."

She leaned on her elbows, peering at the inked script. "Renounces? Why would he do that? God, what would someone have to do to be renounced by their own father?"

"It doesn't say ... Wait a second. 'Daughters Rachel and Mrs. Elmer Nations,' it says. Why isn't Rebecca mentioned?"

Natalie shrugged. "Maybe she got married."

"No, because a married daughter *is* mentioned."

"Then maybe she died."

Mark shook his head. "We'll have to figure out somewhere else to look. Maybe another record will shed some light on it."

"Can I help you look?"

"Sure." He gestured to the shelves by the door. "Start on those marriage records and see what you can find." He turned back to the probate ledger.

Brother and sister were silent for some time, poring over the yellowed pages. After fifteen minutes, Natalie tugged at his sleeve and pointed to an entry.

"She wasn't dead when the codicil was made. See? John A. Chapman and Rebecca Lavinia Giles. It's dated June 4th, 1861. Then it says the return is June 5th, 1861. What does that mean?"

"The marriage license was obtained one day and the wedding was held the next." He scrawled the new information into the notebook, then looked up. "Both James and Rebecca were cut out of the will. Did they both do something to offend him? Was she engaged to someone her father didn't approve of, and James supported her?"

Natalie shrugged and flipped to another entry. He peered over the book sideways, leaning on his elbows, and exclaimed as he spotted a familiar name. "Hey, look!"

"You can read upside-down?" Natalie asked.

"This is a record of the marriage of James S. Giles to Alice Rose Parker on February 9th, 1861, with Samuel Giles as bondsman. Our however-many times great-grandparents."

Natalie discovered an entry written four months later, in which Samuel Giles again acted as bondsman for the marriage of Beatrice Lavinia Giles and Elmer Nations. Mark copied the entry, then pulled out his pocket watch. "It's nearly three. We should wrap this up soon so you'll have time to study for your exams."

She sighed and nodded. "But let's see if we can find out anything about that guy who didn't believe in the curse. He had a really funny name--Oh, yeah, Demarcus."

"Ha, ha. You're a laugh riot. Okay. Let's find probate records after 1909. That was when the pamphlet was published."

Natalie cleared her throat loudly after opening the 1910 probate ledger. Mark raised his eyebrows and moved to her side as she leafed to the appropriate page. "Index says Demarcus Giles, but it only references Orphans' Court records."

He found the volume and said, "June 3rd. A hearing to assign custody of Clarice Giles."

"Our grandmother? Where was the rest of the family?"

"Doesn't say. Just says she became the ward of Robert Hawthorne, the child's maternal grandfather." A roaring in his ears blotted out the sounds around him as he realized the man must have died within a few months of publishing the pamphlet Mark read in the library.

"Earth to Mark, Earth to Mark." Natalie shook his arm. "You're spacing out, Bro."

"Sorry. It's just--I hoped--"

"You hoped I was wrong. I knew it. We're cursed," Natalie said. "How did he die?"

"It doesn't say. We'll have to check newspaper accounts, find an obituary. Is there a library around here?" Mark wondered.

"Whoa, I thought you said we were going back--"

"Later. This is important." He copied the probate record information into his notebook and dashed to the counter in the hallway. "Excuse me, is there a local library that might have back issues of newspapers?"

The woman nodded. "Public library's just down the street. Oh, but sir, wait--"

He turned back. "She closes at noon on Fridays."

Shit, he thought. He wasn't sure if he said it out loud.

Natalie handed him his briefcase. "Watch your language, Bro. I've never heard you talk like that before. We'll just have to--"

"Why do they have to close early on Fridays? I have to wait all weekend? I need to know this now," Mark said. "Do you have the librarian's home number?"

"Sir, I don't--"

"Mark. *Demarcus*. Calm down." Natalie jerked on his arm. "Sorry, ma'am. He's under a lot of stress lately."

Mark allowed his sister to drag him away toward the car.

"I can't take you anywhere," she grumbled, throwing his briefcase in the back seat as he unlocked the car. "Do you have to make such a public display?"

Public display, he snorted. I wasn't even near that level yet. He was dimly aware of his sister turning on the stereo as he drove out of town. His head buzzed with questions, an almost audible hum: I have to find out what happened to him. He couldn't have died of natural causes. And what about James and Rebecca? Why would their father denounce them both, write them out of his will? What did they do? Was that the origin of whatever is going on in this lunatic family of mine? Why--

Gravel flew toward his face and the buzz in his head grew louder. He winced back in his seat before he remembered there was a windshield between him and the flying debris. The buzz resolved into Natalie's voice shouting, "Mark! Mark, listen to me! Stop the car! Stop the car!"

CHAPTER 18.

Peeling white slats of a wooden fence loomed before him. Mark stomped the brake pedal, wheels catching at last on the gravel surface. He jerked the car into park and sat clutching the steering wheel. "Where are we?"

"I've been yelling at you for the past five minutes," Natalie said. "I thought you were going to crash into that fence. What do you mean, 'where are we'?"

To his left a steeple stretched toward the blue sky from a tiny church's slate roof. The front bumper of the car rested five feet from a white fence, beyond which rose uneven rows of limestone and granite headstones. A holly hedge obscured the view to the right. The car stopped on grass, and clouds of dust obscured the view of the gravel road behind them.

He pried his fingers from the wheel, swayed out of the car, and hauled his watch from his pocket. His hand trembled as he noted the time--he drove without conscious thought for at least thirty minutes. He leaned forward, hands on his knees, breathing deep gasps of pine-scented air. The loss of control was as terrifying as the visions and blackouts. Mark shuddered, then kicked the front tire, reveling in pain as a reality he could deal with.

Natalie stroked his back. "Are you okay?"

He looked up at her sideways, then straightened and shrugged as his heartbeat slowed. "I have no idea what just happened," he admitted. "I have no clue where we are."

His sister wrapped an arm around his waist. "You really scare me, you know that?"

Mark looked down into her wide eyes. "Honey, you can't be more scared than I am." He squeezed her shoulders. "But we might as well make the best of this. Let me catch my breath. Old cemeteries are fascinating, no matter who's buried there."

He took her hand and wandered through the gate toward the graves, calmed by the poignant peace between the stones. He reveled in the unspoken stories represented by the terse captions on headstones of infants who died before they could walk, sentimental expressions of love untouched by death, and pious homilies requesting entrance into the afterlife.

"Sis--did Dad ever talk to you about the second death?"

"Second death? What do you mean?" Natalie asked.

"His rant that we're supposed to remember our ancestors or it's like they've died twice."

"That's interesting. No, he never did. What else did he say about it?"

Mark shook his head. "I don't know. I never wanted to listen to him. Now I wish I had."

"Stop that. You'll make me start crying. I'm gonna go look at headstones." She pulled away, running to examine the taller obelisk monuments in the center of the cemetery.

He glanced at the names to the right and to the left, and stopped dead in his tracks as he read on a small limestone-incised block, "Lucinda Lavinia Giles, beloved daughter of Samuel and Lavinia Giles, born 1843, died 1844." Next to it rested the body of "Rachel Lavinia Giles, 1841-1931, aged 90 years, 3 months."

He jogged back to the car for his notebook. How did I know to come here? I realize family history can become an obsession, but I never heard of anyone blacking out and coming to in a cemetery they didn't know existed, full of dead relatives they'd been tracking down.

When he returned to the Giles graves, Natalie said, "You know how weird this is? Finding these people buried here?" She stooped down, tracing the letters in the stone with a forefinger, and added, "Rachel wasn't cursed, was she? She was old, by anyone's standards."

He stepped over to the next pair of sandstone markers. One of them was harder to read, the incised letters spelling out "Samuel Giles, born Sept. 30, 1820, died June 2, 1861." Next to him was "Lavinia Giles, beloved wife of Samuel Giles, born Dec. 3, 1821, died April 5, 1871." "I can't believe it," Mark marveled, lowering himself to one knee and steadying his notebook on the other. "This is just about the whole family. All the people I read about in the census record."

Natalie dropped to the ground, arms clasped around knees, gazing at the row of stones. "I'll bet Rachel was a 'beloved daughter' too, but by the time she died, no one was around to remember that." She leaned back on her hands. "So how did you know to come here?"

Mark stared up at the patch of dazzling sky that peered down on them like an eye between the swaying tops of the tall pines. "Damned if I know," he answered.

~*~*~

Natalie insisted on driving. Mark stared out the window. His head ached with the effort of understanding what was happening to him. He wiped moisture from his chin and recoiled at the red smear on his fingers. The throbbing pain in his lower lip and the salty taste—

"Mark! What have you done to yourself?"--and Natalie's startled exclamation told him he had bitten through his lip. "Natalie," he breathed, "am I insane?"

His sister surveyed him over the top of her mirrored sunglasses, startling him with a glimpse of his bloody face. He dug in her purse for a tissue. "You are if you think you can find anything in that purse," she answered.

He balled up the tissue after scrubbing away the blood. "I'm scared, Natalie."

"No, you're my big brother. You don't get scared. You're just tired." He could tell she was struggling to maintain her "grown-up voice."

"You must've read about the location of the cemetery and only remembered it on a subconscious level. You'll be okay. You're tough." She reached over and patted his knee. "You always were the strong one when we were kids. Nothing ever got to you."

Mark snorted. "Oh, yeah, that's me. I don't think Demarcus is really my name. Suppression, that's what it should be." He realized he was still laughing and wasn't sure if he could stop. He bit down hard on his split lip. After a deep breath he forced a steady smile and found he could keep his lips from trembling if he concentrated. "So," he said at last. "How far are we from home?"

Instead of answering, Natalie asked, "Why have you never talked to me about your visions?" Knuckles white on the wheel, she stared straight ahead at the road, the grim set of her lips more familiar on his mother's face.

"How do you know about them?"

"Janet told me. Mark," she dragged his name out to two syllables, "I'm your *sister*, for God's sake. You can tell *me*."

"Honestly," he said, wondering if she could tell he was lying, "it never occurred to me." You're still my baby sister, he thought. I'll shield you from life's ugliness as long as I can. "I don't like to talk about it, especially not after what's happened today."

"After what's happened today and what happened to me the other night, you need to tell me," Natalie said.

"I don't think so." He grabbed the dashboard when she slammed on the brakes in the middle of the highway. "Shit! What the hell are you doing?"

"I'm not moving this car until you tell me about the visions." Natalie put the car in park and folded her arms across her chest.

"Move the damn car!" he shrieked as an eighteen-wheeler keened past them, horn blaring.

She shook her head, still staring at the horizon.

"Okay, okay! I'll tell you!" he snapped. "Just move the car before we get killed!"

Natalie snorted and dropped it into drive, steering to the shoulder of the road. "I wouldn't get us killed." She turned off the engine. "Now, spill it, Demarcus, or you'll spend the night in this car."

"Damn, you're bossy." He unlatched his seat belt. "Okay, what has Janet told you?"

"Not a lot," she said. She copied his action with the seat belt. "That you've had these episodes where you go unconscious and have, like, horrible nightmare experiences."

Mark shrugged. "That's a pretty good description."

"You didn't ever do LSD, did you?"

"No. I don't know what causes them. But it isn't drugs." He shuddered. "I'd hate to think how drugs would affect me."

"So tell me about one of the episodes."

Mark blew out a breath through his teeth. "The first time I actually saw something, I was in a conversation with Janet. No, not a conversation," he amended. "A major argument. I don't remember now what about, probably the usual about her trying to control my life."

He ignored his sister's outraged exclamation, studying the outline of the trees against the sky. "Suddenly, I was running through a forest, running like my life depended on it." He felt the blood in his throat pulsing against his shirt collar. "Someone was trying to kill me. In the vision, I knew who it was. It was someone I knew, someone I was related to ... maybe even married to. The thing of it was ..."

He rolled the window down as he tried to draw a deep breath. He'd never told anyone this part. "The thing of it was, I felt ... guilty, like I deserved to be murdered, to be chased down like a--no, I was going to say like a mad dog, but a mad dog isn't responsible for its actions. Chased down like a thieving fox, I guess. It's hard to explain to you the feeling ... the feeling that I had so wronged someone, so violated their existence, that they hated me that much."

Mark bowed his head.

Natalie was silent. Vehicles arrowed past, intermittently rocking the car like a rowboat in a gusty breeze. She reached out and stroked his hair.

"Needless to say, that stopped that particular argument," he finally said with a chuckle. Mark wiped his sweaty palms on his jeans. "It's happened three times. So far."

Natalie rested her hand on his arm. "Was it the same every time?"

Mark shook his head and described the latest visions of the Yankee patrol and the lynching. He grabbed Natalie's hands. "The scary part is, I never know when they'll happen."

"Mark, you're hurting me!"

He released her. "Sorry. I got freaked out just thinking about it." He rested his elbow on the window frame, fingers tapping on the car roof.

"What does it mean? Have you wondered that?" Natalie examined the impression her ring made on her finger from Mark's grip. "See what you did to me?"

He patted her hand and said, "Of course I've wondered about it."

"It sounds like an out-of-body experience. Or do you think it's something that will happen to you in the future?"

"I don't know what it is." He leaned his head back, eyes closed. "Can we go now?"

She started the engine. "Sure. Thanks for telling me. *Finally*. Don't you feel better?"

"Not particularly. Now let's just get back in one piece, okay? No more stopping in the middle of the road?"

She grinned. "I promise."

The hum of the wheels and the warm sun through the windshield soon melted away his anxiety. He slipped into semi-consciousness, until Natalie started talking again.

"--for her sake and all you've meant to each other. You really should."

Mark yawned. "Sorry, Nat. I fell asleep. What are you on about now?"

"You and Janet. I said you should get back with her."

He tucked his hands into his armpits. "Whose sister are you, anyway?"

"She's my *friend*, Mark." Natalie stuck out her lower lip. "All couples fight. Just buy her some flowers and make up."

"So speaks the woman who considers three dates a long-term relationship." He ran his fingers through his hair. "It's not that simple, Sis. I don't know ... maybe I married her too fast."

"But you've been married to her for eleven years. Does it really matter how long you knew her before?"

Did it? He'd met Janet in his senior year of college at the bookstore, which she hadn't owned then, and they'd dated for three months before he

85

popped the question.

"That was my first--okay, my *only* serious relationship."

She slipped him a glance. "I dated more in *middle school* than you did in college."

"Thanks, Sis. I can always count on you to bolster my ego," Mark said.

"I remember how surprised Mom and Dad were when you announced you were getting married," Natalie said. "They hadn't even met her. I told them it was so romantic--you know, love at first sight."

"Yeah, but after we married I got to know her. We fought. A lot. She was always trying to tell me what to do. Always controlling me." He stuck his arm out the car window, feeling the wind rush between his fingers. "She's never satisfied with what I do. Always wants me to 'do something.' Well, I *will* 'do something,' but according to *my* timetable, not hers."

He was angry again.

Natalie glanced over at him. "So why did you stay married?"

He flipped his hair out of his collar. "I don't know. Because it's ... easier." Janet's face flashed into his mind and his tone softened. "I do love her, Natalie. I just ... need to find out what are my ideas about things and what are hers."

"You do tend to let events control you, rather than you controlling events," Natalie said.

Mark glanced at her. "That's pretty insightful, Nat. Are those *her* words?"

His sister shrugged, setting her earrings bobbing. "I've heard her say that, but it's what I've thought for a long time."

"I think this conversation's gone on long enough. If I need psychoanalysis, I'll go to a shrink. But I *don't*." Mark shifted in his seat, turning away from her to stare out the window. He didn't think there was anyone who could help him.

CHAPTER 19.

Saturday, May 8.

"You've really got it bad," Kynon said, laughing. "Two Saturdays in a row. Or are you here to see Victoria? I heard you walked her out to her car the other day."

Mark scowled. "This staff's got mouths as big as the ones at my library. Look, I need to find an obituary in a Marengo County newspaper, 1909 or 1910. Any chance you have backfiles?" He held his breath in anticipation.

"Sorry, man. None for Marengo County."

"Damn!"

"Hey, take it easy," Kynon said. "Let me finish. We do have a compilation of obituaries from the *Marengo Courier*. Seems like it's ..."

He consulted his screen. "Yeah, it's 1900 to 1950," he said, and handed Mark a scrap of paper with the call number scribbled on it. "You're really getting into this research. It can't be *that* serious."

"You just don't know. Thanks, Kynon." Back in the stacks he found the book within minutes. Get a grip, he counseled himself. You're scaring people. Including yourself.

The thick volume consisted of poor-quality photocopies of obituary clippings from the *Marengo Courier* and the *Demopolis Herald*, including an index of the names of the deceased. Mark quickly located Demarcus Giles. Three related news articles were included with the obituary. The headline of the first announced in bold type, "Brutal Murder of Woman and Children. Husband Missing."

The text detailed the discovery of Clarice Giles of Jefferson County and her young children Demarcus, five, and Elizabeth, four, in their family home, stabbed to death by person or persons unknown. The husband Demarcus and eight-month-old daughter Clarice were missing. The second clipping reported the discovery of little Clarice safe and sound at her grandparents' home where she was staying while her mother recovered from an illness. The baby's father was found hiding in the basement of the house, covered in blood, but denying any knowledge of what happened. The last clipping described the funerals of Clarice and her children, and a report of the suicide of husband Demarcus. He killed himself before he could be tried.

"Found out you're descended from horse thieves?"

Mark dropped the book. "Oh, hi, Victoria," he said, picking the book up again. "I wish it was horse thieves."

She pulled out the chair next to him. "Nothing you've read could be that depressing. You should see your face."

Mark blew out a long breath and pointed at the page of clippings. "That was my last hope. My last ... log to hang onto. Now it's gone."

"You can't hang onto a log. You probably mean plank. Or better yet, life preserver."

His annoyance faded as he saw the twinkle in her eyes and the Mona Lisa smile on her lips. "It's just that ... a curse? It's a hard idea to accept. It's not ... it's not logical."

"Do you really think anything in the world is logical? Logic is just an illusion your brain pieces together from fragments of insanity, to try and explain it all, make it--force it to make sense." She pulled the clippings book closer to her. "Demarcus Giles. Ancestor of yours?"

"My great-grandfather."

Her long red fingernail skimmed the lines of the newspaper account. "Your great-grandfather murdered his family? Not good. Is that what you mean about a curse?"

Mark shook his head. "It would take too long to explain. Besides, you probably have to get back to work."

"Take me to lunch and explain. You intrigue me."

He shut the book and said, "I've never intrigued anyone before. Sure. Let's go to lunch."

~*~*~

Natalie approached the young black man. Despite her brother's profession, she always felt awed by large libraries and wanted to avoid looking foolish. He didn't look too scary, though, with that cute little earring.

"Excuse me, sir--"

The man laughed. "Sir? I'm not old enough yet to be a sir. What can I do for you?"

"I know a lot of people come in here," she said, "but I thought you might know him. My brother, I mean. I figured he might be here. His name's Mark Richards."

"Oh, you're Mark's little sister?" he said, his tone putting her at ease. "You obviously got all the looks in the family. Yeah, he was in here, but he left about a half hour ago."

"But I saw his car in the parking lot ..."

He raised his eyebrows. "Well, he left with a woman who works here, so they must have taken her car. My name's Kynon, by the way. I've known your brother for many long years."

She shook his hand. "Nice to meet you, Kynon. You know, while I'm waiting for him, I might as well do some research. Was he working on anything?"

"He was looking at books on Marengo County." Kynon pointed to a table nearby. "That's where he was sitting. If you have any questions, ask away, okay?"

"Thanks." She sat down at the table, and opened the large volume at random. To her surprise, she read the headline of a 1931 article reproduced from the *Marengo Courier*: "Miss Rachel Giles Passes into History."

Skimming the story, she learned the ninety-year-old woman lived in the old family home until the day she died. She'd become a historian of the area, author of a little book entitled *My Memories of Marengo*. Other family members were mentioned: her father Samuel, who died when she was twenty, her mother Lavinia, whom she nursed until her death in 1871, her sister, Mrs. Elmer Nations of Galveston, Texas, who survived her mother by only fourteen years, and her siblings James and Rebecca, about whom little was known. The article mentioned a rumor James was disowned by his father and later murdered during the Civil War by marauding Yankees. Rebecca married John Chapman and moved to Baltimore.

The last sentences about Rachel's family intrigued Natalie. "'I haven't told you everything I know about my family,' Miss Giles said in an interview after the publication of her book. 'You'll just have to read what I've written. Some things a young lady doesn't talk about, but some things an old lady just might write about.'"

Natalie begged Kynon to help her find a copy of Rachel's book. To her utter astonishment--and his as well--the library owned a copy of it. She flipped to the section of Giles family photographs. Samuel and Lavinia appeared in a wedding portrait, young people aged by their somber expressions and formal attire. The next photograph showed the entire family, three girls and a boy, all below the age of ten. Separate portraits of Rachel and Beatrice followed, young women with dark hair and eyes and serious expressions. But the last of the older photographs made her gasp.

The caption read, "James and Rebecca, age 17." James stood in profile, Rebecca close beside him with her hand on his arm. James' dark hair was cut short, but a wavy lock fell on his forehead. His eyes sparkled with an inner amusement, and Natalie noticed in his facial structure and coloring he strongly resembled Mark. Rebecca's hair was long and curly, her eyes haughty and challenging, thin lips turned up in a mysterious half-smile. Her fingers, curving along the dark fabric of James' sleeve, were long and elegant.

Wow. She's not really beautiful, Natalie thought, but there's something about her ...

She dug in her pocket for change and photocopied the picture. Then she flipped through the pages of the little book, scanning in the absence of an index for any mention of Rebecca.

"My sister Rebecca was a year younger than I," Natalie read. "But she always seemed to be years older. She was very intelligent and so interested in learning that at last Papa engaged a tutor for her, a Mrs. de Graffenried, all the way from Nashville. Unfortunately as her knowledge grew, her Christian charity dwindled. She could be very cruel and spiteful, especially when she was determined to have her way. Rumors spread that Mrs. de Graffenried was a witch, who taught wicked things to Rebecca, but I never believed it could be true.

"My sister was especially fond of James, doting on him in a way almost unseemly. That fondness made it all the more shocking when she and James had a falling-out. Rebecca was very ill for some time after that with some sort of mysterious female trouble. A wicked friend of mine thought she was with child and lost the baby, but I pointed out that was not possible since Rebecca was not married. At about the same time, my father disowned my brother after a terrible argument. Papa had been dangerously ill for some months before the argument, and sickened again afterwards, never quite recovering. I never knew why they fought, and I never saw James again until his body was brought back for burial. Rebecca married a Yankee man after knowing him less than a month and they moved away up north. I never saw her again."

Natalie closed the book and stared at the photocopy of the picture. It must have been very hard to be a smart woman back then, she thought. I'll bet she stood up for herself and that's what got her into trouble. They probably thought getting an education was the same thing as witchcraft. I wish I'd known her. She looks like someone I could learn a lot from.

~*~*~

The restaurant Victoria chose was reached by a series of curving roads off the main highway. Mark doubted he would ever find the place again alone and was pleased that she drove. He felt somewhat uneasy being with her, but dismissed the thoughts: What harm can it do? An innocent lunch with a friend in front of other people. Who could object? Besides Janet.

"Aren't there any tables more out in the open?" he asked as they sat at a table in a dim nook. A curtain cut them off from the other customers.

"All the tables are private," Victoria said. "Discretion is their byword."

"But I don't have any reason to be discreet."

She smiled that maddening smile and picked up the menu.

The waiter approached and before Mark could speak, Victoria ordered grilled chicken and a bottle of wine. "Wine at lunch? Don't you have to be back at work?"

"No. I only worked the morning shift today. Now ... tell me about this curse."

He sketched the particulars for her, emphasizing it was his father's theory, not his. "I've tried--thank you," as the waiter poured wine into their glasses, "I've tried to disprove it by doing research on the family ..."

The wine was tart on his tongue. "This is the first time I've had wine for lunch, except for a few champagne brunches," he added. "Anyway, all I've done is prove him right."

"Is your separation a symptom of that curse?"

He watched the tip of her tongue lick a stray drop from the rim of her glass. "What? No, just a symptom of my inability to conform to the personality she wishes I had."

"And what personality is that?" Victoria asked.

"Ambitious. Proactive. Knowing exactly what you want out of life, then going for it." He sipped his wine. "I shouldn't be telling you this if I'm trying to impress you."

Her smile illuminated the golden glints in her eyes. "You're the opposite of that?"

"Frankly, yes. I prefer to ... see what comes along, weigh the options, make up my mind slowly. She calls it letting things happen to me and not being willing to make decisions." He fell silent as the waiter brought their meals. This woman is actually listening to me, he thought, without telling me what I should be doing and when and how and why. He tasted the chicken. "You're right--this is delicious."

"Would I steer you wrong?"

"Apparently not." Mark ate a few more bites and asked, "Do you ever feel ... I don't know, like you're a pawn on a chess board--to use an old cliché--a pawn everyone else can move around to their satisfaction but not necessarily to yours?"

She plowed lines in her rice with a fork, watching her food. "You don't know what an apt description that is for my life." Looking up, she asked, "Is your life that way?"

"I think so. Maybe that's why I've always resented my father going on and on about our ancestors, like their actions ... predestined mine. If you don't leap to decisions and conclusions, people assume it's because you want them to make them and reach them for you." He took another sip of wine. "My wife's particularly bad about that. Definitely a control freak."

"My Aunt Sylvia is that way." Victoria nibbled at her bread. "Well, she's not really my aunt. She raised me after my parents died when I was six. Everything I've ever done has been tightly controlled by her. Everything."

Mark laughed to ease her tension. "Not meeting me. She can't control that."

She blinked and repeated, "Everything."

He raised the glass. "To kindred spirits, then."

"Kindred spirits." She drank. "I don't intend to be controlled anymore. *My* future will be shaped by *me*."

He chewed, taken aback by her sudden intensity. "You know ... I think if I knew the future, it would be easier to make decisions."

She laughed, scooping up a forkful of rice. "You mean if you knew the outcome, the consequences of your actions, you'd be more ambitious and decisive?"

"I'm serious," Mark said. "That would be a great skill to have."

"You'd rule the world."

"Sure, with all the money I'd make--" he said, laughing.

"Now *I'm* serious. If you also had the ability to control the future, actually influence the consequences instead of being ruled by them ..."

The look in her eyes was somber, but he smiled when he said, "Do you have any secret knowledge I should be aware of?"

"Maybe." She set her fork down on her plate and brushed her fingers across the back of his hand. "I might be persuaded to share it with you."

Her touch sent a charge through him and he gazed into her eyes until the waiter coughed. Mark ignored Victoria's offer and replied to the waiter's question, "No. Just the check."

"I'd like to know the future to figure out what effect this curse will have on me," he said. "If there *is* a curse. I'm not ready to concede that yet. The future wasn't kind to my ancestors."

He wrote in the tip when the waiter brought the bill and scribbled his name on the credit card receipt, thinking, The lady's not cheap. But then, he hadn't been on a date for over a decade, so how would he know?

Victoria leaned forward to smile at him. "Thanks for lunch, Mark. Now you really must come over for dinner, so I can make this up to you."

"I'm not sure it's a good idea."

"Do you know what time it is?" she asked when they reached her car. "Oh, you're not wearing a watch."

"1:15."

"What a beautiful pocket watch! May I look at it?" Victoria leaned on the car. She ran her fingernail across the dent in the case. "How was it damaged?"

"My father ..."

He cleared his throat. "Had it in his pocket. When he was killed. A train. Hit him."

"I'm very sorry," she murmured, opening the case and examining the face. Then she snapped it shut and, still clutching it, went around to the driver's side of the car.

Mark climbed in, reluctant for their time together to end. He expected her to return the watch, but it lay cradled in the Y-shaped intersection formed by the wrinkles of her skirt as she pulled the seatbelt between her breasts and started the engine.

"So what are your plans for the evening?"

He stared as the watch in her lap quivered with her breathing.

"I'm having a tarot reading done by a friend of my wife's. My wife's ex-lover, I guess I should say. He's a psychic counselor," Mark added with a snort, "whatever that means."

"Well, that's one way of finding out about your future." She gunned the engine as they sped through a yellow light changing to red. "Although it won't help you control it."

Mark peeled his fingers from the dashboard when he realized they weren't crashing within the next few seconds. "You know, I think maybe what I need control is the past. Change what's already happened. If I could change whatever happened between James Giles and his father, my life might be totally different."

Victoria whipped the car into the library parking lot and turned off the ignition.

He felt her eyes boring into his, an almost-palpable sensation. His skin prickled with the electric warmth of her body. "My watch," he whispered, his gaze slipping from her eyes to her lips to her breasts. "Can I have it now?"

Victoria smiled and said, "That's not what you're thinking about," and drew his wrist down toward her lap. His mouth dry, Mark slid his fingers beneath the brushed gold case. She folded her hand around his and said,

"Your life *will* be different, Mark. I promise you that."

CHAPTER 20.

That evening, Mark parked his car at the bottom of the steep hill, not trusting his brakes to hold on the incline. Hiking up to the Victorian house, he caught his breath at the view of the city lights. The cast-iron statue of Vulcan rose atop nearby Red Mountain, its arm outstretched in pagan benediction.

The house needed a coat of paint and new shutters, but the carving on the porch railing and the gingerbread on the eaves looked original. Warm yellow light streamed out through the open screen door. Mark knocked, and a male voice invited him in. As he stood in the entryway, he heard Janet's laugh somewhere within.

A man appeared in the doorway, smiling. "Mark? I'm Daniel O'Brien."

Mark shook his extended hand, unused to the sensation of looking up at anyone. Daniel's grip was firm and strong. Okay, so the guy works out, he thought. Big deal.

"Come on in, and we'll get started," Daniel said, leading him into a high-ceilinged room dominated by a large black lacquer coffee table. Overstuffed black cushions stenciled with Chinese characters were arranged around the table. Mark's eyes were drawn his wife, sitting on the red couch on the opposite side of the table.

Her hair, shining in the lamplight, fell loosely around her shoulders, and she wore the blue blouse he gave her for her last birthday. They had argued at length over the color of that blouse. He insisted it was just blue, while she claimed it was "cobalt, edging toward royal."

"Hi, Janet," was all he could think of to say. "Good to--uh--see you."

95

She smiled, but that vertical crease appeared between her brows. "Thanks for coming, Mark. I was afraid you wouldn't."

Daniel waved Mark to one of the cushions. He sank down cross-legged while he watched the other man take a small wooden box from a bookcase.

"Where are the candles?" Mark asked.

"Do you prefer candles?" Daniel set the box on the lacquered table and lifted the lid, extracting a rectangular bundle wrapped in green silk.

"Uh, no, this is fine, but I thought--"

"He's not some fortuneteller out on the highway, Mark," Janet interrupted. "He doesn't need fake atmosphere."

"This is the Aquarian deck," the blonde man explained, folding the square of green silk and setting it back in the box. The cards were slightly larger than a typical deck of playing cards, with brilliant blue backs and elegantly painted fronts.

Mark wanted to ask Janet if they were cobalt or royal blue.

Daniel placed the deck in front of Mark and sat cross-legged on his left. Mark shifted. One leg was going to sleep. "How can these help me with whatever you think is wrong? Are you going to predict my future or something?"

He watched Daniel and Janet exchange glances, but Daniel's voice held no condescension. "I believe the cards serve as a conduit for subconscious thoughts as well as psychic energies. The patterns on the cards depict many aspects of the human condition."

Mark nodded and the man continued. "They free your mind to express what lies unrevealed, sometimes even psychic forces at work. Please understand, though--"

He leaned forward. "Your future is what *you* make of it. The cards can suggest paths and possible outcomes, but it's up to you to make the choices."

Mark grinned. "'He's got to follow his own path. No one can choose it for him.'"

"Mark!" Janet snapped. "This is serious. Stop with the movie quotes."

She's really edgy tonight, he thought, scowling at her.

Daniel checked her anger with a raised hand. "*Star Wars?*" He returned Mark's grin. "You have the right idea, actually."

"Kind of like therapy without the couch." Mark shifted again, wondering how Daniel managed one position for so long.

"Kind of. Shall we try it?"

Mark shrugged. "Okay. What do I do?"

"First, I'll choose a card to represent you. It's called the Significator." Daniel glanced at Mark and riffled through the deck. He selected a card and placed it face up in the center of the table. It depicted a man facing left, wearing a plumed helmet and carrying a budding stalk resting on his shoulder. The caption read "Knight of Rods."

"Now shuffle the deck while clearing your mind of everything but your question. You don't have to tell me what your question is."

Mark shuffled the oversized deck and wondered what to ask. For a split second he was tempted to ask what Victoria meant by her cryptic remark this afternoon, right before he climbed out of her car. He refused to even consider asking about a curse on his family, and settled for what would happen to him during the upcoming summer semester. He cut the deck into thirds as Daniel instructed and watched the man pick up the three stacks in the opposite order to Mark's cut. Daniel dealt the cards, placing one atop the Significator, one crosswise across it, then one below, to the left, above, and to the right, forming a cross. Four additional cards were laid in a vertical line to the right of the cross, starting in front of Mark and continuing away from him. Daniel stared at the layout, and Mark glanced at him as he sucked in a breath.

"Something wrong?"

"No, maybe not," the blond man said, clearly shaken. "I--I've just never seen this many Major Arcana cards in one layout before. Seven out of ten cards."

"And what does that mean?" Mark was almost afraid to ask. He noticed Janet slide down from the couch onto the floor to his right, her eyes transfixed on the cards.

Daniel clawed his hair out of his eyes, not looking at Mark. "These events are out of your hands, for the most part. Forces are acting upon you that you cannot control."

"But I thought you said--"

"I know, I know." He sighed and glanced sideways at Mark. "Let's look at the cards in detail before we jump to too many conclusions, though. I'll explain their meanings individually, and then weave them together to help you understand the message they bring."

Daniel pointed to the first card, covering the Significator. "This card, the Moon, represents the general atmosphere surrounding your question, the environment."

Mark peered at the depiction of a white crescent moon, its thoughtful face gazing toward the brilliant blue surrounding it.

"You are experiencing perils that you are unaware of. This is a card," he explained, "of deception and change. What is interesting is that this card, especially in this position, suggests the realization of psychic abilities in you."

"Psychic? Me?" Mark drew his knees up to his chest. "You mean like the weird visions I've been having?"

Daniel rested his chin on his fingertips, elbows on the table. "That makes sense." He tapped the card crossing the Moon card. "This represents the forces opposing you."

"The Devil?" Mark yelped, picking up the card and staring at it intently. A strange animal-like skull with bat wings dominated the picture, an inverted red pentacle on its forehead between small pointed horns. Below it, to the left and right, stood a female and a male figure, facing away from each other and each sporting a curved tail. Red flames or peaks reached up from the bottom of the card. "This cannot be good." He replaced the card on the table.

"Its primary meaning is temptation, an emphasis on the material aspects of life. There is also black magic at work in opposition to you, which you must resist at all costs. But you are not alone in your journey. This next card, the High Priestess, represents your experience, something that forms a reliable foundation." The card depicted a woman gazing at a flower she held in her hand. She wore a robe patterned with oak leaves and a priestly headdress. A scroll stood beside her. "She signifies an understanding and supportive woman, as well as hidden influences and secrets you may not yet understand."

Mark glanced at Janet. A slight smile crept across her lips as she studied the card. Her gaze flitted up to his; she colored and looked away when she realized he was watching her. She thinks the card refers to her, Mark thought. I'm not so sure it does.

Daniel indicated the upside-down fourth card, which showed a man of kingly expression seated on a throne decorated with rams' heads, holding a scepter terminating in an ankh. "The Emperor, reversed. This is in the position of an influence or experience that is passing away, a man of limited self-control, a man who has been injured or killed--"

"My father," Mark interrupted, his mouth going dry. "My father died-- maybe killed himself--recently. I'd say that indicates limited self-control."

The man beside him bowed his head. "This card can indicate one's father," he said. "I'm sorry about your loss."

Mark nodded curtly and pointed to the companion card, the Empress, also reversed. "Does this represent my mother?"

"No. The position is that of the present, things occurring now or shortly to occur." The card showed a woman with a headdress of stars, holding a scepter and a shield inscribed with the symbol of Venus. "The Empress reversed indicates--"

Daniel cleared his throat and stretched one leg out before him. "It indicates poverty, destruction, psychological problems leading to instability ... and infidelity."

"Well, this reading is certainly making me feel better," Mark snarled, avoiding even a glance at his wife. Victoria's face popped into his head at Daniel's last word. "I see three other reversed cards further on. I'm sure that means good things," he said.

"Reversed cards are not always bad," Daniel said. "If you wish to discontinue the reading, though--"

Mark shook his head. "Oh, no. I want to know the worst." He glanced at Janet. "Are you enjoying this? It was your idea."

She said nothing. Her lips and face pale, her fingers interlaced in her lap.

"The two of Cups, reversed, is in the position of the future," Daniel said. A man and woman faced each other, looking into each others' eyes, each raising a goblet. Daniel closed his eyes momentarily as if collecting his thoughts, then said, without opening them, "We see here a misunderstanding with someone you value, a loss of balance in a relationship. This can denote a passion that is too violent."

He opened his eyes and gestured toward the cards to the right of the cross. "We move on to the card representing you and the fears you have about your question. The Sun, reversed, signifies a troubled marriage, cloudy future plans, failure."

Mark kept his eyes on the bright orange rays surrounding the sun's face. He felt as if he were descending in a very fast elevator. Daniel's reading was hitting much too close to home for his comfort. Janet's presence did not help either.

"The influence of family or friends on the matter is the next position," Daniel went on, gripping the edge of the table. Mark leaned forward to study the card, again reversed. A figure, back to the viewer, head bowed, stood near the edge of what appeared to be a swamp. Birds flew overhead, and below were three spilled goblets the figure seemed to contemplate. Behind him stood two additional cups, just above the lettering: "Five of Cups."

Daniel smiled, easing his leg back into a lotus posture. "This card shows what I meant when I said reversed cards are not all bad news. It signifies the return of hope, the forming of new alliances, and courage summoned to overcome difficulties."

Mark heaved an exaggerated sigh and said, "Well, at least one card is positive."

"This next one is, too. The ten of Pentacles. The position of the card is your hopes and ideals. The primary meaning, as signified by the man, woman and child beneath the arch, is the settling of family matters in a satisfactory way. It often denotes an inheritance, or other gains."

Maybe things will work out after all, Mark thought, massaging his cramping calf muscle. Maybe the curse isn't real. I doubt it, though, with all these other negative cards. With an effort he focused his attention on the final card, a mighty tower stretching toward the sky. Waves swirled at its base, flames leaped from upper windows and its crown, and lightning stretched down on either side.

"This card represents the final outcome." Daniel cleared his throat.

Mark glanced at his sharp-featured profile. His face seemed drawn and drained, as Janet's was. "The Tower represents the overthrow of selfish ambition, of existing ways of life. Change and conflict. But it isn't a totally negative card. Change and conflict can bring enlightenment. If reversed, it would also indicate freedom of body and mind at great cost, but I think there is some element of that here in its upright form."

Daniel rose to his knees and looked at Janet. "I'm sorry to ask this, but would you leave us now, dear? I'd prefer to do the final summation privately."

Janet shrugged, grabbing the couch for support as she stood. "I'll be in the kitchen."

Mark eased up onto the red and black loveseat behind him. "This sounds intense."

Daniel nodded. "It is. Let me collect my thoughts, and then I'll sum up for you." He stood lithely, obviously used to sitting on the floor in pretzel-like positions, and began pacing.

Mark leaned back, draping himself over the back of the loveseat, staring at the ceiling twenty feet above him. This was definitely not what he anticipated. His thoughts were interrupted by Daniel's reappearance on the cushions at his feet. Mark slid down beside him.

"I hope you don't mind my dismissal of Janet," he began. "There are some things in this reading you might prefer she didn't hear. She may already have heard more than you'd like."

Daniel cleared his throat and pointed to the cards. "You are entering a period of great change and upheaval in your life. It sounds melodramatic, but I read great danger ahead for you as well. Hard as this may be for you to believe, someone is using powers of black magic against you. The death of your father is somehow involved. Trouble in your marriage is abundantly indicated, as well as temptation and infidelity." Daniel looked at Mark eyes sternly. "Do not have an affair with this woman. It will contribute to the peril that surrounds this period of time."

Mark flinched away from his intense gaze. Heat tingled along the rims of his ears. "Sure, sure. No affairs. Right."

"Don't take this flippantly," Daniel replied. "There are many indications here of a violent passion, as well as a serious misunderstanding, a rift between yourself and your wife. The future is cloudy and uncertain, but the outcome will be conflict and change, although whether positive or not I cannot tell. Your salvation lies in your family and friends, who will make great sacrifices for you during this time. The woman represented by the High Priestess card I believe to be Janet. Her understanding and support will be crucial in these matters."

Mark rested his chin on his fist, elbow on the table, as he stared at the cards. The heat suffused his face. "Where does the black magic fit in? Could it be--"

He cleared his throat, nervous about actually saying the words. "Could it be a curse?"

To Mark's relief, Daniel didn't laugh. "Possibly. These forces are directed toward you, and apparently your father as well, a continuing threat. Somehow there is also some ... unhealthy family relationship. I can't quite understand what it is. The temptation and infidelity are in your path," he pointed to the two of Cups reversed, "but also your father's, along with psychological instability, as indicated by the Empress reversed so close to the Emperor reversed."

Mark looked at Daniel out of the corner of his eye. "Are you saying that my father was unfaithful to my mother?"

Daniel glanced away. "That is one interpretation, yes."

Mark was silent, but his mind raced. That would explain his mother's suspicions and Antonia's son's report of his father being seen with someone the day he died. "What was that you said about an unhealthy family relationship?"

"I can't point specifically to any card, but it's an impression. Do you have a sister?"

Mark nodded. "Yes."

"I think it involves her. Are you close?"

"Yeah, but--not that way. What are you getting at?"

"Please, don't get angry. As I said, it's just an impression, something to watch out for."

Mark's mind buzzed with incoherent thoughts, and he struggled for words. "You've given me a lot to sort out," he said at last, proffering his hand. "Thanks, Daniel."

The man shook it. "Now I'm afraid I sound like a fortuneteller, but you ignore these warnings at your peril. Very real peril, I must add. Be strong, and lean on family and friends for help." Daniel folded his arms. "I've never done a reading this ... powerful, this definitive before. Be careful, Mark. Although you have no control over these forces, you do control how you react to them. Your decisions and actions control the outcome, control whether the change and conflict will end beneficially--or in disaster."

Mark reached back toward the loveseat and pushed himself to his feet. As he did, his watch slipped from his pocket and bounced on the floor. "I need a chain for that," he muttered as Daniel reached for it. He stared as the man clutched the watch. "Dan? What's wrong?"

Daniel's voice was strained. "This watch ... Death surrounds it. Three, maybe four of its owners died violently." He thrust it into Mark's hand. "There's blood on it."

"Well, I guess you could say that," Mark answered, thrusting the watch into his pocket. "My dad had it in his pocket when he died."

"No, I mean literally. Psychically, as well. In the crevices, around the face." Daniel was trembling as he sank onto the couch. "You probably cannot see it, but it is there nonetheless. I see a train ... a suicide ... a drowning ..."

"The train. That would be my father. How could a drowning get blood on the watch?"

The psychic counselor sighed. "A severe injury preceded the drowning. A shipwreck, perhaps? It is powerful, Mark. Do not let it out of your sight. Guard it well."

Mark nodded, anxious to escape this strange man. "Would you tell Janet I said good-bye? I'm not quite ready to face her."

Daniel agreed with a tilt of his head. "But you must face her soon. You two have some issues to deal with."

"Thanks again, Daniel." Mark strode out into the night air.

~*~*~

"Did he leave?" Janet asked, frowning as she heard the screen door slam.

"He wasn't ready to face you yet," Daniel explained. "He clearly has much on his mind."

Sighing, she skirted the lacquer table and sagged onto the couch. Daniel sat beside her and took her hand in his. "He's going to need your strength, Janet," he said. "The reading indicates great danger ahead for him."

"And temptation and infidelity." Janet leaned against him, resting her head on his shoulder. "I'm assuming that means he's going to cheat on me."

She felt Daniel shake his head. "Not necessarily. The temptation is in the cards. How he reacts is up to him."

"Well, he's never been exactly a ladies' man. I've always suspected, though I never asked, that he was a virgin when I met him." She sat up and stretched, hoping to ease the kinks in her neck muscles. "He's always seemed so helpless to me. He's accused me in the past of trying to run his life, but if he would ever take action, I wouldn't have to."

"You don't have to defend yourself to me. But could it be he just doesn't take action as quickly or in the same direction as you would like?"

She straightened. "So you're saying I *am* trying to run his life?"

He patted her knee. "No, I'm just saying be patient with him. Let him work things out for himself. Give him space to do it." He folded his arms, chin on his chest. "But I'm not sure he took my warning seriously enough. He really could be in danger. From forces he doesn't understand, or even necessarily believe in." Daniel looked into her eyes.

"You have to help him through this, Janet."

CHAPTER 21.

Sunday, May 9.

Mark spent most of Sunday in his office, poring over the grant application. Barbara wanted the first draft tomorrow, but he found concentrating difficult. His thoughts kept bouncing back to last night's tarot reading. In the darkness he was convinced of the truth of Daniel's reading, but in the light of day he wasn't so sure. Several times he caught himself staring off into space, visualizing the images on the cards and wondering what Daniel meant by "black magic." By eight o'clock he was nodding off more than working and decided to pack it in, praying he would not fall asleep on the way back to Dave's.

Dave's red Escort was the only car in the driveway as he parked on the street. He fumbled for his key to the front door, yawning as he shoved it open. "Hey, Dave, I'm--"

He stopped. Dave and Tina were locked in each others' arms on the couch. "Er, I'm home. Oops, sorry."

Dave, his shirt lying in the middle of the floor, sat up, scowling. "Great timing. Tonight you come home early. Thanks."

Tina pulled her blouse closed, her cheeks red, but said nothing.

"I'll just go in the den," Mark muttered. "I'll turn the TV up real loud." He hurried into the next room, scrounged without luck for the TV remote, and punched it on manually. Some reality show was on, but he only saw five minutes of it before he fell asleep in the recliner.

~*~*~

Natalie closed her book with a sigh, and glanced over at her snoring roommate. That girl could sleep through the wreck of the Titanic. The numbers on the bedside clock read 11:55. The words of Rachel Giles' book echoed through her head, distracting her attention from her history textbook. She leaned over the side of the bed, dragged a notebook from beneath a pile of books, and slipped a single sheet of paper from between its leaves.

The image of the Giles siblings stared out at her, Rebecca's dark eyes full of challenge.

What was it really like to be an intelligent woman in the 1800s? she wondered. You must've been about my age when this photo was taken. Seems to me from what your sister wrote that you were misunderstood. I'll bet you really weren't a witch at all. People were just jealous.

The buzzing sound crept into her head again, as it had periodically since last week's blackout on the quad, this time forming into words. '*Witch' is merely a label, branding someone whose philosophy people do not understand. When the powerless seek to obtain power, the powerful feel threatened and lash out. The gaining of power is important. The wresting of control is imperative. Do you understand me, sister?*

Natalie shook her head. "I'm not sure ..."

You will. Trust me, my sister. Soon. Very soon.

~*~*~

Monday, May 10.

Mark blinked his eyes open and stretched. He was really getting old if he was this sore after sitting for a few minutes. Then he jerked back the curtain of the window next to him. Sunlight flooded the room. Uh, oh. He hauled out his pocket watch. That's a.m.

By the time he showered, changed clothes and shaved--grumbling the entire time about how Dave should've awakened him--it was a quarter to nine. Mark jumped into his car and turned the key in the ignition. The engine sprang to life, but just as he moved his hand to put the car in gear, it died. He tried again, with even less result. What the--oh, shit. The gas gauge read Empty. He meant to fill up yesterday. Damn it to hell. He tried to think of anyone he could call for help, but they were all at work or in class already.

The carillon on top of the building chimed ten o'clock as he walked through the front door of the library. The three-block walk to get gas for the car did nothing to improve his mood or his appearance, and the ten minutes driving in circles to find a parking space on the crowded campus did little to improve his dark mood. The hair around his face and neck was plastered with sweat; the rest stuck out in random formations from running his hands through it. Sweat stains ringed the underarms of his blue shirt, and his hands reeked of gasoline. The smell transferred to his neck as he attempted to massage away the pain from sleeping in the recliner. All he wanted to do was escape into the stairwell and vanish into his office, but Tina intervened.

"Aren't you a sight for sore eyes?" she called across the foyer as he stepped through the security gate. "What did you do, walk to work?"

Mark glared and turned toward the stairwell. "Hey, come over here," she persisted. "We have a major network problem. We've been trying to call you for nearly two hours."

"I ran out of gas."

"Oh. I'm sorry," she said, not sounding at all sorry.

I understand why people bring rifles to work, Mark muttered to himself. Although why they don't bring weapons of mass destruction is harder to comprehend.

"The system is down. It's giving all kinds of weird error messages. Barbara's going nuts. She had Christy calling all over the place trying to find you."

"Oh, great."

Tina paused dramatically. "She called Janet."

"Oh, great." Mark closed his eyes and sucked in a deep breath.

"Neither Barbara nor Christy knew you and Janet have split up. Janet told them."

Mark slumped over the counter, resting his forehead on the countertop, groaning, "So now it's all over the library."

"What do you think?"

He slipped behind the main desk. Various keyboard commands failed to correct the problem, and he guessed something was wrong with the server.

It was close to one o'clock before Mark managed to convince the network server it was not permitted a vacation and was supposed to be running the library's online catalog. Networking, one of the truly great marvels of the twenty-first century, he snorted. His mood had improved some, thanks to a washed face and hands, combed hair, and two Cokes, but the sad, pitying glances and prying questions of his coworkers during lunch sent his anger boiling again.

Mark returned to his office and shut the door, savoring the quiet for all of twenty minutes, until Dave stuck his head in. "I need to talk to you," the man said, squeezing his bulk through the opening. He closed the door behind him and sat down.

"I appreciate the wake-up call this morning," Mark grumbled.

"Waking yourself up is your problem," Dave shot back.

Mark jumped at the angry tone in his usually easygoing friend's voice.

"This arrangement isn't working out. I never knew you kept such weird hours."

"But I don't usually--"

Dave held up his hand. "I'm sorry about whatever happened between you and Janet, but I cannot condone your having an affair with someone while living at my house."

"An affair?" Mark repeated, bewildered. "What?"

"Tina told me about you and that woman. The least you can do is plan your rendezvous out of sight instead of in the library. It's immoral, and you know it."

Mark gripped the arms of the chair. He was proud of how calm and even he kept his voice. "I am not having an affair, Dave. I told Tina, it was an accident. I dropped some stuff and fell as I was picking it up."

Dave stared at him, doubt flickering in his eyes. "Well, it still doesn't look right."

"Is this because I walked in on you and Tina last night?"

"We can't ever get a moment's privacy," his friend replied, adjusting his glasses. "She has a roommate, too. Your popping in at all hours makes me feel like I'm still in high school, sneaking around behind my parents' backs."

Mark leaned back in his chair. "When do you want me out?"

"Tonight."

Mark gave a sharp nod. "Fine. I'll pick up my stuff after work."

Dave grunted as he stood up, but said nothing more. Mark watched him until the door shut behind him, then picked up a book and threw it across the room. It bounced off the far wall and slapped with a metallic echo on top of a stack of CPUs. Great. Now I've either got to shell out money for a hotel room or go back to Janet. Maybe that's what I should do.

The ringing phone cut through his reverie.

"Mark, this is Barbara. I have some free time now if you'd like to bring me the first draft of the grant application."

"I'll be right there." He slammed the phone down and fumbled on his desk for the report.

He returned after a brief dressing-down from his boss. She accused him of turning in shoddy work and reminded him of his deadlines. When Mark said the library wasn't his entire life, Barbara replied in a frosty tone, "It won't be any of your life if this attitude continues."

The phone was ringing as he slammed the door shut behind him. "Mark

Richards," he snapped into the receiver, throwing the grant folder on the floor.

"Ooh, somebody doesn't sound too happy today."

He slid into his chair. "Sorry, I've had a rough day."

"Did you remember tonight?" Victoria's cool, calm voice was like lotion on sunburn.

"Tonight?"

Her chuckle caressed his ear through the phone line. "I invited you to dinner tonight. You didn't say no."

"I didn't say yes, either. Did I?" he asked.

"It'll do you good. I'm cooking something simple. I'll see you at, what, six-thirty?"

"I'll be there at six-thirty." He hung up the phone, a smile creeping across his lips. At least somebody wants my company.

~*~*~

He was back at Dave's by four-thirty, anxious to be out before his friend returned home. Packing his few belongings took little time, and he took a quick shower and changed into a dark green polo shirt and jeans. His wet hair clung to his neck and collar. Dave pulled into the driveway as Mark stepped out of the house.

"I'm sorry about this, man," Dave began, even before he had climbed out of his Ford.

Mark shrugged. "It's probably for the best. Nobody can stand to be around me these days. People don't like to have a guy around who'll mess up their day with his problems."

Dave slammed the car door. "Quit feeling so sorry for yourself. Janet didn't do anything to you. You just 'needed your space.' I think you've brought on your problems yourself."

"Oh, really?" Mark dropped the suitcase and clenched his fists. "My father killed himself a couple of weeks ago. Did I bring that on myself? He might've been murdered. Is that my fault?" He knew his voice was getting louder, but the tirade felt good. "I'm having blackout spells and seeing visions that could mean I'm a schizophrenic. Did I bring that on myself?"

Dave stepped closer, pushing his glasses up on his nose. "Mark, I--"

"You accuse me of having an affair while my wife's hanging out with some psychic who's nearly conned me into thinking my family's cursed, and in her spare time she's thinking up new ways to control my life. And you have the nerve to talk to me about morality when last night you were fucking Tina on the couch--"

The world spun, and Dave grew very tall. Mark rubbed his aching jaw, and realized he was sprawled on the grass, looking up at the man who had just slugged him in the face. Hot liquid dripped from his nose. Dave strode toward the front door as Mark dabbed at the blood with the back of his hand and climbed to his feet, his head pounding.

"Thanks for the hospitality!" Mark called. Dave glared back and slammed the door.

CHAPTER 22.

"Mark, what happened to you?" were the first words out of Victoria's mouth when she answered his ring. He was early, but his head ached too much to drive around any longer.

"My best friend, the guy I was staying with, just punched me in the face." He stepped inside, tasting the faintly musty, cinnamon-scented air as he breathed through his mouth. "I see you got your door fixed."

She led him to a big sofa draped with a quilt. "Sit down and I'll get you some ice."

The couch dragged his body down like an anchor in deep water. He savored the coolness of the deep cushions against his hot clothing, blinked at the wing-backed chair beside a large fireplace. Blue and terracotta pillows dotted the floor in front of the fireplace. Brass candle stands on the raised hearth gleamed warmly in the sunshine filtering through the picture window.

The rustle of ice on ice snapped Mark's attention from the furniture to Victoria's bare legs and feet beneath a billowing ankle-length gauze skirt. She leaned over him, affording a tantalizing view of black fabric molded to pale, full breasts. A gold charm bracelet tinkled as she applied the plastic bag of ice to his chin. He sucked in a breath through his teeth as the ice burned, then numbed his cheek.

"I'm making a great impression on you," he joked. "First I pass out when your boyfriend threatens you, now I come in after being on the wrong end of a fist. I should at least have bruised knuckles to show off my manliness."

She lifted the ice bag and examined his face. "Well, you'll have a bruise. Just be glad he didn't hit you that hard. You'd be in the emergency room getting your jaw wired together." She handed him the bag. "Keep that on your face while I see to dinner. It should be ready in a few minutes. Now lay down."

He nodded and leaned over to unlace his boots. His face throbbed. He kicked the boots to the floor and swung his feet onto the couch. As he replayed the day's events, eyes closed, his anger mounted. He was tired. Tired of his job, tired of being told what to do, tired of nosy coworkers prying into his life. Tired of--

"What is it?" he snapped. He relaxed at the sight of Victoria's startled expression. "Oh, sorry. I was just--never mind."

"You're really wound up tight as a bug in a cocoon, aren't you? I just came in to ask if you mind if we eat in here. On the floor. A picnic."

He handed her the ice bag. "Sure. Sounds fun. Need help?"

"No, you're my guest. I'll be right back."

She returned with a tray laden with bowls of salad and pasta, a loaf of crusty bread, a bottle of wine, and two glasses. He took it from her and set it on the foot-high hearth. Victoria gracefully folded herself onto one of the pillows and passed him the bottle, a strangely colored wine he first thought was pale pink, but then decided was golden. He wrestled with the corkscrew, grateful he opened it without spilling any, while she lit the candles on the hearth with a fireplace lighter.

"What is this?" he asked, pouring the golden --or was it icy clear?--wine into the elegant crystal goblets she provided.

The candlelight accented the gold flecks in Victoria's green eyes. "Secret family recipe. I managed to snitch some from my aunt's stock." She raised the glass in a toast. "To us."

"Uh--how about 'To the abolition of Mondays'? I'm afraid there isn't any 'us.'" Mark studied the liquid in his glass.

"You can't eat standing up, Mark," she said. "Do I make you nervous?"

"Of course not." Mark awkwardly sat on the floor and leaned against a pillow. What you make me is horny, he amended, and drank a healthy swig of the wine. "This is good. Very refreshing."

"Was your day awful besides getting punched?" She handed him a bowl of salad.

"Depends on what you call awful," he replied, setting down the glass. "Getting punched was the climax. It started with oversleeping and running out of gas."

"Then I'm surprised you'd come over here." She nibbled at the salad.

"Wouldn't you rather be far away from people?"

Mark poked at the leaves, noticing Romaine, radicchio, and even some dandelion leaves. His usual idea of a salad was iceberg lettuce and maybe a carrot or two. "People, yes. You, no." Their eyes met and he laughed. "I didn't mean it that way. I mean I'm tired of all the people I know. They all want something from me, or want to change me, or want to improve me." He chewed, wiped vinaigrette from his chin. "So what do you want from me?"

He held his breath as she stared into his eyes, her face solemn. A truck rattled past outside. A siren keened somewhere in the distance. The watch in his pocket pressed into his thigh as the silence seemed to coalesce between them.

"The same thing you want from me," she whispered at last.

Mark choked as salad dressing burned his throat. He gulped wine to cover his confusion.

Her Mona Lisa smile crept across her lips as she set her salad bowl on the hearth. "Be careful how you drink that," she warned. "It has more kick to it than you might think."

He nodded and reached for a bowl of steaming fettuccini in a thick alfredo sauce, sprinkled with sun-dried tomatoes, peppers, onions, and some kind of thinly-sliced sausage. "You're a great cook. I feel like it's been forever since I had real food."

She rolled a noodle around her fork. "How long have you been separated?"

"About a week and a half. But she's not terribly creative in the cooking department. Neither am I, for that matter."

She murmured sympathetically and refilled his wine glass.

At last he set aside the bowl with a satisfied sigh. "I feel a lot less like murdering passers-by with a chainsaw." He lolled against the pillow, sipping at the wine and studying the strange iridescent color of the liquid. "Wonder what kind of grapes could produce a wine that looks like this. Never seen wine this color before." He stretched out full-length on his stomach, chin resting on his hands atop a pillow. Closing his eyes, he twitched, then relaxed as her hands kneaded his knotted shoulder muscles. "Now that's nice," he murmured.

She tugged at his shirt. "Why don't you take this off and I'll give you a proper massage? I think you need it."

What the hell? he thought. When he sat up, tingling warmth spread through his whole body. He finished his wine with a gulp and peeled off his shirt. Her fingers were strong, and he groaned as she found the myriad knots in his back and shoulder muscles. Her touch aroused him, sent his mind spinning toward dangerous possibilities. A tiny part of his brain still functioned, prompting him to say, "Did you enjoy seeing the campus the other night?"

She paused, her hands resting on the small of his back. She sounded confused. "What little I could see of it in the dark was beautiful."

He twisted around to lean on one elbow. "I got quite a scare when I finally left work that night. I found my sister lying unconscious on the ground."

Victoria sat back on her heels. "How awful! Is she okay?"

"Far as I can tell. She said she heard voices in her head and passed out."

"That's very odd," Victoria commented. "More wine?"

He held out his glass. "This stuff is good."

"I'm telling you, though, be careful with it. You've had quite a few glasses now."

He laughed, drained half the glass, and set it on the floor behind him. "It hasn't affected me in the least. Thanks for the massage. I feel so much better now. I was getting to the tower-climbing-with-a-rifle stage."

She slid down and rested her elbow on a pillow, mimicking his position. Six inches of polished hardwood floor and a cushion of warm air separated their bodies. Her hair flowed over her arm to pool on the pillow, flaxen in the flickering candlelight. The flowery scent of her perfume was aromatherapy to his bruised mind. Slowly, he stretched out his hand, brushed her cheek, slid it to the back of her neck, and drew her lips to his. The kiss began softly and tentatively, but soon his mouth devoured hers as he released the pent-up desires and frustrations of the past few weeks. She arched her body into his, nails pressing into his skin, his low moan echoing hers. His tongue tasted the wine that flamed through his veins. His fingers tangled in the length of her hair, drawing her to him as she ripped at his belt and zipper.

They rolled off the pillow. He barely heard the sudden muffled pop. His panting breath rose into a howl as jagged glass ripped into his bare back. Her fingers were slick and wet as she clutched at him, urging him into her. Fire kindled in his back as a cold wetness seeped through the rents in his skin. His hoarse grunts faded into a roaring in his head as his body heaved with the climax, mingled with a shriek from Victoria, consumed by a brilliant light—

--searing his vision as the sun, clawing down through the dense canopy of trees into the clearing flashed on the upraised knife. He screamed as the steel parted the shabby cloth and sweat-slicked skin on his left shoulder. Blood welled up through the rent. A shiver convulsed his spine as the hot fluid oozed down the hairs on his arm and knitted them to his sleeve. One holed and scraped boot shot out from under him, sliding on leaves and underbrush like a hound on ice, as the stretching fingers of his other hand flailed for a tree trunk just out of reach. The toe snagged a lurking root, ripping the rotted stitching of the boot. The sole parted from the worn leather upper with a dull ripping sound; the root scraped across his exposed toes and the ball of his foot. He skidded to one knee. Pain skewered his ankle and a lurking rock peeled layers of skin and rotten fabric away from his knee. The man flung himself behind a fallen tree trunk as the blade flashed down again, ripping away buttons and scoring a trail of red across his chest before slashing the hem of his shirt. Dark drops of blood slung off his fingers, pattering on the leaves like rain. He found himself staring up into—

--Victoria's eyes, huge pupils surrounded by dark green and white. Her hair was tangled around her bare shoulders as she moved out of his line of vision. "God, Mark, I thought you were dead," she gasped. He pushed the damp washcloth off his face with a nerveless hand, and she draped it across his forehead.

He shoved himself up off the floor. "Lie down," Victoria insisted. "You'll start bleeding again--see, I told you," she said as he yelped in pain.

"What ... happened?" Mark gasped, rolling onto his side. He pushed back the soft quilt and gingerly felt the bandage on his back. Blood and glass were still spattered and scattered across the floor. A bloody handprint, too small to be his, marked the hardwood floor beside him. The spilled wine was gone, absorbed into his skin and pants. He sipped the water she offered.

His stomach went cold as the memory engulfed him. "Oh, God," he moaned under his breath. "Not again." His hands trembled as he handed the glass back to her.

She held it tightly in front of her like a wedding bouquet. "Well, the sex was great, but I've never had anyone pass out on me before." Victoria's hands trembled too. "You ... we rolled over the wine glass. I patched you up with some of those butterfly bandages, so I don't think you'll need stitches, and the wine sterilized it. But something happened--I felt it, too. What was it, Mark? What were you seeing?"

"Help me up," he breathed. She hauled him up onto the couch, brushed his hair out of his eyes, and tucked the quilt around his trembling shoulders where he sat. He stared at a framed poster on the wall for a full two minutes until he could control his chattering teeth. "I had another vision, like the other day when your boyfriend chased us."

Mark winced as he eased his back against the couch cushions. "I was being attacked by someone ... someone I knew, although I couldn't tell you who. A definite presence--a female presence was there too. I don't know if

114

it was the attacker, or someone watching. Whoever it was had a long knife ... no, maybe it was a short sword." He shuddered. "Whatever it was, it slashed my shoulder ..."

He flipped his hair out from under the quilt around his shoulders. "I slipped on leaves, in a forest. I think I was about to get cut again." He dropped his head back, eyes closed. "That's the most vivid it's ever been."

"Mark, I felt something too. For an instant, in some corner of my mind, I had an overwhelming sensation of fear and pursuit and being in a dark forest. This has happened to you before the time with me? My God, who did you scare that time?"

"Well, the first time I was just at home talking to my--uh--wife." He forced Janet's worried face from his mind. "I had something like a nightmare, running from someone who wanted me dead. I passed out, like this time and last time. Well, not as spectacularly as this time. When I came to, I was on the floor of the living room. I'd been out for an hour. No wounds, no injuries--unlike this time. Janet said it seemed like I'd passed out in mid-sentence."

Victoria held his clammy hands in hers. "Exactly like this time. Although not exactly in mid-sentence. But these weren't the only times it happened?"

"The next one was at work, when I was walking up the stairs." He dashed the hair out of his eyes and pointed to the healing scar on his forehead. "That's how I got this. I had a little warning that time. I seemed to be a Rebel soldier and ran into a Yankee patrol. They wanted to hang me, just like the last time over here."

Victoria tucked her bare feet beneath her on the couch and snuggled into his armpit. "That is extremely strange," she said. "What do you think it means?"

Mark shifted, wincing again. "Daniel thinks I'm receiving psychic messages."

"Daniel?"

"Oh, sorry. You don't know him. Daniel O'Brien. He's my wife's ex-lover that I mentioned when we had lunch. He did a tarot reading for me Saturday night and basically scared the shit out of me. He predicted that--"

He stopped, Daniel's warnings ringing in his head.

Victoria grasped his arm. "Mark? What is it?"

He buried his head in his hands. "The reading had several cards indicating temptation and infidelity. He flat out warned me not to have an affair with you."

"What else did he say?"

"He said," Mark sighed and looked into her green and gold eyes, "I was in great danger."

A drying streak of blood stood out in relief on Victoria's cheek. "Danger?" she croaked. "From whom?"

He shrugged. "He didn't say. Something about black magic being involved. I think it was psychic talk to scare me." He reached out and wiped the smear from her face. "But he was right, Victoria. I've been unfaithful." Mark heaved himself up with one hand on the back of the couch. "I'd better leave."

Her fingers on his arm were strong and insistent. "No, Mark, not now." Her voice compelled him to resume his seat an instant before his legs threatened to buckle. "If your friend hit you, I doubt he still wants you to stay with him. Where will you go? Back to your wife? Back to being controlled every step of the way?"

The vein in his left temple throbbed as he pressed his fingers against it. "I don't know ..."

She grabbed his chin, jerked it toward her, the nails biting into his bruised jawline. "Something happened tonight, Mark. I've seen a lot of weird shit in my short life, but I've never experienced anything like this. You need to face up to it. Running away won't solve anything."

"Don't pressure me." He seized her wrist, jerked her fingers from his face. "I will deal with it, in my own way. If I want advice, I'll go home to Janet. If I want to run away, I'll run away. Believe me, it's solved a lot of problems in my not-so-short life. However--"

His angry gaze took in the tangled mass of blonde hair, flushed cheeks, the tight white curving skin of her breasts. Gripping her wrist until she gasped, he levered her onto the couch beneath him. "However, running away is not an option right now," he whispered, crushing his lips and body against hers.

CHAPTER 23.

Natalie woke from a sound, dreamless sleep. She peered around the room, eyes adjusting to the darkness. Patterns of light slipped around the edges of the curtains from the street light outside her window. The ceiling fan squeaked, but she heard no other noises.

Weird. She yawned and climbed out of bed. The carpeted floor stretched before her with an elasticity it never exhibited before. What in the world? Her vision swam as the floor curved upward, then bounced back to normal. With a surprised cry, she collapsed onto the bed. Her mind altered, thought patterns changing ...

The warm air was thick with smells of hay and manure. She stood beside a stack of hay bales in a loft, her back to the man with whom she was speaking. But she knew what he looked like, as well as she knew her own reflection in the mirror. She couldn't hear what he was saying to her, or what she said to him. When she turned, his face was clouded, scowling, his arms folded across his chest.

She patted her belly, concealed beneath her voluminous skirts, smiling with joy as she revealed her secret to the man. He shook his head, his face pale. He grabbed her, shook her, rattling her teeth. His wild expression and angry words frightened her. She still couldn't hear his words and he wouldn't stop shaking her. He shouted, she shouted, and they were falling-

Falling from the loft to the barn floor far below. Falling alone. He clung to the edge like a spider, his white face twisted in horror, watching her plummet to the hay-strewn floor ...

Natalie's eyes flew open wide, gasping and staring into the darkness.

~*~*~

"I don't understand why you're so angry, Sylvia." Victoria clutched the receiver. "Isn't seduction the whole idea? Isn't this why you trained me?"

The woman on the other end of the line exhaled sharply. "Don't you understand what has occurred? You mentioned the wine and blood so off-handedly. You obviously don't understand the significance of your actions."

"Then for once in my life why don't you try to explain it to me?" she said, her voice rising in exasperation.

"You cut yourself on the glass. Correct?"

Victoria glanced at the small bandages affixed to the backs of her hands. "So?"

"Your blood mingled with his. Correct?"

Victoria struggled to remain calm. "You don't have to act like I'm a complete dolt--"

"Answer the question."

"I guess it did," Victoria said. "My hands were cut and covered in his blood. I thought at first I was hurt worse than I was."

"Allow me to be the first to extend my congratulations," Sylvia said. "You and

Mr. Richards are joined."

"What?"

"You have completed the first phase of the ritual of joining. Your souls are now married. Unfortunately, it's ten days too early."

"Married?" Victoria clenched her jaw. "If you informed me of your plans instead of keeping me in the dark, I might be able to help. I'm sick of you always controlling me."

Sylvia's tone was the one that always accompanied a slap in the face. "There are larger issues than your adolescent struggles against discipline." Her voice softened. "But something else has happened, hasn't it? The reason you called."

"He had another vision. And I was part of it. This time he was being chased by someone in an old uniform with a very long knife." She clenched her fists, caught up in the memory, and winced as the skin under the bandages pulled. "The attacker slashed at him, actually cut his arm. I was there, watching. What does this mean, Sylvia? I've participated in all kinds of weird out-of-body experiences before, but nothing like this."

"He is reliving James' life," she said.

Victoria sucked in a sharp breath. "James?"

"I really do not have time to discuss ancient history with you. Suffice it to say he was the person on whom the Giles curse was bestowed." Victoria heard the snip of embroidery scissors through the phone line. Even at this time of night Sylvia was stitching. "Is there anything else you wish to tell me?"

Victoria suppressed a yawn. "Someone apparently predicted our affair. A psychic named Daniel O'Brien did a tarot reading for Mark on Saturday."

"You'll recall I phoned and warned you Saturday someone was investigating us."

"That's right, you did," Victoria said, annoyed Sylvia was always right. "He said the cards revealed temptation and infidelity. And O'Brien warned him he was in great danger, and black magic was involved."

"Black magic," Sylvia sneered. "I'll have Mr. Sweeney deal with Mr. O'Brien. I'm very glad you told me, dear."

"I'm glad you're happy." Victoria yawned again. "Now, I'm going to bed. I'm worn out. Mark's asleep already."

"You have done all the hard work," she said, her voice heavy with sarcasm.

"Oh, and what have *you* contributed? I still don't understand all your little machinations."

"You are not required to understand," Sylvia said.

The younger woman sighed. "I'm just getting tired of all this mumbo-jumbo."

"Sometimes I find it difficult to believe you're descended from Rebecca."

"I'm descended from her. I'm not *her*." Victoria leaned back on the couch. "He just seems so, I don't know, helpless. And inoffensive. He's a *librarian*, for God's sake."

"You aren't becoming too attached to him, are you?"

"No. But he's so much like his father." She clamped down on the sudden wave of tears the memory of Tom's death evoked.

"Why don't you invite him over here for dinner? I'd like to meet this helpless, inoffensive Giles who is a librarian." Sylvia's tone held more than a hint of sarcasm.

"All right. I'll invite him."

"Remember, Victoria. No matter how inoffensive he seems, he is a Giles. He is dangerous to our plans--"

"I know. One hundred forty-seven years of planning. I know." She hung up and groaned, thinking, Sorcery is hell, and wandered into her bedroom, where Mark slept peacefully.

CHAPTER 24.

Tuesday, May 11.

"Good morning, dear. How do you like your eggs?"

Mark stared. The light in the kitchen hurt his eyes, but squinting sent daggers of pain through his skull. He propped himself on the doorframe. A protest against the strangeness of the situation formed in his mouth, but all that came out was, "Eggs?"

Victoria laughed, cracking one into a bowl. "No, that's not the right answer. Sit down, I'll fix you some coffee."

He staggered to a chair and lowered himself into it. No one had cooked breakfast for him since he left home for college. He felt like he'd stepped into a 1950s movie, complete with housecoated Stepford wife. Although, as Stepford wives go, he thought, she's certainly attractive. "Sorry. I'm not well-versed in the repartee of the morning after."

"Are you always so restless when you sleep?" She poured coffee from the glass carafe into a shiny gold mug. "Cream? Sugar? Sorry about the tough questions."

"Two sugars." Mark ground his teeth, wondering why he always ended up with women who were perky morning people. He was transfixed watching the spoon circling the liquid, then tore his gaze away and frowned up at her. "I had a bizarre nightmare. It kept repeating itself, over and over ..."

Victoria glanced at him over her shoulder, scrambling the eggs. "A nightmare? What kind of nightmare?"

"I was walking in a field somewhere." He took a sip of scalding coffee. "Scattered out in the field were people I know--Janet and Daniel and Natalie--and people who seemed vaguely familiar, maybe ancestors?" His head ached with the memory. "This huge dark cloud blew up, all black and green. A tornado dropped out of it and roared toward me, devouring the people farthest away, getting closer and closer and growing with every person it scooped up. I woke up before it reached me, but when I went back to sleep, it started over again."

"How weird." She slid the eggs from the skillet onto a plate, added two slices of toast, and set the food in front of him. "You were mumbling in your sleep, but I couldn't tell what you were saying. Do nightmares run in your family?"

"Well, I think my father--"

He stopped. "Why would you ask that?"

"I don't know," she said with a shrug. "I once dated a guy who suffered from nightmares. He was afraid it was genetic. I don't think it's possible, though. Do you?"

Mark tore a slice of toast in half. "It's hard to say what's genetic and what's not." He chewed without tasting the food. The dinner and the lovemaking, with its spectacular climax of horrific vision and ecstatic pain were clear in his mind, but after that, things were hazy. He thought he remembered making love again, maybe, but--

"Did you drug me last night?"

She paused, coffee carafe in hand. "Beg pardon?"

"The wine. I don't remember very much after--"

"Why would I drug you?" Her laugh echoed inside his head. "I warned you last night that wine was strong. Do you think that's how I get my men?" She poured herself a cup of coffee and stood next to him, stroking his hair. "I didn't drug you to get you to come to dinner. Now eat your breakfast. You'll be late for work."

The coffee--or was it her fingers in his hair?--cleared his head. Half-forgotten details of the previous night filtered into his consciousness. He glanced up at the wall clock and wondered if they had time to find out if she had anything on under her robe. The idea of making love before work--something he and Janet had never done--sent an agreeable shiver through his groin.

"My aunt wants us to come to dinner tonight."

"What?" With a mental curse, Mark dragged his mind from his erotic fantasies of taking her there on the kitchen floor and muttered, "Uh--sure. What time?"

"Six o'clock. Precisely. She's strict about punctuality. Numbers are important to her."

"Is she a mathematician?" He speared the last lumps of scrambled egg.

"Sort of. It's a hobby of hers."

He finished his coffee and stood up. "I'll be home by five." 'Home'? Listen to me, he thought. She's got me thinking I'm in *The Brady Bunch*. Mark took the mug from her hand and set it on the table, then gathered her to him. Her satin robe was cool against his arms, her lips warm on his. No, not *Brady Bunch*. More like *Bewitched*.

~*~*~

Natalie dropped her exam paper on the professor's desk and shuffled out, sagging against the wall. What is wrong with me? Her skin crawled at a touch on her shoulder. She looked up and realized she was sitting on the floor. A girl squatted next to her, frowning in concern. "Nat? You okay? You're white as a sheet!"

What is her name? I should know this. Carmen? Carlie?

"Not sure, Carla." Carla, that's it. "I feel really weird."

"Well," Carla said with a frown, "we did stay up studying pretty late last night."

That's how I know her. We studied together. Natalie eased her head from side to side. "No, I don't think that's why. It's not just being tired. I feel empty inside ... sort of ... hollow ..."

"Hollow?" She felt Carla's arm around her shoulders. "Let me help you back to your room. You need to rest."

Natalie leaned against the other girl and swayed to her feet. "Thanks, Carla, but I can make it back--"

"Nat!" she yelped. "What kind of a best friend would I be if I let you go by yourself?"

Best friend? What's wrong with me that I can't recognize my best friend? A wind whistled past her ears, setting up a roaring inside her head. She lurched down the front steps of the building into the mid-morning sunlight. "I thought you said you were okay after that fainting spell the other night. Maybe you have a concussion." Carla pulled her along the sidewalk toward the girls' dorm.

Natalie lurched to a halt. Carla staggered. A wave of something close to relief washed over her as she reached a startling conclusion. "No," she began. "It's not a concussion. Carla--"

"What? What is it?"

"I feel like--I know this sounds weird, but ... I feel like my soul is gone ..."

CHAPTER 25.

After all her years with the woman who'd raised her, Victoria noticed what no one else would. When presented with Mark's hand, Sylvia's cheek muscle twitched ever so slightly, and she hesitated as if steeling herself before grasping his hand and shaking it.

"So you're Demarcus Richards. Victoria speaks of you often." Sylvia sounded short of breath. Victoria thought Mark would attribute it to old age, but she knew it was the old woman's sensitivity to psychic energy. Sylvia eyed Mark after stepping out of his aura. Victoria suspected she did not approve of the length of his hair, nor his casual attire.

Victoria thought he was almost handsome tonight, although he kept flipping his hair out of his collar. His eyes reminded her of Tom Richards', the same dark blue with silvery glints.

"Thank you for inviting me," Mark said. "Ms.--er--"

"Miss Dee." Sylvia motioned him toward the chair while she retired to the couch and picked up her needlepoint.

Victoria perched on the arm of the chair beside him. "She's married only to her work," she giggled, ruffling his hair.

A dark flush spread across his cheeks. "Mrs. Work."

"Victoria," Sylvia snapped. "None of your impertinence in front of our guest."

"Speaking of work, Victoria mentioned you're a mathematician?" Mark ventured, running a finger under the neck of his black collarless shirt.

Victoria wondered if she would merit a slap later for telling him that. "I dabble in the art," Sylvia said with a slight frown. "What do you do for a living, Mr. Richards?"

"I'm the systems librarian at Beason University. In other words," he said with a smile, "I fiddle with computers."

"Have you lived in Birmingham long?"

"All my life." He crossed his legs, ankle on knee.

"And what about your family? Have they always lived here? Or don't young people care about family history?"

Victoria shifted in her chair. "Aunt Sylvia, why the interrogation? Give him a break."

The old woman rummaged in her sewing basket and produced a skein of dark green yarn. "It's called making conversation, young lady. Forgive the questions, Mr. Richards. I'm something of a scientist and become quite analytical when meeting new people." She threaded the tapestry needle with all six strands of yarn. "I believe I asked you a question."

"Well, I am interested. I've only started investigating my family recently, in the past couple of weeks. Fortunately, I found a pamphlet at the library, the day I met Victoria--"

He blushed again, "--that was written at the turn of the century about the Giles family. My dad wrote an account of his parents, and I've filled in a little beyond the pamphlet."

"That's interesting, Mr. Richards," Sylvia replied. "I'm a genealogist myself."

"Please, it's Mark. I don't think even my dad was ever called Mr. Richards."

Sylvia wove the needle through the holes in the canvas. "I prefer the formal modes of address, Mr. Richards. People in this day and age do not seem to realize the power inherent in given names. Victoria, perhaps you should look at this pamphlet. It might have something of your family in it."

"No, it's only on the Giles family," he corrected.

"Mark, you don't know my last name, do you?"

His face reddened again and he plucked at the laces of his boots. I did my job well this time, Victoria thought. He's so smitten he never asked my last name.

"Sorry, Vic, I guess I never did," he said at last.

"Well, sweetheart," she grinned, enjoying the effect she knew her words would have, "we just might be related. My last name is Giles."

~*~*~

Mark eased out of the chair and glared at Victoria. The heat in his cheeks only aggravated his rising anger.

"Very funny. This is rather embarrassing, pulling this in front of your aunt," he said.

Victoria rummaged through her purse, producing a rectangular plastic card. Victoria Rebecca Giles, he read. Oh, my God, she wasn't lying. "Okay, so your driver's license says Giles. Couldn't you have told me before today?"

"And would it have made any difference if you'd known?"

Seeing her perched on the arm of the chair, short blue skirt hiked up, head cocked at a perky angle and eyes sparkling, his anger drained away. He shrugged. "As long as you're not about to tell me you're my long-lost sister--"

"I'm not," she said with a reassuring smile.

"Okay." Mark relaxed a little. "Giles is a fairly common name anyway."

"Forgive the interruption, but I think it's time I started dinner. If you'll excuse me,

Mr. Richards?" Setting aside her needlepoint, Sylvia struggled to her feet. "Victoria, why don't you show him my genealogy database?"

"Need any help with dinner, Miss Dee?" Mark offered.

"No, but thank you for asking. Run along now. I'll call you when it's ready."

Victoria took his hand and pulled him toward the hallway. "You'll want to see her computer setup anyway."

The study was the first door on the left. Victoria shut the door behind them and pinned him against the wall with her body. "Alone at last," she murmured, pressing her lips to his.

"Not here," he protested, sliding his hands down the small of her back. "No?"

"No. Over there." He sat in the typing chair and pulled her into his lap. "So is this her computer system?"

"Do you like it?" Victoria asked.

"I certainly do--oh, you mean the computer?" Mark reached around her and clicked the mouse button. Several icons on the desktop were familiar, but he gestured to a couple that weren't. "That one must be the genealogy program," he said, "but what's that?"

She nibbled at his neck. "Don't mess with that. That's her calculation program."

"Strange hobby," he said. Her lips sent chills down his spine. "What's it for?"

"Who knows?" She pulled away. "I don't do math. Strange graphs and weird equations, like calculus on steroids. I don't understand it, but she

125

apparently does. Just don't mess with it."

He noted fear in her eyes. "Okay, I won't pry anymore. Now, let's see if your family links up with mine at any point." He double-clicked the mouse button on the genealogy icon. The program was laid out intuitively, and he navigated his way through until he found a multiple-generation chart. The response was rapid. "So far, so good," Mark grinned. "I don't recognize any of these names."

"Each screen goes back four generations," she said, pointing with a long red fingernail. His mind wandered as she caressed his cheek. "Gabriel and Gerda Giles were my great-grandparents. Click there to see farther back."

"Ebenezer and Rebecca Giles were your great-great grandparents on the Giles side. I see my family's not the only one with strange male names." He clicked onto the next screen. "John and Amanda Allen are the next generation, and--another Rebecca Giles? Whose father was--"

Samuel Giles, born Sept. 30, 1820. No. It can't be, Mark thought. He read further, eyes widening. Married to Lavinia Jones in 1838. Children: Rebecca, James, Lucinda, Rachel, and Beatrice. "Where--where did she get this information?"

"What's wrong?" She gripped his hands. "Mark?"

"Common ancestors, multiple-great grandparents. We *are* related."

She sat very still. "It doesn't matter. That's a long time ago."

"Did you know all along?"

She shrugged, but didn't look at him. "I knew vaguely. I don't keep up with all this. It's Sylvia's work. I have more important things to do."

"But why didn't you tell me?" The hairs on the back of his neck stood up.

"It honestly never occurred to me. What's the big deal? Everyone's related if you go back far enough." She gave him a wide-eyed innocent look and rested her fingertips on his arm.

He moved away, her touch rippling his skin into goosebumps. "So many weird things have happened to me lately that involve my family history that I'm paranoid." He licked his parched lips and stared into her eyes. "It's just one big coincidence that we met, right?"

He wanted to believe it, more than anything else; he wanted her to be the one thing that was okay, because so much in his life wasn't right--his dad's suicide, his leaving Janet, the fainting spells and visions ...

She smiled. "One big coincidence."

He thrust away his doubts and responded to her insistent lips on his, losing himself in the taste of her mouth, the warmth of her skin--until he realized someone was calling her name. "I think Sylvia's yelling for you," he managed to gasp.

Victoria pushed away from him and rearranged her tousled hair.

The delicious warmth faded after she walked out of the room. Mark wiped his mouth with the back of his hand, then switched his attention with some difficulty to the computer screen. He minimized the genealogy program and looked at the icon for the mysterious mathematics program. Unable to resist the temptation, he double-clicked the mouse button.

The image on the screen was completely foreign, despite his experience with a wide variety of computer programs. Green lines on a black background curved in labeled arcs, spiraling back on themselves, marked at intervals with Greek letters and strange hieroglyphs. He peered at one of the labels, reading the tiny letters that spelled out "Awareness tr051799." He clicked on the menu at the top of the screen and chose "Time Series."

This screen consisted of a mosaic of tiny squares, with a line of numbers forming a grid across the top. Mark glanced at the printer to his right, hesitated for a scant moment, and clicked the print command.

When the printer stopped, he exited the mathematical program and returned to the genealogy one. He had just folded the sheets of numbers and arcs when the door swung open. He stuffed them into his pocket and smiled at Victoria.

"Dinner's ready," she announced.

~*~*~

Janet knew her eyes were still red and puffy. Her face was clean of makeup and still damp along her jawline, but she was proud her voice was steady as she asked him into the house. "Thanks for coming, Daniel. I know it's late."

He waved aside her apologies. "I was up anyway. I've always been something of an insomniac, and it's worse these past couple of days. I'm getting fleeting glimpses of some sort of psychic attack, but nothing really tangible." He joined her on the couch. "How are you?"

"I'm better now," Janet assured him. "I had my little cry. But I can't stop worrying about Mark. Like I told said on the phone, no one knows where he is, not his mother or sister. I called the friend he was staying with, but Mark wasn't there. Dave threw him out yesterday. The arrangement wasn't working. Mark was verbally abusive, according to Dave, and stormed off."

"Did Dave know where he went?"

She shook her head. "No. They avoided each other at work today, so he has no idea where he is."

"Perhaps a hotel?"

Her blood pounded in her ears. "I called them. All of them. He's not registered anywhere. Nobody knows where he is."

"Janet." His commanding tone cut through her rising panic. "Take a deep breath."

She obeyed, filling her lungs with air. "Sorry. Ever since that tarot reading--"

"I'm worried about him, too. I have a nagging feeling that he's in over his head."

"In what?"

Daniel sighed, shook his head. "That, I do not know." He twisted sideways, and she could see his face better. "You have phoned all the hotels and his sister and his mother. What about other friends?"

She squeezed a throw pillow, arms wrapped around it. "He has no other friends I know of. Not close friends, anyway. He's always been sort of a loner. Although he's always been a sucker for anyone who would listen to his problems. If someone lends a sympathetic ear, he's theirs for life." The corners of her mouth sagged. "Well, maybe not for life."

Daniel pried the pillow from her arms and tossed it to the floor. "I am afraid that may be what has happened. Listen to me carefully, my dear. His soul is in jeopardy, of that I am convinced. I read temptation and infidelity in the cards, but I think it goes beyond that. There's a devious purpose at work here. We must find out what is happening to him or, at the risk of sounding melodramatic, your husband is doomed--body and soul."

CHAPTER 26.

Wednesday, May 12.

Every time Mark started work on the grant proposal, his attention strayed to the two printouts. Somehow he knew they were extremely important to his future well-being, but they still made no sense. He counted 48,545 squares on the page. Counting that many squares might be bordering on the obsessive, but he shrugged away the thought. He peered at the sheet of paper until his eyes hurt, and was almost grateful for the interruption when Fran stuck her head into his office.

"Here's the reference desk schedule for the next month," she announced, handing him a sheaf of papers. She peered at the printout. "Is that a crossword puzzle? Or a calendar. If it's a calendar, that'll never work. Those squares are too small."

He blinked at her. "Huh? Calendar?"

"Well, whatever, but I'd never be able to see anything in squares that small. See you later." She bustled away.

He picked up the sheet again. Calendar? How could it be a calendar? Wait a second ...

He clicked the calculator icon on his computer and divided 53,655 by 365. The result was 147. Then he entered the current year and subtracted 147, resulting in 1863. He dragged his notebook out of his briefcase, flipping through the pages. Eighteen sixty-three was the year James and Alice Giles were murdered. But what did it mean? Why would Sylvia keep up with the days since a nineteenth-century murder? It must be a

129

coincidence, he told himself, and yet ... yet he couldn't believe that.

He glanced at the digital clock at the corner of his computer screen. Two-thirty, he muttered to himself. And what have I accomplished on this grant? Zilch. So what if it's due in five days and if I don't finish it my career is ruined?

A tentative knock sounded. Startled out of his reverie, Mark pulled open the door and was even more startled to see Antonia standing outside, clutching a manila envelope. "I'm sorry to disturb you, Mark, but may I come in a minute?"

"Uh--sure, Antonia. What can I do for you?" He cleared a stack of software manuals, electronics catalogs and old mail from the second chair in the room and motioned her to sit.

"Mark, I'm sorry I was so ... tactless when you came back to work after your father's funeral," she stammered, opening and flattening the little metal wings of the clasp on the envelope in her lap. "I've been thinking about it ever since."

He hardly knew what to say. "Well, Antonia, I--"

"So I got this for you." She handed him the envelope. "It's from Billy. He talked with the reporter I mentioned, the one who had information about your father."

"Your son got this for me? I really appreciate this." He slid the single sheet of paper from the envelope.

Antonia stood and shrugged. "I hope it's helpful to you."

Mark detained her with a hand on her arm. "It means a lot to me. I'm sorry I was rough on you. I had no right to be."

She smiled as she left. He sank back into his chair and read the typed page. A brief note at the top detailed the origin of the interview, made on April 27, the day after his father's death, with a man named Joe Booth. The reporter's signature was scrawled beneath the note.

Booth saw the photo of Thomas Richards in the morning paper's article about his death. He contacted the newspaper and told the reporter he'd gone into the café for a cup of coffee the previous day at 3:15 p.m. At the same time, an older man entered with a good-looking blonde in a red-miniskirt. He never saw her face, but he studied the man, envious of someone his age with such a young, attractive companion. They were still there when Booth left thirty minutes later. Mark noted the café was located in the Five Points area, not far from Sylvia's house.

So his dad was with someone else the day he died. But in Five Points? That's a good thirty-five miles or so from Helena. Why would he go from Birmingham to Helena with someone? Mark draped an arm over the back of the chair and stared at the ceiling, wondering why Tom Richards went so far afield. Unless he was reminiscing. Mark recalled how his father talked to anyone who would listen about watching trains when he was growing up in Helena. He felt an overwhelming urge to go there, to revisit the place his father was born--and died.

~*~*~

Mark forced himself to stare at the yellow railroad crossing sign. He rubbed his sweaty palms on his thighs and concentrated on slowing the pounding of his heart. What's the big deal? he chided himself. It's not like his body's still there. He walked to the place where the train stopped after dragging parts of his father's body down the tracks. In the darkness and artificial lighting two and a half weeks ago, the street had been menacing and portentous. Today, in the afternoon sun, it was all terribly, achingly ordinary.

He swallowed hard against the queasiness in the pit of his stomach and forced his thoughts into an analytical mode. Dad was in a cafe thirty-five miles away until at least 3:45, but he's run over by a train around 6:00. What was he doing all that time?

Mark tried to imagine his father sitting in a café chatting with a blonde and failed. He always thought that his father was about as smooth with women as he was, and occasionally wondered how Dad managed to meet his mother. I know he was human, with the same urges I have, but a blonde in a miniskirt...?

Okay, suppose he stayed in the cafe a little longer than the witness, say until 4:00. At that time of day, in rush hour traffic, it would take him at least forty-five minutes to drive down the interstate. Well, considering the way he drives--drove--I'd better say forty-five minutes tops. Mark stepped over the rails, imagining the dark rusty stains on them were his father's blood. He crunched across the gravel, following the tracks away from town.

I certainly underestimated Dad, he thought, chuckling to himself. Hey, I'm underestimating myself, too. I've got a blonde in a miniskirt as well! What a coincidence. Maybe it's genetic, like the curse. His toe caught on one of the crossties, and he fell sideways against the steep grassy hill that framed the tracks beside him. Well, he laughed, it's obvious you can't walk and think about Victoria at the same time.

He listened for a train whistle as he crossed the railroad bridge spanning the creek, heart pounding at the thought of being trapped and cut in half as well. All he heard was a distant static of traffic, the calling of birds, a faint shriek of children at play. He jogged the rest of the way across the bridge, then slowed to a walk.

To his right, the steep ridge beside the tracks crested into a flat grassy area, sheltered by trees. Mark climbed up in two strides, then turned to survey the little meadow, seeing nothing but sky above and trees curtained around him. He pulled the two computer printouts from his back pocket and sprawled on the grass to study them.

The first printout was the arcs-and-lines one, much like the outer edges of a giant Spirograph design, he thought. Notations in a tiny font appeared at intersections of the lines. He studied one that caught his attention earlier, "Awareness tr051799." It has to be a date, he reasoned, since dates seem to be so important in whatever these calculations are. May 17, 1999. May 17-- Wait a second ... that's the day before I married Janet.

Blood pounded in his ears as he thought of the remarkable ... coincidence ...

The sharp edges of the day were dulled by the passage of eleven years. He remembered how scared he'd been, how his legs shook. Someone later told him his pants legs appeared to be in a heavy breeze during the ceremony. His father acted as the best man, but no one could find Thomas until he slipped in, ashen-faced, as Janet paced toward Mark up the aisle. When the time came to exchange rings, Mark's father stood motionless, eyes fixed, brow furrowed. The minister motioned him to pretend he was slipping the ring on her finger.

After the ceremony, Mark's mother insisted her husband was fine, except for a fainting spell that morning. Mark tracked him down to a back corridor of the church, where he was leaning against a window ledge, staring out at the parking lot.

"They are demanding to be remembered, Demarcus," his father replied when Mark asked him what was wrong. "They want something from me. But I--God help me--I don't know what."

"What do you mean? Who wants something from you?"

"I don't know. A soldier. A Rebel soldier. My kin." He turned from the window. "You can die more than once. Did you know that, Demarcus?"

"Is this more of your ancestor crap?" Even now, Mark felt the echoes of the anger that welled up in his chest. He wanted to strike the man. How did I get stuck with him for a father? We may have been born on the same day, but we're nothing alike.

"Get yourself together, Dad. It's my wedding day, for God's sake. Act like a father for once!" Then he stormed away.

The remembered words hit him with all the impact of a diesel locomotive. Mark stared up at the afternoon sky. "So," he muttered aloud. "The blackouts aren't the only experience we shared. He had the visions, too."

A car horn blared in the distance, jump-starting his heart for an instant before he realized it wasn't a train whistle. He sank back on his elbows and watched sunlight wink on and off through the leaves. Another memory, long forgotten, reared its head.

It was May 21, 2001. "I'll admit a library school graduation isn't the most exciting event, but how many of his children have earned a master's degree?" he muttered to Janet as he kissed his mother after the ceremony.

"Your father ... had a bad night." Delia brushed lint from his black robe.

"Nightmares again?"

Delia nodded. "Please, have dinner with us, dear--"

His sister, then only eleven years old, heard the last bit of the conversation and dashed up and grabbed Janet's hand. "Oh, come on, please have dinner with us!"

Janet smiled and accepted without consulting him. Mark ground his teeth, wishing he could go home and crash for the evening.

"Well, he must be feeling better," his mother announced, coming down the stairs. "He's not in his bed. I'll go fix dinner and you see if he's in the basement."

As soon as Mark turned the knob to the basement door, he knew something was wrong. He creaked the door open and snaked his hand around to feel for the light switch, an old childhood habit for scaring the monsters lurking in the dark basement away before he saw them. Beside the landing hung a rope, looped over the pipes and trailing down, ending-- Oh, God--

"Demarcus? Is something wrong?"

"Mom--don't come down here. Just call 911. We need an ambulance-- quick. It's Dad."

Just before the paramedics loaded the man into the ambulance, Thomas opened his eyes and focused on Mark's face. "Didn't work, did it?" he whispered. Mark leaned close to hear him. "You stopped me too soon. Still cursed."

Mark snatched at an overhanging branch, and ripped a leaf in half along its central vein. I can't believe I'd forgotten about that, too, he thought, especially after I had the vision about the Rebel soldier being hanged. But he'd thought his father was just babbling, even though he said the same thing the next time he tried to kill himself.

Mark closed his eyes and recalled that day. His father regularly underwent therapy for five years, and Mark shoved the experience into the back corner of his mind. Mark took a day off to work in his yard, and mid- day let himself into his parents' house to borrow a Weed-Eater when no one responded to his knock. Inside the house, he stumbled over his father, who lay on the floor of the downstairs guest bathroom.

Why on earth is he painting the bathroom red? was Mark's immediate thought. Mom's going to be so mad when she sees he's spilled paint all over the floor ... all over his wrists ... Mark called the paramedics and slowed the bleeding before throwing up on the living room couch. The date was May 21, 2006.

In the hospital, when his father regained consciousness, Mark hovered at his bedside. "I'm tired of this, Dad!" he said, fists clenched, tears rolling down his hot face. "What are you doing to me? Damn it, next time you can just go ahead and die. I won't be there to stop you."

Thomas Richards sighed, his face gray, his eyes sunken. "It's not your fault, son. It's mine. I'm not the one to stop it." He rolled his head from side to side on the pillow, back and forth. "I'm not the one to stop it. It just won't work."

Cursing under his breath, Mark stormed out of the room. He refused to speak to his father for two years, until his mother called him about the fourth suicide attempt.

Mark squinted at the tiny letters, trees casting a shadow over the paper. The date of every suicide attempt was there on the page: tr080199, tr052101, tr052106, tr052008. T. R. There was no doubt left in his mind. The initials meant "Thomas Richards."

He followed the lines to another intersection, "Awareness mr032110." March 21, 2010. The day of my first blackout. M. R. is Mark Richards. What the hell is being traced here? It was important he figure this out, he had to--

A blast rent the air. Blood pounding in his ears, Mark leaped to his feet and staggered against a tree, printouts fluttering to the ground. He breathed again only when the sound repeated and revealed itself as a train whistle. The thunder of the train's passage vibrated the soles of his feet, the nerves in his thighs, rattled his teeth. Mark slid down to the ground, laughing at his awe in the wake of tons and tons of hurtling metal. He picked up three pieces of paper from among the dead leaves and brushed them off, shaking off the flat bit of gold that clung to one piece.

Where did this come from? The third piece of paper was a half sheet torn from a notebook, scrawled across in ball-point: "Milk, skim not 2%! Laundry detergent, cheapest brand--Paper towels, the fat roll kind that tears off into small pieces--" Mark chuckled, recognizing his father's handwriting and the elaborate notes he wrote to remind himself of tasks Delia set him. The laugh caught in his throat, came out as a sob as he realized the significance of the note. Dad was here. Maybe he even jumped from here ... or was pushed ...

He folded the note into a small rectangle and slid it into his pocket next to his watch, wiped the tears from his cheeks with the back of his hand, and leaned back against the tree to study the printouts one last time. The sun glinted off the bit of gold beside him. He picked it up. It was a tiny square, about the size of his smallest fingernail, engraved with a symbol, a figure-8 with the top cut off. The little gold ring for attaching the charm was twisted open, snagged onto the bit of paper. He slipped the charm into his pocket.

Turning his attention back to the page, Mark noticed on the right side of the printout the tiny, scattered squares formed a curving line. Three-quarters of the way down, one square protruded farther than the others and was shaded. Beneath it was written "Ter052110."

He flipped to the sheet crisscrossed with arcs, scanning the coded dates. In the lower right quadrant he located "Terminal mr052110." There were no dates later than May 21, 2010. Okay, he thought, the word "terminal" appears before my initials and a date less than two weeks from today. But what the hell does "terminal" mean?

Terminal. He blinked, went numb.

The sky still glowed, high clouds tinged with pink, but the sun had dropped behind the ridge of trees. The terminal date was the same date, or the day after, his father tried to kill himself, three out of four times.

CHAPTER 27.

"But you do know how to do one, don't you?"

Daniel frowned at the receiver in his hand. "Yes, Natalie. I've conducted many séances in my time. I suppose I could get together some people, but I can't do it tonight ..."

"Oh, please? I've been reading about my ancestor Rebecca lately, and maybe if we could contact her or some other dead ancestor, they might help Mark out with this curse business."

"Very well." He was not overly fond of Mark Richards, but his sister's winsome pleading was difficult to ignore. "Tomorrow night at eight o'clock. Will that work for you?"

"Thank you, Daniel. I owe you one."

He gave her his address and directions and hung up. Something in her tone bothered him.

~*~*~

Thursday, May 13.

"Who is this?" Mark frowned at the handset. His gaze strayed back to the computer screen. After three hours of intense concentration, during which he thought of the previous day's excursion to Helena only ten or twelve times, he completed Barbara's requested revision of one section of the grant proposal. His eyes wandered to the wall calendar. Eight days to the 21st. A little over a week until ... what?

"Your sister, Natalie. Remember me?"

"Oh, sorry, Nat. You don't sound like yourself."

A little sigh drifted through the telephone lines. "Everybody keeps telling me that. I'm just tired. End of the semester stress. Thank God exams are over. Finally." Another sigh, then, "I'm glad I found you at work. No one seems to know where you're staying."

"I'm staying with a friend."

"But not Dave." A flat statement, but he could tell she wanted to know.

"Dave and I had a ... falling out." He propped his feet on the other chair, knocking off two manuals, some unopened junk mail, and a plastic box of floppy disks. The box clattered to the floor and snapped into pieces. "Sorry--I didn't catch that. What'd you say?"

"You're knocking things off furniture again, I can tell."

Mark wondered why she sounded so subdued.

"I said, you should have told someone where you're staying. We were worried. Mom was ready to call the police."

"Sorry, Nat. I forgot my obligation to report my every move to her."

Yeah, he added to himself, and when's Janet going to track me down and tell me I haven't done laundry for a week?

"Forgive us for caring." Her voice was flat and emotionless. "Anyway, I called to ask you if you want to go to a séance with me tonight."

"A séance?" he laughed. "Why are you going to a séance?"

"I convinced Daniel--you know, Janet's psychic friend?--to have one. I thought it might help figure out what's going on with the curse."

Daniel's name jarred him. "I'm not sure it will, but whatever you want to do, Sis. Where's this séance going to be held?"

"His house. Starting about eight o'clock. Can you come?"

"Sorry, but I can't," he said. "This proposal I'm working on is due Monday, and I'm not anywhere near finished. I'll be here into the wee hours, I'm afraid."

"Well, don't spend your time talking about computers, or you'll never get it done."

Mark laughed. "There won't be anybody to talk to. I'll either be in my office or down in basement storage digging through some old files for a CD with yet another new section on it I have to add to the report."

"Basement storage?" she echoed. "That isolated place down there with the rickety old shelving and all the bats and spiders?"

"There are no bats down there, Nat. Spiders, yes. Bats, no."

"Somebody could attack you down there," she said in a flat voice, very unlike hers, "and no one would know."

"Thanks for the mental image," he told her. "Your imagination is running wild again. Who'd want to attack me? Listen, thanks for the invite, but I must regretfully decline."

"Sure?" Her voice still held hope.

"I'll make it up to you. I promise. Say hi to all the ghosts for me, okay?"

"Don't joke, Mark. You be careful walking out to your car if you stay late."

"Thanks for caring. I appreciate it. Call me tomorrow and tell me how it went."

He hung up the phone and turned back to the computer screen, scowling as he read the last paragraph he'd written. Utter crap. Dammit, Jim, I'm a computer geek, not a writer. The offending paragraph disappeared with a sweep of his mouse.

~*~*~

"No, I have to go back to work," Mark insisted, squeezing Victoria's hand across the kitchen table. "Dinner's delicious, by the way."

"You've really been a delightful companion these past two days," she said with a twist of her lip. She slid her hand out of his. "You were so quiet when you came back from wherever you were yesterday, I felt like I was alone in the house." Her bird-wing eyebrows gathered above her nose. "Admittedly I'm not letting you stay here because of your brilliant conversational abilities, but a few words now and then would be welcome."

He set his fork down. She sounded like Janet. "I'm a little distracted right now," Mark said, barely disguising his annoyance. "I'm sorry if I've been ignoring you."

"At least tell me what's bothering you." She tossed her blonde hair. "Men don't usually tire of me this quickly."

"Tire of you? Hardly. That's a major part of my problem. I can't get you off my mind, Victoria. I can't tell you the number of times this afternoon I mentally undressed you."

The Mona Lisa smile crept across her lips. "It doesn't have to be just mentally."

"I know," he said with a heartfelt sigh. "But I have to get that proposal done. If I'm not thinking about you, I'm puzzling over those damned printouts--"

"Printouts?"

Mark felt his face turn red. "Oops. I didn't mean to say that. I guess I'm busted. I printed off a couple of charts from Sylvia's computer."

Deliberately, as if afraid her knees might break, Victoria crossed her legs. "I'm certain I told you not to mess with her calculations."

"I didn't mess with them. I got curious. They have something to do with me and my family, don't they?"

138

Her eyes on him were like green ice. "You have a vivid imagination, Mark. Why would Sylvia's calculations involve you? Does that really make sense?"

"No, I can't say it does." He leaned his elbows on the table, tangled his fingers in his hair. "Nothing does anymore."

"Don't worry about it. Sylvia's calculations are her own business. Trust me, darling. You don't believe there are evil machinations afoot, do you?" She laughed. "What do you think I am, a black widow spider?"

He smoothed his hair. "I have to run. No, I don't think you're a black widow spider."

Her deep, lingering kiss almost convinced him to stay. "I'll be back very late, unless a miracle happens and aliens have finished the proposal for me. If you try to call me and I'm not there, leave a message on voicemail. I'll be down in storage going through some files."

She stood and molded her body to his. "I won't wait up, then. But you owe me,

Mr. Richards, big time. You have duties to perform."

"See you later." Mark strolled out to his car, yawning. He slid into the driver's seat, thinking, Another exciting night in the life of Mark Richards, Boy Systems Librarian.

~*~*~

Natalie stifled a yawn and tried not to think about crawling onto that red couch and sleeping for about a week. The séance was not quite what she expected. After thirty minutes of sitting around an arrangement of flickering candles on the low table, listening to Daniel drone on about the spirit world and guides and whatnot, they'd still not seen one ghost or even heard a rap or a trumpet sound. As far as entertainment value goes, she thought, this ranks up there with TV gardening shows and documentaries on World War II.

She shifted position on the black cushion, coaxing the blood back into her tingling ankle, and glanced at Daniel. His eyebrows were drawn together over his pointy nose, his lips pursed.

"Please forgive the delay, but my guide is not appearing tonight. I don't understand--this has never happened before."

Natalie noticed a quaver in his voice.

"There is another presence requesting--no, insisting on admittance." His chest was heaving, eyes now squeezed shut. "I cannot prevent--"

A rush of howling wind flattened the candle flames as if under an invisible plane of glass, then coaxed them upward into one vast white-hot column. The small circle of participants winced away from the heat. The flames whirled and writhed and formed a translucent sphere, hovering three feet above the center of the table. A pearlescent glow blanched the faces of the six watchers, filmed their wide eyes, bleached their hair.

They look like zombies, Natalie thought, her heart thudding. Well, you wanted something to happen. Daniel's head craned forward, eyes wide and mouth hanging open. Her spine tingled with a thrill of horror and excitement as the sphere slowly rotated. Five pairs of eyes swiveled toward her as a metallic voice echoed in her head.

"You have gathered here to help my brother James," the voice drawled in a distinctive southern Alabama accent. Where is it coming from? Natalie wondered. It sounds like she's next to me, but I don't see anyone. "But I'm afraid James is beyond help. He is marked for death, and no one can save him now."

"We are here to help Demarcus Richards," Daniel corrected firmly, his face glowing in the pale green-white light. "We don't know anyone named James. No one is marked for death."

Wait a minute, yes, we do, Natalie insisted. James was my however-many-times-great grandfather. It must be Rebecca. Why won't my mouth work? I can't make them hear me.

The voice went on. "Oh, of course. I've been out of the world for so very long. James is long dead." She laughed. "I killed him myself. It is his filthy descendent who will die soon. Except I intend to kill him first and put an end to the Giles line forever."

Where is she? Natalie asked herself. Why is everyone staring at me?

Daniel seemed to recover his senses. "Why would you want to kill this descendent? What harm has he done to you? If you have indeed been dead a very long time, he could not possibly have harmed you."

She spat out the words like sour milk. "He harms me by living--by existing! And he will die. I have not laid plans for all these years for nothing. What year is this?"

"2010," a frowning Daniel answered. The light of the sphere grayed his hair, transforming him into a very old man.

Her voice was quieter. "It is a very long time since I killed my brother."

Daniel stood, the light casting his face into a weird mask. "You must leave this assembly," he intoned. "We cannot allow this talk of death and murder."

Her sharp laugh rang in Natalie's head. "I will leave. But I will not be gone. You will hear of me again."

The sphere winked out of existence. A buzz filled the room as Natalie's vision blurred and the muscles in her legs collapsed. The sound set her teeth on edge, like blowing on paper wrapped around a comb. She clamped them together and still it resounded, sizzling in the bones of her face. The

140

concept of "body" lost meaning as the Natalie-consciousness that gave her identity retreated to a corner of the vast dim theater-like space in which she found herself. It occurred to her that, in her acting classes, she'd never completely lost herself in a character before, not understanding how to submerge her personality into someone else's life. Now, as the blackness swallowed her, she understood ...

Rebecca summoned her last reserves of strength and shoved the heavy bureau in front of the door with a grunt.

"There," she said, sinking onto a pile of blankets on the floor. "That should prevent anyone from sneaking up on us in the night." Her brother slept fitfully on a featherbed by the fire. The homemade herbal salve she applied to his neck would ease the pain of the rope burns, and was already drawing the swelling from his broken arm.

She was grateful for a night's rest in the abandoned cabin, a night in which she did not have to sleep with one eye open, watching for the enemy. The journey from the clearing where she found James to the cabin nearly two miles away was a blur of vignettes: the flour sack sound of his body crumpling to the ground as she cut him down, the muscle-tearing agony of half-dragging a semi-conscious man nearly twice her weight, the raw tang of terror as a Yankee patrol passed within six feet of their hiding place. The blur became a whirlpool, dragging her weary body into sleep.

James' muttering awoke her sometime later while it was still dark outside. Joints popping in protest, Rebecca climbed to her feet, and added another log to the fire. Her brother, in his restless feversleep, pushed the blanket from his tanned chest and injured arm. She straightened it, pulling it up below the darkening welts on his throat, and retreated to her makeshift bed.

Conflicting emotions chased through her head. She wanted desperately to kill him, but not here, not when he was helpless and unaware, not without his precious Alice to die at his side. She wanted just as desperately to be joined with him again, as on the night their ill-fated child was conceived, the night he thought he was loving someone else. She searched her heart for a trace of remorse for the destruction of her family's harmony and peace during her pursuit of power, but she found none there.

~*~*~

Mark interlaced his fingers and stretched his arms with a grin. That's what I needed, he thought, a good four hours of uninterrupted work and I'm nearly halfway through this thing. The clock on his computer screen said ten-thirty--a good time to look for that old report and stretch his legs. He locked his office and strode toward the elevator. Despite the late hour,

141

or maybe because of it, most of the tables on the third floor balcony overlooking the reading room were filled with students engrossed in studying before the final day of exams. He pressed the button for the lowest level of the building.

A long corridor stretched to the left as he stepped out of the elevator. The hum of the air conditioner masked any noises in the immediate vicinity. To the right was a darkened office and a hallway leading toward an older part of the building. Mark glanced at his reflection in the office window, a tall, translucent figure, isolated from the rest of civilization.

He dragged open the door leading into the basement storage area, a cinder block-walled room filled with old wooden book stacks from some previous incarnation of the library, reaching nearly to the ceiling and arranged in rows at right angles to the wall. The air down here was chilly and musty, and Mark laughed at himself when he realized he was scanning the exposed pipes on the ceiling for bats.

Emergency lights burned at either end of the room, shadowing the shelving closest to the wall. The light switch barely illuminated the room. This place still feels like a cavern, he thought. All it needs is a few stalagmites to complete the picture. The cement floor muffled the sound of his boots as he paced toward the center.

Mark skimmed the hand-lettered labels pasted to the ends of each stack. Some were as old as the shelves themselves, the script elegant in an inked copperplate hand. He found his row, marked "Librarians' Files," and his allotted section next to the wall, two shelves up from the floor. The aisles were only wide enough for him to walk without turning sideways. He leaned over to open one of the boxes, helpfully labeled "Mark's Old Files," and backed into the stack behind him, sending several large volumes bouncing from the top shelf to the floor. Mark dodged the books and noticed a row of five-pound pharmaceutical reference books had worked their way to the edge. Another nudge would do some serious damage to anyone standing beneath. The stacks were bolted to the cement floor, but the upper shelves tended to sway.

He prowled through the file folders inside the storage box. "I have got to label these things better," he told himself aloud. He knew the old report was there on a CD somewhere, along with a rationale for acquiring additional online databases he wrote the year before. He'd saved the older files to CD when he got a new computer.

Mark finally slid the lid back on and moved to the next box, also labeled "Old Files." He looked up at the faint "snick" of the door opening.

"Hello? Don't turn off the light, I'm in the stacks." He listened, but heard only a sigh of the door closing again and the white noise of the air system. Shrugging, he returned to the files.

The cinder block wall smashed into his face. He tasted wet iron. What the hell--?

He was pinned against the wall by a hand shoved into the small of his back. His first attempt at speech failed. He cleared his throat and tried again.

"Who's there?" he demanded. "What do you want?"

Small but strong hands gripped his arms to turn him and shoved his back against the prickly cinder block wall. Mark stared in utter amazement as he recognized his attacker.

"I want you to become my lover," she smiled.

CHAPTER 28.

The attacker twined her arms around his waist, pressing her body against his, and wiped the blood off his scraped cheek.

"I--I hate to break this to you, Natalie," Mark stammered, shrinking as far away from her as the wall at his back would permit, "but contrary to popular opinion, incest is illegal in this state. Not to mention disgusting."

"Demarcus ... we were meant to be together."

Something about her eyes was strange, he thought. Her voice was different, too. The skin-tight T-shirt she wore could've been selected from Victoria's wardrobe, but not Natalie's. Revulsion warred with a faint tingle of desire.

"Natalie, you're not acting like yourself. You're--" That's what it was. Her hazel eyes were now unmistakably green. Contact lenses? "Just back off and get a grip."

She smiled an unfamiliar wickedly arch smile. "I'd be glad to. Just tell me where."

He grabbed her shoulders and shoved her away, fighting off the rising panic. "Stop trying to seduce me. That's not what sisters do, okay?"

"It's what Isis did, and she was a goddess. Don't you think that makes it all right?"

"Isis? I'm hardly Osiris. Or Tutankhamen. Or any other dead Egyptian who married his sister. Now let's get out of here and get you some help." He tried to shove past her, but her grip on his arm bit into his flesh. "You been working out lately?"

Her green eyes bored into his, snapping with a golden fire. Just like

144

Victoria's eyes, he thought with wonder. "You've never taken me seriously, big brother. I'm offering you an opportunity for greatness," Natalie hissed. "Don't make me angry."

"I take you seriously when you deserve to be taken seriously." He pried her wrist from his arm, his hands shaking. "This is not one of those times."

She stepped in front of him again, a very Victoria-like smile playing across her lips. "I'm sorry, Demarcus. I guess I haven't given you enough time to get used to the idea. I don't think you know what power is accessible to us. Open your mind to the possibilities. Don't you want to be powerful, to control your own destiny?"

"Natalie," he said shakily. "Right now all I want is go to bed."

"See? I knew you'd like the idea." He pried her arms from around his neck.

"Alone. As in sleep," he said with a shudder. There was a cold knot in the pit of his stomach. "Did I suddenly become so irresistible to women that my own sister wants me? I think your exams have unhinged your mind."

Her eyes flashed, lips twisted into a snarl. "You're making fun of me again. I won't have that." She reached to the back of her jeans and whipped out a long knife. "You're just like *him*. What's wrong with the Giles men?"

"Calm down." Sweat sprang out on his forehead. "I'm like who?"

"Whom." She tapped his chest with the tip of the knife. "James Giles."

Mark stretched a trembling hand toward her and struggled for a calming and reasonable tone. "Come on, Natalie, give me the knife."

An explosion of sound followed his words: a shrill scream--a slashing of the air--an echoing ring of metal on wood. He stared at his sister, who was panting heavily and nursing the hand that clutched the bloody knife. The vibration of the wooden shelving subsided. She must've hit her hand against it when she slashed at him. But where did the blood on the knife come from? He looked down at the torn fabric of his shirt, red with his blood, and staggered back against the wall. "Natalie ... why did you--"

She shook her head and advanced. He watched a drop of his blood drip from the knife to the concrete floor. "Oh, no. You had your chance. Don't try to make it up to me now."

Somewhere beneath the horror, an idea was forming. Ignoring the pain in his chest, he braced his hands beside him on the wall. "You won't get away with this," he said, wincing at the B-movie dialogue. "Someone checks this room frequently for intruders."

"I do not believe--"

Mark launched himself sideways into the shelving, swaying the wood against the floor bolts with a groan. Books rained down like a meteor

145

shower. Natalie howled in fury and alarm. One of the large, fifteen-pound books smashed into the side of Mark's temple, slamming him to the cement floor.

Mark peered up at her through the haze of his pain, knees, head and chest throbbing in concert, bracing himself for a fatal slash he could not avoid in these cramped quarters.

Natalie clung to one of the empty lower shelves, blood dripping from a cut on her arm. The knife lay on the floor between them, its long blade glistening blackish-red in the dim light. Her face was turned away from him, her back heaving.

He fought the nausea the blood invoked. "Natalie!" His anguished cry tore his throat, twisting into a sob. "Why are you doing this? What's wrong with you?"

His sister retrieved the knife with the wary gaze of a hunter too close to dangerous prey. With a deft kick, she shoved him onto his back and grabbed a handful of his hair and exposing his throat. Blood from the knife splashed on his cheek. The corners of the books beneath him dug into his skin.

"For revenge, big brother. No one spurns me and gets away with it. No one."

CHAPTER 29.

"Daniel?" Janet held the door open as the man pushed past her.

"I'm sorry to come by so late without calling first." He grasped her hand and pulled her toward the couch, not releasing his grip as they sat, knees touching.

She brushed a strand of hair from his eyes. "What's wrong? Your hands are trembling."

"Janet, something happened tonight, something unexpected." He closed his eyes, sucked in a deep breath and slowly exhaled. "I held a séance tonight, at Natalie's insistence--"

"Natalie's? Why would she want you to hold a séance?" His grip on her hands was painful, but she couldn't slide them out. She'd never seen him so agitated before, and his intensity frightened her.

"Please don't interrupt me, Janet." She could tell he was holding his temper in check with great difficulty. "She said it might help Mark. I didn't question her motivation. If you'll allow me to continue, I usually work through Deirdre, my spirit contact. I felt, instead, the presence of someone else, someone very powerful who blocked Deirdre. The spirit did not identify herself, but referred to her brother James."

"Daniel--you're hurting me."

He released her hands.

"I don't understand--" she began.

The man shuddered, shaking his head as he buried it in his hands. "This should not have happened. All the books, all my teachers--they all say there is no evil that can manifest in a séance, that there is no possession with intent to harm."

"Possession?"

"This spirit possessed Natalie and spoke through her during the séance." He ignored her gasp. "It happens sometimes, with no harm or difficulty. But I felt evil in this spirit, a dark intent. It's related to the danger in Mark's life."

"Is she all right?" Janet asked, her hands raised to her mouth.

"She was apparently oblivious to what happened. When I told her the spirit was not *behind* her, as she thought, but speaking *through* her, she said, 'Cool'."

Janet said, "That sounds like Natalie. Was she all right afterward?"

"She seemed so. I offered to drive her home, but she refused. Said she felt better than she had in months. This isn't the only thing that worries me, though." The knuckles of his clenched fists resting on his knees were white. "I haven't slept in ... I do not know when I slept last ... three, maybe four nights ago. Someone is attacking me psychically. Very subtle, but very powerful. I've felt the presence since the tarot reading."

Janet dragged a pillow into her lap, wrapped her arms around it. "Who would do that?"

"Someone I have never met before. He seems to be extremely powerful, both physically and psychically. I've read of people who are imperceptive psychically, but who have the ability to attack with great ferocity. He must be one. And I think it's related to the curse on Mark's family. He and his sister are in grave danger. And so are you."

He looked at her and she felt his fear, something she'd never seen in him before.

"You need protection."

A wave of helplessness washed over her. "Should we call the police?"

Daniel laughed a short humorless bark. "They wouldn't be much use against these forces. Janet, I think I need to stay here tonight. Someone will be attacked, and I don't want it to be you. I can sleep on the couch--if I sleep at all ..."

She hesitated, looking at Daniel's anxious face. "If you really think it's necessary."

"Thank you, Janet." He smiled, sagging against the cushions. "It is necessary."

She leaned against him, aware of his body, but craving only closeness to another human being at that moment. "I'm sorry I dragged you into this, Daniel."

He shrugged. "When you called that night, I was trying to convince myself not to call you. I have missed you, Janet. No one else can ever take your place in my life."

Their faces were so close she felt the warmth of his breath on her lips. She knew he was about to kiss her. Her heart beat faster and she wasn't at all sure she would resist him.

The front door flew open. Mark stumbled across the threshold, his shirt stained with blood. He swung on the doorknob to ease his fall and panted, "Honey, I'm home!"

CHAPTER 30.

Andrew paused in the aisle and surveyed the tableau at the opposite end. A slender young woman with short dark hair knelt on the arm and chest of a man she closely resembled. The fingers of her left hand tangled in his long hair, twisting back his head to expose his neck. The other hand grasped an antique knife, its long blade poised against his jugular vein.

"For revenge, big brother," he heard her say as he edged closer. "No one spurns me and gets away with it. No one."

Andrew had to put a stop to it.

"He's gonna get away with it for now, babe. Put the knife down like a good girl."

Natalie gasped and whipped her head around to look at him, her teeth bared like a vampire in a horror movie. "Whoever you are, get out now. I'm busy."

"Natalie, stop--" the man on the floor pleaded.

Andrew recognized him as the man with Victoria the day she ran away from him. Is that all he does, collapse on the floor? What a pansy, he thought.

"I'm warnin' you, missy. Put the knife down or I'll have to hurt you."

She jerked Richards' head back harder. Richards cried out as the blade bit into his flesh.

Andrew would've enjoyed watching her off this wimp, but he knew how Miss Dee would react. He shut his eyes and released a burst of dark air toward Natalie's consciousness. Her cry of pain fed into his energy, coursing through his veins like good bourbon. He heard the knife rattle on the floor. When he opened his eyes, she was staring at him, green eyes

150

wide, hands clutching her head.

"Why did you stop me?" she shrieked. "I was so close!"

Andrew reached down and grabbed her wrist in his powerful grip, jerking her to her feet. Richards' body relaxed with a sigh. Andrew quickly probed Richards' psyche. The man was only unconscious. Strong barriers prevented Andrew from doing anything more. The slash across Richards' chest was still bleeding, but not enough to kill him.

"Lucky for you he ain't dead. Miss Dee would have a shit fit." He walked toward the aisle, dragging the girl behind him.

"Who are you?" the woman demanded.

Andrew stopped halfway to the door. "You sure remind me of Victoria." He spun her against his chest, one arm firmly around her waist, and peered at her. "It's the eyes, I think. Miss Dee wants to know who *you* are. She's gettin' some weird vibes from you."

"I don't know what you're talking about. Let me go."

He shook his head. "I don't think so. You're comin' with me for now. Leave the poor guy alone. You already cut him up pretty good."

She wriggled in his grasp. "Not good enough."

Her struggles aroused him, but Miss Dee's short leash wouldn't allow him any pleasure until this business was over.

"Miss Dee wants to see you. And she don't want you killin' him too soon. Now come on, or I'll have to sling you over my shoulder and carry you."

~*~*~

At Mark's entrance, Janet and Daniel leaped from the couch. "Mark, what happened?" she cried as they each slipped an arm around his shoulders and eased him toward the couch.

"Sorry--for the dramatic entrance--Jan--But my--sister just tried--just tried to kill me--"

Mark's words made no sense. "What? Your sister? Natalie?"

"Only one I got--"

He broke off, hissing through his teeth, face screwed up in pain as Daniel lowered his head onto a pillow.

"Janet." Daniel's firm hand dragged her back to reality. "He's hurt. Get some bandages."

When she returned with first aid supplies, Daniel had removed Mark's shirt, exposing an eight-inch slash across his chest. "It's not very deep."

The psychic counselor backed away, and Janet took over.

"'Not so deep as a well,'" Mark quoted, "'but 'twill serve'"

He screamed through clenched teeth as she wiped alcohol over the wound. "I've been tortured enough tonight, Jan."

"Would you prefer an infection?" Anxiety sharpened her voice, and she added, "Now tell me what happened."

He closed his eyes while Janet applied the bandages with numb fingers. "Natalie cornered me in the basement of the library and ... well, to put it bluntly, she tried to seduce me."

"What?" Janet's hand froze, and she had to force herself to continue her ministrations.

"Yeah, well, that was my reaction too. Then when I wouldn't--uh--cooperate, she flew into a rage and pulled out a knife--this knife--"

He dragged it from his belt. "You see the results. I don't know why I brought this thing with me," he added, handing the knife to Janet. "It seemed important."

"How on earth did you get away from her?" Janet asked, dropping the knife on the end table. She dabbed blood from his stomach and chest and cleaned the small cut on his neck.

"That's the weird part--well, it's all weird, but--I thought I was dead for sure. I had the bright idea to knock books off the shelves to distract her, but it clobbered me, too, so I was kinda vulnerable. She was about to slit my throat when out of nowhere comes Victoria's boyfriend Andrew and drags Natalie away. I passed out, and when I came to, they were gone."

Janet folded the bloody washcloth into a small square. "Who's Victoria?"

She watched her husband's cheeks redden as he straightened away from her. "A friend--uh, colleague. I met her at the library recently. Her boyfriend was chasing us--"

He shook his head, tried to fold his arms across his chest, but winced and shifted position on the couch instead. "Long story."

She felt Daniel move to stand just behind her.

"Has your sister ever displayed these ... tendencies before?" Daniel asked.

"Hell, no!" Mark exploded.

"Daniel didn't mean any insult," Janet said, rubbing a hand across her stomach. "He's trying to help."

"Yeah, but help himself to what. I saw you two on the couch when I came in."

"Demarcus." Daniel's tone was firm and commanding. "This is no time for petty jealousy. Something serious has happened to your sister."

"No shit," he replied. "And it's Mark, okay? Not Demarcus."

"I came over here to tell Janet what happened tonight to your sister. She was possessed by a spirit--one intent on evil."

Mark glanced sharply at the blond man. "Possessed?" He swung his legs to the floor, leaning forward. "I don't understand--"

"What happened to your back?" Janet cried when she saw the bandage on his bare skin.

"What? Oh, nothing. I'm--uh--accident-prone these days."

Janet looked at him, eyes narrowed. "You didn't have another vision, did you?"

"Actually I did. Look, can we talk about Natalie? What happened to her, Dan?"

Janet perched on the edge of the couch beside him. Daniel sat cross-legged on the floor. "Someone has been attacking me psychically, as I told Janet. My attacker, from what little I have been able to glean, is a man with a very powerful will and natural ability to hurt and destroy. He erected strong barriers to prevent me finding him. And after what happened tonight, I think there is some connection between my attacker, the curse, and Natalie's possession."

"A connection?" Mark asked.

"I've done some investigating on the astral plane, trying to find my attacker. In the course of it, I found Natalie's aura is somehow linked with his--and with two other women, neither of whom I know. But one of them is not as heavily shielded, and I may soon be able to find out who they are."

Mark sat up, alarming Janet with the thought he was in pain. "No, I'm okay. I think I know who it is, but he doesn't seem bright enough to be able to attack someone psychically."

"Intelligence has nothing to do with psychic power, unfortunately. The kind of power of which I am speaking is an innate power the person was born with, and has learned to control for his own--or someone else's--ends," Daniel explained.

"I think Andrew is the person who's attacking you. I'm not quite sure why I think that, but if he's linked with Natalie, that may explain why he showed up tonight."

Janet saw Daniel's gaze sharpen. "Do you know his full name? Where he lives?"

Mark shook his head. "Sorry, Dan. I could ask my friend."

"It would help. But I don't understand why he is attacking me. I do have a certain prominence as a counselor, but ..."

Mark shrugged and winced. He reached for his torn, bloody shirt. "Don't put that thing back on," Janet said, glad for the chance to do something instead of just listening to this incredible story. "Let me get you a clean one."

~*~*~

"I'm afraid I can't help you with why he's doing it."

Feeling strangely detached, Mark watched Janet bustle out of the room. "But he's a pretty mean-looking dude. If he's as mean psychically as physically ..."

"Have you heeded my advice, Mark? Stayed away from the woman I warned you about?" Daniel asked.

He wondered how exactly to answer that. Tell him it's none of his damn business? Confess? Have him tell Janet? Instead Mark said nothing and looked away.

"I see."

Mark frowned. "But I didn't say--"

"You didn't have to. Is that where you are staying?" Daniel bowed his head. "This is not a wise course of action."

Mark squinted up at the ceiling, watching the ceiling fan. "See, you don't understand. She's different from anyone else I've ever met. It's like ... she's in my head ... I--Thanks, Jan." He pulled the shirt on to cover his reddening face and buttoned it over the wound.

"As you were saying," Daniel said, "we must figure out what is wrong with your sister. She mentioned killing her brother James. Does that mean anything to you?"

"Her brother ... James?" Mark clutched the edge of the couch as the floor tilted for one brief second. "My God, I think I know who that spirit is, folks. Rebecca Giles. Sister of my great-great-great grandfather. And she's possessed my sister."

Despair welled up inside his chest like bile. Mark launched himself from the couch. "This is all insane! Stuff like this doesn't happen. It just doesn't! Where does it all end?" He laughed. "Oh, I forgot. With my imminent demise."

He realized Janet and Daniel were staring at him, both frowning in concern. "Don't worry," he said, massaging his tense neck muscles. "I'm not going postal or anything. Can you help my sister, Dan?"

The blond man climbed to his feet. "We'll find a way. I need to do more research first."

"I thought you were staying," Janet objected.

"Staying?" Mark raised an eyebrow.

"I didn't like the idea of her staying alone when I have been the object of attacks and so have you. Janet could be in danger. Since you weren't staying here--"

"I am now." Mark wasn't about to let Daniel stay here with his wife.

"Mark?" Janet's face brightened.

"Well, it's late--it's--" He patted his pockets. "My watch--I must've left it at Vict--uh, at--uh--I need to go back and get it."

"But it's after midnight, Mark," his wife objected.

Daniel stared at him. "You left the watch there?"

"Well, my clothes are still there, too. What's wrong?"

Daniel sighed. "Never, and I do mean never, leave possessions--especially that one--where someone you don't know well can access them. It can give them power over you. Don't you remember what I told you about the watch?"

"But I don't see any danger from--"

"The danger is there, Mark, whether you see it or not. I know these things. It's what I do, remember?" Daniel paused, one hand on the doorknob, his pointed face suffused with righteous anger. "Do not go back to get it by yourself. And do not leave Janet alone."

The door slammed behind him.

"Are you really staying?" Janet asked.

He bit his lip, considering. "For now, I think so. I still don't have things clearly sorted out in my head--"

She tugged at the couch cushions, brushed off crumbs invisible to Mark's eyes. "You were staying with that woman you mentioned."

The iciness of her stare as she peered at him over her shoulder froze his heart, snapping off little bits of it like brittle icicle shards. His lips worked, but his brain, sorting through excuses and reasons and platitudes, rejected them all and simply shut down.

"I assume you slept with her." She slapped the decorative pillows into shape, her gaze sweeping away from him. Her jaw quivered.

"Janet, I--"

"Under the circumstances, I think it would be better if you slept in the guest room."

A solitary tear, melting away from her icy eyes, dropped with a tiny splat onto the couch. Janet paused in the doorway. "You remember where the towels and things are."

He rubbed a hand across his chest, winced, and wandered into the guest room. I'm lucky I got this instead of the garage, he thought, emptying his pockets onto the dresser. The little gold charm winked in the lamplight and he stared at it, wondering again where it came from.

His head ached, his brain rebelling. No more puzzles, it told him. Sleep.

CHAPTER 31.

Friday, May 14.

The only way Mark knew he'd slept was the succession of vivid dreams. At least twice, he dreamt of the huge vortex sucking up his family members into its gigantic blackness. The other dreams began as seriously erotic adventures with Victoria, but ended with him being chased by some chitinous, multi-jointed creature. The details were hazy, but he awoke drenched in sweat, his heart pounding.

A shower and change of clothes revived him a little, but he ached in every muscle and he broke out in a cold sweat when he examined his wounds in the mirror. The gold charm on the dresser distracted him. He fingered it, puzzled over it again, then shoved it back into his pocket with the coins, resolving to worry about it later.

Janet's note on the kitchen table informed him she'd gone to work. As he munched on a cold grape Pop Tart and absorbed as much coffee as his system would allow, the telephone rang.

"Mom? What's wrong?"

Delia Richards sounded upset. "Oh, Mark, I'm so glad you answered. I didn't want to alarm Janet. It's Natalie."

"What about her?" he said warily, hating the thought of telling his mother what happened.

"She didn't come home last night. She said she was going out with friends to a movie, but this morning her bed hadn't been slept in. I called her friends, and they said she didn't go out with them. Where do you think

156

she could be, Mark?" The anguish in Delia's voice tore at his heart. "Oh, hold on, someone's at the door."

He heard a muffled conversation, then, "Hi, Bro!"

"Natalie?" Mark nearly dropped the phone. "What the hell did you-- Where did you--" He stopped as the words tumbled out and tried again. "What the hell's wrong with you?"

"Wrong? What are you so upset about?" she answered. "Stop yelling at me. I'm fine. I just got sleepy after the séance and pulled the car over on the side of the road. Post-traumatic exam syndrome. No big deal."

No big deal. Had she forgotten what she tried to do, or was she lying?

"That's a long sleep, isn't it?" During which you tried to kill me, he added to himself.

She answered him with, "Where are you staying, Mark? You're elusive these days."

"Oh, you know, here and there," he hedged. "You take care, Natalie. Don't scare Mom anymore." Or me, he added to himself, hanging up before she could say anything else.

Sleeping in her car beside the road? The idea was ludicrous coming from a person who claimed she couldn't sleep in hotel rooms on family vacations. He wondered if she didn't remember being in the library. Of course, he told himself, what did you expect her to say in front of Mom? 'Oh, hi, Mark. Sorry about trying to seduce and kill you. No hard feelings?'

He tried to imagine how Andrew was involved. What possible reason would Victoria's ex-boyfriend have for saving him from a knife-wielding maniac?

He gulped the last of his coffee and glanced up at the wall clock with a yelp. The mug clattered as he dropped it in the sink and dashed for his car.

~*~*~

Mark swallowed twice. "You wanted to see me, Barbara?"

His boss motioned him into a chair and shut the office door. "I understand at you are experiencing some difficulties at home." She sat behind her desk, folded her hands. "And that you've had some health problems, in addition to being separated from your wife. And the recent passing of your father."

"I'm back with my wife now, though." He knew saying it wouldn't help, but he wanted the people there to know.

"Nevertheless, the quality of your work has suffered lately. The proposal is ... adequate, but I'll have to spend some time on it myself to get it in shape to present to the President."

"But I--"

She ignored him and kept talking. "It's not up to your usual standards, Mark. And you've neglected your other duties as well."

He stared at her solemn face. "You're not .... you're not firing me, are you?" He felt like he was about to step off a cliff. He held his breath ... waiting ... waiting ...

A sad smile lightened her eyes. "You're too valuable for that. I'd like you to take an unpaid leave of absence to get your life sorted out. A month should do it. Take the rest of the day to wrap things up here, and start your leave on Monday. Does that sound reasonable?"

He exhaled. "Yes, ma'am, I guess it does. I'm really sorry--"

"I know. It's partly my fault. I shouldn't have put so much pressure on you so soon after your father's death."

He nodded. "I appreciate that, Barbara. I'll see you in a month."

If I'm still alive in a month, he added, staggering out of her office.

~*~*~

Sunday, May 16.

His throat was raw from screaming, but at least his eyes were open now, and he knew he was finally awake. He glanced at his biceps, untorn by the talons of the hard-shelled, bug-like creature that held him in its grip during the nightmare. Janet, her hair tousled and eyes squinty with sleep, stood in the doorway.

"Mark? Are you all right? I heard--"

"Sorry," he croaked, massaging the knots in his neck. "Bad dream. Go back to sleep. It's not even dawn yet."

"You don't have to snap at me," she muttered and disappeared down the hall toward the room they'd once shared. Mark slid back onto the pillow as his frantic heart slowed. For the second night in a row, his nightmares kept him from restorative sleep. The juxtaposition of the erotic beginning of his dreams with the miniature horror movies, complete with the ghastly bug-thing that snatched him from Victoria's embrace to tear out his entrails while he watched in excruciating agony, was wearing on his nerves, sapping his energy during the day. He was increasingly irritable, lashing out at Janet with little provocation.

He realized the ghastly bug-thing wore his wife's face.

He climbed out of bed and padded into the dark kitchen. Yawning, he made coffee, randomly leafing through the phone book while it brewed. The first ad he saw was for "Daniel O'Brien, Psychic Counselor. Tarot card readings a specialty. Dreams interpreted. Curses revoked. Hidden matters revealed. All transactions strictly confidential. By appointment only." The telephone number and address were given.

Mark chuckled at the last line: "VISA, MasterCard, and Discover accepted." *I guess it really is all in the cards.*

He poured steaming coffee into the largest mug he could find, and inhaled the aroma. A scuffling sound made him jump before he realized it was Janet's house slippers. She clinked and clanked her way to a cup of instant coffee, ignoring the freshly brewed pot, then slid into the chair opposite him.

"I'll never get used to this decaf," she mumbled.

"So don't drink it. Is it more of Daniel's New Age bullshit that's got you swearing it off?" He winced at his harsh tone, but retracting it was too much effort.

"No. It's healthier for the--for me." She took another sip and glanced at the open phone book. "Looking for anything in particular?"

"Just trolling. I happened upon your boyfriend's ad."

"He's not my boyfriend," she said.

"Does he know that?"

"You haven't been sleeping well, have you?" Janet asked. "Is the bed too hard?"

"Don't change the subject. If I hadn't stumbled in the other night, I'm sure he wouldn't be sleeping in the guest room."

Coffee sloshed over the edge of the mug as she slammed it on the table. "Stop that right now, Demarcus Richards. You're trying to pick a fight. You have no right to criticize me, and I have no reason to feel guilty. You're just trying to make yourself feel better because you slept with that--that woman."

He slammed his mug down, too. "I'll tell you one thing about her. She doesn't try to control me the way you do."

Janet stared at him until he looked away. "I'm going back to bed. I don't know what your game is, but I'm in no mood to play it right now." She poured the rest of her coffee down the sink, placed the mug in the dishwasher, and scuffed out of the room.

Mark sucked down his coffee, tasting nothing but hot liquid that burned his tongue. He knew he was behaving like a complete jackass, but he couldn't seem to stop it. *Maybe I need to get out of town,* he thought, *away from all women.*

Maybe then the dreams will go away.

CHAPTER 32.

Monday, May 17.

Mark cocked an eye toward the sky, as he had many times since leaving the records room at the Marengo County Courthouse. Waves of dark, substantial-looking clouds rolled in moment by moment. He smelled a tang of ozone on the strengthening breeze, alternating warm and cooler gusts of wind blowing across his clothing and skin as he stood in the dust. The photocopied description of the land once owned by his four-times-great-grandfather Samuel Giles threatened to fly from his hands.

A growing sense of urgency compelled him to locate the land owned by his ancestors in this county. He packed a small suitcase, left a note for Janet, and drove down to the county seat of Linden. Twice during the two-hour trip from Birmingham, he nearly drove off the road when he dozed off. The nightmares continued even in the musty rented room in a tiny motel off the courthouse square. He spent the next morning at the courthouse, and fell asleep over the massive volumes of deeds and land descriptions until a probate office employee startled him awake.

Thunder rumbled in the distance like an unquiet stomach protesting a rich meal. I think that storm's going to snack on me next, Mark thought. He glanced over his shoulder at the white picket fence a few hundred yards away and shivered again. The fence enclosed the cemetery he'd somehow found on his last trip here with Natalie. No wonder we recognized the names on the tombstones, he realized. It's the churchyard closest to where the family lived.

He scuffed his boots across the dusty ground, breathing hard in the hothouse warmth. A bulldozer stood nearby, a spot of color in the darkening landscape. A large wooden sign at the edge of the excavated area proclaimed the new location of the Marengo College Library. According to the map, somewhere in the section was the house where James Giles grew up.

A sudden thunderclap drowned out his thoughts. Instinctively, he grabbed the knife in a scabbard on his belt, the knife left behind by his sister. As the wind strengthened, he relaxed his grip on the hilt and clutched his hair into a ponytail at the nape of his neck. Behind him the dark stand of pine trees gyrated, their sighing whispering on the wind. Mark walked closer to the center of the field. No matter which way he turned the sheet of paper, he couldn't orient himself. Thunder and lightning rent the air simultaneously with the scent of hot iron. A spray of rain rattled in his face, accompanied by another groan of thunder. The sky was one big bruise.

The wind snatched the sheet of paper from his grasp and whirled it across the field. He ran after it as rain slashed his face like sea spray, plastering his hair into a soggy helmet. At the edge of the field, he paused beside a puddle where the photocopy came to rest, floating on the deepening water. He squinted around for something to fish it out with before it disintegrated completely, and squatted to retrieve a peeled stick protruding from the muddy ground.

When he touched it, he knew it wasn't a stick. This is a bone, the words formed inside his head. A human bone.

His vision tunneled. A metallic hum echoed, volumed into a roar. His hands and knees slammed to earth, columns of pain. His teeth snapped shut. The roar clotted into bursts of sound, rising and falling in a familiar rhythmic pattern. Speech? His vision blanked. Warmth and wet soaked his left side from wrist to ankle.

Demarcus. You must listen t' me.

"Do I have a choice? Have I ever had a choice?"

This is important, damn it. You must stop her.

"Who? What's this all about? Who are you?"

I think you know who I am, Demarcus. I've been communicatin' with you, tryin' to help you understand the danger you're in.

"The visions--"

Yes. I tried talkin' to your father, but he wasn't as ... as able to hear me as you are. You have t' stop my sister an' her bitch teacher from workin' their evil magic. They cursed me, son, cursed us. All of us. An' you're the end a' the line. Do you realize you're dead in a few days?

Mark couldn't believe he was talking to whatever – whoever this voice was, but he couldn't seem to stop. "Well ... I got that implication ... How many days?"

I don't know. I don't know time anymore. It's like a big ol' red ink stain on your lifeline.

"How am I supposed to stop her?"

Do you have the watch, son?

"Dad's watch? Yeah ..."

It was mine. I gave it to my son when we shipped him off t' his aunt's, when the war started. All our blood is in that watch, all but mine--and yours. You gotta complete the chain.

"But--your blood? How do I do that?"

You'll know when you get to my cabin. That's where it all started. That's where it has ta' end.

"Your cabin? Excuse me for saying so, but you died in 1863. That cabin's probably not there anymore."

It's there, whether the timbers are still standin' or not. The ... the soul of it's there. Demarcus, I did a wicked thing, although I didn't know at the time how wicked. I thought she was a neighbor woman I'd ... dallied with. It was my own sister. My sister, Mark. No matter, either way I was wrongin' Alice. I must atone. The only way I know t' do that is to save you. Powerful forces are at work here. Powerful. If she succeeds in what she wants t' do, your body will be dead, but your soul will be hers forever. Like a slave. Worse. A slave could run away up North. You won't be able t' run nowhere. It'll be the second death.

"The second death?" The words seemed to echo, and he recognized them as his father's.

Don't you folks read the Bible in your time, son? The book a' Revelation. "An' the sea gave up the dead which were in it; an' death an' hell delivered up the dead which were in them: an' they were judged every man accordin' to their works. An' death an' hell were cast inta the lake of fire. This is the second death." She's judged us all, every one a' us Gileses, but accordin' t' my works. She'll use you t' gain her twisted pagan power, an' use you for her purposes until the end a' time. Bondage, son. Endless bondage.

"Okay, okay, you made your point! But if she's so powerful, how can I defeat her? Especially if I'm doomed to die."

She's not God, Demarcus. She's not omnipotent. There's a way. It'll take great sacrifice from you, more than you think you c'n bear--the ultimate sacrifice. You have power a' your own, maybe because you're a Giles. I had power too, which is why I'm talkin' t' you now, but I didn't have a chance to use it. You do. You must act, Demarcus. You already have somethin' that may help you fight against her. She left it for you without meanin' ta.

"But where was your cabin?" Mark stared around him.

North a' the Tennessee River, not far from Bolivar. Jackson County.

"Alabama?"

162

A' course Alabama.

"But you were buried here, weren't you?"

The house where I was born was right through them trees. Mother brought me back after my father died, had me buried here. She never really knew what happened between me an' Rebecca. Her mind was too pure to think a' such ugliness. All she knew was that my father hated me an' forbade me t' come home while he was alive. I never did.

"I'll do what I can."

You'll do what you think you can't, Demarcus. You're a Giles. Blood's more'n just somethin' t' hold your veins open. It's life an' kin an' love an' sorrow ... It's what makes you exist. It's what makes you real.

"Oh, God, not you, too. My father always used to say that." He could remember Thomas's words all too well.

Your father was a wise man, Demarcus. See if he didn't write some a' that wisdom down for you. It will help you defeat her. Remember my words, son. Remember ...

CHAPTER 33.

"I'm really not sure this is a wise course of action, Janet."

Daniel swung into an empty space, shifted the car into Park, and turned to face her. "You don't know how she might react, and she's on her own turf, so to speak."

Janet sighed, knotting her fingers in her lap. "I have to see her, Daniel. It's not really because I'm jealous ..."

She raised her eyes to his. "I don't think I feel any jealousy anymore. I'm scared for him, that he's in the clutches of someone who wants to use him ... Do you understand what I mean?"

He unfastened his seat belt. "I think I do. Does Mark know about the baby yet? It might change his attitude."

"No ... I haven't had a chance. He's been so damn obnoxious, I--Daniel!" She grabbed his arm. "There she is!"

"But how do you know--"

"I just do."

"Janet, don't--"

Ignoring him, she threw open the car door and flung herself across the library parking lot. "Excuse me, we need to talk."

The tall blonde-haired woman spun toward Janet, eyes wide and startled, the key in her hand poised over the lock. "Do I know you?"

"I'm Mark Richards' wife, Janet."

The other woman sagged against the car. "I've been working all day. I'm not in the mood for a confrontation."

"Has Mark been living at your house?" Janet stared into the dark green eyes, searching for a clue to this woman's power over her husband.

The woman stared back. "Yes."

The nausea Janet felt all morning settled into a knot in the pit of her stomach. "What do you want from him?"

A half-smile, half-smirk played across the other woman's lips. "I want," she brushed blonde strands from her face, "his soul."

The knot expanded into a wave of rage. Janet lunged toward Victoria, words pulsing out like bursts of water. "You can't have it."

"Too late. Technically, I already have it." Victoria laughed.

Her wave of rage became a brittle icy calm. "Do you mean you slept with him?"

"Oh, definitely. But not just that." She held out her hand, the knuckles pink with healing cuts. "We've been joined together. Forever."

"I don't understand," Janet said.

"My blood. His blood. Joined together. We are related, you know."

"If you hurt him--" Janet felt the rage, held by her cold calm, but still there.

"It was accidental. We rolled over a wineglass while making love. Does that upset you?"

Janet listened to her heart beat once, twice, again. This time she's gone too far, a voice in her head giggled. She sprang at those green eyes, dimly aware of arms flailing before her face, skin splitting on her knuckles, a shrill keening in the air. As she reached the end of the hazy black and red tunnel that engulfed her, something jerked her backwards.

"Janet! Stop it, Janet!"

Black and red sharpened into asphalt and blood. "Daniel?"

He pulled her away several steps. What was that white and purple and red thing on the ground? The giggle shrilled through her head again. Whoever was holding her arms behind her shook her. The edges of the image sharpened, resolved into Victoria's white face, blotched with purpling knots. The younger woman swiped at the red stream trailing across her lips, and hauled herself up on the fender of her car.

"Stay away from Mark," she heard herself hissing at Victoria.

The green eyes, one nearly swollen shut, burned into hers. "You'll pay for this, I swear you both will," she croaked through split and bloody lips. She winced as she jerked the car door open. "In four days, Mark is mine forever. And there's nothing you can do about it."

Within moments, the car roared away.

The pavement beneath Janet's feet turned to jelly. She sagged back against Daniel. He cradled her in his arms for a moment before leading her toward his car.

"Daniel--I actually--"

"Beat her to a bloody pulp, yes, I know."
"I've never, ever before--I don't know what--why I--"
She gave up trying to talk and collapsed against his chest.

~*~*~

For an instant, Mark looked down at himself from somewhere above. His body lay full length on his left side in the mud, arm flung over his head. His hair clung around his white face and blue lips. One hand clenched the sodden sheet of paper. His clothes were soaked through. With a bone-jarring thud, he fell back into his body and blinked up at the leaden gray sky.

The rain slowed to a drizzle. James' voice wallpapered the inside of his skull. He wanted to rationalize it away as just a dream or another vision, but he knew down where he stockpiled the realities that made him *him*, he had conversed with his great-great-great-grandfather, dead for one hundred forty-seven years.

This is all true, Mark thought. The visions, the tarot reading--Good thing Grandpappy Giles came to set you straight, otherwise you'd've dropped dead and never understood why.

He sat up in the squelching mud, shivering, and brushed against the scabbard at his waist. He pulled out the long, plain knife and studied it. James' words rang in his head: *You already have somethin' that may help you fight against her. She left it for you without meanin' ta.*

Mark stood, swaying, sheathed the knife, and crossed the sodden field to his car.

He found an old newspaper in the trunk to protect the seat from his mud-soaked legs. When he slid behind the wheel amid the crackle of paper, the lines on Sylvia's printout popped into his head. The cryptic letters and numbers meant something. "Terminal mr052110." Mark was certain the last day of his life was May 21, 2010. He had four days to live.

CHAPTER 34.

No one answered his repeated rings on the doorbell, although her car was in the driveway. He tried the knob and pushed open the unlocked door.

"Vic? You home?"

The house was silent except for the whump-whump of the ceiling fan in the living room and the squelch of his muddy shoes on the hardwood floor. "It's me! Your door was unlocked."

A thought kick-started his heart: What if Andrew's come by and done something to her--

He dashed toward the bedroom, catching the doorframe with both hands to stop his mad flight as he saw her sitting on the bed, her back to him. "Oh, thank God, you're all right," he breathed. "I was afraid Andrew had--"

She turned and he saw her swollen, purpling eye, and split lip. In one stride, he reached her, kneeling before her, heedless of his mud-caked pants.

"Who did this to you? Andrew? I don't care how big he is, he can't get away with--"

Her reply was faint and soft.

"I'm sorry, I didn't hear what you said."

She licked her lip. "Your wife did this to me."

Mark recoiled. "Janet? Janet did this to you?"

She nodded. Forming words was clearly painful. "They were waiting for me when I came out of work. She and that blond man. She attacked me for no reason."

Mark enfolded her in his arms and rocked her like a child.

Victoria pushed him away after a moment. "What happened? You're all muddy."

He clenched his fists. "Doesn't matter right now. She cannot get away with this."

~*~*~

Mark pounded the door with his fist, kicked it, rattled the knob. "Daniel! Let me in! I know she's in there!"

Finally the door swung open, and he glared up into Daniel's eyes. He scanned Mark up and down, but did not comment on his sodden appearance.

"What do you want?"

Mark pushed the taller man hard in the chest and stalked past him. "Where is she?"

Daniel grabbed his arm with one hand, shut the door with the other. "You do not need to see her with this attitude."

"Attitude? Oh, you haven't even begun to see attitude yet."

Mark shook off the restraining hand and strode into the living room. "She wasn't at home or at the bookstore, so she must be here. Where's she hiding?"

Daniel spoke quietly. "Sit down, Mark."

"I'm not going to--"

"I said," the taller man grabbed his shirt front, shoved him onto the couch, "sit down."

Mark's anger was replaced by sheer amazement. Where is the mild-mannered Daniel O'Brien, he wondered, and what have you done with him? T he psychic counselor sat on the low table. "Did it occur to you to ask what provoked Janet to attack Victoria?"

"She had no right--"

The other man cut him off. "Do you realize what you are entangled in? Victoria is evil. Do you understand me? Evil."

Mark's hands clenched, but Daniel's intense gaze warned him against standing. "You've got it all wrong. Victoria's not the threat. Rebecca is. Rebecca in the form of my sister."

"Victoria said you and she have been joined together by blood." His voice dropped to a whisper that drilled into Mark's brain. "And that in four days, you would belong to her. That your soul would be hers."

He felt his cheeks flush. "She's just trying to hurt Janet. That can't possibly be true ..."

"Do you remember what the cards held when I did the reading?" Daniel asked.

"Well ... yeah ..."

Daniel shook his head. "Obviously you didn't pay much attention to their message."

Mark squirmed under Daniel's holy glare. "You talked about temptation and black magic and--"

"Victoria is using you for some purpose, possibly some sort of sacrifice--"

"Sacrifice." The word set up an ache behind his eyeballs.

"The length of time she mentioned, four days, is obviously significant."

"It's sure as hell significant. That's my last day alive."

Daniel looked puzzled. "Why do you think that?"

Mark fished in his back pocket for his wallet, feeling the scabbard scrape against the side of his pants, and produced the folded printouts. His frown deepened as Daniel studied the water-stained sheet. "See that date? Terminal. That's me. James as much as confirmed it."

"James?"

"My great-great-great-grandfather. I spoke with him today." It didn't sound as funny as it should have.

Daniel's gaze was fixed on the wall as he said, "'It is his filthy descendent who will die soon. Except that I intend to kill him first and put an end to the Giles line forever.'"

Mark shuddered. "What?"

"During the séance when the spirit spoke through your sister--"

Daniel's voice faltered, and he shuddered. "That was one of the things she said. Mark--she was talking about you."

Mark's cheeks felt stiff and cold, as if he had dunked his head in ice water. "That explains why she tried to kill me that night," he whispered.

Daniel buried his head in his hands. "It's my fault--I let her come through--"

Mark picked up the two printouts from the floor where Daniel dropped them. "It's not your fault, man. It's Rebecca's fault. It's her hate that's caused all this."

Daniel sighed and looked at Mark. "You're right. I know that. It's just so hard--"

"To realize you're not perfect? Sorry, that's just something I've wanted to say since I met you." Mark handed the printouts back. "Do these have any other significance to you?"

"This is a diagram of psychic energy field fluctuations."

"Psychic energy field fluctuations." Mark repeated the words, but they meant nothing to him. The icy coldness had spread to his brain.

"I studied under Professor Stanley a few years ago. He specialized in studying psychic energy fields and produced diagrams resembling this. Where did you get this?"

"I printed it out at Victoria's guardian's house. She has a computer program that generates this stuff. But what does it have to do with--"

Mark snapped his fingers as a new idea occurred to him. "The curse. Is it possible a curse could ... I don't know, take on a life of its own?"

Daniel stood lithely and began pacing again, his Sherlock Holmes profile dark against the brightening light through the huge window. "Theoretically, it would create an energy field that could be mapped."

He stopped and stared at the printouts. "As you surmised, these numbers are obviously dates. The only ones known for certain would be the initial and terminal dates, with the other dates calculated by someone with remarkable stochastic abilities."

"That sounds like Miss Dee. She's apparently a math whiz."

"I would venture to guess, if you're correct, and the curse is an entity, an…energy force, someone's psychic energy and fury have been lending it strength through the decades… fueling it, as it were."

"That someone has to be Rebecca. Maybe she hasn't had enough power to do more than influence my ancestors' deaths until now," Mark suggested.

Daniel resumed pacing. "I am not sure her direct power caused or contributed to their deaths. The curse would take care of that. It's like--"

"Like she programmed it!" Mark leaped to his feet. "It's exactly like a computer program. Rebecca initiated the program by killing James and his wife, giving it the parameters, you know, something like, 'I curse thee down to the sixth generation.'"

"What is this, *Moby Dick*?" Daniel gave him a puzzled look.

"*Star Trek: the Wrath of Khan*, more likely. Anyway, after she's gone, the curse--or the program--keeps on running, killing people, and--"

"Adding their psychic energy to fuel it."

"Right! Then it's programmed to stop. With me." Mark dropped limply onto the couch, the meaning of his words striking him like a fist in the stomach. "The last line of the program is 'Kill Mark Richards and then terminate.' Or 'Terminate him and then terminate,'" he giggled.

The other man stared down at him. "I really think you're carrying this programming metaphor too far. But I'll play a little longer. How do you stop a computer program?"

Mark was still giggling. "Make it sing 'Daisy.'" He rolled on his side on the couch, more witty rejoinders reeling through his head.

"You're getting hysterical," Daniel warned, peering at him.

"Sorry, sorry." He wiped tears from his eyes, taking deep breaths. "Didn't you ever see *2001: A Space Odyssey*?"

"Do you always face adversity with old movie titles?"

170

Mark nodded. "Maybe I need a drink."

"This might help." Janet stood in the doorway, holding an old-fashioned glass with an inch of amber liquid in it.

"Were you eavesdropping?" Mark knocked back the contents of the glass and shuddered.

"Basically." She sat next to him, an arm's-length away. "Mark ... I'm sorry I hit your-- um, I'm sorry I hit her. I just completely lost it when she said you two had ... you know ..."

"She said that? To your face?"

Janet nodded, eyes shining wetly, bright against her pale skin.

The whiskey flushed his cheeks as he stammered, "Look, I--I didn't plan for that to happen, Janet. I had a horrible day and she was so ... so kind and ... and desirable ... And it's been so long since we--"

Janet took the glass from his hands and set it on the table. "I'm not really sure I want to hear this right now."

"I think you'd better tell me what happened between you," Daniel said.

Choosing his words carefully, Mark outlined the events of that night, about the strange wine, rolling over the glass, his intense vision. "Sounds like some sort of sacrament to me," Janet observed as he finished, her voice calm once more. "More binding than our wedding ceremony was."

"But Janet--"

"I'm serious, Demarcus. You shared wine, blood, other bodily fluids--"

The ice in her voice cracked on the last word.

He wiped his forehead with his sleeve. "I wonder how this fits in with the nightmares I've been having lately."

"Nightmares?" Daniel asked, leaning forward.

He recounted them in as much detail as he could remember while Daniel unfolded himself from his perch and paced across the room again. "I think it must be hereditary," Mark finished. "My mother mentioned my father having nightmares."

"Is that why you couldn't sleep?" Janet moaned. "Why didn't you tell me?"

The pain in her words intensified his despair, and he shrugged and looked away.

"The tornado dream is the more intriguing of the two." The man stopped and stroked his blond beard. "Let's talk about the second one first. Did it occur to you that Victoria may be causing these dreams?"

"Now why would she do that?" Mark demanded. "And how?"

"Have you retrieved your watch yet?" Daniel asked.

"No ..."

Daniel flicked him an exasperated look. "I warned you if she retained any of your possessions she would have power over you. She is more than likely enticing you to return to her by presenting Janet in a negative light. This woman is using you for some purpose."

Daniel sat on the edge of the lacquer table again. "I think the tornado dream is linked with the other dream, although not directed by her. I think it signifies that your ancestors have been sacrificed--are being sacrificed--to this curse."

"So what do I do now?"

"I'll reiterate my earlier question," Daniel answered, "and hope to get a slightly more constructive answer. How do you stop a computer program once it's running?"

"Well ..." Mark stood up, claustrophobic between Janet and Daniel, and paced to the window. "You introduce an element it doesn't expect. Confuse it. Captain Kirk did it enough times--sorry, Daniel. No movie or TV references," he said. "Introduce a virus. Convince it to commit suicide--"

Suicide? The word reverberated in his head, oddly familiar.

"Mark?" Janet frowned at him.

"No, I'm okay. I just thought of something, but I'm not sure what it means yet."

Daniel reclaimed Mark's attention. "Did James have any advice?"

He slid the knife from the scabbard and held it up. "He said to use this."

"Where did you--"

"It's what Natalie tried to kill me with," Mark explained. "She left it behind when Andrew dragged her away. James said it would help me fight against her, that she left it for me without meaning to."

Daniel pressed him for details, and Mark dutifully recounted his conversation with his dead relative. "He said he wasn't sure how much time I have left--but I think Sylvia's charts make it obvious," he sighed, closing his eyes. "I guess now wouldn't be a good time to renew my subscription to *Computer Gaming World*."

"Don't joke about this," Janet said.

"Do you have any better suggestions?"

Daniel leaped up. "Sylvia! That's where I have heard that name."

"What? You've heard of her?"

"What is her last name?" Daniel asked.

"Dee."

"When I studied with Professor Stanley," Daniel said, "he was researching a pioneer in energy field research, although it certainly wasn't called that in her time. Her name was Sylvia de Graffenried, and she was a mathematical genius who was said to be able not only to forecast events with her calculations of the energy fields, but to actually influence them."

Mark thought for a moment. "Can you call this professor? Find out where this woman lives? Maybe it's her."

"Not possible. Professor Stanley passed on several years ago. I think I have a book somewhere in my library that discusses her and her theories."

Mark stood and stretched. "Well, I can't spend my last ninety-something hours on earth sitting around speculating."

Janet's face twisted in alarm.

"If I can think of any way to help you, I'll call you. Where will you be? At Victoria's?" Daniel's arms were folded in that Old Testament prophet look he should get royalties for.

Mark swallowed. "No, my mother's. I think my dad was trying to tell us something all those years, and I need to find out what it was. I guess I'll end up at James' cabin. If you come looking for my--"

He cleared his throat. "--for my body, it'll be there, if his cabin still is. If it's not still there, who knows where I'll be?"

Tears streamed down Janet's face. She wrapped her arms around Mark. "Don't say that," she said. "We'll think of something."

Mark wiped away her tears and smiled at her. "Thanks, Janet, but I'm not too optimistic, given my family's track record."

He kissed her and walked out.

~*~*~

Janet dropped to the couch, wondering, How can this be happening to us? She rested her hand on her abdomen. What kind of world am I bringing a child into?

The front door slammed. Daniel sat down next to Janet. "He's very scared right now, but he puts up a brave front."

"He always does. Isn't there anything we can do? I feel so helpless just sitting here."

He scratched his bearded chin. "I really need to find out more about this de Graffenried woman. Why don't I cook us a quick supper and then you can help me with the research?"

"Sure," she said, nodding. "It sounds like a plan."

After a meal of vegetarian stir fry and steamed rice, they piled the dishes in the sink and headed for Daniel's study. Bookshelves lined every available wall surface, crammed with paper- and hardbound books from pamphlet to unabridged dictionary size. Even the desk held a small two-shelf bookcase.

"I thought Mark and I owned a lot of books," Janet said. "Have you read all of these?"

"Not every word of every one," the man admitted. "I've only skimmed some of them."

"So where do we start?"

"I'm looking for *Psychic Energy Field Theory* by Meyer. It's a red book, about half an inch thick."

She stooped to read the titles, running her finger across the spines. "*Secrets of the Golden Dawn* by Anastasia Sunstone--Great name, huh? *Channels of Life* by T. P. Mitchell. *Rosicrucian Doctrine and the Expectation of Divinity* by Madame Z. I won't even comment on that one." Janet laughed, stretching to read a title on the top shelf. "*Mystic Origins of the Tarot* by Oscar ... Richards ..."

She trailed off, the smile vanishing, and sank to the floor.

"Are you all right?" Daniel knelt beside her.

"I'm just thinking about Mark and all he's going through." She rubbed her belly.

"If we find that book, you won't have to worry. It--Ah, here it is."

The volume was indeed as he had described it. He opened it, crossing his legs into a lotus position while thumbing through the pages.

"--Sylvia."

"What? I'm sorry, I wasn't listening."

"'Sylvia de Graffenried was an unsung pioneer in energy field experimentation. She was a gifted mathematician who perfected a technique for forecasting events as well as influencing their outcome. After the publication of her pamphlet *The Influence of the Mind in Predicting Future Occurrences* created a storm of controversy in Massachusetts, she disappeared from the public eye, becoming a teacher and tutor in Alabama, Georgia, and Tennessee.'"

Daniel fell silent.

Janet looked up. "What is it?"

"This next sentence is rather interesting."

Daniel glanced at Janet, cleared his throat, and read, "'Miss de Graffenried is thought to have died in 1875.'"

CHAPTER 35.

Mark parked the car in the driveway at his mother's house and sat a moment, wondering how to break the news that her only living son would be dead in three days.

Simple. By not telling her.

Delia Richards held him at arm's-length and surveyed him critically. He knew that look and could almost mimic her words before she said them. "What happened to you? Have you been rolling in the mud? Your clothes are filthy. And you don't look well. Have you been getting enough sleep, Demarcus?"

"Mom, did Dad ever keep a journal?"

Delia folded her arms. "His therapist encouraged him to, but, you know your father ..."

"Mind if I look through his things in the study? It's ... sort of important."

"Help yourself," Delia answered. "You can take a shower, too, while you're up there. Some of your old clothes are in the closet in the spare room. Can you stay to dinner? Natalie will be back soon and--"

"Natalie? When will she be here?"

His mother sighed. "Fifteen, twenty minutes. Who can tell with your sister?"

"Mom, has she seemed... well...normal to you lately?"

"She's tired and run down after her exams, if that's what you mean."

Mark shrugged. "No, I--Never mind. We'll chat about it later." He dashed up the stairs, two at a time, dragging himself to a halt in the doorway. His heart thumped hard once in his chest as he saw the train set again. I always thought I'd inherit his stuff when he died, but now ... who'll inherit from me? he wondered.

The bookshelves lining the room were crammed with papers and notebooks and boxes rather than actual books. Mark sat in the squeaky desk chair and frantically plowed through the debris. After clearing off one shelf and finding nothing, he stopped. This isn't working. Use your alleged brain, he chided himself.

Now if I were Dad's journal, where would I be? He laughed. Probably propping up the corner of the train set. His thoughts trailed off as he realized there actually was a thin, hardbound book under the left corner of the base of the setup.

He slid it out carefully so the delicate buildings and snaking track and tiny pedestrians would stay intact. Across the front of the blue notebook were large ballpoint-written letters proclaiming, "CHEM 100, Property of Mark Richards, Mr. Mattacks' home room."

Inside, the first third of the book was devoted to long-forgotten equations and red Xs. After that, Mark's high school scrawl became his father's sprawling script. Dated entries covered a period of ten years, skipping weeks and even months between writings. The first, written a week before Tommy's death, merely said, "Purchased new CSX engine. Added trees and stream." The next was dated August 1, 1999, two weeks after the accident ending his brother's life. The day of Thomas Richards' first suicide attempt.

"The truth is evident to me now," Mark read, deciphering the shaky letters. "Tommy's death woke me from this fantasy world I was living in. I can deny it no longer."

The next sentence was written in heavily-inked capital letters: "I murdered every one of my brothers and sisters. Mother was right," the shaky cursive resumed. "The curse is real. I had no memory of the deeds, though I often wondered that I was present for every death. Now that I am responsible for," the last three words were crossed out and after them written, "have murdered my own son, I must find a way to end it. Before I kill again."

Mark's hands shook so much reading was difficult. He leaned the notebook on the table edge and scanned the remaining entries, stopping at an almost illegible one toward the end.

"May 20, 2008. I don't know what else to try. How amazing that it's so difficult to end one's life. Life persists. The curse persists. I couldn't save Tommy and I can't save Demarcus. The closest I came was the blood route--I almost sensed it breaking then. This must be part of the curse, the inability to stop it. I live in fear the symptoms will manifest in Demarcus, and the end will be worse than it has ever been before. He is the seventh generation from the curse, according to my mother. He is the one who will either end the curse--or be destroyed by it. I cannot bear to tell him he must end his life by his own hand. He's been so ashamed of me. But he's beyond listening to me now."

Mark wanted to scream. He wanted to cry. He wanted to tear his heart from his chest to stop its frantic beating. Instead he gripped the slim blue notebook before him in both hands like a shield, and walked down the stairs to the kitchen.

His mother was pulling a dish of steaming macaroni and cheese from the oven. As she caught sight of him, she almost dropped the casserole, lowering it to the top of the stove with a cry. "Demarcus? Are you ill? Your face--"

"Mom. Why didn't you tell me? You must've known." The cardboard edges of the notebook scored his fingers. He gripped it tighter as the only tangible thing in the universe.

She drew off the oven mitt and turned away. "You didn't need to know."

"Didn't. Need. To know."

His body sagged as he felt rage simmering through his veins. He scaled the notebook across the table like a Frisbee. It smashed a glass tumbler into the wall in a shower of glittering shards. "Didn't need to know? That my father was a serial killer? That it's hereditary?"

"Demarcus--"

He seized the dish of macaroni. The hot glass sizzled against his skin as he imagined himself heaving it toward the wall, imagined the glass and pasta exploding outward--but he didn't throw it. Instead he set the casserole back on the stove, curled his seared hands to his chest, and sank to his knees.

"Mom--" he whispered, his throat so tight. "I needed--to know."

He sobbed as she picked up a tube of aloe vera from the counter and knelt beside him. The cream soothed his burns as she spoke softly.

"As far as I can tell, Mark," his mother said, "this is the first time you've cried since the funeral...since I can't remember when. You're so much like him, whether you believe that or not. He kept things inside him. I guessed the truth, long before he ever said anything about it, and his mother confirmed it. I thought it was long over, some childhood aberration--until Tommy died. I knew--I don't know how I knew-- your father killed him. It was no accident. But no one else ever suspected."

"I read--" Mark took a deep, shuddering breath. "I read in the notebook...the day he ran his car into tree...he realized what happened, that he'd killed Tommy."

"He was so afraid the curse would settle on you, that you'd start killing as well."

Mark pulled himself up on the oven door, wincing as the handle scraped his burned hands. "But he could have told me ..."

"Would you have listened?" Delia asked. "To anything he had to say?"

"The family he thought was so important to remember ... he couldn't remember he'd killed them. God, no wonder he tried to commit suicide all those times. His link to the past betrayed him." He wiped his eyes with the back of his hand. "Thanks, Mom."

"Thank you for not destroying dinner." A glimmer of a smile sparkled in her eyes as she climbed to her feet. "I'm so sorry, Demarcus. We should have told you sooner."

He kissed her on the cheek. "Now I know what I have to do."

He retrieved the notebook from behind the table and brushed shards of broken glass from it. "I'll clean this up for you."

"No, don't worry about it. I'll take care of it." She grabbed his shoulders as he passed. "Don't follow in your father's footsteps, Mark. Don't give in. Fight it."

"Believe me, Mom, if there's another way, I'll take it." He smiled and hugged her. But he didn't think there was.

~*~*~

Janet echoed the last phrase Daniel read. "'*Thought* to have died?' How mysterious. Wait a minute--*eighteen* seventy-five? Then ... she can't be the same person ... can she?"

Daniel didn't answer, but said, "The author goes on to discuss her theories, including one that a curse, when properly bestowed, takes on physical form, creating its own energy field that acts to perpetuate itself. It then feeds on the life energy of its victims, strengthening until it totally annihilates the object of the curse."

"But how do you stop it?"

"I'm not sure." He flipped over several pages, grunting to himself. "Here it is."

He leaned back against the desk and read aloud, "'Many theories have been advanced for the counteraction of the energy field created by a curse. The essential point is that in no circumstance should any negative energy be contributed to the field. For example, any acts of violence committed within the field will contribute to the strength of the field, increasing exponentially the amount of power required to negate it.'

"'Destruction of the field is accomplished through entrance to that field, location of the center, usually an astral body or spirit generating the field, and expulsion of the body from the field through the direction of personal psi energy.' That seems clear enough."

"I'm glad you understand it." She climbed to her feet.

"This is fascinating. He has an appendix giving more biographical information on Sylvia de Graffenried. She was a devotee of Isis--although no Isis cult I'm familiar with--and was extremely interested in brother-sister incest and its connection to the development of psychic power. The author quotes from another of her pamphlets about the joining ceremony in which the blood of two related individuals--it doesn't have to be as close as brother and sister--is exchanged, imbuing them with incredible amounts of power. 'It is also during the joining that the spirit is vulnerable to usurpation,' he writes here. 'The body of one of the individuals participating in the ceremony of joining may be taken over, permanently evicting the spirit and transferring the power to the new owner.'"

"How weird. I--"

She sniffed the air. "Do you have something on the stove?"

"No." His attention remained focused on the book.

"Maybe we forgot to turn off the burner. I'll go check."

An acrid tang hung in the air as she neared the kitchen. She glanced up at the smoke alarm in the hallway, thinking, Can't be anything too serious, or that would've gone off.

She slipped into the room. The smell was stronger, but the stove was off. A faint eddy of cigarette smoke hazed the ceiling. Janet noticed more smoke wafting from under the cellar door.

~*~*~

Daniel set the book on the desk. Janet should've been back by now. Halfway down the hall, he swayed with an onslaught like a scream in his mind, braced himself against the wall before his knees buckled. The vein in his right temple throbbed as pain arrowed through his skull. He staggered into the kitchen.

Wisps of smoke swirled near the kitchen ceiling. Now he heard a muffled banging from the other side of the door, and Janet's voice screaming his name. "Daniel, the door's stuck! There's a fire--"

"Coming, Janet! Com--"

Her terror snaked through his head, winding tighter and tighter, filling his senses, overflowing until it was all he could hear, all he could experience. He jackknifed to the floor, struggling to fortify his defenses against the psychic assault. Through the glittering, agonizing fog, Daniel saw the source of the assault standing over him. He reached out with one trembling hand, his psyche an actinic flare of pain, his body a bow strung too tightly, bending double.

With a twang the string snapped, and he catapulted into the black vortex of oblivion.

~*~*~

Andrew laughed, high with the rush of absolute power swelling his chest.

"Miss Dee will be very pleased tonight," he said aloud. "Strike one, strike two. And Mark Richards will be strike three."

He dropped the cigarette in the sink with a smile at the rattling doorknob, stepped over O'Brien's inert body, and strode from the house.

~*~*~

Mark was so wrapped up in his thoughts, he'd turned off the ignition and climbed out of the car before he realized he was parked at Victoria's house. She's got me on auto-pilot already. I didn't develop that with Janet until months after we were married. He chuckled, remembering the angry expression on his wife's face when he tried to explain why he kept ending up at his mother's house after work.

"No, honest, I'm not trying to avoid you. I keep forgetting I live here. My auto-pilot hasn't kicked in yet."

She was waiting for him in the bedroom. Shades of green and purple splashed her right eye and cheek, and narrow scabs zippered her lip and neck. "Thank you for coming back, Mark," she whispered as she peeled his stiff, dirt-caked shirt from his body.

He laid the notebook on the antique dresser and unbuckled his pants, setting the scabbard atop the notebook. "I didn't have a choice, did I?"

"You've always had a choice in this, Mark." She dropped the shirt beside the closet door and knelt to untie his boots. "I haven't coerced you in any way."

A penny clanged against the wood and rolled to the floor as he dug the change out of his pockets. "Is that part of the ritual, for you to say that?"

Her fingers dug into his bare arms. "Hear me, Mark. You made the choice yourself. You don't have to be here. You're free to leave any time you want." Her voice was husky, and her lip trembled. "You cannot blame this part on someone else. Granted, there are forces at work outside your control--but you're here with me of your own free will."

He snatched his arm from her grasp and rummaged through his suitcase for a clean pair of boxer shorts. "I don't believe that."

"I think it's time you faced the truth, Mark. You have to decide whose

180

side you're on. You have to make that decision. Your feelings for me have nothing to do with the curse. When you accept it, the next few days are no longer your fate, but your decision. *You* will be the one in control, Mark. *Not* Sylvia. *Not* the curse. *You.*"

Mark didn't look at her. "It's just semantics. I can't avoid dying by Sylvia's hand, can I?"

Her eyes were intensely green, her lips compressed. "We've been over this before, darling. *I* will have the power. *I* will decree who lives and dies. When we are formally joined, you will not be the one dying, I swear to you."

"Victoria. I think ..."

He took a deep breath. "I think in spite of everything that's happened, in spite of Daniel's warnings and my common sense, I may be seriously in love with you."

Her expression did not change. "That is your decision. I have not forced you to say it." She kissed him and smiled. "You know I love you, Mark."

CHAPTER 36.

Tuesday, May 18.

Mark stretched and pulled the sheet up over his nakedness. He glanced at the blonde hair and the pale limbs of the woman beside him and rolled on his side away from her. *Why did I make love to her again? I know what she is, what she'll do to me, but I want her now more than ever,* he groaned.

And I actually told her I love her. Which I do.

I think.

He lay still as she molded herself against him. Her breasts were warm against his back, her thighs wet on the backs of his thighs. Desire stirred inside him again. He bit down hard on his lip until he tasted blood, trying to convince himself that she was manipulating him, no matter how much she tried to deny it. *In four days--*

He glanced at the clock beside the bed. *In three days, she and Sylvia are going to kill you. She's not irresistible.*

"No, Victoria," he snapped, clenching his fists.

Her lips brushed his ear. "Mark ... you don't realize the power we'll share. We'll be together forever. You'll control the future--and the past, if that's what you want."

He sat up, rubbing his ear. "Okay, what is the deal with this power stuff?"

"I don't know what you mean." She yawned and stretched, toes pointed beneath the sheet and hands reaching for the headboard and body arching.

Mark blinked, but said, "Oh, don't give me that empty-headed bimbo crap. I may have only known you for, what is it, two weeks? But I know you well enough to figure out you're not the mindless seduction machine you try to pretend you are. If you don't know exactly what this power trip is about, you've got a pretty shrewd idea."

Victoria sighed and sat up against the headboard, tucking the sheet up over her breasts. "Okay. Here's the party line. 'Victoria,'" she began in a fair imitation of Sylvia's voice, "'you will be the instrument of Rebecca's revenge. You will join with the terminal ancestor and control time and space, blah blah blah.' That's all she'd tell me."

"Did you ask?" Mark prompted.

"I asked. As you said, I'm not stupid. Well, I was pretty stupid until about six months ago. I was pretty angry when she made me seduce Andrew—" She saw his look and shook her head, blonde hair flying. "No, don't say it. Turns my stomach too. I took my mind off cruise control and started puzzling over this. From what I can determine, the curse generates an energy field, which she measures with her computer program. There's a special chip in it she got God-knows-where. The field originated through the negative psychic energy of Rebecca, who killed someone to whom she was already linked psychically, i.e., her brother. With me so far?"

Mark nodded, crossing his legs under the sheet and leaning on his elbows. "I think so."

"Okay. She was also linked to him by semen--sorry, am I shocking you?"

"No, 'fraid not. I've sort of gotten used to that particular family aberration."

Victoria smiled and went on. "According to something I found in one of Sylvia's books, *The Tenets of Isis*, the remaining step is the joining by blood and wine."

"Like what we did."

She cocked her head and looked at him sideways. "Well, yes, I guess so. But the formal ceremony has not yet been performed. Anyway, I haven't exactly figured out the physics of it, but the interaction of all these links with the temporal-spatial qualities of the curse field itself releases a tremendous burst of energy--"

Mark stopped her. "I think you lost me there. Temporal-spatial?"

"Time and space. The curse originated at a specific time in a specific place, but transcends time and space in ever-increasing spheres of influence as it increases in power. This resulting energy burst will allow for all sorts of amazing power transfers. Personally, I think it creates an alternative universe that--"

"Whoa," he objected, resting his hand on her thigh. "You're getting way too science fiction-y for me."

She put her hand over his for a moment. "Are you sorry you asked?"

"No. I'm tired of people keeping secrets from me. So you don't plan to kill me?"

She laughed and slid her arms around his waist. "Why would I do that? I told you I love you. Besides, you're much more entertaining alive." Her tongue traced the curve of his ear. "After that little joining ceremony, you'll be my ... consort."

"Don't you mean your property?" He frowned.

"What's the difference? Does it really matter? Let go, Mark, just let it happen. You told me you wanted to control the past, right? Besides, we love each other. Why fight it?"

She trailed a fingernail down the middle of his chest, over his stomach. He shivered, pinned her shoulders to the headboard and buried his tongue in her mouth.

~*~*~

"Because I don't have to go to work," Mark answered, shrugging into a short-sleeved shirt, his back to her. "My boss suggested I take an extended leave of absence without pay."

"She fired you?" Victoria stepped into his field of vision.

"No. But she might as well have."

She pointed to his chest. "Your shirt's buttoned wrong. Why are you getting dressed?"

"Because I have three days to live. I can't spend this entire day making love to you."

"Why not?"

He pulled on his pants, and threaded the scabbard through his belt. "It's very tempting, don't get me wrong. But I intend to do something to stop this curse."

"Sweetheart, I thought we settled this last night." She wrapped her arms around his neck. "Just relax and let go. You have nothing to worry about."

"I can't just relax and let go. I have to try to do something. For once in my life. If it doesn't work out, then maybe I'll relax." He slipped his wallet into his pocket and reached for the pile of change on the dresser.

She darted her hand toward the tiny gold charm amid the coins. "You found it! I've looked everywhere for this. It was a gift from Sylvia."

Mark stared at the charm, trying to remember where it came from. The memory left him feeling as if someone punched him hard in the solar plexus. Sweat sprang out on his forehead. "Victoria, I found that in Helena ... by the railroad tracks ..."

He gasped for air. "It was hung on a scrap of paper with my--with my

184

father's handwriting on it ..."

A scene from his childhood flashed in his head. Natalie was five years old. Mark walked into her room where she was playing with one of his mother's cherished porcelain figurines along with her Barbie dolls. At the instant he walked in, the figurine slipped to the floor and shattered. The expression on her face was the one Victoria wore as she clutched the charm. "Mark ..."

He sagged back against the dresser. "No, please don't bother to deny it. You were with him in the café." He wrapped his arms around his stomach. "I am unbelievably thick-headed. I should have seen it. Just answer me truthfully. Did you kill my father?"

He watched her voluptuous lips, almost mouthed along with her as she said, "Yes, Mark. I killed your father."

Mark swayed, catching himself with his arms flung out behind him against the dresser.

"You aren't going to protest it was an accident, are you?" he asked, his voice flat.

Victoria shook her golden hair. "No, it was intentional."

She dropped the charm into the pocket of her robe. "But I did it for his own good, honest. I cared very much about your father, Mark. That's what attracted me to you. You're so much like him."

He was sliding, rolling down an icy mountain slope. "So," he whispered, barely moving his numb lips. "My mother was right. He was having an affair. With you."

Victoria talked very fast. "He was an assignment at first, nothing more. Sylvia sent me to seduce him, to gain his confidence. He was the next Giles in line, maybe the last, for all we knew. That's how I found out about you. He told me all about you."

His whole body went numb. "But ... but you killed him."

"I swear to you, Mark Richards, it was the hardest thing I've ever had to do. I can't tell you how many times I've relived the moment he fell--okay, that I pushed him under the train. I had to kill him--so he wouldn't kill the rest of his family--"

Mark staggered toward the bathroom and vomited up his breakfast. His stomach continued to heave long after nothing remained but bile. He hung over the edge of the toilet, watching sweat drip down from his face into the water. I've slept with the woman who murdered my father. Not once, but repeatedly. And enjoyed it. And fell in love with her.

It was so obvious. Why didn't I see it?

He wiped his mouth with the back of his hand.

He was proud of his calmness as he walked back into the bedroom. She was sitting on the edge of the bed, tying the satin belt of her robe into knots. He sat next to her and put on his socks and boots. "You said you killed him so he wouldn't kill the rest of his family. He told *you* about killing his brothers and sisters? You? His mistress." He spat the words out, twisting away from her grasp and striding to the doorway. "He never told *me.*"

Mark heard her calling after him as he slammed the front door and climbed into his car.

Mark let himself into the house, calling his wife's name, and peering around the door. The air smelled of Lysol and cinnamon and vanilla candles. She was nowhere to be seen. He wondered what time it was, patted his pocket, and realized Victoria still had his watch.

He dialed the bookstore number and Daniel's house, but got the answering machine both places. Mark unfolded the copies of Civil War era maps he'd photocopied in the library after leaving Victoria. One showed Bolivar—the location James mentioned—located between Stevenson and Bridgeport, three or four miles north of the Tennessee River. The other was a more detailed map, "Sketch of Reconnaissance from Stevenson to Cross' Island, at Mouth of Crow Creek." There were enough landmarks in the form of creeks, islands, ponds, and springs that Mark hoped he would be able to find the general area.

After refolding the maps, he leafed through his father's journal, re-reading the section about his attempts at suicide. The words echoed in his head as if he was hearing Thomas Richards speaking them. So, Mark thought, if I don't kill myself, I will kill my family without even realizing it. Or maybe that ceremony involves my conversion to mass murderer.

He stretched out on the couch, staring at the ceiling. My father thought by killing himself, he could prevent the curse from passing to me. He was wrong. Then he met someone who actually made him happy. She killed him.

I met someone who made me happy. Now my alternatives are to kill myself, wait until I axe-murder Mom and Natalie, wait until Victoria kills me, or wait until I drop dead from the curse. Or some combination of the above.

Ah, the smorgasbord of choices.

He rolled off the couch and stood, fists clenched. No, he thought. I'm not going to just wait to be killed or drop dead. At least I can do some damage on the way out--really give them a reason to kill me. He paced across the carpet.

How do you stop a computer program? Maybe you erase its hard drive?

The shrilling of the phone broke into his plotting. "Hello?"

"Mr. Richards? This is Penny, from the bookstore? I'm so sorry to hear about Janet and Mr. O'Brien, and I wanted to find out how they're doing.

She's not home from the hospital already, is she?"

Mark gaped into the phone.

"Hello?" The girl's voice returned his attention to the phone.

"Yeah, I'm here, Penny. Hospital? What are you talking about?"

"You don't know? Mr. O'Brien's house caught on fire and--"

"What hospital?" Mark broke in.

"St. Vincent's."

He hung up without another word, dug out the phone book and called the hospital. "Janet Richards' room, please."

"Hello?" Her voice was hoarse.

"Jan? My God, what happened? Are you all right?"

"Sort of. Daniel's house caught fire. I smelled smoke in the cellar and went to check on it, and the door got stuck--"

She broke off to cough. "I don't know what happened after that. I woke up here."

"How's Daniel? Janet?"

Her voice was thin and tight. "I heard Daniel's voice calling to me, and then ... nothing. They found him unconscious in the kitchen. He's in a coma."

CHAPTER 37.

"I find it hard to believe this is a coincidence, Jan," Mark said.

Her face was pale as she sat on the hospital bed, feet dangling off the side. "Who would want to hurt Daniel--or me?"

"What were you doing when it happened?"

She paused, coughing before answering. "Researching Sylvia de Graffenried."

"That's why," Mark said. "She must have known and didn't want you to discover the truth about her."

Janet leaned back against the pillow. "But it can't be the same woman. The one Daniel was researching died in 1875."

"I'm beginning to believe just about anything at this point." He wandered to the window and looked out over the parking lot far below. "Victoria killed my father."

A squeaky cart rolled down the hall. An electronic voice paged a doctor.

Mark jumped at the sound of her voice when Janet finally said, "She killed him? And this is the woman you can't seem to stay away from?"

He whirled. She stared at him, eyebrows halfway up her forehead. He felt an irrational urge to defend Victoria. "But she said she did it to protect us--"

"Oh, come on, Demarcus. What are you saying--that she did it for his own good?"

"Well, no--uh--"

Janet lowered her head, peering up at him through her eyelashes. "You don't--you're not in love with her, are you?"

"No, I'm not." He sagged against the windowsill. "Okay, maybe I am. Or I thought so. I don't know anymore."

"Daniel warned you, you know."

He nodded. "Yeah, and this is your polite and tactful way of telling me 'I told you so.'"

She took his hand. "Let's see how Daniel is. Then I have something I need to tell you."

~*~*~

The man lying on the bed was hardly recognizable as Daniel. His face was pale, furrowed as if studying some inscrutable document.

"The doctor's not sure what's wrong with him. I was treated for smoke inhalation, but he had no signs of it. They can't find anything wrong. He's just ... just comatose."

Mark paced to the tiny window and stared out. Daniel's view was more impressive than Janet's, and he couldn't enjoy it. "This must have something to do with the psychic attacks Dan complained about," he said.

"He looks so ... so fragile."

Mark peered over his shoulder at his wife. Might as well clear this up now, he thought, summoning his courage. Last chance. He cleared his throat twice before swinging toward her. "Jan ... are you in love with him?"

Her whispered reply jolted him more than an ear-splitting scream. "Yes, Mark. I am." She stared at him with glistening eyes. "And I think I always have been."

"So ... you never really ..." He cleared his throat again. "Never really loved me."

"I'm not sure." She peered at the man in the bed as if judging how much she should say in front of him. "I never should have--no, never mind."

"Never should have married me?" He thought after Victoria's revelation he was too numb to feel anything. He was wrong.

Janet wheeled toward him. "I mean for your sake, Demarcus."

This suicide idea was becoming easier to contemplate. He chewed the inside of his cheek, and sagged against the windowsill. "I understand," he said. "I'll even save you the cost of divorce proceedings. I'll be dead in three days, so you won't have to worry."

"Demarcus!" She stamped her foot.

"What? One way or another I'll be out of the picture." His voice was matter-of-fact. "Current thinking on the subject indicates I should off myself to cancel the curse. I have some ideas on how to short-circuit this thing, but I'm not real sanguine about my chances."

She trembled. "Now just stop it! You're trying to guilt trip me."

"No, I'm really not," Mark said, surprised to realize he wasn't lying, to her or himself. "If anyone's going on that particular cruise, it should be me. I screwed up royally, and now I have to live with--and die with--the consequences."

He grasped his wife's hands. "Janet, I am sincerely sorry for all the pain I've caused you, but I don't think that's nearly enough. I have to ... I have to atone for my sins ... and maybe I'll come back from it alive and maybe I won't."

Her face was so lovely and pale and sad.

"I'm not sure what you mean, but killing yourself won't solve anything," Janet said.

"Not according to my father--and my great-great-great grandfather. But Sylvia and Victoria can't kill me without a fight. I have an idea that might work. Emphasis on *might*."

"Mark, don't do anything crazy."

"No, I think it's about time I *did* do something crazy. Haven't you been telling me since the day I met you I should take charge of my life and *make* something happen? Well, this is it. I'm taking charge." His heart beat faster as the numbness gave way to anger. "I may not have anything to live for, but I'll give them something to kill me for."

She stared up at him. "What on earth are you planning?"

He leaned against the windowsill, his back to her. "I'm going to try to stop the curse. Just a little computer work. Don't worry. There's very little danger. I just plan to make some people very unhappy. Mind if I help myself to some tools from the house?"

"Do you need me there?" Janet asked.

The tiny cars far below reminded him of his father's train layout, distant and uncomplicated. Yes, I really do, he wanted to say. I need your strength and hardheadedness and sense of reality. "No, better not. I don't think it'll be dangerous, but you never know."

Mark kissed Janet gently on the lips and stepped to Daniel's side, taking his hand. The fingers were icy cold. "Sorry you can't hear me, man, but this happened because of me, and--"

A peculiar sensation flooded through his body, his nerves tingling and prickling.

"Mark? What's wrong?"

Janet's voice was a distant buzz. He felt a pressure deep in the recesses of his mind, sensed a consciousness floating aimlessly nearby.

Dan? What happened to you?

A psychic attack of some sort. I've never felt anything like it before. I just can't find my way back. All the landmarks have disappeared. Help me, Mark.

But I don't know how to help you. I'm not a psychic.

You have a power of your own. That's why Victoria is drawn to you, why she needs you. Stretch out to me. Give me a line.

What, "use the force, Luke"?

Your humor is a good shield, but you cannot use it against everything. Help me, Mark. I'm growing weaker and weaker.

An image surged into his mind: a man with feet firmly planted, hair blowing wildly, standing on a promontory overlooking a crashing surf. It was himself, he realized who defied the howling wind and gathered it in to himself, transforming it into flashes of silver. He perceived a drowning man far below, helpless in the ferocious and chaotic sea. Awkwardly at first, then with growing confidence, he wove the silver flashes of the wind into a rope and hurled it out to the man, praying it would reach him before the waves dragged him under for the final time.

He lost sight of the man for the space of several heartbeats, until a fierce tug on the rope almost pulled him over the edge. He saw a flailing arm as the drowning man bobbed to the surface. Sweat and salt spray drenched his face and neck and arms as he hauled on the rope with all his might. Sparks of silver flashed off the rope as it scraped on the cliff edge, igniting tufts of sea grass in transitory flares. His arm muscles wrapped with strands of pain until he thought he could no longer bear it--and the man's hand appeared over the top of the promontory.

"Demarcus?" Janet peered at him, puzzled. "What are you doing?"

He still held Daniel's hand.

Is it my imagination, he thought, or does he feel warmer?

"I'm not quite sure," Mark murmured. "I think I helped him find his way back to himself." He released Daniel's hand and stepped back with a shrug. "Although I don't know if it worked. He thrust his trembling hands in his pockets. "I'd better go now. If I'm successful, I'll let you know. Take care, Janet."

"Mark, before you go, I have something to tell you. This isn't really the best time, but there might not be ..."

She studied the linoleum. "Mark, I'm pregnant. You're going to be a father."

He stared at her, wondering when the English language became such a difficult concept. "I don't understand ... How--When--"

"I won't take up the 'how' part. You were there. I think you know how. 'When' is ten weeks ago. About a week before your first blackout."

"How long have you known?"

She shrugged. "Since all your testing. The time never seemed right, and then you left"

"You're sure."

"Oh, yes." She twined her fingers across her stomach protectively.

He sagged back against the bed. "I can't process this, Janet. It's not sinking in. I've had a lot of shocks today--I think I've reached system overload." He ran his fingers through his hair and looked up at her. "I know I'm supposed to hug you and be happy, but it doesn't make sense." He touched her arm with his fingertips. "I need to go now. I'll call you later, when it sinks in."

At the door he paused. "I'm going to be a father?"

Her smile was wan as she nodded.

"I've heard a lot of weird things lately, but ..."

He shook his head. "This is the weirdest of all."

~*~*~

Mark's muscles were stiff from sitting in his car for two and a half hours, watching the front of Sylvia's house. He grabbed the steering wheel, instantly alert, when he saw movement at last. The old woman waddled out onto the tiny porch, followed by Andrew, whose hand rested on Victoria's shoulder. Resplendent in a dark purple tunic and red miniskirt, Victoria shrugged off his touch and stepped from the sidewalk to the grass. Andrew opened the front door of the white Lincoln for Sylvia, then climbed into the driver's seat. Victoria got into the back seat. For a second, she glanced Mark's direction and he could have sworn their eyes met. Did she nod?

When the car pulled away, Mark hauled a plastic grocery sack from the back seat, crossed the street, and crept between the houses to the small back porch. He set the bag on the floorboards and stared at the screen door for a full five minutes.

Why don't they teach you useful things in graduate school, like breaking and entering?

The rusting handle refused to budge when he yanked on it. He wiped his hands on his jeans and picked up a keyhole saw from the plastic bag. The saw slipped through his fingers and clattered on the porch. Mark cursed under his breath, retrieved it, and pushed the thin blade through a small hole between the wooden frame and the screen. The rasping metal on metal grated on his nerves until he was certain someone would hear it and report it to the police.

Sawing through the screen was harder than he anticipated. Metal filings sifted onto his hands and dusted his boots. When he judged the opening sufficiently large, he peeled up the screen and slid his hand through, unlatching the door. The raw points of wire scraped lines into his skin. He bit back an exclamation, swung the screen open, and twisted the knob of the back door. It was unlocked.

Mark counted ten thuds of his heart before slipping in and latching the screen door. It was dim inside, but his eyes soon adjusted to the light seeping around the edge of the curtains. He recognized the kitchen. Halfway out into the hallway he realized he was holding his breath. He opened his mouth and let it out, irrationally certain the tiniest sound would give him away, although he knew no one was in the house. The scabbard on his belt thumped reassuringly against his thigh, his fingers resting on the warm wooden hilt.

A short sharp blast echoed in the dim hallway as his thigh flared in pain. As he clapped his hand to the injury, he thought he'd been shot. He sagged against the wall as the echoes died away. You ran into the credenza, you idiot, he snapped to himself.

No one dashed down the stairs to apprehend him. He skirted the furniture and reached the intersection of the front door, an archway to the living room and a short staircase.

He glanced to the right. The curtains were parted, and the late afternoon sunlight illuminated an old framed photo on the wall. Mark caught his breath as he knew with certainty he was looking at the face of Rebecca, nemesis of his family for generations. He almost faltered in his resolution as he gazed into those eyes.

No, I can't let you win, he snapped. You've won for too long. He caught a whiff of Victoria's familiar perfume as he turned his back on the photo and crept up the stairs to the study.

The self-satisfied hum of the computer filled the room. Mark closed the door behind him and slid into the chair. The monitor was on. He stared at the snaking green lines against the black background of the psychic energy field program until a sharp snap somewhere in the house refocused his attention on the task at hand.

Let's try something simple, shall we?

He pressed the Escape key, hoping it would bring up a menu. Bingo! Now we just close you down, like so--Oh, I see. Apparently psychic prediction programs don't run under Windows, huh? Must report that oversight to Bill Gates.

He clicked the mouse on the "Start" button. Let's just see how you like having your hard drive reformatted, Sylvia.

He clicked the mouse button several times, performing the required steps, and was rewarded with a stern warning message. Just click "Yes" and your troubles are solved. The thought of unleashing total anarchy on the computer system bothered him a bit, and he swallowed hard, finger poised for the death blow.

A faint snick behind him and a slight change in air pressure diverted his attention. Simultaneously the chair skidded backward on its casters and something fleshy, hairy, and unyielding slammed across his windpipe. He sucked futilely against the sudden loss of breath, his heart flailing in his chest. The arm choking off his air rammed against his chin as he felt himself heaved bodily from the chair and slung like a garbage sack against the wall.

Ears ringing, shoulder on fire, he shoved his feet hard against the floor and slid up the wall, squinting at the dim bulk of Andrew in the green glow of the monitor.

"Miss Dee won't let me blast your mind like I did your psychic friend--" the man snarled, "or roast you like I did your wife, but she didn't say nothin' about not poundin' the shit out of your little body."

Plasterboard exploded as the huge fist missed Mark's head by millimeters, showering him with white dust. Mark hurled himself, ripping his shirt sleeve on the desk and falling across the chair, scrabbling for the mouse. Andrew grabbed the back of his shirt and hoisted him away.

His vision exploded in red and white flashes as the fist buried itself in his face.

Every nerve in his face throbbed. He wiped at the warm liquid dripping from his nose, grabbed for the chair, and slipped in his own blood.

Mark lay where he fell, unable to remember where he was and why he couldn't die on command. His head felt huge and light enough to bear him away toward the ceiling, but was anchored to earth by the throbbing fire in his nose. As his forearm lashed against the arm of the chair, he realized Andrew had hefted and thrown him again.

Squinting through a red haze with the only eye that seemed to work, Mark saw a length of rope in the man's hands. An instant of clarity pierced the pain. Andrew intended to tie him to the chair. He screamed as he lunged for the mouse and clicked the button, gratified to hear the hard drive chuckling in its contented way. He clenched his jaw and shoved the chair toward the opposite wall. The chair impacted with a satisfying thud against Andrew's legs.

Damn! He's quick for a big guy, Mark thought as the chair sailed perilously close to him through the doorway, embedding itself in the wall at the top of the stairs. His right arm went numb, although he barely felt the chair hit him. Mark half-slid down the stairs and flew toward the back door, bouncing off the wall. His head rang with Andrew's outraged roar. Air cooled the sweat on his back as he heard his shirt rip. The man back-handed him across the face.

His chest burned with ragged gasps as he collapsed in the corner of the kitchen. Feebly he raised his arm over his face as Andrew swung a frying pan from the countertop toward him.

Death sure hurts more than I thought it would, he thought, steeling himself for the blow.

Instead he heard Sylvia's voice calling to his attacker as he slipped into the sucking whirlpool of unconsciousness.

CHAPTER 38.

The panic subsided as Mark realized he wasn't paralyzed--he wouldn't hurt this much if he were. He lay on his side on the floor, wrists and ankles bound behind him. He pulled his wrists against the ropes, and white hot agony blazed in his right shoulder. The pain in his jaw and nose had subsided to a dull throb. He suspected his nose was broken. One eye was still swollen shut--at least he hoped that was all it was.

A voice cut through the roaring in his head. "Mr. Richards, you seem to be all right."

All right? The woman has a truly twisted sense of humor, he moaned to himself. If I were dead, I'd be all right.

"Would you care to explain your actions?" Twisting his head toward the source of the voice hurt too much, and he gave up trying.

Licking his dry lips, he discovered a broken tooth in front. "I stopped the curse," he mumbled. "I reformatted your hard drive."

Her laughter bounced around the inside of his brain like a hyperkinetic pinball. "You are fortunate I can still find some humor in this situation, and that I need your physical presence for the ceremony Thursday night. Otherwise I would have let Mr. Sweeney finish what he started."

Sylvia's face snapped into focus. "Yes, you reformatted my hard drive. Did it not occur to you that I maintain backups?"

"Yeah, leave it to you to be the one person in a thousand who actually backs up her files."

Talking was an effort, and his jaw popped with every movement. It dawned on him that she wasn't upset about the loss of the data. "Are you saying it had no effect on the curse?"

196

"Now why would it?" she asked in a gentle tone, as if leading a class of very young students through a logic exercise. "Would destroying a television set destroy the networks? Would smashing a telephone kill the person at the other end?"

The kindly schoolteacher tone melted away like ice from a heat lamp. "The computer is merely an analytical tool. You have temporarily cost me the ability to judge the precise timing of the ritual. The chip within is still intact, and that's what is important."

"If I was sorry, I'd apologize. Do you plan on freeing me any time soon?" He squirmed. The ropes chafed his wrists.

Her angry eyes bored into his. "I will release you when we leave for the ceremony and not until. Now if you'll excuse me, I have files to reconstruct."

"Are you Sylvia de Graffenried?" he asked before she could leave the room.

"I am amazed." She stared at him. "How on earth did you arrive at that conclusion?"

"Let's just say I have intelligent friends."

"Daniel O'Brien. I should have had Mr. Sweeney destroy his mind much sooner." She sighed and shook her head. "I suppose at this point it doesn't matter if you know."

Mark lowered his head, his neck aching from craning to look up at her, so he was unprepared when her foot caught him squarely in the stomach. He groaned. "*That* is for destroying my data, Mr. Richards," she snapped as he curled up in fetal position. She drew back her foot again.

"Sylvia--don't you dare!" Victoria shoved past the older woman.

"You're--a little--late," Mark wheezed. "She's already--done it once."

"Why is he tied up?" Victoria demanded.

"I don't want to have to track him down when we need him."

"You didn't have to hurt him." She knelt beside him. "Are you all right?"

"Oh, sure. I-I enjoy being kicked in the stomach." His vision settled back into single images. Victoria helped him sit up.

"Sylvia, this is cruel," she protested.

The older woman ignored her. Victoria sat on the floor next to him.

"Thanks for calling her off me," Mark snarled. "But I don't see why you're sticking up for me. Is it because there's a shortage of trains around here?"

"I guess I deserve that," Victoria said with a frown.

"You *guess*? She didn't force you to kill my father. You had a choice."

"Mark, you just don't understand."

"No, I sure as hell don't." This woman evoked extreme emotions.

Anger boiled inside him, as strong as the lust he felt before. "Rebecca and that *fucking* curse ruined my father's life, with Sylvia's kind assistance, no doubt, and you topped it off by screwing him and shoving him under a train, leaving him in three nice neat pieces for me to identify. I do not understand that. At all. And, gee, don't take this the wrong way, but I don't want to understand." He clenched his jaw until his teeth hurt.

"Mark, you know how the curse acts, what it does, how it warps the mind." He watched the tear quiver on her lower eyelid, spill over and trail down her cheek, along the line of her jaw. "He would have started on your mother and sister next. I had to stop him. I couldn't bear to see him go through it again."

"But you're still working for Sylvia." He hardly recognized the flat voice as his own.

"She raised me, Mark. She's the only family I had. My parents were killed when I was six years old--"

"Oh? And who do you think was responsible for that?" Mark countered. "I'll bet my life, for what that's worth right now, Sylvia had a hand in it. Go on and tell her, Sylvia. Tell her you offed her parents, too. How many Gileses have you killed in your time?"

"Keep your mouth shut, Mr. Richards, or I shall have Mr. Sweeney shut it for you," Sylvia responded. "The ceremony does not require that you have a tongue in your head."

"You didn't answer him, Sylvia." Victoria stood. "What did happen to my parents? You always said it was a car crash. Was it?"

"The car crashed, Victoria. They died in the crash. He is trying to manipulate you into turning against me."

"That still doesn't--"

"Victoria. Hush. I must repair the damage he caused. Now, where is Mr. Sweeney?"

Mark heard the door slam. Sharp and acute disappointment, as palpable as the ache in his eye and his shoulder, twisted his stomach. It didn't work, he thought. Why did you think it would? Did you think you'd be exempt from the curse?

Janet's parting words flooded him with the force of Andrew's fist. He wasn't the last of the line anymore. If he let Sylvia go on with her twisted plot, the curse would carry on to his child. Looks like the suicide option is the only thing left, he told himself. He swallowed hard against the rising bile. But I don't think choking on my own vomit is the way to go. He shoved aside the memory of his father lying on the floor of the bathroom draped in his own blood. How in the hell am I supposed to get to Jackson County and kill myself if I'm tied up like an extra in some kind of bondage movie?

~*~*~

Janet jerked awake as the nurse entered the room and retrieved her book. "I'm sorry, Ms. Richards, did I startle you?"

She tucked a strand of dark hair behind her ear and listened to Daniel's steady, regular breathing. "I fell asleep. How is he?"

The nurse picked up his wrist and consulted her watch. Her eyebrows shot up. "I think--excuse me ..." She hurried out of the room, returning seconds later behind the doctor.

"What's wrong? Is he worse?" Janet panted. "Please, doctor, tell me."

The doctor smiled and shrugged. "I'm not sure why, but he's out of the coma. He's sleeping normally now. I couldn't explain why he slipped into the coma in the first place, but ... " He broke off as Daniel's eyes fluttered open, focusing first on the doctor's face, then on hers. Her heart skipped a beat as he recognized her.

The doctor examined him and stepped away with a shrug. "Damnedest thing I ever saw. I'll come back by in the morning and see how you are."

"Thank you, Doctor," Janet said.

"Don't thank me. I didn't have the slightest thing to do with it. It's just ... well ... one of those amazing things that reminds us we don't know everything." He returned her smile, patted her shoulder, and left the room with the nurse trailing behind him.

Daniel tried to speak. She poured him a glass of water and helped him drink. "Where's Mark?" he croaked at last.

"I'm not sure. He said something about stopping the curse with a little computer work."

"He saved my life, Janet."

She propped pillows behind his back. "Saved your life? How do you mean?"

"I was lost, out on the astral plane. The attacker sent me there. I--" He shuddered. "I couldn't find my way back. Mark reached out to me, helped me ..."

She wondered if he was delirious. "But how?"

"He used his powers, threw me a ... a psychic line and dragged me back to myself."

"His powers?" she echoed.

Daniel smiled and shook his head. "Do you think I'm the only one with psychic ability in the world? You vastly underestimate your husband. But no more than he underestimates himself. I don't think he realized he had the ability."

Janet sank into the chair, wondering when was the exact moment the bizarre became normal. "And he did this for you after I told him ..."

"Told him?" Daniel asked, his voice stronger.

"I ... told him I love you. And he still helped you." She twisted her fingers in her lap until her knuckles turned white. Daniel was silent. At last she could stand it no longer and darted a glance up at him.

"It wasn't a secret, my dear," he said with a smile. "I've known for some time. You know the feeling is mutual." She wanted to leap up and throw her arms around his neck, but restrained herself as his expression became serious. "However ... I think we must discuss something else first. I did not realize until this ... experience ... that Mark's potential power was so strong. The danger to him is even greater than I supposed. Can you remember everything he said to you?"

Janet related the conversation. "I've never seen that expression on his face before," she finished. "So ... determined."

"Is that all he said?"

"Yes, I--" She broke off as something else he said popped into her head. "I can't believe I forgot this. He said, 'I may not have anything to live for, but I'll give them something to kill me for.'" Her bottom lip quivered. "Daniel, what do you think he might do?"

He said grimly, "A man that desperate is capable of anything."

~*~*~

Wednesday, May 19. 7:25 a.m.

Fred Troxell climbed down from his tractor and wiped his brow with a red bandanna. He cocked an eye at the line of cumulonimbus clouds gathering toward the west. Already the forest bordering his property swayed as one dark mass in the stiffening breeze.

"Just what we need," he muttered under his breath. "More rain." He was already late plowing the field because of the unusually heavy storms during the past two weeks.

"Dad?" His six-year-old son, dressed in overalls identical to his father's, trotted across the field, skipping through the deeper puddles. "You gonna get much plowin' done this mornin'?" He jumped as a crack of thunder pealed earthward.

"Doesn't look like it, Bo. Haven't seen this much rain since ... well, I don't know when."

"I saw Billy yesterday, y'know he's been visitin' his gramma in Decatur? An' he said they ain't had no rain atall!"

"Haven't had any rain," he corrected absently. "Seems like it's all coming through and staying in Jackson County. I could almost swear the

200

clouds hover over the forest, too." A bolt of lightning shivered through the sky toward the trees.

"One Miss'sippi, two Miss'sippi--" Thunder interrupted Bo's counting. "That was close. Do you think it struck any trees out there?"

"Might have. Let's go in now. It has to stop sometime." Fred climbed into the seat of the tractor and helped Bo up into his lap. "You'd almost think this area's cursed."

"Cursed? What does that mean?"

Fred laughed. "It means your old man's getting as crazy as Mrs. Bailey. She swears she saw fireballs hovering over the forest the other night. UFOs, she said." His son whipped his head around, eyes wide. "It's all nonsense, Bo. She's also claimed to see a cabin out there in the woods, and you know nobody's lived out there for decades. It's all in her head."

The boy giggled. "A cabin? If there was one, I'd'a seen it. She's bonkers."

"Don't say that to her face."

"I won't."

"Now let's get the tractor in before that lightning hits us."

~*~*~

1:00 p.m.

"Quit arguing with me, Mr. O'Brien," Janet said in mock severity. "I will not allow you to stay in a hotel until the repairs are finished on your house when I have a guest room."

"I appreciate your kindness, Janet, but won't Mark object?"

"At this point, I doubt it." Janet opened the car door for him. "I think you've grown stronger since we left the hospital. You certainly stumped the doctor. He didn't know what to make of your recovery." Daniel leaned on her as they walked toward the front door, but strength was returning to his legs. "He'll probably write an article about you. 'Amazing Recovery from Deep Vegetative State,' he'll call it."

Daniel sank onto the couch as Janet closed the door. "Sounds like something for the *National Enquirer*, I'd say." He took her hands in his, pulling her down beside him. Deep lines creased his forehead. "I'm worried about Mark. It's no wonder these people want him. In fact, they may not really know why they want him, just that they do. My theory is the energy field produced by the curse enhanced his latent psychic abilities."

Janet sighed. "I don't understand any of this." She noticed the blue notebook on the floor next to the couch. She picked it up and laughed at the youthful scrawl on the cover. "I wonder why Mark had this out. I've never seen it before."

"A chemistry notebook?"

"Apparently." She flipped to a couple of crumpled pages and smoothed them out. "This part isn't Mark's handwriting. It looks like his father's."

Daniel peered over her shoulder. As his breath gently warmed the top of her left ear, she longed to fall back into his arms and forget about Mark and psychic energy fields and all the insanity and anger and pain of the past weeks. She wanted to lose herself in the comfort and care of someone who loved her unconditionally and devotedly.

The words scrawled on the page shook her from the dream of security: "August 1, 1985. The truth is evident to me now." She read Tom Richards' confession of murdering his son with a chill of horror. How could this be the same quiet, gentle man she'd had pleasant conversations with over the last eleven years? The phrase blazed in her mind: "... seventh generation from the curse." When she read her father-in-law's desperate assertion that Demarcus had to "end his life by his own hand," her heart gave a sickening thud.

"Janet, where is Mark now?" Daniel gripped her shoulder.

"I don't know," she said.

"Think. This is important. You told me back in the hospital he wanted to give them a reason to kill him. Did he say anything else that might tell us what he's doing?"

She closed her eyes, rubbing the pain in her temples. "He said something about current thinking being he should ... what word did he use? 'Off' himself to stop the curse. I told him killing himself wouldn't solve anything, and he said, 'Not according to my father and my great-great-great grandfather.'"

"He's not--do you know what he plans to do?"

Janet did know, but she couldn't bear to say it aloud. "No. Why? Do you?"

Daniel took the notebook from her. "His father tried to kill himself?"

"Several times. Pills, hanging, slitting his wrists--"

"That's what he means here by 'the blood route.' He thought by killing himself, he could end the curse, but he was not the one to succeed. He practically tells Mark to commit suicide."

She grabbed his hands and whispered, "My God, Daniel, is that what he's going to do?"

"I wouldn't be surprised. Especially after he read his father was a murderer, if he didn't already know. It would come as quite a shock."

"It's certainly a shock to me," Janet said. "I don't think he knew. In fact, I'm sure of it."

"We must find him." He flipped through the notebook. "Wait a minute, though. If the curse is going to kill him anyway, as he seems to believe, why kill himself? He would merely be ending his life a day or two earlier. Maybe there's nothing to worry about."

"But, Daniel, did you forget? He's not the last one."

He blinked at her. "What?"

She patted her belly. "I told him about the baby before he left. He knows he's not the last in the Giles line."

"Janet, I am not entirely certain, but I don't think his suicide will destroy the curse. We need to find him before he makes an irrevocable mistake."

CHAPTER 39.

1:45 p.m.

The bruised cloud boiled, exuding a sinuous shape slipping silently earthward to the grassy field. Rows of men and women with vaguely familiar features, their hair and vintage clothing blowing in the strengthening wind, stood in the center of the field. His father, mother, sister, and brother stood nearer to him, wearing modern clothes and gazing straight ahead, unconcerned. A scream of warning choked his throat as the twisting vortex slurped up the back row, but no sound emerged as the tornado sucked closer and closer to the front.

Tommy was the first to go. One moment he stood there, with that worldly-wise-teenager look he always affected, wearing jeans, filthy tennis shoes and a T-shirt, and the next he was gone. The vortex skipped around his mother and hovered over his father. The man glanced around, puzzled, before he, too, was borne into the cloud.

Natalie watched her father disappear. Her lips curved into an enigmatic little smile as she stretched her arms over her head and leaped upward into the tornado. Mark screamed and screamed as the whirling column of dark air bore down on him, but the soles of his boots melted into the ground, anchoring him to the earth--

He jerked awake, the rasp of rope on his wrists grounding him in reality again. His heart racing, blood pounding through the veins in his swollen nose. He blinked against the dimness in the room. He'd been moved from the floor to the bed, additional ropes fastening him to the bedposts. A sliver of brightness from the sunlight striped the bedspread, glinted on the eyelets of his boots, up the rope securing his ankles to the bed and across two white columns by the door.

The columns rippled forward, closer and closer, until he realized they were Victoria's legs beneath a dark skirt. A thrill of desire coursed through his body as he stared into her green and gold eyes. Her hand clutched a knife, and for one insane second, he thought, If I could have her one last time, I'd gladly let her kill me.

Her body heat burned through his pants leg as she sat on the edge of the bed. He gasped as she rested the icy blade just under his chin, right over the small cut his sister bestowed on him. "Mark," she whispered in his ear, "I want you to understand what I am about to do." He shivered as she drew the tip of the knife around his jawline. "I am, metaphorically speaking, slitting my own throat. If she gets the chance, Sylvia will kill me. Or have me killed. But--" she stretched up, her breasts rubbing against his face as she sawed through the rope tying him to the bedpost. "--I can't let her do this to you." He muffled his cry at the sudden release of his shoulders. She cut the rope binding his wrists together, then moved to his ankles. "She's trying to change what's supposed to happen. I can't allow it."

"Thank you," he croaked, wondering at the inadequacy of the words. He reached down and rubbed feeling back into his legs. "I'll never forget this, Victoria."

"No. You won't." She touched his swollen nose and cheeks. "When Andrew bragged about beating you up--I couldn't stand it. You know, I think your nose is broken." She reached into a pocket and handed him something oval and metallic. "Take this. To prove my good intentions. I relinquish my power over you, Mark."

His hands trembled as he clutched the watch. "Give this whole thing up, Victoria. It's a fight between people long dead. It has nothing to do with us."

"And what would I do? Stand trial for murdering your father? Spend the rest of my life in jail? Or run away and hide forever--and do what?" Her fingernails bit into his palm as she clutched his hand. "I don't think you fully comprehend, Mark. This is my whole life. I was trained to seduce, to kill, if necessary. Until I met Tom, it never bothered me, never occurred to me there could be anything else. And when I--" Her voice broke. "--Killed him, when I shoved him under the train with these hands and saw his head hit the rail--" Her tears fell on his hand. "I knew my life was one short hollow emptiness and no one, not even you, could change that."

Her voice was almost inaudible. "I loved Tom, and I love you. But it doesn't matter anymore. This horrible curse is very effective. It's destroyed me as much as it's destroying you--and destroyed your father, and your grandfather ..." She stood. "I have to go, Mark. Run, now. The back door's unlocked. You'll see me again, at the cabin, under your own power."

"Wait--what about the fire at Daniel's house? Did Andrew do that?"

She nodded. "I overheard him talking with Sylvia. I called the fire department. Neither of them deserved to die that way."

He grabbed her arm. "Come with me."

"No," she answered, her eyes wet. "It can't happen that way. I know how all this turns out. Sylvia was trying to subvert the process, but she can't. It's ... well, it's destiny. Rebecca set it in motion long ago." She kissed him and whispered, "Whatever happens, Mark, be strong. Do what you have to do. Understand?"

"No, I don't understand. I'm tired of everyone's cryptic messages. Speak plainly."

"If I spoke plainly, you wouldn't believe me. Just remember: bear what you think you can't bear. You'll understand. Soon."

"Tell me one last thing. How much of this was intended just to set me up? I feel like a pawn, a really stupid pawn."

Frowning, Victoria folded her arms. "I know you don't want to hear this, but our meeting was planned. Sylvia sent me to library school so I could get the job at Birmingham Public."

"So you could get a job in a library." His arms tingled as the blood returned.

"No, she had that specific job in mind. She reasoned eventually you would come in that library looking for information on your ancestors."

He was afraid to ask, but he had to know. "Was falling in love with me part of the plan?"

She dragged him off the bed, pressed the scabbard holding James' knife into his hand and shoved him toward the open door. "No, Mark, it wasn't. Get out of here before they return."

He kissed her. "Thank you, Victoria."

Then he ran.

~*~*~

Sylvia and Andrew returned thirty minutes later. He carried a large box with a computer manufacturer's logo on the side.

"We've bought a laptop, Victoria," the old woman explained. "It won't be as powerful as the desktop, though, until I transfer the chip. We must have something to take with us to the cabin. What's wrong?"

She was sitting on the couch, leafing through a magazine. "Nothing.

I'm thrilled for you and your portable curse-detection."

Sylvia followed Andrew up the stairs.

Victoria braced herself, a detached sense of calm settling over her as she waited for--

"Victoria! Come up here immediately."

She set the magazine beside her on the couch and strolled up the stairs. Sylvia's eyes were dark and angry as she stood outside the door. "Why, Victoria?"

She stepped into the room. Andrew stood by the bed, arms folded across his huge chest. A gleam of excitement twinkled in his eyes.

"It wasn't right," Victoria said, glancing from one face to the other. "This wasn't the way it's supposed to happen. He will come to the cabin of his own free will. You didn't have to imprison him here, drag him like some animal."

From the doorway, Sylvia nodded. Andrew stepped closer, until Victoria felt the heat of his body on her skin.

"I see my instincts were correct," her guardian intoned. "I've determined the substitute will perform the function better than you ever could. Your participation is no longer required."

"Substitute? Mark's sister?" A little vein somewhere under her scalp throbbed.

"She seems amenable to the idea," Sylvia said. "She will perform the ritual instead."

"Are you saying--"

"I'm saying good-bye, Victoria. Oh, one last bit of information you might find interesting. About your parents," Sylvia said. "Mr. Richards accused me of killing them. He was completely wrong. That privilege was yours."

Victoria laughed uneasily. "Oh, no way that can be true. I was six years old--"

"The curse works on you as well. You deliberately stepped out in front of the car. Your father swerved off the road and directly into a tree, killing him and your mother."

She shook her head. "No. That's ridiculous."

"Mr. Sweeney, she's yours to do with as you wish. Please ensure she does not leave this room alive. But do try to keep the noise to a minimum, for the sake of the neighbors."

Sylvia stepped outside the room, pulling the door shut.

Andrew's mustache partially obscured his toothy smile. His hands darted toward Victoria before she could react, pulling her against him. Something hard in his camouflage pants pressed into her abdomen. She prayed it was a wrench.

"You know I've wanted this for a long time, babe," he whispered in her ear. "The first time was a setup, and you stopped just when it was gettin' good. I ain't gonna stop this time."

She squirmed, struggling to ram her knee up into that hardness. He thrust his leg between hers and wrapped it around her ankle, pinning her tightly to him. She clamped her teeth shut against his slithering tongue writhing across her lips. She wondered if she could die of revulsion, steeling herself as he slid his hand down her thigh and beneath her short skirt.

He bent to gnaw at her neck. Victoria banged his chin with her head. Blood sprayed as his teeth clamped down on his tongue. Cursing, he slapped her hard across the face, flinging her against the bedpost. He sprang on her like a feral beast and pinned her to the floor.

"I knew you liked it rough," he said in her ear.

"Go--to--hell," she panted, her head spinning.

"Only if you come with me." One large hand fastened her wrists above her head while the other unbuttoned her blouse. "This is what all chicks want, Vicki. They all wanna be fucked by a guy like me that'll overpower 'em. Then they'll call it rape if they enjoy it too much."

She tried to spit in his face, but her mouth was too dry. As he shifted to pull her blouse from the waistband of her skirt, she jerked one hand free and raked her long nails across his face. Blood welled up from the parallel lines on one cheek and the side of his nose. He roared, both hands clamped to the wound, and she wriggled out from under him.

Andrew grabbed her ankle, his blood smearing her leg through her hose. "No, you little whore, you ain't getting away that easy."

The rug bunched up under her as he dragged her toward him. His hands clamped around her throat. "Now you're gonna die, bitch."

Victoria sucked desperately for air, squirming vainly against the insistent pressure of his body on hers. A roaring in her ears blotted out the sounds of his grunting.

~*~*~

4:30 p.m.

Janet hugged the small blue notebook to her chest. "Can't you sense where he is? You've been trying for hours."

He leaned on the map spread out before him on the floor and sighed. "And all I have received for my efforts is a massive headache. It's too soon after the attack, I'm afraid. I can barely sense you." Smiling, he added, "No, we don't have time for that."

"You can't read my mind," she laughed.

"No, but I sense your emotions, and your passions. Are you blushing?"

"No," she snapped. "It's a hot flash." She tossed the notebook on the floor where it slithered across the map. "My timing isn't very good, is it?"

Daniel stretched his legs out. "There will be time for us to be together when this is over. Be patient. I've waited eleven years for you. I can wait a few days." He pulled the map toward him. "I am surprised the person at the public library gave you Victoria's address."

"He's known Mark for years. I explained it was an emergency. But no one answered at her house. And Sylvia's not listed in the phone book."

"Mark's father was seen in a café in that same area before he was killed, correct?"

"Seen with Victoria." A sudden rage boiled inside her. "That bitch killed my father-in-law. And seduced my husband. Who knows what else? We have to stop her, Daniel."

"We will, dear, we will."

"Don't patronize me," Janet snapped. "I hate it when you do that. Makes me feel like 'the little woman.' I have a right to be angry."

Daniel circled her shoulders with his arm. "I am sorry, Janet. I didn't mean it that way. You do have a right to be angry. You have suffered greatly the past two months with very little--if any--support."

"Thank you for understanding." She kissed his lips quickly, then passionately. He responded with his old familiar intensity. The eleven intervening years melted away as she remembered the taste of his mouth, the gentle strength of his fingers. At last she pulled away, gasping. "Sylvia de Graffenried must live near Victoria."

He blinked at her. "What?"

"I'm sorry, but it just popped into my head. Sex tends to free my unconscious mind. I'll bet Sylvia lives somewhere in the area where the café is and where Victoria lives."

"You're correct," he said, panting, "you do have a bad sense of timing." Taking her hand, he added, "Perhaps we should drive around that area. I can get a better sense of the location that way. If we stay here, your unconscious mind will have plenty of opportunity to be free."

Grinning, Janet grabbed her purse and keys from the end table while Daniel gathered up the map and notebook. "I'll drive. You keep an eye open and intuit, or whatever you call it."

CHAPTER 40.

5:00 p.m.

The hotel room smelled of stale cigarettes and the icy tang of old Freon. Mark dropped the suitcase and briefcase on the floor by the bed, slung his keys across the table under the window, and collapsed across the shiny orange and green-striped bedspread. The drive up from Birmingham was a two-hour blur of rush hour traffic and tree-crowded interstate and county road ascending the foothills of the Appalachians. He amused himself by trying to recall a time when some part of his body did not ache or burn.

He'd only reached the outskirts of town when a new pain struck him, a band around his throat so sudden and intense he swerved off the side of the road, afraid he would pass out. After about ten minutes, the tightness eased, leaving him dazed and gulping air. He'd wondered if Victoria was in trouble, but the feeling slipped away as he worried about the hours ahead .

For several minutes he savored the weight of his tired body sinking into the mattress, the silence of the room roaring in his ears. Outside a car door slammed. A child's voice yelled, "Mom! Which suitcase is my swimsuit in?" He willed his tensed knees, shoulders, neck to melt into the softness beneath him, without success. While I was driving, he thought, all I wanted to do was sleep. Now I can't even relax. He wondered if the hotel bar was open yet, then remembered it was a dry county. Yawning, he ambled to the sink to wash his face—

--and slipped in his own blood that slicked the dead leaves scattered between the trees. He tried to lever himself to his feet behind the rotting log where he'd taken refuge. A stab of pain lanced his ankle as he lurched upright, chest heaving. He peered around him through the sparkles of light obscuring his vision, wondering why the attack had broken off as suddenly as it started. His attacker was nowhere in sight; he heard a crashing through the underbrush disappearing swiftly into the distance.

He sagged against the tree, his mind registering one strip of skin on the back of his right arm that didn't throb with pain. I should just lie here and die, he thought. This is my just reward. Maybe I'm already dying. Alice will wonder what happened--Oh ... my ... God ... Alice. He realized his attacker was running in the direction of his home.

Heaving himself to his feet, he discovered a falling run that propelled him through the forest. He staggered into trees, once nearly passing out as his shoulder slammed into the rough bark, cracking the bloody glue knitting his sleeve to the hair on his arm. The pain in his ankle tunneled his vision at every misstep on the stones hidden under the leaves and roots and vines.

An eternity later, he flung himself into the edge of the clearing and gazed blankly at the wooden cabin, bracing himself against a tree to keep his knees from buckling under him. He knew he was there for a reason, but was momentarily uncertain what it was. He struggled to sort out coherent thoughts as he stared at the wide open door of the cabin. Something was wrong here. Alice would never leave the door open-- A shrill scream, abruptly choked off, slapped his face. With a burst of energy he lurched past the well and onto the planks of the wide porch.

He fell against the door frame, left arm flung out across the planks of the wall he'd planed himself. His breath whooped in great gasps as he dashed stinging sweat from his eyes. The little front room sprang into definition as he adjusted to the change in light: the chairs that were a wedding gift from her father, the table with the one wobbly leg he could never quite get even, the pale yellow muslin curtains she sewed. He released the outside wall and stumbled across the rag rug.

"James!"

The whisper halted his steps, jerked his head toward the fireplace to his left. His wife sat perched perfectly still on the stool, hazel eyes wide with terror, neck twisted at an angle, dark brown hair clenched from behind by his attacker. The knife smeared with his blood was tilted against the tanned skin of her throat, exactly in the spot where she writhed in ecstasy when he brushed his lips across it. Her fingers were spasmed in the fabric of her skirt.

"James--" she gasped. "Don't--"

He watched, almost in fascination, as sunlight between the yellow curtains glittered on his wet blood on the knife. Slowly the blade slipped around the curve of her throat, hidden by the gush of liquid, as bright and red as the squares of the quilt lying across their bed. The blood dyed the worn brown calico of her bodice, spraying across her clawed hands.

James' hands flailed uselessly toward the sagging body on the stool. His vision tunneled, the roaring in his ears so loud he couldn't hear his own screams as he staggered toward the stool.

His calf muscles gave way and he slammed to his knees, crashing face down onto the plank floor.

CHAPTER 41.

5:15 p.m.

Janet drove to Victoria's address, a quiet empty street after the frustrating stop-and-go traffic of the interstate. She was relieved Mark's car wasn't parked there. "Where to now?"

"This headache is affecting my range," Daniel muttered, snapping the map into shape. "I suggest we drive to the café and work our way back from there."

They found the coffee shop about five blocks away. Janet parked on a side street at Daniel's suggestion. "I think we'll have better luck if we walk." He helped her out of the car and held her hand.

"Under other circumstances, this would be very nice," she said, smiling. "A stroll down a quiet street on a beautiful spring evening--"

"We're close," he interrupted in a low, tense voice. He pulled her across an intervening road then paused, stroking his beard. "Stay alert. I do not want them to surprise us."

She noticed a white Lincoln and a blue Honda in a driveway two houses down from them. "Daniel, that's Victoria's car, the one she drove off in after I beat her up."

"We'll approach slowly. We can--Someone's coming out of the house." They ducked behind a tree, crept under cover of a hedge.

"Do you recognize him?" Janet asked, watching as a man loaded two suitcases into the Lincoln's trunk. "Daniel?" She turned and saw him hunched on the ground, head in his hands.

"It's him," he said through clenched teeth. "The man who attacked me. I can feel his mind. Janet, I have to concentrate, protect myself from him. Keep watching what he does."

She nodded, alarmed at the fear in his voice. The man--Andrew, Mark called him--returned to the house twice, putting strangely-shaped packages into the trunk. On the third trip he carried a briefcase or laptop computer case and was accompanied by a short, plump woman whose braided white hair was piled on top of her head. He opened the door for her, helped her inside, then deposited the briefcase in the backseat.

"Don't worry, that Natalie Richards kid will show up for her part in the ceremony. If she doesn't, I'll find her and drag her," Janet heard him say before he slammed the car door and climbed behind the wheel.

"They're gone, Dan--" Now he lay curled on the grass in fetal position, eyes closed. She shook him. "Daniel, Mark might be in there." Shaking him harder had no effect. The hedge shielded them from the street, and large bushes between them and the house would prevent him from being seen. "Sorry, but I have to find out if Mark is in there. I'll be back as soon as I can."

She dashed from behind the hedge and sprinted across the yard next door, veering into Sylvia's backyard. Creeping onto the small back porch, she almost tripped over a plastic bag of tools. "Richards" was written in black permanent marker across the handle of the saw. You'd make a great burglar, Mark, she snorted. She noticed the cut in the screen and used it to slip her hand through and unlock the door.

The hallway was dim as she skirted a credenza and paused at the intersection of the front door, living room and stairs, feeling as if she were being watched. She whirled and found herself face to face with a framed photo of an old woman with marcelled hair. The eyes were very familiar, intelligent but with an almost-intimidating willfulness. Janet was relieved she was seeing a portrait and not the real woman.

A huge ragged hole gaped in the plaster at the top of the stairs. She stepped into the room across from it. The curtains were open, and the waning rays of the sun shone across the parts of a disassembled computer. The wall in this room also held a hole, this one fist-sized, and a spray of dried blood. On the wooden floor next to the computer chair was a large smear of blood like the imprint of a boot.

A low moan prickled the hair on the back of her neck. She turned, unsure of the direction of the sound, and heard it again from across the hall. A large four poster bed dominated that dark room. Ropes were tied to both posts of the footboard and one at the headboard. Someone moaned again. Janet looked down. In a heap on the twisted rug lay

Victoria, blouse torn, short skirt twisted, large bruises darkening her throat.

~*~*~

Mark blinked his eyes open, the prickle of carpet fibers under his cheek instead of the planed and sanded wooden planks he expected. He rolled to his side, gingerly probing for the bloody rent in his shoulder and finding only smooth, whole cotton. His shirt was wrinkled but uncut, the buttons intact. Working off his boot and peeling down the sock underneath, he stared at the pale skin of his ankle, unpurpled by any sprain. He dragged himself backward across the floor to lean against the bed.

"I'm not James," he told himself as his eyes darted to the stool next to the fireplace, no, the TV sitting on the dresser. No fountain of blood down a calico dress. "--and I don't have a wife named Alice. I didn't build a cabin." He flipped his hair from his collar and hauled himself halfway up on the bed, but the throbbing in his nose and head forced him back down onto the floor until it subsided into a dull ache. "I thought the visions were over," he panted. "That one was a doozy."

He shuddered as he relived the horror of the knife sliding across her throat. The eyes of the woman holding that knife were the same as those in the old woman's photo on Sylvia's wall.

Mark took out his pocket watch. He'd been out for about an hour. Stroking the dent in the back of the case, he asked aloud, "Why didn't you tell me about this, Dad? How could you live with this horror and never tell anyone?" He grimaced.

"Yeah, so different from the way I've handled it." He collapsed across the bed.

~*~*~

Janet wiped Victoria's face with a wet washcloth, somewhat surprised she was doing it. The day before yesterday she had put some of those bruises on her face.

The woman moaned again. Her eyelids fluttered. When she focused on Janet's face at last, she shrank away, green eyes wide with terror.

"It's okay, I'm not here to hurt you. Can you talk? What happened?"

Victoria shook her head, long red-tipped fingers rubbing her throat.

Janet helped her off the floor and perched beside her on the bed. "And what were these for?" she wondered, picking up a length of rope still tied at one end to the bedpost.

Blood stained the pillowcase.

"I ... released Mark," she whispered. A coughing fit racked her body. At

215

last she gasped, "Sylvia was holding him...for the ceremony."

Janet gasped. "Oh, my God, was he hurt?"

The other woman rubbed her throat again and looked at Janet. The golden flecks against the dark green were almost hypnotic.

Janet began to understand the woman's hold over her husband. "Andrew beat him up...broke his nose...don't know what all else." Victoria winced. Janet found a glass in the bathroom, filled it with water, and handed it to her.

"Thank you." Her voice was still a hoarse whisper, punctuated by coughs. "When they found out what I'd done, Sylvia said...said she ..."

"What? I'm sorry, I can't hear you."

"Sylvia said she no longer had any use for me." A tear trailed down her cheek. "Said she'd found a substitute. That Andrew could ... could do with me what he liked." She sipped water and cleared her throat. "He tried to rape me. I scratched the hell out of his face, so he tried to kill me. I guess he thought he had."

"Where are they now?"

"Gone to the cabin for the ceremony. Jackson County."

"Victoria, I'm not entirely sure this is the right thing to do, but would you be willing to help us follow them, rescue Mark?"

She thought a moment and nodded. " I'll do it. If only to settle things with Mr. Andrew Sweeney." Looking around the room, she added, "Where's your boyfriend?"

"He's not my--oh, he's outside--" Janet dashed out the door and down the stairs, nearly running full tilt into Daniel. "I was just coming to find you. Are you okay?"

He stroked his beard. "Yes, I am. I'm sorry I deserted you. I was terrified of him attacking me again. What is she doing here?"

"Helping us find Mark. I'll explain in the car."

"There's no real need to hurry." Victoria's voice was still a husky whisper. "We have until midnight tomorrow before the ceremony begins."

"We think Mark plans to circumvent the ceremony," Daniel put in. "By killing himself. Call it a pre-emptive strike."

The blonde woman's eyes widened. "But that's not supposed to happen. He can't. Or can he?" She smiled a mysterious little smile. "He's cleverer than I gave him credit for. That might work. If Sylvia doesn't stop him first, that is."

She excused herself, saying she wanted to change clothes and freshen up first.

"Do you trust her?" Daniel asked when she left the room.

"I'm not sure. But I don't think we have a choice."

Victoria joined them twenty minutes later wearing jeans and a T-shirt, her hair brushed back into a ponytail, her face freshly made up. When Daniel opened the front door for her, she stared at the empty driveway and said, "I hope one of you has a car."

"I drove us here," Janet answered. "Why?"

"Because someone has stolen mine."

"But it was there when we arrived," Daniel recalled. "We were watching the house and saw the old woman and the man leave in a white Lincoln."

Victoria grimaced. "You saw Sylvia and Andrew. Then who stole my car?"

"That was Sylvia de Graffenried?" Daniel asked.

"No, Sylvia Dee. My guardian. My *former* guardian, I should say, since she gave Andrew permission to kill me."

Daniel raised an eyebrow. "I think we need to inform you of what we discovered concerning your guardian."

Victoria frowned and said, "Okay. It's about a two-hour drive. We should have plenty of time to talk. I suggest we get going. Where did you say your car is parked?"

CHAPTER 42.

Mark soldiered through a dinner of country-fried steak, mashed potatoes, green beans, and squash casserole in the hotel's restaurant, but tasted little of it. Nourishing his body seemed pointless when he was contemplating suicide. The very word sent a shudder down his spine.

What I really need, he thought, digging bills from his wallet and handing them to the waitress, is to get seriously drunk. Unless he happened upon some moonshiners in this dry county, he didn't think there was much chance of that. Although it was just after six, the sun was already hidden behind the mountains. The allure of the honeysuckle-scented air convinced Mark to change to running shoes and venture back outside. He jogged toward a wooded area behind the hotel, relaxing as the breeze whipped his hair and fanned his face.

The litany that haunted him on the drive up returned in a sing-song echo to his jogging footsteps: Ja-net's preg-nant, Ja-net's preg-nant. That scared him worse than the thought of facing Andrew. If the curse ends with me, he thought, and I can find some way to defeat it without killing myself, great. If it doesn't end with me ... I may have to kill myself to stop it.

But I don't want to, another part of his brain whined. If I'm actually going to be a father, I want to see the child.

James didn't live to see his child grow up. Being a father? That's too much reality. I don't think I can handle it.

So is offing yourself. That's about as real as it gets.

He shuddered as he flashed back to all the times his father attempted suicide, especially the time he slashed his wrists--the 'blood route,' as the journal entry referred to it. Mark stumbled into a tree trunk as he recalled dreaming in red for months afterward, nearly passing out when his sister spilled crimson fingernail polish. The thought of actually sliding the knife across the thin skin separating life from death--

He slumped against the tree, chest heaving, legs cramping. Blood pounded in his swollen nose, shooting waves of pain through his head. He stretched his aching leg muscles and headed back toward the building at a slow limp. Halfway across the parking lot he stopped in his tracks at the sight of a familiar car parked in front of the hotel in the registration area. He nodded, convinced it was Victoria's dark blue Honda. From his angle, he couldn't see if she was standing in the lobby. A thrill of ecstasy mingled with fear coursed through his body as he hobbled to his room and unlocked the door.

Calm down, he counseled himself. So what if she's found you? She can't break the door down. He tossed the key onto the table by the window and headed for the shower, dropping his clothes in a trail on the floor.

He was rinsing off the soap when he suddenly shivered, certain someone had entered his hotel room. He wrapped a towel around himself and peered out of the bathroom. The front door was shut, the room still and dark. He strained his ears but could hear nothing above the roar of the shower. Great, he thought. Someone's hiding out there, and I'm in here naked.

Silence yawned around him as he spun the taps off. The air conditioner masked any sounds from the street. He felt drawn toward the bed. The room's only illumination came from the bathroom light, shining across the shape of a body under the covers. His shoulders relaxed as he crept toward it, knowing it had to be her. No burglar would hide *in* the bed.

"I know you thought you'd surprise me," he grinned, slipping under the sheet. "But I saw your car outside. I don't know how you managed to find me." He wrapped his arms around her, stroking her short hair and kissing her lips with an intensity--He froze, leaned away from her so the light from the bathroom shone on her features, then yelled and catapulted backward as he saw the face of his sister. He scrubbed his hand convulsively across his mouth.

Natalie laughed at his horror. "You're quicker than James was, or maybe not as amorous? He didn't find out until I told him months later."

"Natalie. No, I guess I should say Rebecca." He sidled toward his suitcase, pulled on underwear and jeans with shaking hands and weak knees. "You stole Victoria's car?"

"I was visiting Sylvia, my dear former teacher," she spat. "I wanted a souvenir."

With a T-shirt covering his chest, he felt less vulnerable. "Did you hurt

Victoria?"

"Why should I? We're on the same side. We both want to kill you."

He snapped on the lamp. "I'm really confused about this, Natalie--"

"Rebecca."

"Sorry, *Rebecca*, but you are wearing my sister's body. I'm confused about this, because if you both want to kill me, why are you doing it separately?"

"James--"

"Mark."

She sighed. "It doesn't matter much. You're all Gileses. Come over here where I can talk to you. I won't bite."

The instant he sat on the edge of the bed, she pounced, catlike, grabbing his hair and arching him over the side. He felt the cold edge of a knife against the skin of his painfully extended throat. "Oh, God, not again," he groaned.

"There. I like you much better this way." Very old green eyes bored into his from the very young face. "I swore, many years ago, I would extinguish your line because you spurned me and killed our baby. I don't really care who else is doing what. Any last words? This time I plan to finish what I started."

Mark swallowed, his Adam's apple bobbing against the sharp steel. "Wouldn't it be more appropriate to kill me at the cabin where it originally happened?"

He winced as the blade nicked his skin as he spoke.

"It's a thought, but also an incredibly transparent attempt to escape your fate."

"N-no, it isn't. Would you get that thing off my throat so we can talk properly? I have a bargain for you."

She released his hair, but grabbed his right wrist, sliding the blade against the vein. He sat up, rubbing his throat with his free hand. "I think Sylvia and Victoria are using the curse for their own ends, in some kind of power play. It involves my death, and I suspect the cabin is the designated site for that ever-popular event."

Natalie/Rebecca narrowed her eyes. "That sounds rather like Sylvia. She was my teacher. Taught me everything I know, although I think I've learned more since then." The woman in his sister's body leaned back, legs folded, the knife he took from her at the library lying beside her hand. To his intense relief, she was not naked, but wore shorts and a tank top. The idea he almost repeated his distant ancestor's mistake shivered through his mind. He promised himself he would never crawl into bed with anyone again without first seeing her face. "Go on," she said.

"Well, frankly, I want to put an end to this curse. I think it's become more than you ever intended it to be."

Rebecca/Natalie shrugged. "It has more power than I expected it to have at this point."

Mark took a deep breath. Revealing this to Rebecca might ruin his chances altogether, but he wasn't sure how else to get what he wanted. "Here's my bargain. I intend to subvert Sylvia's plans by killing myself in the cabin before they can kill me. If it works, you get the pleasure of seeing me end my own family line." No sense in telling her about the baby, he added to himself. "If I hesitate and can't do it, you can kill me, and you make Sylvia really mad by ruining her schemes. Either way, you win. How's that for a deal?"

Rebecca traced the point of the knife across the skin of her inner thigh, leaving white lines. "I certainly don't owe Sylvia anything anymore. She's the one who told me about the power I could have if I slept with James."

"That was her idea?"

Her bottom lip stuck out in a Natalie mannerism that tugged at Mark's heart. He wondered where his sister's consciousness was. "It was my idea. She told me over and over the story of Isis and how she was married to her brother Osiris and how she was called the queen of the words of power. Sylvia initiated me into the worship of Isis and said if I carried out the ritual of joining with someone I was related to, I would have the power to control the future, essentially to control time."

"Why would you want to do that?"

"Control the future?" She snorted, slipped off the bed with the knife, and began pacing around the room. "You're a man, so you wouldn't understand. You don't know what it was like to be a woman during the time I lived, controlled by your father, your brother, your husband. By stupid men fighting a senseless war. James had it all. He could do anything he wanted, go anywhere, be anyone. I hated him for it, for the way our father treated him. But I loved him, too. I tried to show him, but he rebuffed me, screamed at me."

"But why--"

Her eyes narrowed as she paused, fist clenched around the knife hilt. "Don't interrupt." She took a deep breath and continued conversationally. "He was engaged to marry that sweet and pure little Alice Rose, but he was satisfying his lusts with the woman who lived down the road from us. I saw her sneak into his window many times. So one night I caught her and killed her and hid her body. Then I put on her clothes and lay with James myself. I later spread the rumor his lover had run off with someone else."

She slammed the knife into the wall up to the hilt in a spray of sheetrock dust. Mark leaped to his feet.

"When I found out I was with child," she continued, leaning against the chest of drawers, "I told him. I was so happy and proud, but James wasn't happy. He shoved me. Hard. I fell, and lost the baby that night. Father saw the whole thing. He heard our argument and banned both of us from his house. He disowned James and pretended I never existed."

Mark's stomach churned as he eased back onto the edge of the bed.

"If Sylvia was your teacher, or your priestess, or whatever," he managed at last, "why do you always say her name as if you were eating live spiders?"

His sister's face clouded. She stroked the knife handle sticking out of the wall with her index finger, absorbed in the motion. "Well, since I've told you this much ... How should I phrase this? Your little sister would probably say, She screwed me over, that's why."

Her smile chilled his blood. Again he was struck by the resemblance of her eyes to Victoria's. "Are you sure you're up to another story? You're looking rather pale."

He swallowed hard as she wiggled the knife out of the wall. "I'm fine. Please go on. Family history fascinates me." Although, he added to himself, I think Dad's view of family would have changed if he'd heard this.

Rebecca shook her head, squinting at the light glinting off the edge of the blade. "No, I don't think I'm in the mood to tell that story right now."

She threw the knife toward him.

Without thinking, he reached out and grabbed the knife, catching it by the handle.

She raised an eyebrow. "Impressive. Didn't know you had it in you."

"Didn't know I did, either."

He placed the knife on top of the dresser, wondering if he had passed some secret test. She bounced onto the bed in a cross-legged posture in a very Natalie fashion. The weird mixture of the familiar and the alien proved unnerving.

His head ached.

"Aren't you worried Sylvia will double-cross you as I assume she's done before?"

"Possibly." She shrugged. "I haven't yet decided how to deal with her."

"But the bottom line is--and I can't believe I'm actually saying this-- you'll kill me only if I back out. Right?"

"It'll be my pleasure. And I mean that sincerely."

"Can I ask you one more thing?" Mark asked.

"And that would be--?"

"Can I have my sister back?"

She smiled then--not Natalie's smile that sparkled her eyes and crinkled her forehead--but a thin cold smile that frosted her eyes and arched her brows. "Your sister is safely tucked away, Demarcus. Let's call her my hostage. I have the power to restore her consciousness to this body. I also have the power to banish her from this body forever." Leaning forward, she stroked his cheek with a cold finger. "The choice is yours. When you die, I release her. If you don't die, you'll be stuck with me, dear brother. For a very long time."

CHAPTER 43.

Thursday, May 20, 2:15 p.m.

Bo Troxell stumbled across the room where his father sat at the rolltop desk. "Dad! There's a man on our porch! I ain't never seen him--haven't ever seen him before!"

Fred frowned. He took his son's hand and walked to the front door. The rain still rumbled on the roof like an endless animal stampede, interspersed with trumpeting thunder. He wondered how much money he'd lost today because the constant rain made plowing impossible.

He opened the door and peered through the screen. Sure enough, a gaunt figure leaned against the pillar of the porch, facing away from the house, hunched shoulders and back pasted over with a dark shirt. He wore jeans and hiking boots, and his hands were tucked under his arms. Rain-slicked dark brown hair concealed his collar.

"Can I help you, sir?"

The stranger's feet nearly left the ground at the sound of his voice. He whirled, hand dipping toward the handle of the old knife hanging from his belt like Dirty Harry reaching for his handgun of choice. Fred frowned at the weapon and stepped out onto the porch, shutting the screen door between himself and his son. "Name's Fred Troxell. What can I do for you?"

"The rain--I was just--I got caught in the rain. My car stalled about a mile back." The young man flipped his hair from his collar. "Your porch was the only shelter I saw."

"Dad, what happened to his nose?" Fred realized Bo had joined him and was staring at the stranger. The child's stage whisper carried over the static of the endless rain.

The stranger shifted his weight, touched his nose. "Somebody wanted to improve my looks," he laughed. "Think it worked?"

The greenish-purple bruises ringing his eyes contrasted with his pale face. Despite his flippant tone, the young man wore a grim expression and Fred thought his eyes looked haunted. Under Fred's scrutiny he folded his arms across his chest, then unfolded them and thrust his hands in his wet jeans pockets, and leaned against the pillar once more. Fred decided the other man did not pose any threat despite the knife.

"You're welcome to wait it out here. Seems like the damn rain's been falling forever."

"Really? We've had hardly any rain at all at home."

"Where would that be?" Fred asked politely.

"Birmingham."

"I didn't think you were from around here. I keep watching the weather reports on TV, and we're the only place in the state getting any rain."

"It's probably the curse," he said with a faint snort.

"Beg pardon?"

"Oh, nothing. Normally a little rain doesn't bother me, but this downpour--I thought I would drown out there."

"So what brings--"

"Where'd you get the knife?" Bo inquired, venturing nearer the dripping man and peering curiously at the weapon.

"Don't be rude, Bo."

The young man smiled, slid the length of steel from the scabbard and squatted, holding it flat across his palms. "It's an old family heirloom, I guess you'd say. Civil War vintage."

"Wow. Did it ever kill any Yankees?"

The smile vanished. "Not any Yankees. Not that I know of."

"My dad says you should be careful with knives. You can cut yourself with them."

The young man slid the knife back into place and stood, jaw muscles clenching. "Your dad's right. Knives can cause a lot of damage."

"Son, why don't you go back in the house. See if your mother needs any help."

"Okay, Dad. Bye, Mister. Thanks for showing me your knife." Bo sprinted inside.

"Hope you didn't mind Bo's inquisitiveness."

"No problem. He seems like a bright kid. Oh, sorry, I didn't introduce myself. Mark Richards." He stretched out a hand, which the farmer shook firmly. "My hands are still wet, sorry about that."

"Would you like to come in, dry off?"

"Oh, no thanks. I need to be going, if this rain ever stops."

"What brings you up here? Hunting?"

"In a way." He scuffed his boot against a splinter in the planking. "Looking for the land my ancestors used to own."

Fred narrowed his eyes. "Oh? Any particular reason?"

Mark laughed. "No, no, I'm not making any claim on any land."

"I don't know of any Richards family around these parts."

"The family name was Giles. But it was back during the--"

"Civil War."

"How did you--"

"When I was young, about Bo's age, my grandfather told me a story about a man and his wife murdered by marauding Yankees during the war. They lived in a cabin somewhere in those woods." Fred pointed to the dark line of trees skirting the edge of his rain-soaked field. "Their name was Giles."

Mark sighed and folded his arms. "Except it wasn't Yankees. It was a very scary woman. Looks like the rain is easing up. I need to get to that cabin."

Fred chuckled. "You must've been talking to Mrs. Bailey."

"Mrs. B--"

"There's no cabin in those woods. At least, not anymore. Mrs. Bailey lives just the other side of my property. She's always complaining about weird lights over the trees, says it's UFOs. Says there's an old cabin deep in the woods that glows with an unearthly light. I've never seen anything myself, and Bo plays in the woods all the time and says he's never seen a cabin."

Mark nodded his head, his face gray, his lips twisted into an ironic smile. "That sounds like the place." He shook Fred's hand. "It was nice meeting you. Thanks for the shelter." He stepped forward and swayed, clutching the porch railing for support. Fred steadied him.

"You sure you're okay?"

"Just tired. Didn't sleep last night." He went down the steps and into the misty rain.

Fred watched him trudge across the yard and down the muddy path alongside his field. "Looks like a man going to meet his doom," he thought and nearly laughed aloud, yet he could not shake the feeling something was wrong, that the very sky was poised and waiting ...

~*~*~

The brief human contact both encouraged and depressed Mark. Fred

Troxell's friendly smile and hospitality made him realize how isolated he'd become, wrapped up in the cocoon of his own problems. There actually were people who didn't worry about what other sick and twisted things their ancestors did that they hadn't discovered yet. He wondered if Troxell would find his body someday, or if Bo would stumble upon the animal-eaten corpse.

He shuddered, wrenching his mind back to the immediate task of finding the property. According to the Geological Survey map, this dirt road alongside Troxell's property was the closest to the land where James built his cabin. Mark spent the morning unsuccessfully trolling through record books in the Scottsboro courthouse. He was ready to scream with frustration until his sleep-deprived mind informed him he was consulting estate ledgers instead of land records. After that, he located the record of James Giles' 1860 land transaction in moments.

He fell asleep while waiting four minutes for the Probate Office copier to warm up. A passing clerk startled him awake. Cursing Rebecca, he quickly copied the document. She took over the bed in the hotel room, so he spent the night sitting in a chair watching her, terrified of falling asleep for fear he'd wake up next to her. He dozed near dawn and woke at the sound of Victoria's car pulling out of the parking lot. The knife pinned a note to the top of the dresser--"Good-bye, big brother. I sharpened the knife for you. Your loving sister."

The track wound deeper into the woods. He wondered why the only noises were the breeze sighing through the trees and the scuff of his boots against the earth and grass. Shouldn't there be birds at least?

An icy breeze chilled his wet skin, blowing thoughts not his own through his mind, "--get to Alice before it's too late--can't let them find me--", then receding like a train in the distance. He squinted down the trail, glimpsing a vaguely man-shaped brightness between the shadows of the trees. A sense of urgency gripped him, and he hurried through the underbrush to the banks of the Tennessee River.

The voices growled just below the threshold of his hearing, interspersed with the clear and anguished voice very like his own: "--not a bushwhacker--Let me go--I have to get to my wife--But she's sick--"

A human howl axed the air, scraped through his nerves. Mark collapsed to the ground, curling up as fiery pain like lightning burst through him. He barely heard the raw, whispered words, "You can't hang me. Please, I'm not a bushwhacker."

More of the muttering hum. Mark concentrated hard against the pain and climbed to his feet, clutching at a boulder for support, swaying. Suddenly, he clawed at his throat as the air supply choked off. He could feel strands of a rope biting into his skin, crushing his esophagus, but his hands found no rope.

It's just James' vision again. The words struck him with clarity as sparks flew before his narrowing view. Only you're not unconscious this time, not yet anyway. Fight it!

In the deep recesses of his mind he pulled at the sparkles as he slipped closer to the void, weaving them into a tiny twisted wire. Hurry, you can't hold your breath forever. He gathered other wires together, weaving and grasping and fitting into a line that stretched into the darkness, as when he'd rescued Daniel. With a final gasp he secured one end of the wire to a post by his feet and hurled the other end into the void. It crackled and flared with a green burst of fireworks.

The gentle lapping of water against smooth stones echoed in his head as he opened his eyes. He lay spread-eagle on his back, panting, pebbles digging into his skin.

What ... in the blue hell ... was that about? He sat up, felt for his knife, and scanned the tree line. The chill breeze and driving rain were gone, and the afternoon sun warmed his hair and arms and clothes. He stood and stared out over the gray waters of the Tennessee River.

Shaking his head, he walked back among the trees. The narrow trail had vanished, but he knew the direction as well as he knew the stairwell to his office. Intermittently he had a sensation of following a slightly-built figure in a gray uniform, half-carrying half-dragging a much larger unconscious figure. He saw the ghosts disappear into a hazily indistinct cabin, and then, in what Mark knew was a collapsing of time, one of them reappeared and dashed away through the forest, soon followed by the other.

He consulted his pocket watch--three-fifteen--and tramped through the thick underbrush, the silence broken only by his footfalls. Gradually he became aware of a very high-pitched hum, like standing too close to a transformer. It emanated from the very air itself, setting his teeth on edge like a dentist's drill.

The gnarled vines and leafy mulch thinned as he staggered into a clearing. The tiny cabin appeared exactly as it had in his vision, right down to the curl of smoke from the stone chimney. Mark tripped on the step and almost sprawled on his face across the porch. Recovering, he pushed open the door and walked inside.

This cannot be real, he thought. The floor was swept, crisp yellow curtains hung at the window, and the handmade furniture gleamed with beeswax. Mark closed his eyes. His temples throbbed like a hot poker through his head. When he squinted at the room, his vision doubled. Instinctively, he knew in a moment he'd see Rebecca cutting Alice's throat as James watched.

The pain in his head was agonizing. Mark sagged to the floor, palms jammed against his temples. This has to stop, he thought, and the moment he did, the tidy appearance of the room flickered for an instant, the agony ceasing for a single second.

He cast his mind back to the feeling of intense psychic pain that accompanied the experience at the river. Just behind the pain was a pocket of nothingness, of non-exertion, almost non-being that held the key to seeing what he knew he shouldn't be able to see. Grasping for that pocket pushed it farther away. After several frustrating attempts at *not* grasping something not perceptually there, he reached just past it, like looking to one side of a faint star. Like a cloak, a sensation of energy settled around his shoulders, silver sparkles licking at the edges of his vision, prickling his skin like tiny needles. The pain ceased. Mark opened his eyes.

Dust sifted through rotting floorboards, tattered wisps of dingy gray fabric twisted idly in the slight breeze, and a warped old table leaned precariously on three legs and a broken fourth.

He let out a long breath, massaged his corded neck muscles. "That's better. I'll get the hang of this weird reality yet." His voice sounded too loud in this silent place. He traced a line in the dust beside him realized he was outlining a dark stain of long-dried blood. "This must be where Rebecca killed James' wife."

The knife slid easily from the old scabbard. Mark gripped the hilt, the dark wood warm against his palm. "You're in the right place," he whispered. "You have James' knife. You have a relatively firm grip on reality. What are you waiting for? The blade's sharp enough, since Rebecca thoughtfully sharpened it for you. Two quick slashes, and the curse is gone." He crossed his legs, resting his left hand palm up on his knee. The dark vein in his wrist pulsed under the pale skin. The blade was an icy line depressing the flesh. He felt a pressure in his mind, a pressure there since his father's death. As he tightened his hand, the pressure increased to an almost unbearable level of tension, and his stomach felt as if he were plunging into an endless abyss. Mark clenched his teeth, sucked in a breath, and held it.

CHAPTER 44.

5:00 p.m.

Janet spoke quietly to avoid waking Victoria, who slept in the back seat. "Mark really wouldn't try to kill himself. There's no way he would. If there's anything in the world he has a horror of, it's suicide." She searched Daniel's profile for some confirmation of her assertion.

"Desperate people will try desperate things," he said in a neutral voice.

"That's not the answer I was looking for, Daniel." She wrapped her arms around her knees and leaned her chin on them, staring through the windshield. "He experienced it so many times with his father. Even when the subject came up in a movie or on TV, he'd go pale and talk about something else, like he was trying to drown out the sound of the words. It wouldn't have surprised me if he'd covered his ears and started humming."

Daniel shrugged. "You know him better than I do, but I think the danger is very real."

"You know this is my fault. I told him about the baby." She laughed bitterly. "Leave it to Demarcus. When he finally decides to take action on something, it's to end his life. I'm just not convinced he'll carry through on it." The trees sped by as the highway arrowed to the northeast, interspersed with farms and tiny settlements. "He didn't want to have a baby, Daniel. He said he didn't want to pass on his heritage of suicide and blackouts. We couldn't even have a straight conversation about it. He wouldn't be serious."

"He cares, Janet, or he wouldn't put himself through an experience that horrifies him."

She forced herself to say the words she'd been thinking since they started driving. She whispered them, though, as if that would negate their power. "What if he's already dead?"

"I don't think he is. I am sensing a ... a presence ... growing stronger the closer to the area we get. I'm certain it is the energy field. If Mark were dead already, the field would be dissipating. He's still alive. The question is, will anyone else find him first?"

~*~*~

6:30 p.m.

The light streaming through the window of the cabin shifted, so he knew at least an hour, maybe two, passed. And still he sat, cold stones of the fireplace burning into his back, the knife blade an enormous weight against his wrist. His cheeks felt stiff from the tears that coursed down his cheeks and into the stubble on his chin. His teeth chattered uncontrollably.

The movie of that most graphic of his father's suicide attempts replayed endlessly through his mind--the bloody steak knife on the fluffy yellow bath mat, framed by glistening red fluid spilling from gaping wounds in his father's wrists, dyeing the pale linoleum.

"Damn!" he grated at last, slinging the knife across the floor with a ringing clatter. It clanged to a stop against the leg of the old table. "Janet's right. I can't act on anything, not even to save my unborn child. I'm a coward down to the bone." He scratched the line on his wrist made by the blade. "I'm not sure why they call it 'the easy way out.' I didn't have the strength of will to resist an affair with a woman I barely know, and now I can't even kill myself on cue."

The sound of mocking applause shocked him to his feet. "What a pretty speech, James. I had a feeling you wouldn't go through with it. Now I get the pleasure myself." Natalie slammed the door of the cabin behind her and strode across the room. She looked like a petite mercenary, clad in an olive drab tank top, camouflage pants, and black boots.

"So Andrew is setting the fashion trend these days I see."

She stooped to retrieve the knife and smiled up at him. "I actually served in the army of the Confederate States of America, James. Did you know that?"

"I'm not James. I'm Mark."

"I was a damn good shot." The woman inhabiting his sister's body straightened and advanced toward him. "Probably would've been at the battle of Chickamauga if I hadn't found you. If I hadn't sent that message

231

your wife was ill and you should go to her immediately."

"In case you've forgotten, you killed James. I'm not James."

She tapped the knife against her thigh. "Oh, no. I haven't forgotten. I was only doing my duty. Killing a deserter. Who also happened to be the man I loved." He winced as she raised her hand, stroked his shoulder. "Now, I believe we had a bargain, big brother. Why don't you kneel down, so I can reach your throat? You're much too tall."

He succumbed to the pressure of her hand on his shoulder until he felt the wooden planks through the knees of his jeans. You made a bargain with her. You couldn't do it yourself, a voice in his head reasoned. But you can't let it end like this. Fight her, now, another voice said.

Shaking his head, he closed his eyes, biting the inside of his cheek. "Go ahead, Rebecca. We made a deal."

Instead she pulled on his arm. He opened his eyes, and she shoved the knife into his hands. "They're coming, Sylvia and that trained pig of hers. I don't want her to know who I am yet. She thinks I'm your sister. I may yet see you die in a more entertaining way, and kill her as well. Hide the knife and play along."

"But how--"

Mark heard footsteps on the porch and thrust the knife into his back waistband.

The cabin door swung open, and Sylvia hobbled in, clutching the handle of a laptop briefcase. She was followed by Andrew, who carried several large packages. They stopped at the sight of Mark and his sister.

"See? I told you I would meet you here," Rebecca crowed. "And look who I brought."

"Well done. How nice to see you again, Mr. Richards."

The old woman set the briefcase on the table.

"Where's Victoria?" Mark asked.

"Her presence is no longer required. She betrayed me by freeing you. I have found a more suitable partner for the ceremony."

Andrew smiled broadly. "I killed her. Strangled her to death."

"No, you didn't," Mark blurted before he understood how he knew. "She isn't dead."

The man set the packages on the floor and straightened, fists on hips. "Want me to show you how I did it?"

"They were joined, Mr. Sweeney," Sylvia interrupted. "He would know whether or not she is dead."

"But I--"

"It does not matter. She will turn up here eventually. She cannot stay away. Then you may finish the job I set you to do. Do not fail me again, Mr. Sweeney."

"No, ma'am," Andrew answered. "I won't."

"Now set up the equipment for the ceremony."

"Yes, ma'am. What do you want me to do with them?" He pointed to Mark and Natalie.

"Tie him up. I don't want to have to track him down when we need him. Miss Richards, come here by me."

"I'm really tired of being tied up," Mark said as Andrew advanced, a coil of rope in hand. "Why don't you let me be the dominatrix for a while?"

"Shut up, Richards, or I'll put a gag in your mouth and see how well you breathe through that broken nose."

"You have no sense of adventure."

Andrew scowled and secured Mark's wrists behind his back, then helped Sylvia set up the laptop. Mark lowered himself to the dusty floor and leaned back against the wall. "Why isn't she being tied up?" he asked, playing along with Rebecca's game.

"She is important to the proceedings here this evening," Sylvia answered.

"Don't be so difficult, " Rebecca said.

"Traitor." He scowled, hoping his sister's consciousness was safely tucked out of harm's way. Sylvia smiled smugly and motioned Natalie into a chair.

Mark wondered what time it was, but with his hands bound, retrieving the watch would be difficult. Can't be too many more hours until the sun goes down, though, he reasoned. If this curse is real, then I'll be dead within six to eight hours.

~*~*~

6:15 p.m.

"How are we going to find this place?" Janet peered at the road ahead, then glanced at Daniel when he did not answer. His brow was furrowed in a grimace. "What's wrong?"

"I don't think it'll be difficult to find. My head is aching. I think we're at the periphery of the energy field now. Where are we?"

She studied the road atlas. "On ... umm ... highway 117. That was the Tennessee River we crossed about a mile back. Stevenson should be up the road about four miles. I don't see Bolivar on the map, though. That's the place Mark mentioned."

"It may not exist anymore. Believe me, Janet, we'll find it. It's--it's like a tornado on radar. We cannot see it yet, but it is there nonetheless. The field's signature on my brain is unmistakable." They drove on in silence for several minutes before he said, "When we do find the place, I want you to stay with the car. If I'm not back in an hour, go for help. Victoria can stay with you."

"Wrong, Mr. O'Brien. I'm going with you."

"So am I," Victoria chimed in.

"But it may be dangerous. Sylvia could be there, and that hulking brute Mark talked about. In your condition--"

"In my condition, women used to plow fields all day. If Sylvia and Andrew are there, that's all the more reason for me to come. You can't face them alone."

"You don't know what they're capable of," Victoria said.

"You're a dear and brave person, Daniel," Janet said, nodding, "but in case you haven't noticed, you aren't Arnold Schwarzenegger."

He smiled, his sharp profile silhouetted against the glare from the late afternoon sun, and turned the wheel as they approached a larger highway. She consulted the map. "This must be ... yeah, Highway 72. It goes to Bridgeport. You do know where you're going."

"I may not be Arnold Schwarzenegger, but he doesn't possess my psychic ability. Although," he frowned, "at the moment I'd be much more comfortable if I didn't possess it."

Janet abandoned the map twenty minutes later when the man veered off the highway onto a two-lane road, potholed and patched many times to little positive effect. Houses were spaced far apart, two-story brick structures alternating with sprawling ranch styles and mobile homes propped up on cinder blocks. The mailboxes bore rural route numbers. After another twenty minutes' travel, Daniel abruptly pulled off the road and buried his head in his hands.

"You...must drive now. I will...direct...you," he panted.

"Is there anything I can do to help you?" Janet asked, distressed by his obvious pain.

"No...I will be fine if I...can...erect some barriers. I just did not...did not expect it to be so...powerful. We must be very close."

Janet opened the door on her side, eased him into the passenger seat, and slid in behind the wheel. She pulled back onto the bumpy road, slamming on the brakes when a barking hound dog dashed out in front of her. She resumed travel, muttering under her breath.

"Ease off those negative thoughts, please," he said, his eyes closed. "It's only a dog."

"Does that affect you?"

"It doesn't help. Turn left at the next road. It should be gravel."

She obeyed, wincing as bits of rock rattled against the fender. "I hope we don't have to stay on this road for long."

"Left ... at intersection by ... by two-story house ... porch roof collapsing ..." His voice was an expressionless drone, and she glanced at him in alarm. In her anxiety she went through the intersection. Janet slammed the car into reverse, evoking a startled exclamation from Victoria, and retraced the route to turn by the house Daniel indicated. Sure enough, the porch roof had caved in.

"No wonder Andrew attacked you," Victoria said. "I thought I'd seen demonstrations of clairvoyance before, but you're the real thing."

Janet shivered, wondering how he was doing it. She'd never known him to evince this much ability before.

"The field is heightening my perception," Daniel said in the trance-like drone, answering as if she'd asked the question aloud. "Although I am not certain how long I can stay in the field and keep up these barriers before I go mad. This road will wind around alongside this field and then end. We should see Mark's car parked sometime before that."

She looked in the rear view mirror at the clods of red mud flying up in their wake. They passed fewer and fewer houses as trees and muddy fields flanked them. "You're right, Daniel. Mark's Saturn." They drove on for another mile before passing a neat, whitewashed farmhouse. A little boy played on the wide front porch. He regarded them solemnly, and she waved.

Driving on the muddy road felt like bouncing on a particularly springy trampoline. At last Janet pulled the car to the side near the woods. "Do you want to get out, or would you rather I left you alone for a while?"

He opened his eyes and swiveled his head toward her like an automaton, but his voice was more normal. "We should walk into the woods. I'll meditate there for about fifteen minutes, gather my strength, and then we will search for Mark. We must be careful, though."

"What time is it now?"

"Six-forty-five," Victoria answered. "We don't have that much time to waste."

Daniel fixed her with a stare. "I must take the fifteen minutes if we are to succeed."

Victoria folded her arms. "We'll have to hurry after that, then. I'd hate for us to be this close and have him--"

"Don't say it!" Janet said, panic washing over her like a bucket of cold water.

Daniel walked through the mud to the edge of the woods. Janet got out of the car at the same time as Victoria, who reeled against the side of the car. "Are you all right?"

"Maybe a little carsick," Victoria answered, brushing hair from her eyes. "Or maybe the curse field is affecting me, too."

235

"Now just where do you think you're going?" a voice behind them demanded.

The two women whirled. Behind them, hands on hips, stood a scarecrow of a woman, her gray-streaked hair tied back with a bright orange scarf. Her rubber galoshes were caked with red mud. "You lookin' fer the UFOs, too?"

Janet sighed out the breath she'd been holding. "UFOs?"

"If yer lookin' fer the other members of yer party, they've gone on in there. I thought about followin', but that big redneck guy glared at me pretty mean-like."

"Was he wearing camouflage pants?" Victoria asked, exchanging glances with Janet.

"Yeah, he was. Got that same stupid mullet haircut as my brother Ernie. You'd think he could decide if it was s'posed to be long or short. Ernie's gotta have it both ways. I tol' him, I said, 'Ernie, I don't care if your wife is a beauty operator, don't let her practice on ya. But Ernie, he don't listen. I tell ya--"

"Was he with an old woman?"

She nodded. "Yer pretty early, though. The fireworks don't start until dark."

"Are you saying there are UFOs in these woods?" Victoria asked.

"Ain't that whatcha came to see? Great balls of light hangin' over the treetops, that ghostly cabin ..."

She snorted, and thrust her hands into the pockets of her mud-spattered jeans. "'Course Fred Troxell--that's his white house just the other side of the woods--says I'm nuts. He ain't never seen nothin'. *He* don't even believe there's a cabin. People only see what they wanna see, if you ask me. And *don't* see what they *don't* wanna see."

"Did you see another man come through here?" Janet ventured. "Tall, with longish brown hair, lots of gray in it."

She shook her head. "Can't say as I did. I was off to Wal-Mart though, so I mighta missed him. Y'all aren't havin' a UFO convention, are you?"

"No, we're just trying to find our friends. We aren't trespassing, are we?"

"Naw. Not sure who owns these woods anymore. Giles family did, years ago. Got murdered by Yankees."

"We'd better go now, Janet." Victoria tugged on her arm.

"Nice to speak with you, Mrs. ..."

"Emma Bailey. I live in that house on the other side of the woods there. If you see the actual spaceship, you be sure to tell me, okay? I seen the lights, but I never seen the ship itself. Ner the aliens neither. Little gray guys--not green, like they try to tell you."

"Thanks, Emma."

She saw Daniel beckoning to them from the edge of the woods, his meditation period over. "I'll certainly let you know."

CHAPTER 45.

Mark could see himself, so he decided this was a dream and not another vision. God, I look horrible, all haggard and drawn, he thought. They never tell you about this little side effect of saving the universe. He looked around, recognizing the little cabin in its earlier days. Three people occupied the room.

Near the fireplace, a stool lay on its side. Beside it was the crumpled mass of blood and cloth that was Alice. She lay in a fetal position, appearing peacefully asleep, except her eyes were wide open and staring, her face was chalky white, and she seemed to float in a darkening, coagulating red pool.

The second occupant of the room was James. Mark knew who he was even though the man was face down, sprawled full length just inside the door. Blood soaked the torn sleeve of his right shoulder, and his pants were threadbare and mud-streaked. The third person, slightly built, dark-haired, and dressed in a Confederate uniform, hunched over with a grunt and dragged the inert figure across the room, very near where Mark stood by the window. The soldier straightened, panting with the effort. It was Rebecca.

She rolled James over on his back and knelt beside him, tenderly stroking his disheveled, sweat-soaked hair. Her expression was so familiar it shook Mark to his soul: Victoria's Mona Lisa smile. He shivered as his third-great aunt's hands caressed her brother's face, one blood-spattered finger tracing his cheekbone. James' eyelids fluttered.

"Welcome back, James. I despaired of you ever regaining

238

consciousness," Rebecca said, smiling.

"Get your hands off me, you sorceress from hell." He tried to shake her fingers from his arm, but they gripped him fast. "Where is Alice--" Mark saw the recollection dawn on him, his face twisting in horror. "You murdered her."

"Forget her, James. We can be happy together. Complete the ceremony with me." Rebecca's hands pressed his shoulders down, one close to the knife wound she inflicted. Her face was inches from his, and Mark strained his ears to hear what she said. "Become one with me, physically and spiritually, and the ancient power of the spirits of Isis and Osiris will be ours."

James spat in her face.

Rebecca's scream slashed the air. Her face twisted in hatred, feral and inhuman. "I curse you, James Giles, you and your descendants through the seventh generation!" she shrieked, whipping a knife from the sheath at her waist, the knife Mark knew had cut both James' shoulder and Alice's throat. Lightning seemed to flash through the window and course down the knife blade as she raised it with both hands and brought it down squarely in the center of James' chest.

Mark awoke abruptly and fought against the gag reflex, the image vivid of blood welling up around the knife and spilling down over James' shoulders and sides to seep between the floorboards. He lay very still, eyes closed, listening to the muted conversation between Sylvia and Andrew. Peering through his eyelashes, he saw Natalie seated on the floor several paces away, bent knees supporting her head.

He lay on his left side, cheek against the floor, left arm completely numb. He managed to wriggle into a seated position, wincing at the needles piercing his arm as the blood flowed back into it. Mark realized he was lying where James died. The words he heard echoing in his head in the storm-swept field came back to him: "All our blood is in that watch, all but mine--and yours. You gotta complete the chain."

Now he knew where to get that blood.

"Hey, come over here and loosen this rope." Andrew glanced at him contemptuously. "My arm's gone to sleep."

The big man shrugged. "I don't care."

"Look, there's nothing to do but sleep until you're ready to sacrifice me, right? But I'm having a hard time sleeping with my arms tied behind me."

"Loosen the ropes, Mr. Sweeney," Sylvia directed, annoyance crossing her features. "It is a reasonable request."

Andrew grunted, crossed the room, and knelt behind Mark. He untied the ropes and retied them around his ankles. "Is that better, whiny boy?"

Instead of, No, you asshole, he said, "Sure, thanks. You're a real humanitarian."

The feeling slowly and painfully crept back into his arms. He blotted blood from his chafed wrists on his shirt, then lay back down. The energy field made his skin crawl, like tiny invisible insects he couldn't dislodge. He began working at a loose thread securing a button to his shirt. When the button slid away from the thread, Mark used its edge to scrape at the accumulated grit between the floorboards. The top layer was dirt and crushed leaves, but below that, the substance was an iron oxide red.

He scraped until his fingers ached, flexed his hand a few times, then resumed work. When he finished, he had a small pile of reddish dust beside him. Stretching, he pulled his pocket watch out--six-thirty. Then he scooped up as much of the dust as he could, patted it down across the face of the watch, and snapped the cover over it. When he slipped it back into his pocket, an intense feeling of satisfaction washed over him from somewhere outside his body. Someone was very pleased with what he'd done.

~*~*~

Janet squinted through the darkness in the direction of the cabin, wishing her flashlight could penetrate the walls. Dampness from the dirt and matted pine straw seeped through her jeans. Despite the absence of the moon and the surrounding thick shield of trees, the area glowed with a faint greenish luminescence. She shivered.

"How long are we going to wait out here?" Victoria asked, her voice still hoarse, snatching the words from Janet's mind.

"I assume. The ceremony. Takes. Place at. Midnight." Janet knew Daniel's defense against the constant psychic pressure of the field was sapping his energy. "I don't want to move too soon. We still ... we still do not know what is happening."

"You've been very quiet since we arrived, Victoria," Janet said. "Are you all right?"

The young woman shifted on the ground, brushing clingy pine needles from her jeans. "*I* should be in there. I've worked all my *life* for this." Janet could see her hands clenched into fists, pale green in the dim light. "She *abandoned* me. What am I supposed to do now? What kind of life am I fit for?" Her voice broke and she scrambled to her feet. "Excuse me," she sobbed.

"Don't go too far," Daniel cautioned.

The woods fell silent around them, then the sounds of crickets and frogs resumed their medley. Janet leaned her head on Daniel's shoulder, and he drew her close to him.

Her eyes flew open. "Did I fall asleep?"

"For about fifteen minutes. I didn't want to wake you."

"Where's Victoria? Hasn't she come back yet?"

"No, she--" The unmistakable slamming of a door echoed through the stillness. "Janet--"

"I know. She's gone into the cabin."

~*~*~

10:30 p.m.

Mark looked up as the door slammed. His heart lurched against his ribcage as he saw who'd come in. Sylvia, fussing with an intricately-stitched tablecloth, said in a pleasant voice, "Hello, Victoria. Nice of you to join us."

Victoria folded her arms, her wing-like eyebrows low over her nose. "Yeah, go ahead and pretend you aren't surprised I'm still alive. I intend to stop this ceremony."

"And how do you plan to do that?" Sylvia turned her attention to the objects on the table. "There is nothing you can do to stop it."

"Well, you already tried killing me, and that didn't work. This time I have help. That psychic and his girlfriend are outside. So just--"

Andrew loomed behind Victoria, gripping the barrel of his gun.

Mark scrambled to his feet and yelled, "Victoria! Look out!" just she turned her head, catching the full force of the gun's grip on her temple. She crumpled to the floor.

Mark launched himself forward, shouting her name, forgetting the ropes around his ankles. He crashed down, his teeth clacking together painfully. Andrew stomped hard on his back to stop him from crawling toward the unconscious woman, then retied Mark's wrists in front of him and shoved him back down.

Sylvia spoke to Andrew as if nothing had happened. "I want you to prevent anyone else from entering this cabin. The field must not be disturbed. I want psychic barriers erected. And move her out of the way, over in a corner somewhere. We'll dispose of her later."

~*~*~

10:50 p.m.

Daniel wiped his arm across his sweat-beaded brow. "I can't get through anymore," he said, shaking his head. "Something's happened."

Janet wrapped her arms tightly around herself. "Isn't there anything we can do?"

Daniel paced, hands clasped behind his back. She'd never seen him so agitated. "Defending myself from the emanations of that curse field is difficult enough." He stopped and stroked his beard. "I fear we aren't a very effective rescue party."

She looked up through the treetops at the black sky and saw one tiny, faint star. "I wish I could help."

"Maybe you can," he said.

"But I don't have any psychic ability."

"No, but perhaps the child does."

Janet clasped her hands across her belly. "Daniel, what on earth are you suggesting?"

He tugged on her arm until she sat cross-legged on the ground beside him. "With the ability Mark has, surely some of it has been passed on to the child. If we channel that ability through you, and combine it with what little strength I have remaining, we may be able to break through Andrew's barriers."

Janet hoped Daniel's mind hadn't been damaged by constant guarding against the field. "Are you sure the baby won't be harmed?"

"If the latent ability is there," he began, taking her hand in his, "then he will come to no harm. If the ability is not there, he will not have the capacity to be harmed. But there is a slight amount of risk in any venture of this kind."

"Okay, let's try, if it's the only way we can help Mark. What do we do?"

"Calm your thoughts as much as possible. Then search inside you for the baby's consciousness. Link yourself to him--you have probably already done so--then channel that power through you into me. I will do the rest."

Calming her thoughts was easier said than done. She concentrated on slowing her frantic heartbeat, breathing deeply and listening to the rustling of the breeze through the trees. Searching for the baby's consciousness was simpler. She'd done it hundreds of times since the doctor confirmed what the home pregnancy test announced.

The tiny spark glowed within her mind like the little star above the forest. Tentatively she stretched out her thoughts toward him, uncertain of the results, and was surprised by a strong surge of energy, a torrent of inarticulate emotions. The leaves and trunks and tangled vines were bathed in pale silver, the sky brightened with thousands of stars. The little spark glowed like an ember, and as she wrapped it with her own strength, it flared into a white-blue ball. Daniel's presence blazed beside her. She gasped as energy from the child-presence sluiced through her astral body into Daniel's. Every neuron tingled, every cell lit with ecstasy. She laughed aloud, and the laughter of a child echoed through her senses.

Slowly, gently, the torrent of psychic energy slowed to a trickle, then ceased altogether. The glowing ball within her did not die out, but dimmed once more to a tiny star. Janet opened her eyes, and found herself looking up at the night sky once more. Daniel lay beside her. He wrapped his arms around her and held her close.

"I think we did it," he whispered. "We broke through the barrier."

"Did we? Oh, Daniel, it was wonderful!"

He kissed her until they both gasped for air. "Thank you, Janet. You do know I am doing all this for your sake, and the baby's."

"I know, darling."

"I must hurry now before Andrew realizes what we've done and re-erects the barriers. He may already know." He helped her up, then paused a few yards away from the door of the cabin. "I want you to stay here. If anything happens, go for help. Go to that white house we passed. Call the police, the sheriff, whoever you can get. Under no circumstances are you to enter the cabin. Don't try to be a hero. Do you understand me? You *must* protect the child at all costs."

She bit her lip and nodded. "Daniel. I love you. Please be careful."

"My heart is yours, Janet. It always has been, and always will be." He disappeared from view into the cabin. She counted her heartbeats, racing, racing in the silence.

Moments later she heard Daniel shout, but his voice was cut off by a sound like a short, sharp thunderclap. Janet fell to her knees without realizing it, hands clasped to her mouth. The roar of blood in her ears and the echo of the blast was all she could hear. She scrabbled on the ground beside her for the flashlight, vision blurred with tears, and dashed through the woods in what she hoped fervently was the direction of the white house.

CHAPTER 46.

11:05 p.m.

Sylvia and Natalie sat engrossed in the lines on the laptop screen.   Andrew hunched in the corner by the door, his eyes closed.

Minutes flowed past and still Victoria did not move. Mark knew she was alive, but the flicker of her consciousness was fading. The constant hum of the curse field clicked up a notch, like turning the volume knob on a stereo receiver. He knew something was about to happen, felt it in some primal depth of his brain.

The crackle of the ether ceased for a split second, then resumed.

Andrew's eyebrows shot toward his hairline, eyes staring and wide.

A few heartbeats later, the door to the cabin sprang open and Daniel strode in.

"Mark!" he shouted. "Listen to me! Don't--"

The gunshot was loud, rivaling his sister's accompanying scream. Daniel's mouth widened in complete surprise. He staggered backward, fingers swiping at the red hole in his chest, and crumpled to the floor.

Mark blinked at the widening stain, the roar of the gun reverberating in his head, vying with the intensified hum of the energy field. The field split his nerves like overstressed rope.

"You killed him, you son of a bitch!"

He surged forward, straining his hands against the ropes, and lurched to a halt in the face of Andrew's pistol. "You won't shoot me. I'm too important to the ceremony."

"Nobody said you had to walk." Andrew lowered the barrel toward his kneecaps.

"Mr. Sweeney, that's quite enough shooting for now," Sylvia said. "Put the gun away. It's giving me a headache. And move that refuse from the floor."

"He's not refuse! He's a human being!"

Mark was dimly aware he was shouting. It felt good, eased the pain from the field's vibrations. Rage boiled through his veins, evaporating the blood and leaving only pure adrenaline. "How many more people are you going to kill in this--this mad power binge? It's all your fault, Sylvia, and yours too, Rebecca, especially yours. You started all this. You and your-- your sick desires and your lust for power--your damned Isis worship--"

Pain exploded in his cheekbone as Natalie slapped his face.

"That's enough of that," she said. His chest heaved as the adrenaline rush snapped off like a switch. Blood trickled down his arms, his wrists worn raw from gesturing against the rope.

Sylvia peering intently at the young woman, who retreated toward the table. "Thank you for that lovely speech, Mr. Richards," she said. "I knew something was amiss somewhere. I just wasn't sure what it was. Rebecca. You've somehow found a way to inhabit Miss Richards' body. Congratulations! However did you do it?"

Rebecca smiled. "Oh, just a little trick I picked up in the Great Beyond." She swayed from the table, hands behind her, to stand in front of Mark. "You know, Teacher, we have a matter to discuss."

Mark almost dropped the knife when she slipped it into his hands. He looked at Andrew, but the man hadn't noticed.

Rebecca continued, "Why did that body transference work for you and not for me? I don't believe that was an accident."

Mark swallowed hard, still shaky from the shooting and the intensification of the curse field. He gripped the knife, shielded by his sister's back, praying he would not drop it or stab himself, and began sawing on the ropes. Andrew's attention was focused on Sylvia, his big hands clenching and unclenching.

"But of course it was an accident, Rebecca. Why would I want to double-cross you?"

Blood and sweat slicked the hilt. Slowly the strands parted. Much too slowly. With accusations like that, he thought, she can't stall them forever. Andrew met his eyes and frowned.

"Why, indeed, Miss de Graffenried? Didn't want to share the power? Afraid I would double-cross you first?" Rebecca asked.

"What's she talking about, Miss Dee?" Andrew broke in, his gaze switching away from Mark. "Who is she?"

"She's Rebecca Giles. Originator of the curse. My former pupil."

"The dead chick in the picture? But how--"

Mark suppressed a grunt as he snapped the last strand of rope, dropping it to the floor. There was only one thing left to do, while attention still focused on Rebecca.

He watched with calm detachment as the fingers of his right hand grasped the knife's hilt firmly. The edge of the blade buried itself in the skin of his left wrist in a diagonal line of red. Mark shivered as the metal scraped on bone, but the fire of severed nerves belonged to someone else. As the warm red ribbon snaked down his arm to nest on the wooden planks at his feet, he switched hands and slashed the right wrist as well.

~*~*~

For the first time since Andrew started working for Miss Dee, she looked afraid. Natalie Richards turned her green eyes on the old woman, who shivered visibly. Andrew recoiled at the palpable psychic force of the girl's gaze and knew Miss Dee was right. The expression in her eyes, the sensation of her aura were very old. He started toward Miss Dee when he heard a faint hiss of indrawn air from behind Natalie.

Andrew shoved the girl aside as Richards dropped the knife, blood flowing down his arms to splat in great red drops on the wooden floor. Richards stared glassily into Miss Dee's eyes for a long second, dropped to his knees, folded himself prone on the floor next to the knife.

"Andrew," Miss Dee snapped, an edge of panic in her voice. "Stop him--revive him now! He must not be allowed to die!"

A chilling laugh spilled from Natalie's lips and echoed through the still cabin. "Oh, have I ruined your plans, Miss de Graffenried? I let him kill himself. Was he important to you?"

The air blurred between Andrew and Natalie as he narrowed his eyes, lashing at her with all the force of his psychic blast. Natalie reeled back a step, nearly slipping in Richards' blood. But the smile was frozen on her young face as she retaliated. Andrew's head rang as he catapulted through the air and crashed against the wall. The entire cabin shook as he slid down in a heap. Dust sifted down from the rafters onto his head.

"You're next, Miss de Graffenried," the girl smiled, advancing on the older woman. Andrew struggled to protect his employer, but his limbs were leaden. Then Natalie stopped, the smile vanishing. She cocked her head, listening to something Andrew faintly sensed, but could not hear. "No," she whispered. "He cannot be doing this. I must stop him—"

Her young body went rigid, her eyes closing. And Andrew figured out, a moment before his consciousness snuffed out entirely, that she'd turned her attention to the astral realm, to do battle with Mark Richards.

~*~*~

Standing was too much effort as the energy flowed out of Mark's body along with the blood that pattered to wooden planks. He thrust his hand into his pocket and grasped his watch as the world beneath his boots pulsed, convulsed, twisted into a red whirlpool of screams and flashes of light. He shook his head, trying to clear the double vision. He saw the room around him like a single frame sliced from a reel of movie film, the actors frozen in mid-action, and another room, misty and indistinct, immense and cavernous. Some instinct told him this foggy room existed in an astral plane generated by the curse, where the actions of one hundred thirty-three years ago played out endlessly through time. The screech of the energy field crescendoed impossibly until, after one last spasm, his vision cleared—

--And he stood in that immense and cavernous room, now clearly distinguishable as a large barn, the air dim and cool. He smelled hay and manure and sweat, and the clean scent of his sister's hair. She stood so close to him he could feel her warmth through his shirt. Her eyes, so hypnotically green, narrowed in unmistakable desire. He stepped back. "Rebecca, what was it you wanted? I got chores to finish."

"James." She took the hay fork from his hands, tossed it aside. "I think you know what I want. You've been avoiding me for days and days. You don't have to be afraid of me."

"That Graffen woman filled your head with evil thoughts."

"Miss de Graffenried. And they ain't--aren't evil. Just different."

"What you're talkin' about is sin. I won't have any part of it." He turned away angrily and reached for the fork.

Rebecca leaned close to his ear. "And you don't call what you and Miss Taylor been doin' a sin? I wonder what your sweet little Alice Parker would think if she knew."

James/Mark grabbed her wrist hard, hoping it hurt. "Stay away from me, do you hear? I will not have anything to do with your pagan ideas. And stay away from Alice. If you so much as speak to her, I'll--"

"What will you do?" she demanded, green eyes boring into his soul.

He dropped her wrist and stalked out of the barn—

--And a wave of guilt drenched him like the drying perspiration on his naked body. He stepped across the floor, shivering in the breeze, and closed the shutters. The bedclothes were twisted from the heat of their passion. He'd resolved to stop their late night trysts, but Susannah Taylor excited him in a way dear Alice never did. Besides, he'd ask Alice to marry him soon, and then he'd never see Susannah again.

Tonight she was different--silent, intense and savage. He surveyed the gashes her nails left on his arm and crawled back into bed, thinking maybe the strange wine she gave him made everything seem different. He shook his head, trying to clearly remember their joining and—

--Stared at her as if she were speaking in a strange tongue. "You are not makin' any sense, Rebecca. Susannah Taylor ran off. Months ago." Without even sayin' good-bye to me, his brain retorted.

"I'm trying to explain it to you, my thick-headed brother." She crossed to a stack of hay bales, her back to him. "Miss Taylor is dead."

"How do you know that?"

"Because I killed her."

"What? Look, girl, you been studyin' too long. Your brain's addled." He folded his arms in challenge. "When?"

"Six months ago. August the twenty-second."

"That's impossible, because I--"

"Slept with her that night? No, my dearest brother James. You did not sleep with Susannah Taylor. You slept with me." She patted her belly. "I'm carrying your child."

"No." Mark shook his head. "It ain't possible. It was Susannah."

"The wine is potent, is it not? Miss de Graffenried made it. We are joined now, you and I, and now--" She broke off in surprise as he grabbed her and shook her.

"No! It ain't true! It *cannot* be true!"

"James, stop it!"

"You're lyin' to me! Alice agreed t' marry me last night, and you ain't goin' t' mess it up with your wild tales."

"Let go of me. I am not lying. How could you possibly marry her when you have me--"

"I don't have you. I won't believe--"

"James--Stop--We're too close to the edge--"

He almost fell with her, clutching empty air at the edge of the loft, scrabbling for purchase with one foot hanging into space. She screamed, tumbling from the loft to the barn floor below as he watched in horror. And then he saw the drawn white face of his father standing nearby, close enough to have heard every word—

--But he didn't blame his father for disowning him. Hell, he deserved it. He heard Rebecca was sick for months afterward and nearly died. She was too ill to attend the wedding, and when she recovered, she married some peddler from Maryland and moved away. He and Alice bought land up in north Alabama, near the town of Bolivar, built a little cabin, bore a precious baby boy. He never told her what really happened between him and his sister, but he wondered if she somehow knew. And then the war broke out—

--And they sent little James Stuart away to Alice's sister's home, away from the possibility of fighting. Mark drilled with the local militia. One day he came home to the cabin and Alice told him about a visitor. "He said his name was Gillette Samuelson, on his way to join another regiment. I asked him to stay to supper, but he said he had to go." She laughed in that childlike giggle that warmed his heart. "He must have been very young. I think he was wearing a false mustache, to make him look older. He did ask about you, though. Said he knew you."

"No, doesn't sound familiar--"

--The eight words of the message scared him worse than the coming battle at the bend of the Tennessee River, at the town of Chattanooga. "Your wife is very ill. She may die." He wasn't certain who brought it to camp. It passed through many hands on the way to him. Without another thought he grabbed his rifle and slipped past the sentry into the night, determined to find his way back to Alice's side.

The terrain was rough, made all the more dangerous by the Yankee patrols searching for the bushwhackers who'd been destroying train tracks and burning supply depots. Time blurred into an infinity of hiding and running and scavenging. He pictured her dying alone, calling his name. He imagined her already dead, her last thoughts feelings of contempt for leaving her. He grew careless. He stumbled into the midst of a Yankee patrol. Mark pleaded with them, desperate to escape, but they shoved a noose over his head, dragged him toward a tree at the edge of the clearing, and suspended him by the neck until he was—

--Awakened by someone very close to his ears, breathing loudly, rasping with each indrawn breath. His eyes snapped open and he wondered why he was still alive. His hand strayed to his tortured throat, remembering his stark terror as the rope slipped over his head. He flinched and closed his eyes as the slightly-built man in a dusty Rebel uniform gently rubbed ointment from a small leather pouch into the burns on his neck.

"I thought I was in heaven," he croaked. "I thought an angel was flyin' me away. But you don't look much like an angel this mornin'. How did I get here?"

"I rescued you from whoever left you for dead. The name's Gillette Samuelson."

"I am very grateful to you, Mr. Samuelson. My name's James Giles." He smiled and moved his arm as if to shake hands, but winced and stopped. "Sorry I can't greet you properly. I think it's broken."

"Does it still hurt badly? I've been applying a salve to it."

Mark flexed the arm, surprised. "Not as badly as I feared. I fell across my rifle barrel onto my arm when the Yankees caught me. They thought I was a bushwhacker."

"You're lucky I came along when I did. A half hour later and you would be in heaven."

"Thank you, sir." He sat up, studying the young soldier's face. "I appreciate your kindness. You seem familiar. Have we met before?"

Samuelson shrugged, "Not sure," and stood, turning away his face and replacing the salve in his belt. "What company are you with?"

"Eighteenth Alabama Battalion, attached to the Thirty-third. Except I've deserted."

"Deserted? What for?"

A thrill of remembrance coursed through his chest. "I received a message in camp, two, maybe three days ago. I've lost count. It said my wife was very ill, maybe dyin'. I must go to her!" He tried to stand, slipped and fell. The soldier lowered Mark back onto the featherbed.

"You're not ready to travel in this condition. You must rest a little longer."

Mark nodded and lay back. "Not much longer. No one else is there to take care of her."

"What's her name?" Samuelson asked.

He smiled, eyes closed. "Alice. Alice Rose, really. She's so beautiful, beautiful as her name. But she's had to bear so much ugliness."

"How many children do you have?"

"Only one," he said with a sigh of regret. "Named for me. He nearly cost us dear. Alice almost died bearing him. But he's safe now, stayin' with her sister away from all the fightin'."

He noticed a twisting of anger in the soldier's face before he turned and rummaged in his provisions bag. He knew he'd seen the man somewhere before. A distant conversation with Alice in which she told him someone named Samuelson was looking for him?

"Are you hungry?"

Mark nodded. "I'm not sure how long it's been since I last ate. Before I deserted, I guess. Some berries along the way. I think I remember shootin' a rabbit." He looked around the room. "Speaking of which, where's my rifle?"

"I didn't see it anywhere. The Yanks must've taken it."

They finished the provisions, some dried corn and a little squirrel meat, in silence, washing it down with water from his canteen. As they sat, Mark studied the fastidious way his savior ate, his profile, his hands.

"Where's the rest of your family live?" the soldier asked. "You from around here?"

He had it. He knew where he'd seen the other. Mark stretched from a cross-legged position, pulling on his shirt. "Further south, Marengo County. My father disowned me, though, so I don't go down there. He's dead now anyway, I heard. But why am I tellin' you? You know this already, Rebecca."

The soldier narrowed those smoky green eyes. "When did you figure it out?"

"A little while ago." Mark climbed to his feet, clutching at the mantel for support. "I'm surprised you'd rescue me. When last we spoke you swore t' kill me."

Rebecca stood also. "That's because you killed my baby--our baby."

"That was an accident--"

"No, my darling brother, I don't want to debate that subject." She stepped closer, stretching out her hands to him. "We still have a chance together. The power we could share, the unlimited power of Isis and Osiris--if I could make you understand--"

"I don't want to understand," he spat. "I don't know where you learned these twisted ideas. Probably from that teacher of yours, that old witch. I will feel unclean until my dyin' day for what we did together."

"But, James--"

He gestured with his injured arm, winced. "You're not even sorry for ruinin' the lives of an entire family! What kind of monster are you?"

She cried out, running to him with tears in her eyes, clutching at the lapels of his shirt. "I'm not a monster, James, please understand--"

He shoved her hard, and she fell to the floor in a heap.

"James, you can't hate me," she wailed.

"I do, Rebecca." He strode to the bureau and struggled to push it away from the door. "But no more than I hate myself."

She was on his back in an instant, clawing and screeching. He grappled with her, backhanding her across the face with his good hand. She spun backwards, crashed into the opposite wall and slid to the floor. He ran—

--And the seeds of panic buried themselves deep in his psyche, growing, fed by his adrenaline with each frantic dodge through the underbrush. He desperately felt the loss of time, time that slipped away from him, from Alice, whose face grew sharper and dearer in his mind with each moment.

The thought of dangling once more from a Yankee noose dogged his steps. He swept blindly at overhanging branches as they whipped his face and clutched his clothes.

When his fear of dying of a burst heart grew stronger than the panic, he collapsed against a massive rock at the edge of a clearing. His throat-searing gasps for air trumpeted his presence to the world, but he was beyond caring. At last he was breathing normally, and with the return of normal breathing came a clarity of mind. He peered through the treetops at the sky above, reckoned his position and the direction of home. He patted his pocket for his watch before he remembered giving it to his baby son when he sent him off to safety.

A rustle from the top of the rock was all the warning he received before she leaped down upon him with a cry that would have done any Rebel credit. A shaft of light flashed on the naked blade she brandished toward him, narrowly missing his back. He ducked, rolled, scrambled to his feet, and the chase began.

She cornered him when he reached the limits of his endurance, the knife slashing his chest and shoulder as he slipped on the rotting leaves underfoot. Pain shot through his ankle. The next slash would finish him off, of that he was certain.

Mark glanced around, peering through the sparkles of light obscuring his vision, wondering why the attack had broken off as suddenly as it started. Rebecca was nowhere in sight, and he heard a crashing through the underbrush, growing fainter.

He sagged against the tree, his mind registering a strip of skin on the back of his right arm that didn't throb. I should just lie here and die, he thought. This is my just reward. Maybe I'm already dying. Alice will wonder what happened--Oh ... my ... God ... Alice. Rebecca was running in the direction of his home.

Heaving himself to his feet, he discovered a falling run that propelled him through the forest. He staggered into trees, nearly passing out as his shoulder struck the rough bark, cracking the bloody glue knitting his sleeve to the hair on his arm. The pain in his ankle tunneled his vision at every misstep on the stones hidden under the leaves and roots and vines.

An eternity later he flung himself into the edge of the clearing and gazed blankly at the wooden cabin, bracing himself against a tree to keep his knees from buckling under him. There's a reason I'm here. But I can't remember. He struggled to sort out coherent thoughts as he stared at the wide open door of the cabin. Something's not right here. Alice would never leave the door open. A shrill scream, quickly choked off, slapped his face. With a burst of energy he lurched past the well and up onto the planks of the wide porch.

He fell against the door frame, left arm flung out across the planks of the wall he'd planed himself. His breath whooped in great gasps as he dashed stinging sweat from his eyes. The little front room sprang into definition as he adjusted to the change in light: The chairs that were a wedding gift from her father, the table with the one wobbly leg he could never quite get even, the pale yellow muslin curtains she made. He stumbled across the rag rug.

"Mark!" The whisper halted his steps, jerked his head toward the fireplace to his left. His wife sat perched perfectly still on the stool, green eyes wide with horror, neck twisted at an angle, long blonde hair clenched from behind by his attacker. The knife smeared with his blood was tilted against the tanned skin of her throat, exactly in the spot where she writhed in ecstasy when he brushed his lips across it. Her fingers spasmed on her jeans. "Mark," she gasped. "Don't--"

He watched, almost in fascination, as sunlight between the pale curtains glittered on his wet blood on the knife. The blade slipped around the curve of her throat, hidden by the gush of liquid, as bright and red as the squares of the quilt lying across their bed. The blood dyed her T-shirt, spraying across her clawed hands. Mark flailed toward the sagging body on the stool. His vision tunneled, the roaring in his ears so loud he couldn't hear his own screams as he staggered toward the stool. His calf muscles gave way and he slammed to his knees, crashing face down onto the plank floor. His last thought was he hadn't witnessed the murder of Alice Giles. Rebecca had just murdered Victoria.

CHAPTER 47.

Andrew's eyes focused with much effort on the Richards girl as she walked over to the chair, her eyes glassy, and sank into it. He dragged his gaze to the laptop screen that had Miss Dee transfixed. Erratic green lines zigzagged across the black background. The green pixels brightened, lines merging, splashing into irregular shapes. The entire screen flashed with a whirlpool of green. Miss Dee staggered backward, her hand pressed against her ample bosom. Her eyes widened in horror as a black spot dotted the center, sucking the green pixels into it until every bit was gone.

He moaned. Miss Dee dragged her attention from the screen and knelt beside him. "Mr. Sweeney? Get up, please."

"Can't move," he whispered. "Her mind-blast ... The battle on the astral plane ..." His lungs labored, his vision flickered. "Took my ... my strength ..."

"I think, Mr. Sweeney," Miss Dee said, "that it would be to our advantage to depart this place. Perhaps another day ..."

"You'll ... have to help ... me ..."

He heard Miss Dee's rasping breath, felt her hands under his arms.

~*~*~

Something dug into his chest. He couldn't move. His mind was a foggy miasma, floating and featureless, until the bloody spray soaking Alice's bodice flickered into view. No, he reminded himself, I'm Mark Richards. That was Victoria.

254

Liquid fire--or was it ice?--sizzled across his chest, spiking him back to full screaming consciousness. He dashed the glass flask of the strangely colored wine from the hand holding it above his chest, spraying both of them in a shower of droplets and shards. His face stung as splinters of glass pricked him.

Rebecca's scowl faded, and she smiled down at him. "Welcome back, James. I despaired of you ever regaining consciousness."

The wine trickled down his side, soaked the back of his shirt. He remembered another time his blood mingled with that same wine, remembered making love-- "You murdered Victoria."

"Forget her, James. We can be happy together. Complete the ceremony with me." Rebecca's hands pressed his shoulders down, her face inches from his, her breath whispering across his lips. "Become one with me, physically and spiritually, and the ancient power of the spirits of Isis and Osiris will be ours."

Mark lifted his hands, worked his fingers into her short dark hair, clenching behind her ears. "I don't think so, Rebecca," he said softly. "It's not going to work this time. As I've told you before--" He threw her sideways off him with all his strength. "I am *not* James Giles." He was no longer replaying past events as a passive watcher, but somehow existing in this alternate reality, this astral plane, fighting for his life against his ancestor--who was completely insane.

She lay on her side, stunned, and blinked at him as he rolled into a crouch. The gold flecks in her eyes flashed against the green with a startling intensity. "That's--that's not possible. It's not supposed to work this way--"

"I have a secret weapon this time. James' watch. And his blood. And the blood of my ancestors. You're not the only one who can work magic."

Her scream of frustration slashed the air, face twisted in a feral hatred as she scrabbled for the knife. "I curse you, James Giles--" She struggled to her feet and raised the knife with both hands over her head. "You and your descendants--"

"At the risk of repeating myself--" He launched himself at her, tackling her and thumping her to the floorboards. "I ... am not ... James Giles. And you *will not* curse my family ever again."

The knife narrowly missed scoring his back before it flew from her fingers to clatter against the stones of the fireplace. Mark rolled over her, pinning her body with his and clamping her wrists over her head in his left hand. He reached for James' watch in his pocket, the watch now containing blood and powerful energy from James, James' son, grandson, and great-grandson, Mark's father, and Mark himself--and felt her writhe out of his grip.

Her nails raked his bare chest, bisecting the bloody half-circle she had carved there. He howled, nerves raw from incessant pain. He heard the watch spin as she kicked it across the wooden floor. Rebecca lunged toward the fireplace, scooped up the knife, and jammed it into her belt. "I really didn't want it to--to end this way, James," she panted. "I'd much rather you joined with me of your own free will. But now ... now I'm going to have to terminate your existence. Painfully and slowly."

His heart raced as fast as his mind as he backed away from her. "Rebecca, you don't want to do this. I'm not James. I'm a very distant relative. I haven't done anything to--"

He darted for the watch, but seriously misjudged the distance and Rebecca's speed. Her foot caught him square in the chest, and as he struggled to suck in air, she jerked him up by the lapels of his shirt. She threw him into the oak table, and it collapsed under his weight. He fought against the tide of blackness lapping at his mind. No, can't pass out now. You'll wake up dead. Daggers of pain shot through his back with each breath.

"I have the watch, James. I'll smash it into a million pieces and start to work on you."

He tried to focus, but produced only a blurred outline hovering above him.

Hang on, Mark. Don't let her defeat you, a voice sounded in his head.

Daniel? His vision cleared, and the man stood beside him, a bloody wound in his chest. What the hell are you doing here? I thought you were dead.

Not yet. Focus your mind. You have the power to defeat her.

No, I don't. She's too strong.

If she destroys the watch, you are doomed, Mark. You and your child. Take my hand. She cannot see me. Open yourself. I'm channeling my strength into you.

Exhilaration swept through his aching body as his mind opened, flooding him with power and strength until every nerve tingled. He snatched the watch from her. "No way, Rebecca. You've overstayed your welcome in my world."

With a roar, she plunged the knife into his chest.

It stopped inches from his skin, skidding across some invisible surface.

She gaped at him, shaking her head in horror. "No. No, this isn't possible."

Mark grabbed the knife with his right hand, flicked open the watch case with his left, and blew the contents into her face. The iron-red dust clung to her skin like a bloody mask, sucked into her screaming mouth. He jammed the watch into his pocket, closed his eyes, set his jaw, and stabbed the knife blade into her heart. This one's for you, James, he thought.

The screams broke off, draping the room in total silence. Time froze.

Her body disintegrated before his eyes, bit by bit dissolving into dust as red as James' blood scraped from the floorboards.

The walls shimmered like clear Mylar, producing a double image of Victoria, one with the horrible red gash in her throat overlaying the other with a bloody wound in her temple. Nearby lay bullet-pierced Daniel. Natalie was stretched out in the center of the room, unconscious or dead, he could not tell which. And across the room lay his own body, blood pooling around his slashed wrists. Andrew and Sylvia were nowhere to be seen.

You've done it, son. You've defeated the curse.

James?

Thank you. You've released me from this damned limbo. That watch trick was inspired. I never thought of your tryin' that.

What am I seeing here? Mark didn't understand what was happening.

Both realities. The present one will fade soon, very soon.

Oh, God, did I kill Natalie by killing Rebecca?

No, she's been released from that bondage.

Was all that talk of power just Sylvia's and Rebecca's imagination?

Oh, no. You have the power, son. Can't you feel it?

But--I look like I'm ... dead.

You have power over time. Don't you understand? You can bring yourself back. You're not dead, but very close.

If I can bring myself back, can I bring someone else back too?

It's your power. But since you didn't complete the ceremony, the power is limited in duration. You don't have much time left. You must make a choice if you're goin' t' bring someone else back.

Mark glanced from Victoria to Daniel. He moaned at the thought of holding her again, ached to take her far away from relatives and killing and death and mystical power.

But Daniel saved his life, gave his dying energies to defeat Rebecca. He'd put his life on the line and been a savior when Mark needed him. And he loved Janet. If I revive him, Mark thought, I'm throwing away any chance of salvaging a relationship with the mother of my child.

Damn! He hated making decisions.

CHAPTER 48.

Friday, May 21, 12:35 a.m.

Natalie sat up and rubbed the back of her neck, peering around the room blearily.

Only time I've ever felt this bad, she thought, was the wrap party for *Dangerous Liaisons* when I thought I was drinking Seven-Up. She shuddered as the full force of the last week slammed into her. Flickers of memory lashed her, memories of Rebecca Giles living inside her, of almost having sex with her brother. Her stomach lurched as she stood and tried to figure out where on earth she'd ended up.

She saw the color first and wondered why Mark lay on his back with a red cape twisted behind his arms, until she focused on the gaping diagonal slashes in both wrists. Olive green smudges hollowed his eye sockets, blending with the swollen purple mass of his nose, stark against the bone white pallor of his skin.

Her mouth opened, closed, but no sound would come out.

Dragging her eyes from her brother, she swiveled her head toward the door. The room swayed as she saw Daniel sprawled in the corner, a red smear across his chest. Beside him was another body, a woman whose blonde hair was streaked with blood on one side of her head.

The wall pressed into her back before she realized she'd moved. She slid down, fists clenched to her mouth.

Why was everyone dead? Did she kill them all? She didn't scream until someone touched the top of her head, and then she couldn't stop screaming.

"Natalie. Natalie, calm down," a voice kept repeating, a voice she knew shouldn't be speaking. She opened her eyes as strong arms enveloped her.

"Daniel? Am I dreaming? You looked--you looked ... dead."

He smiled. "I was dead."

"A gunshot--I remember--I was floating in that limbo and couldn't find my way back to my body. Then I heard a gunshot and was looking out through my own eyes and I saw that man shoot you and I screamed."

Daniel's arms tightened around her as she convulsed.

"It's all right now, Natalie. Mark saved me. Without him--"

"But Mark's dead, too," she wailed, peering over his shoulder at her brother on the floor.

Daniel drew her to her feet, his voice confused. "I thought he was ... He seemed in control. I do not understand ..."

"Natalie! Daniel!"

Janet burst into the cabin, followed by five people in uniforms. Emergency medical technicians knelt beside Mark and the blonde woman while two men in law enforcement uniforms approached Natalie. Another policeman snapped photographs of the room and scribbled in a little notebook.

"Daniel, I heard the gunshot and I thought--"

Janet stopped and pointed at the blood-rimmed hole in his shirt.

"--you'd been shot."

The sheriff frowned. "Mrs. Richards reported gunfire. Open your shirt, please."

Daniel complied, saying, "Mrs. Richards' report was accurate."

Natalie noticed a bright red dime-sized circle amidst the blonde hair in the center of his chest, corresponding to the hole in his shirt. Another red mark appeared on his back with an accompanying larger torn hole in the fabric.

"What happened here?" the sheriff finally snapped in exasperation.

"I'm afraid he's beyond help." A paramedic looked up from Mark's body.

Natalie whipped her head toward the EMTs. "You're wrong! He's got to be okay. He's my brother!" She slung herself away from Daniel's restraining hand and knelt beside him, blood soaking into the knees of her camouflage pants.

"Mark, can you hear me? Mark!"

People kept interfering, trying to pull her away from him, first Daniel, then Janet, then the paramedics. She struck out, rage and tears blinding her so she barely felt the needle prick her arm before she lost consciousness.

~*~*~

"I was afraid she going to hurt herself," the EMT explained, lowering Natalie onto a stretcher. "We'll take her out to the ambulance while we straighten things up in here."

Janet sighed and leaned against Daniel, afraid her legs wouldn't hold her upright any longer. She watched Deputy Jenkins photograph Mark's inert and bloody body from several angles and then gesture to the sheriff. The sheriff nodded and called to the woman EMT. Janet saw her unfolding a long rubber bag, knew what they were doing with it, but shut her eyes tightly and listened to Deputy O'Connor questioning Daniel. O'Connor sounded frustrated.

"Okay, let's try this again. Were you shot or not?"

"Yes." Daniel looked at her and smiled.

"But you were healed." The other man looked like he couldn't put the two things together.

"Yes."

"By that man lying on the floor dead."

Daniel nodded. "Yes."

"Was that before or after he killed himself?"

"After."

Deputy O'Connor threw up his hands. "Sheriff, this guy isn't making any sense." He crossed the room to consult with his boss, who stood next to Victoria's body.

Janet buried her head in Daniel's chest she heard the sound of the zipper on the body bag, like a long dry cough. When she looked up again, they prepared to tuck Victoria into another bag, under the frowning gaze of the sheriff.

"This really can't be happening." She was too tired to cry. She felt the pull of gravity like hands grasping her ankles, and a dull ache pulsed behind her eyes. "So Mark did kill himself after all?"

"It would appear so. I did not witness it." He rubbed the spot on his chest. "Andrew shot me as I entered the room. Janet, Mark saved my life. He had to--"

"Well, open it up, then!" the female EMT was saying.

"--had to make a choice--"

"I can't," the male EMT protested. "The zipper's stuck!"

Janet and Daniel turned to see one EMT watching as her colleague tugged at the zipper on the bag containing Mark's body. The bag wriggled like a mad caterpillar, bulges appearing and disappearing in the rubber fabric.

"Cut it open," the woman said frantically.

"No, I got it!" he answered.

Something thrust its way out of the opening, gasping for air in great whoops.

"Not much ... not much ventilation in those things." Mark coughed and wriggled free, his face shining with sweat.

The room spun. "Mark," Janet cried. "You're alive!"

"Reports of my demise are greatly ... whatever ... whatever." He heaved himself to his feet and shook Daniel's hand. "I'm glad to see you made it back."

"Thanks to you."

"Excuse me," the male EMT interrupted. "I've never had to say this before, so I don't know quite what to, er, say. Um, sorry we put you in the bag, but you had no pulse."

"I guess I'm just hard to kill." Janet saw Mark's joking expression change to panic. "Where's Natalie? Is she okay?"

"She's out in the ambulance."

~*~*~

Mark ducked into the back of the ambulance and sat on the bench next to his sister. He took her hand, stroked her bangs off her white forehead. After a few moments, her eyelids fluttered and she blinked up at him.

"Mark? But I saw you lying there dead." Her words were slurred from the sedative.

"I nearly was, if it hadn't been for Dan. Are you feeling like yourself again?"

Natalie sighed, tossed her head from side to side. "I think so. I'm so tired. I had the worst nightmares, but I'm kind of afraid they weren't really nightmares."

"They weren't, kiddo. I hate to tell you that."

Mark leaned across the stretcher and hugged his sister tightly. "You really had me scared. What's this?" He fished something out of the pocket of her camouflage pants that crinkled when he hugged her. He unfolded a sheet of paper and started violently. "Where did you get this?"

"I copied it out of a book about Rebecca Giles. I don't want it anymore."

"Good." He shredded the black and white portrait of the woman responsible for years of pain and misery in his family and her hapless brother. Then he patted her hand.

"Now you take it easy. I need to see if the sheriff's arrested anybody yet or if he's waiting to arrest me."

He shoved the ball of shredded paper into his pocket and strode toward the cabin.

261

CHAPTER 49.

Janet looked up as Mark walked through the door. She shivered at the grim set of his lips, the purple and green bruises on his face. He glanced at the EMTs re-zipping Victoria's body bag and raised an eyebrow.

The woman EMT said, "We wanted to make sure she's alive, since you obviously are."

Mark's jaw tightened. "She's very dead. She was murdered twice."

"Twice?"

"You'd never believe it if I told you."

The EMT shook her head, muttered something under her breath Janet couldn't hear, and walked over to confer with the sheriff. "I had to make a choice." Mark's voice cracked. He cleared his throat. "I didn't have enough power to raise both."

Janet's heart stopped. "You--chose Daniel? Not Victoria?" He looked away, his jaw muscles tightening and his Adam's apple bobbing convulsively. "But--you love her. Why?"

His eyes were wet when he looked at her. "You love Daniel. Think of it as ... as my gift to you, to try to make up for the way I've treated you. Besides, he saved my life. He gave me his last strength when he should've been fighting for his own life."

"It sounds terribly inadequate to say," she began, squeezing his hands in hers. "But thank you, Mark. I--uh, oh. Here comes the sheriff. I think he's going to want some answers."

"I don't think he's going to like the ones he gets."

"Emma Bailey saw a woman matching the description you gave of Sylvia de Graffenried about an hour ago," the sheriff told Janet. "De Graffenried was supporting a man, but Emma couldn't see his face. We've got men looking for--"

He stared hard at Mark. "Uh, weren't you dead?"

Mark shrugged. "I got better. The witness wasn't sure if it was Andrew with Sylvia?"

"No." The man grabbed Mark's wrists and examined them. "A few minutes ago, you were lying on that floor in a pool of blood, with slashes in these wrists. Now all I see is a couple of red lines."

"I heal quickly."

"Look, I need to get some answers to all this. I got reports to fill out. Mrs. Richards here said she heard a gunshot, but nobody's been shot." He looked narrowly at Daniel. "We have a reported suicide, only now he's not dead and there's no sign he tried to kill himself. All this happened in a cabin that's not supposed to exist." He shook his head, muttering, "And I thought weird shit like this only happened over in Fyffe."

The sheriff sighed and pulled a notepad from his pocket. "Now, Mr. Richards. Tell me about what went on here."

"But what about my sister? Is she being taken to the hospital?"

"Yeah, they're taking her over to Scottsboro."

"Can I go with her?"

"Not until I get your story. You and Mr. O'Brien here may have miraculously risen from the dead, but Ms. Giles didn't."

"I'll go," Janet volunteered. "That is, unless you still need me, Sheriff?"

The man consulted his notebook. "Sure, go on. I know where to reach you if I need to."

Daniel kissed her, then seemed to remember her husband's presence and colored.

"We'll pick you up when we reconcile matters here. Be careful, Janet."

Mark watched her leave with an odd sense of finality. She paused in the doorway and glanced back at him with a quick flash of a smile. He folded his arms, set his jaw, and concentrated on breathing regularly.

Then he turned to the sheriff. "Well, do you want to know what really happened here, or what will make sense in a police report?"

An hour and a half later, the sheriff gathered up his deputies and equipment. He ordered Mark and Daniel to come by his office that afternoon to try again to make sense out of the situation, then left the cabin, still shaking his head. The two men stood in the center of the room, avoiding each other's gaze.

"Mark, I find myself at a loss for words--" Daniel began.

"Don't bother, Dan. I know what you're going to say."

He wandered toward the rickety table, handmade by James Giles, and closed the monitor on Sylvia's laptop. The sheriff assumed the computer belonged to Mark and had no connection to the murder, and Mark said nothing to change his assumption.

"I really don't think I want to examine my decision too closely right now."

Daniel nodded. "Are you taking that computer?"

"I thought I deserved a little souvenir. Maybe I'll show this to the sheriff so he'll believe I'm not making all this up." The two men walked toward the door of the cabin.

"Mark, he won't believe you no matter what evidence you show him. It beggars logic."

Mark rubbed his eyes with one hand and hitched the computer up under his other arm. "You're right. How can they believe Victoria died from being struck with the gun when she really died of having her throat cut? By someone who's been dead for over seventy years?"

He looked back into the room as they reached the porch and the image shimmered like a disturbed reflection in a still pond.

"I saw it too," Daniel confirmed. "Our energy is anchoring the cabin to this existence. When we leave, it will vanish, I suspect."

Mark nodded. "I guess Emma Bailey won't see UFOs any more, not over this forest, anyway. And the sheriff loses his crime scene."

They crossed the porch and stepped into the line of trees surrounding the cabin. He looked back once more. The moonlight illuminated the rusty tin roof, the aging wood, the once-yellow curtains.

Then the vision faded, like slowly turning down the brightness on a computer monitor, until nothing remained but three piles of rock foundation marking off corners, overgrown with kudzu. He glimpsed something glinting in the silvery light, handed the laptop to Daniel, and crossed back into the area where the cabin stood.

The knife was wedged in the ground, blade coated in red dust. Mark tugged it out, feeling like Arthur freeing Excalibur from the stone. He wiped the blade on the grass, slid it into the scabbard on his belt and sighed. The weight of the past hours draped around his shoulders. He patted his pocket to reassure himself he still had the watch, and the two men left the woods in silence.

CHAPTER 50.

Wednesday, June 23, 2010

Mark watched the figure in kerchief and overalls scrubbing moss off an old headstone several yards away, then laid the bouquet of artificial tulips carefully on the mound of dirt. He sat cross-legged on the grass beside the grave.

"Mom says these are your favorite," he said. "They're not real. Sorry about that. Never knew you had a favorite flower." He sighed. "So much I never knew about you."

He leaned over and brushed dried mud off the small funeral home tag so the writing was legible: Thomas Demarcus Richards, 1958-2010.

"I understand now what you were going through. Wish you'd told me." The breeze blew his hair across his eyes. Mark tucked the loose strands behind his ear, and said, "I know, what would've been the point? I wouldn't have believed you. I'm not sure I believe it all, even now."

His knees were stiffening; he stretched his legs out parallel with the grave, leaning back on his hands. "Dad...about Victoria..." The sky was so blue it hurt his eyes. Puffy cumulus clouds gathered at the horizon. "She used me, that's for sure...but...I've thought about this a lot. She loved you, in her own way. She was..."

Mark gestured as if conjuring the right words out of the summer air. "In her crazy way, she was trying to spare you the agony of the curse, killing you for your own good."

He squinted at the mound of dirt and said quietly, "I know what you're thinking. You think I loved her too, the woman who killed you. I don't know if it did. I just know I can't get her out of my head." Mark snatched up a blade of grass. "It's like she said, we were joined. Forever. She's a part of me. Always will be, I guess."

He fell silent, listening to the whisper of leaves, the hum of traffic, a lawnmower coughing to a start in the distance. "James reminded me of a Bible verse, from the Book of Revelation, about the second death," he murmured at last. "I know what he meant now. His death was the first death, the one that started it all. The intervening deaths—his son James, Demarcus, Tommy, you—guess it skipped my grandmother because the next in line was a woman—all of them were caused by the curse, but ultimately by Rebecca's hand."

Mark rubbed his nose thoughtfully. "But my death was the second death, caused not by the curse, not by *her* hand, but by my own decision. You were on the right track, Dad. You came close. I had to murder myself by the means I feared most." He shook his head. "I'm not even sure if James himself really understood what I had to do, and I know Rebecca didn't.

"And now I've got a second *life*. It's time I did something constructive with it," Mark said. "I understand what you meant, all those years ago, when you said family's what makes you real, no matter how strange the family is."

"I never thought of it like that."

Mark looked up with a start at baggy, faded overalls, tanned and slender arms and a tightly-stretched sunny yellow tank top. She folded herself into a crouch, her freckled nose crinkled, her narrowed eyes the color of a clean mountain stream.

"I'm sorry I startled you," she added, tucking a strand of hair like fresh turned earth back under her red kerchief.

"Oh—you were cleaning the tombstone over there," he said, blinking. "Did you hear…?"

"Pretty much everything," she nodded with a smile. "Sound carries on a day like this. Don't worry, I'm not some random stalker. We've met before. But I'm sure you don't—"

He climbed to his feet. "Renata…Frisch." The name popped into his head suddenly. "The library technology conference a couple of years ago. Do you still live in—"

"Huntsville, yes." Renata tucked her hands into her pockets. "I have relatives buried down here," she said, squinting up at him. "I check in on them from time to time."

"Daniel thought we'd find you here."

Mark turned at the sound of Janet's voice, his heart leaping into his throat. She wore a bright blue Empire waist sundress. Daniel's arm was linked through hers, the sunlight shining on his blond hair and beard. They looked like figures out of Greek myth.

Mark nodded. "I just felt I had to…settle things with Dad and get on with my life."

He folded his arms, shifted his weight. "Uh, I haven't seen you since I moved my stuff out of the house."

"The bookstore's been very busy lately," Janet answered. "Did you—" She cleared her throat. "Did you get the papers?"

He swallowed hard. He thought he was well-prepared for this moment. "Yesterday. All signed. You should get them in the mail tomorrow." The toe of his right boot suddenly looked very interesting. The lawnmower had stopped and silence yawned around them. "Eleven years, down the drain."

"They weren't wasted, Mark," Janet said, her hand resting lightly on her belly. "Please don't think that."

"We were just marking time, Jan. Going through the motions. We were never as close as…well, as you and Dan are." He glanced at the large man stooped over the lawnmower a few yards away, his back to them. The man reminded him of Renata; he noticed she had ducked back over to her family's headstones. "How's the, uh, the baby?"

Janet smiled. "Very well. Four months along now. The doctor thinks I'm paranoid, I've gone to see him so many times, but the stress doesn't seem to have affected the baby."

She nudged Daniel. "Didn't you have something …?"

Daniel nodded. "Mark, I asked Janet to become my wife. She accepted."

He knew it was coming, had made it possible. So why did he have that feeling again that he'd stepped into an empty elevator shaft?

He shook Daniel's hand. "Congratulations, man. When?"

"In about six months, after the divorce is final," Daniel replied. "A private ceremony, but we would consider it an honor if you would attend."

Despite the knot in his stomach, Mark had to suppress a smile. Renata had moved where he could see her, and she whipped her head around and stared at him, open-mouthed.

"I'll think about it, Dan," he answered. "Can't make any promises right now."

"We understand," Janet said. "How's Natalie?"

Mark turned away from Renata's body language of disapproving disbelief and shrugged.

"As well as can be expected. She's taking one class in summer school. Still quiet and withdrawn, not at all like her old self. I guess being possessed and un-possessed takes something out of you."

The smile faded quickly. "Sorry, bad joke."

"Your nose looks a lot better," Janet said, breaking the awkward silence.

He touched it self-consciously. "Still crooked, though. Dr. Hollinger's talked about surgery to straighten it out. I'd like to send the bill to Andrew."

"Have the authorities found any sign of him yet?" Daniel asked.

Mark shoved his hands in his pockets and sighed out a breath. "No. That worries me. A lot. No sign of Sylvia either."

"I have ventured psychic sleuthing to determine their whereabouts," Daniel said. "I am able to locate no evidence of Sylvia's presence on the astral plane. Andrew, on the other hand—"

"You've located him?" Mark demanded, grabbing the psychic's arms. He realized how scared he sounded and stepped back, glancing over his shoulder at Renata.

She was frowning at him.

"Do not be alarmed, Mark," Daniel said. "I have caught brief glimpses of him, but he is adept at shielding himself."

"You've made me feel so much better," Mark said quietly.

He pulled out his watch and flipped it open, brushing a stray speck of iron oxide grit from the crystal. "I need to go. I have a job interview in Huntsville tomorrow, and I still have some preparation to do."

Janet raised an eyebrow. "You're not going back to the University?"

Mark shrugged. "Maybe. Maybe not. I'm reassessing my priorities. I do want to be here when my child is born."

He shook Daniel's hand. "Take good care of her, Dan," he said. He hugged Janet and patted her belly.

As they walked away, Renata ran over to him, her expression indignant. "How can they act so civilized?" she demanded.

Mark sighed and looked down at his watch, closing it with a snap. He shook his head. "Not worth the drama," he answered. He smiled up at her. "You know, Renata, I'm not sure saving the world's all it's cracked up to be. I lost my wife, my child, my father, my lover, my life. And for what? A dented pocket watch, an expensive laptop and a rusty knife."

He glanced down at the bright flowers on the grave and added, "Oh yeah. And a second chance at life without a curse hanging over my head." Mark slipped the watch into his pocket.

Renata slipped his arm through his. "I have no idea what you're talking about. But a second chance is more than some people get. Would you like to explain it to me over dinner?"

Mark looked into her eyes and said, "I'd like that. You can tell me all about Huntsville."

~*~*~

The huge man squatting beside the lawnmower tilted back his baseball cap and watched the tall, gaunt man link arms with a voluptuous woman in overalls and stride away from the month-old grave toward a green Saturn parked nearby. He stood, brushed grass from the knees of his camouflage pants and started the mower again, smiling. Huntsville, huh? Andrew thought. He'd always wanted to see the Space and Rocket Center.

END

~*~*~

If you enjoyed this book, look for these books by
Donna K. Fitch on Amazon.com:

The Source of Lightning

The Color of Darkness and Other Stories

Find out more at
DonnaKFitch.com.

For more exciting books, visit the authors of the
Alexandria Publishing Group at
http://alexandriapublishinggroup.com/.

~*~*~

ABOUT THE AUTHOR

Born in Huntsville, Alabama, the "Rocket City," Donna K. Fitch grew up hearing the sound of rocket testing at Redstone Arsenal and graduated from a high school named for Virgil I. "Gus" Grissom, the astronaut who died in Apollo 1. She also heard tales of the ghost of Sally Carter and the "old Grizzard Mansion" near her home, said to be haunted. This background, when mixed with an early diet of Dr. Seuss, the reference section of the Oak Park Public Library, 1930s mystery stories and the Gothic novels of Victoria Holt, set her to writing her own stories at age 13. Later literary influences spilled into Donna's writing--Ambrose Bierce, Edgar Allan Poe, H.P. Lovecraft and Tim Powers--to give it more than a tinge of paranormal and the macabre. Her love of research led her to a Master's in Library Service, and her fascination with HTML led her to switch careers from academic librarian to web designer. For fun, she visits cemeteries--the older the better--and plays roleplaying games.